The Tempter's Bane

The Tempter's Bane

The Drifters' Road Part Two

Kyle McCurry

atmosphere press

Contents

MÛRONDÛN

NORUNGAD

DAIREHAAD

GULGURAD · DAIR IGINA (BLACK MOUNTAINS)

THE GREYLAND

QUICKWATER

KYRRWOOD

SASKYWATER

NORTH FOLD

THE HIGH HALLS

SILVER MOUNTAINS

THE LOWRY MOUNTAINS

THE WOODLANDS

ELVEN ROAD

NORDURA

NORTH RIVER ROAD

BARROWMAR

THE DEAD FOREST

KAELUMEN

NORTH WORLD ROAD

GUNDMAR

HIGHBANK

CORNWALLOANA

ELOTHASIN

THE FORNWOOD

STILLHOLM

KAEMLON

SOUTH FOLD ROAD

SOUTHERN FOLD

NORTHERN ROAD

HOUSE OF ARDEREGEN

ELVEN ROAD

THE ROLLING FELLS

OLD TAOLNOR ROAD

GAP OF GUNDMAR

DWIMORT FELLS

GJEFR FELLS

FOSSCOVE

THE LOST REALM OF HAELNOR

EASTWARD ROAD

HOUSE OF CAVALIERS

VOLLIRHAUST

THE KITROSE VILLAGE

EUSTICLLO

MERILHOLT

CORNALLRO

VALDYRMORK

GAESIR VILLAGE

FRAITI MOUNTAINS

GOLLN REFUGE

SNAEFA SUMAR

Chapter One; A Late Morning

Several days had passed since the goblin chief's defeat. It would have been November the Sixth, by your calendar. Adroegen led his friends as best he could, however, he was not able to travel as quickly as he had the past few months. He had suffered some wounds at the hands of the goblin chief and still suffered greatly, even several days later. The company had been fortunate after the goblin chief's defeat, for it seemed the goblin pack had retreated. But the pack quickly regrouped, and after a few days they returned to the Dead Forest in force and were now pursuing the company again.

"We must make straight north for the mountains," Adroegen said. He was doing a little better by now, but still limped, and on occasion needed help standing. He had no choice though but to press on.

"The pack keeps gaining with each passing night. They will surely catch us soon," said Edelbir as he and Caitren helped Adroegen stand. Adroegen shared Edelbir's worry. The company needed to reach the Silver Mountains and find the door into a hidden dwarven kingdom, the nearest location in which they could find safety from the pack. But the Silver Mountains were still a few days away on foot. In the sky, the sun was setting. The pack was going to be out soon, and they clearly had picked up the company's trail, for the howling of wolves was growing louder with each passing night.

"If I were not hurt, I think we would have reached the mountains by now," said Adroegen, and he was quite right. The company was not traveling swiftly like before, and he was the reason why.

The Dead Forest looked the same as when the company first entered, with no sign of life. The woods darkened as the daylight waned. The company had been traveling alongside some cliffs for several days.

"The pack will be out soon," said Gleowan. "I know not who leads them now, nor where they have been since we defeated their leader, but they have only regrouped and are coming for us."

"Keep making for the mountains," said Adroegen. "We must reach the edge and then turn east. Then we will travel along the mountain walls until we find etched in stone a hammer striking an anvil. If we can but reach the mountains, find the hammer and anvil, and touch it, the door into the mountains will open. Only friends of the dwarves can open the door, for it is a special dwarven magic. We will have no worry once we reach them. However, they cannot shelter us if we do not first make it to their kingdom. We would be there already were it not for me. I am delaying us from safety."

"Don't say such things!" said Caitren. "We would not even know where we are going were it not for you."

"I only hope to reach the kingdom," said Adroegen. "War is on this land's doorstep. Those dwarves could help us. Vyroun knows not of their existence. It could be an advantage. I am just unsure if the king will help us, for he wishes to keep hidden. Still, we must try and seek their aid. It grows clear to me that reaching those mountains is vital. We must not fail in this."

"We will make it there," said Edelbir. "Mark my words, we will not fail in this quest if you deem it so important."

Night soon fell. Adroegen struggled to run. He needed to rest, but for him and his friends, there was no time for resting. Before long the pack was out and searching for the company. The goblin pack was close too, for the howling of the wolves grew louder.

"I had hoped that we would have some relief from those vile creatures after the goblin chief was defeated," said Vaenn.

"They are very close," said Gleowan. "We have to run, for they will catch us tonight."

Adroegen mustered all of his might, but he was not able to run like he once could. His wounded leg only caused him to stumble. The company stopped, and Edelbir came to Adroegen's aid.

"Grab on!" said Edelbir. Before Adroegen could answer, Edelbir heaved him over his shoulder and began carrying him.

The company was on the run without rest for the next several hours. They had not yet been found, but the sounds of wolves continued to grow louder. It would surely not be long before the goblin pack reached the company. It was late in the night. Adroegen hoped morning would come before the pack found them.

Edelbir was a very strong man, and he was able to run swiftly while carrying Adroegen. The company moved a little faster. Adroegen could see what was behind them as he was being carried. He kept watch for any goblins.

Adroegen hoped that their luck would hold and they would reach the morning, but that would not be so. Before long, Adroegen's fear was realized. "They have found us," he said.

In the distance, within the Dead Forest, Adroegen saw several goblins atop wolves giving chase. They gained quickly, and soon the company was within their reach. Gleowan and Vaenn took out their bows out and fired some arrows. They slayed a few wolves and goblins, but there were far too many on their tail. Adroegen's friends ran as fast as they could, but it was no use. They could not outrun wolves. The pack soon caught up and surrounded the company. Edelbir had to put Adroegen down. Adroegen drew Endonhil and tried to stand, and all of the others had their weapons drawn. The company was in a similar position as they had been the night of the goblin chief's defeat. They were cornered, and behind them was the edge of a cliff. This time, though, the company was at least together, and like before, morning was not far.

"Hold!" said one goblin, riding up to the company. He was taller than the others, tall like the goblin chief, though not so bulky. He wore many piercings in his ears and his nose, and sported broad armor. It was not the ragged armor that the hunters wore, for it was much thicker, and more difficult for any weapon to pierce. He was the new leader in the wake of the goblin chief's defeat, though the company had not seen him previously. Adroegen, however, had seen this goblin before, when he had been imprisoned with his mother as a child. This goblin was high within Vyroun's ranks, and he was accompanied by his own small pack that joined the one that had been hunting the company. These goblins were heavily armored and did not appear suited for a hunt, but rather for war.

"Word of you runts has reached our master," said the goblin lieutenant to the company, before turning to the goblins. "He has heard word of the goblin chief's defeat, and that the jewel he sought is gone. We no longer sense that you carry treasure, and my master is not pleased the jewel is lost. We have orders from the dark lord. That mangled vagabond is to die. But the rest of you are to be taken and brought before our master. My master values strength, and admires how long you have been able to last. He will grant you maggots one chance to serve him, and if you accept, all will be forgiven. The vagabond, however, will die. He should be easy work. Look at him! He can hardly stand at all!"

The goblins all laughed. Adroegen's friends closed around him to keep the goblins from reaching him. The news did not surprise Adroegen at all, as he was certain that with the goblin chief dead, and with the Night's Jewel gone, there was no longer reason for him to be kept alive. His friends, however, were in their own danger. Years before, Adroegen had been brought before Vyroun and had dealt with great torment, and was almost killed. Now his friends were to meet the same fate, unless they could escape it.

"They want to take all of us?" asked Kattalin. "Why would Vyroun want us brought before him rather than killed?"

"Vyroun is known by many as the tempter," whispered Adroegen. "He will try to seduce everyone that he can into serving him, and those who refuse are slain. I have seen it before. You cannot be brought before him, for your fate will be too terrible to imagine."

"What must we do?" said Vaenn. "I see little hope of escaping."

"We are well into the night," said Adroegen quietly to his friends. "We were cornered like this before, and then morning came. That is our best hope right now. The sun cannot be far from rising."

"What are you whispering there?" taunted the goblin lieutenant. The rest of the pack laughed. "Perhaps you can find a way to escape? If you could run then you might have a chance! Morning is too far away, and you'll be dead by then!"

"That is our best hope," whispered Adroegen to his friends. "We must make it to sunrise."

"Enough of your bickering!" said the goblin lieutenant. "Yield now and come with us north, and we will not harm you."

Adroegen's friends did not surrender at all. They were prepared to fight. Adroegen, too, was prepared to fight, though he was not as fierce as he once was. The goblin lieutenant looked disappointed, but not surprised, that the company would choose to fight.

"Very well," said the new goblin leader. "Let's make this quick. It's nearly time for war, and we don't wish to be absent. Slay the mangled vagabond, that ought to be simple! And take the others!"

The goblins began their assault upon the company. Gleowan and Vaenn began to fire arrows, while Edelbir, Kattalin, and Caitren did their best to not let any members of the pack reach Adroegen. Adroegen, though he was still hurting, fought with what strength he could muster. He did not want his friends to face the pack without his help, even if he was the one in the greatest danger at the moment. Though the company was outnumbered, and cornered against the top of a cliff, they fought with much courage. Soon several goblins were felled.

Adroegen, though he slayed a few goblins and wolves, could not help but look to the east, hoping that the aid of morning would come. The dark did appear to be lifting. His friends were all fighting and felling members of the pack. The company tried to move away from the edge of the cliff, but this time they were not able to advance against their enemy, and they were still well outnumbered.

"Morning sunrise, you have not failed us yet," said Adroegen quietly to himself. "We need your help again."

Adroegen swung Endonhil and slayed as many goblins as he could. He was having much difficulty walking and oft fell to his knees. Adroegen was not facing as many foes as were his friends, who were guarding him as best they could, for Adroegen was in the most danger, being hurt, and also commanded to be killed under the goblin lieutenant's orders. Adroegen worried greatly that his friends, in trying to protect him, were putting themselves in danger of being taken, and if such took place, Adroegen would feel as if it were his own fault. Adroegen wanted to keep his friends from harm, just as he had sought ever since he was forced to lead them away from their home, yet because Adroegen was wounded, he could not protect them as he once could. Fortunately for him, however, Adroegen's friends were stronger now than they had been when they first left home.

Though the company's luck had held thus far, I am afraid that we cannot always be fortunate. Adroegen continued to fight fiercely, cutting the head off one goblin and then cleaving another. However, he was then knocked off balance and fell. A couple of goblins approached to kill him, and though Adroegen was in great pain, he had no choice but to endure it and roll around to avoid the ragged swords of the goblins.

"Adroegen! Oh, we cannot see you die!" said Caitren, running to Adroegen's aid. The others, too, tried to help Adroegen, though there were still several goblins attacking them. Caitren swung her sword to slay what goblins she could as Adroegen fought while on his back.

Adroegen was able to get a little relief from the goblins' attack and was grateful to Caitren. She tried to help Adroegen rise to his feet, and Adroegen struggled again to get up. Once he was standing, he quickly turned back to the east. He could see a very small gleam of sunlight rising from the horizon. Adroegen's spirits lifted greatly. Help seemed to be on the way, like on the night he and his friends had encountered the goblin chief.

"Morning is near," said Adroegen. "We need not hold for very much longer."

This time, however, Adroegen and his friends would not be so fortunate. After looking to the east, Adroegen faced the goblins again and found that the goblin lieutenant had entered the battle. The new leader of the pack had a sword, but it was sheathed, as he did not want to kill Adroegen's friends. Instead he held a club and made his way to Caitren, whose gaze was on the sunrise at that moment.

"Caitren, behind you!" said Adroegen, who ran towards her as swiftly as he could, but he could not reach her quickly enough. Caitren quickly turned around, but before she was able to react, the goblin lieutenant knocked her over the head with the club, and Caitren fell to the ground unconscious.

"Caitren!" said Adroegen, who had forgotten briefly that he was still greatly hurt. He tried to reach Caitren, but a couple of goblins quickly picked her up and put her on one of the wolves. Caitren was then carried away by a few members of the pack.

"Caitren, no!" shouted Adroegen, who tried desperately to run after the goblins, but I am afraid that trying to catch a wolf on foot was arduous enough even without an injured leg. Adroegen had feared losing his friends ever since leading them from home, and now that fear was being realized, for Caitren in time would surely be slain if the company could not save her.

"We must catch them!" said Edelbir. He and Kattalin ran after the goblins that were taking Caitren away. Gleowan and Vaenn tried to shoot these goblins, however, there was a risk that their arrows would hit their friend instead. Adroegen, too, tried to get Caitren, however, he quickly fell well behind his friends in their chase. It was but mere moments before Caitren was out of their sight and being taken to Vyroun's kingdom.

"Oh, what will we do? She is gone!" said Vaenn as the company tried to chase the goblins and save their friend.

"We cannot abandon our friend!" said Kattalin. Adroegen, who was farther behind, was in despair about what torment and death might await her at the hands of Vyroun. He had hoped that the company would find Huldnar, Caitren's father, as she had been separated from him when their home in a hidden village was destroyed the previous summer. Caitren had been certain she would one day find her father again, but now Adroegen worried that it would not come to pass.

Adroegen's friends went after Caitren. However, in doing so, I am afraid that matters only became far worse for the company. In their pursuit of Caitren, Adroegen had been left alone. Adroegen's friends were fighting desperately through several goblins, but in that moment, several of the goblins turned their focus to Adroegen and instead attacked him.

The company had moved from the edge of the cliff, but Adroegen was still rather close to it, and now surrounded by goblins. If Adroegen were not so hurt, I would say that he would have had a very decent chance of holding off the attack, at least until help from his friends arrived. Adroegen, however, had suffered wounds not only to his leg but to his chest and shoulder as well after meeting the goblin chief one last time, and thus he was not as ferocious as he once was. Adroegen was quickly knocked to the ground, and he had no choice but to again endure the pain and roll away from the swinging goblin swords.

"Adroegen!" shouted Vaenn. Adroegen caught but a glimpse of his friends, who were in a terrible situation, as one member of their company had been captured and another was on the ground and under attack. Adroegen tried to get to his feet but had no chance. To make matters worse, Adroegen was being driven back towards the edge of the cliff.

Adroegen fought as fiercely as he could, and even when wounded, he was still dangerous. A couple of goblins were felled swiftly. Finally, he had a chance to rise back to his feet. His friends were trying to reach him, but they had their own goblins to fight through. Adroegen had trouble standing upright but had no choice but to fight onward.

He grew fearful, as he was cornered by several goblins, and behind him the edge of the cliff was mere feet away. The goblins had inched him to the very edge. At the very bottom was a river flowing alongside a rocky shore. A fall over the cliff would have been more than a hundred feet. Adroegen would surely not survive such a fall, unless perhaps he plunged into the river below, but being as wounded as he was, Adroegen surely would have difficulty swimming to the shore.

Adroegen cut off one goblin's head, but then he was knocked back to the ground. He tried desperately to not fall over the edge, however, he could not keep the goblins from pushing him over. A goblin kicked him, and Adroegen fell off the cliff. A fear took him that his end had come. The last thing he heard was a scream, very likely from one of his friends, and the last thing he saw was the light of the morning sun beginning to rise in the east. In but a brief moment, Adroegen's mind was overwhelmed with thoughts of how he was meeting his end, how Caitren, too, would likely die, and how his friends would be alone in lands they had not before ventured into. All became dark and hopeless. The morning's light had finally come, but for Adroegen it came far too late, as he had taken a tumble over a cliff and fallen a long way into the river below.

Chapter Two: The Company Splits

Caitren was out of sight, and though Edelbir wanted to pursue the goblins that had taken her, more goblins stood in the way. Behind, Adroegen might have fallen to his death, and those who remained of the company needed to find him also. Edelbir was quite overwhelmed, and beyond any doubt the others all were, too. The four of them needed to find their friends but were uncertain of who to seek first. Edelbir cleft one goblin's helm with his sword, but after that the pack chose to fight no further.

"Retreat! The sun has risen!" said the goblin lieutenant. The pack ceased its attack and rode away. Gleowan and Vaenn shot as many goblins as they could as the pack fled. It did not take long though before the pack was gone, and the forest was quiet again. The company was alone, and now they were without two members, one taken, and the other possibly dead.

"Adroegen!" screamed Vaenn, looking over the edge of the cliff. Edelbir ran there and joined the others as they urgently looked below. A river flowed south along a very rocky shore. The four of them could hear and see the flowing water, but they saw no sign of Adroegen.

"Adroegen!" called Gleowan. He tried calling him again, but the four of them heard nothing but flowing water.

"There is a way down over there. We must go find him," said Vaenn. Just a little farther down was a ridge that went right along the cliff and to the bottom, wide enough that they could make their way down.

"But Caitren has been taken!" said Kattalin. "We cannot abandon her! Oh! What woe we have met! Two of our friends are gone! And how can we hope to find both of them when they are now in separate places?"

"Morning has arrived," began Edelbir. "That may buy us a little time to be able to save Caitren. Adroegen, however, has fallen, and we must find him now if we are to save him. If we can find him now, then perhaps he might know where the pack will take Caitren."

The four of them swiftly made their way to the bottom of the cliff. They hastened down the shore, desperately calling for Adroegen but hearing and seeing no sign of him.

"Perhaps he may have fallen into the river. I must look!" said Kattalin, entering the river and searching to see if Adroegen had drowned. Edelbir, Gleowan, and Vaenn made their way down the shore in search of Adroegen as Kattalin swam beneath the water.

An hour or so passed. Gleowan and Vaenn ran farther down the river's shore in case Adroegen had drifted downriver. Kattalin swam in the river, and Edelbir hoped that she would not find Adroegen's body at the bottom of the water. Edelbir searched where Adroegen had fallen over the cliff, in case there might be any sign or clue there as to what might have happened to him. He thought he found some blood on a small rocky slope towards the bottom of the cliff, but found no other possible clue. If it was indeed blood, then it must have been Adroegen's, and Edelbir was very afraid, as there was a good chance that the leader of their company hurt himself greatly before falling into the river, if he fell into the river at all. He was certain there was little chance Adroegen survived, but Edelbir would not give up hope until their friend was found.

Gleowan and Vaenn called Adroegen's name endlessly, but they did so to no answer. Kattalin, after swimming to the bottom of the river and searching for some time, found nothing, and so the four of them could only conclude that Adroegen had not drowned.

"We have looked everywhere!" said Vaenn. "He is not down the river, he is not on the shore anywhere, and when we call for Adroegen there is no answer."

"I have searched the bottom of the river," said Kattalin, shivering terribly and trying to squeeze as much water as she could out of her dress. "I see nothing but rock and sand when I search the riverbed. Adroegen is not there, I am sure of it, for I have searched everywhere I could."

"The longer we are here, I am sure the less chance we will have of finding Caitren," said Gleowan. "I know not what we must do."

"Our friend is dead," said Vaenn, in tears. "For he is nowhere to be seen. The longer we search, the more lost he seems."

Edelbir looked to the north, where, somewhere, a pack of goblins was holding one friend captive. Somewhere along the river, another friend had fallen and might have been dead. Edelbir knew that the company had a very difficult choice to make.

"We do not know that he is dead," said Edelbir. "Until

we find his body, our friend is not yet dead. We cannot abandon Adroegen so quickly."

"But we must also find Caitren," said Gleowan. "For she, too, is in grave danger. The longer we remain here, the smaller the chance we might have of finding her."

"Gleowan is right," said Edelbir. "The longer that we linger here, the more dim any chance of finding Caitren grows. We must go north and find her, before she meets a terrible fate."

"Do we abandon Adroegen, then?" said Kattalin. "What if he still lives, somewhere downriver?"

"No, we cannot abandon Adroegen either," said Edelbir. He was growing certain the four of them would not be able to save both of their friends in time if they remained together.

"How will we go about finding both of them?" said Kattalin.

"I see only one choice," said Edelbir. "Until we find Adroegen, we cannot give up on him, but we cannot delay in finding Caitren, either. And there is still another task we must succeed in, also. Adroegen told us that we cannot fail in reaching the hidden kingdom of dwarves, for there are many more lives at stake than just those of our friends. We must reach the dwarves and seek their aid, for war is coming. This we know from the goblins. We have three tasks. I know not if we can hope to succeed in all of them, but we must try nonetheless. There is only one way I see that we can succeed in each. We must split our company. Two of us search for Adroegen and then head north to find the dwarven kingdom. The other two amongst us search for Caitren."

"No! We cannot break our company!" said Vaenn.

"How would we fare if we are on our own?"

"I do not wish to part at all either," said Edelbir. "For you have been my friends, my only family for all my life. How would we fare if not together? I do not know. But I see no other choice. If we seek to save Caitren, and if there is still a chance that Adroegen lives, then there is no other way for us to find both of them. Either that, or we give up on one in hopes of saving the other. We could stay here in search of Adroegen, hoping that he still lives, but if we do so then Caitren will be pulled well beyond our reach. Even if we find Adroegen, who knows how long it may take, and how long would the search delay us in seeking Caitren? And if we leave here in search of Caitren, then we abandon Adroegen, and even if he lives, no one would be here to save him. But if two of us search for Caitren while the other two find Adroegen, then there may just be hope of saving both."

"We will each be far more vulnerable if separated," said Gleowan. "If peril finds us, we would have a greater chance of facing it together than if separate."

"I must agree with Gleowan," said Kattalin. "It would be a great risk for the four of us to part ways, for we would be easier to defeat if separated. And yet, I am afraid Edelbir is right. I cannot abandon either of our friends, and I see no chance of being able to save both of them if we remain together. Time is against us. We cannot linger here and let Caitren be taken beyond our sight. Yet we cannot abandon Adroegen if he still lives. Only by parting ways would we have hope of saving both."

"I know not if this plan would succeed," said Gleowan. "Saving either of our friends, let alone both, is going to be a grave task."

"Yes, there might be very little hope," said Edelbir. "But if there is a chance, we must take it."

"How would we split our company?" asked Kattalin. Vaenn was silent and in tears as the others spoke on.

"Kattalin is the most natural swimmer amongst us," said Edelbir. "She should be among the two of us who search for Adroegen, I think."

"And what of Vaenn and I?" said Gleowan. "Which task would each of us fare better in taking?"

"I think the two of you should remain together," said Edelbir. "For you are inseparable, as I have come to know. With Kattalin searching here, you should be the ones who search for Caitren. I think it would be best, for the two of you are skilled with bows, and that task will be a hunt."

"Then that would leave Edelbir with me here, searching for Adroegen," said Kattalin. "I can only hope that he lives and that we are able to find him. And after that, what do we do then?"

"Adroegen told us that we must make for the dwarven kingdom," said Edelbir. "We must not fail in this task. We will search and hope to find him. Though if after days of searching we do not find our friend, I know not what we will do."

"If this is decided, then I think we best not delay," said Gleowan. "For the pack will take Caitren north at nightfall, I am sure. Vaenn and I can only hope the pack stops for the day, and that we have time to gain on them and catch them. If we do not find them soon, then they will distance themselves from us, for the wolves are too swift for us to catch on foot in the night."

Vaenn was crying. The others, too, were afraid of what was to come. After all, if you or I were about to be separated from our family, without knowing if we would ever see them again, we, too, would be saddened, afraid, and uncertain of what might be in store. Though Edelbir, Kattalin, Gleowan, and Vaenn were not quite family, they were very close and the only sort of family any of them had.

"Do stay alive, please," said Vaenn to Edelbir and Kattalin. "Whatever you do, and wherever you go next, just remain alive. I do not want to lose you."

"And the two of you must do the same," said Edelbir. "Your task might be far more dangerous than ours. I can only hope that you are ready for it. We all must be ready for what is to come next."

"We all must promise that we will find each other again," said Kattalin. "Whether our paths cross during our next ventures, or whether we cease to have perils to face. We must find each other again."

"We will," said Edelbir. "For we are all bonded in a way that can never be broken. We must fight next, for our friends, should they still live, and we must fight so that one day we can meet again, and in a far better time."

"But now we must part," said Gleowan. "For the longer we delay, the dimmer hope becomes for our friends. This is where we must say goodbye to one another, until the next time we meet."

"Take care of yourselves, Gleowan and Vaenn," said Edelbir. "We hope greatly that you can find Caitren and save her."

"And we hope you can find Adroegen," said Vaenn. "I hope he still lives, somewhere at the bottom of this cliff. I hope he is all right, and that our greatest fear is not realized. Hope wanes, though, the longer you go without finding him, and so you must search. Please find him, and please remain alive."

Gleowan and Vaenn made their way up the cliff. Once their friends reached the top, Edelbir and Kattalin looked upon Gleowan and Vaenn one final time until their next meeting, if there would be a next meeting, and then Gleowan and Vaenn made their way to the north and west, where the goblin pack had taken Caitren. As Gleowan and Vaenn departed, Edelbir and Kattalin turned their attention back to the river.

"We have already searched for some time," said Kattalin. "And yet we have found no sign of Adroegen. Where can we search that we have not yet looked?"

Edelbir looked upon the river. It was not flowing quickly, but the current was fast enough to drift one a decent distance in a short time. "We have only been searching since this morning. I think it may take a few days to find Adroegen, depending on where he is. That is the question. The place where he fell, we have searched thoroughly."

"Where could he be?" said Kattalin. "I have swum through the river and have not found him. Granted, I hoped I would not, as that would mean he has drowned. However, if he is not here, how far away could he be? Might Adroegen be farther down the shore, or could he be close and within our sight, and we simply cannot see him?"

"What I gather makes me believe he is farther down the river," said Edelbir. "Adroegen was wounded, and I think I found some blood up the cliff where he fell. If he were on the shore, we either would have found him or we would have found some kind of trail of blood that would surely have led us to him. I believe he hit he rock on the cliff and fell into the river. However, if that is true, then he may be dead."

"But I saw no sign of him there," said Kattalin.

"I know," said Edelbir, looking suspiciously at the river. The current, while not at all strong, made him uneasy. Adroegen must have fallen into the river, otherwise they surely would have already found him. If Adroegen indeed was in the river, Edelbir was unsure how far it could have taken their friend by now. "That river flows steady, and it flows without stopping. I believe the river must have carried him farther away. That is the only hunch I have, that Adroegen, whether dead or alive, has been drifting down the river since he fell, and he is either still in the water or has washed up on shore somewhere farther down."

"Then we must make down the river!" said Kattalin. "And we must be swift."

"Yes," said Edelbir. "Perhaps I will search along the shores, and perhaps you should swim in the river and search there. Hopefully I will be the one to find him and not you, for if Adroegen is washed up on shore somewhere, then there might still be a chance that he lives. However, if you find him in the river, then he will surely be dead."

"I can only hope that you are correct also," said Kattalin as she went back into the river, while Edelbir went back to searching along the shores. The two of them headed south along the river, hoping to find their friend alive.

Edelbir and Kattalin searched for the next few days. Their task carried them south, which was the direction the river flowed. Edelbir searched the shores while Kattalin swam and searched the bottom of the river. On the shores, Edelbir called Adroegen's name in hopes that his call would be answered. He looked along the shores on both sides of the river.

Kattalin, meanwhile, from morning until sunset on the first day, swam in the river, which was about three fathoms deep. She was a natural swimmer. It was November, and thus the chill of autumn had come. Edelbir did enter the river at times to cross to the other side. When Edelbir had to swim, the water to him was quite cold, although he was not too bothered by it, for there were far more pressing concerns. Edelbir, though, noticed that Kattalin was in the water for hours and yet the cold never seemed to bother her, and he wondered if Kattalin even felt cold while in the water.

Strangely, the water was far warmer to Kattalin, and the chill that Edelbir felt did not smite her at all. She did expect the water to be cold, as it was almost winter. However, despite spending several hours in the water, Kattalin did not shiver so much as once. Whenever Kattalin left the water, however, then the cold really smote her and she shivered greatly, which forced her to go back into the water, whereupon Kattalin was strangely warm again. Kattalin found this to be very queer and thought it was surely unnatural.

"That water is cold!" said Edelbir. "If you wish, I can take your place and search the river, although I daresay that swimming is a greater skill for you than for me."

"No. I would rather keep searching the riverbed," said Kattalin. "I cannot tell why, but the water is far warmer to me than the air. Never have I swum so much before. I have heard of folk dying of the cold when in the water during the autumn or winter, yet that cold has not met me. Upon returning to land, however, I am perhaps colder than I have ever been before."

"That is strange," said Edelbir. "But I know not the reason why the cold of the water bites you not as it bites me."

"I know not either," said Kattalin, who was quite bewildered by this, though she would have been far more so if they were not searching for their fallen friend. Whatever the reason, Kattalin's mind did not dwell on it.

The two of them could search only in the day. As urgent as the matter was, at night it was far too dark and difficult to see. They worried that Adroegen might be lying somewhere and they would pass by without seeing him. Kattalin had a little more trouble seeing beneath the water at night, and she did not want to miss Adroegen if he indeed was in the river. To make matters more difficult, they could not call for their friend in the night, as the goblins were still out searching for the rest of the company. At night they heard wolves howling, although they appeared to be farther to the north. Because Edelbir sometimes entered the water, and because Kattalin was almost always in the water, it seemed that the wolves had not picked up any kind of scent.

Hiding at night was somewhat troublesome. Once leaving the river, Kattalin was cold in a way she had never been before. This did not surprise her, as it was late autumn, but upon leaving the river and becoming bitterly cold, Kattalin was quickly reminded of how much warmer she oddly felt in the water. She had a spare dress, which she had to have Edelbir carry amongst their supplies.

Every night, Kattalin needed to change immediately into her spare, dry dress when leaving the river, as her clothes she wore while swimming were soaked and cold.

As she did so, Edelbir would find some wood and make a fire. Though the two of them worried goblins might spot the fire, Edelbir and Kattalin were at the bottom of what were foggy cliffs, and so they took the risk. Kattalin was so cold when leaving the river that there was hardly a choice but to make a fire, or else she might grow sick or even die of cold. The fog fortunately hid any smoke and helped to veil the firelight. Kattalin placed her soaked dress by the fire each night to dry it, and she herself stayed very close to the fire to stay warm. At times Edelbir even had to give her his cloak. Then, the following morning, Kattalin would have to change back into the dress that she swam in, as she felt it best to make sure that one dress was always dry.

Four days had passed since Edelbir and Kattalin parted from Gleowan and Vaenn. Kattalin had swum through the river for miles without finding Adroegen's body. That was a good thing, but Edelbir, too, had not found Adroegen anywhere on the shores. They had found not so much as a single clue to Adroegen's whereabouts. Still, Edelbir and Kattalin had traveled many miles and were certain that even if the river had carried Adroegen south, he could not have been taken as far as Edelbir and Kattalin had already traveled.

"It is hopeless," said Kattalin from the river. "We have looked everywhere and have found not one sign of Adroegen."

Edelbir, too, was growing very disheartened. He did not want to give up their search, but it had been four days by then. Edelbir had said that until they find Adroegen's body, he is not dead, and that they must not give up hope. At that point, though, Edelbir began to think that if Adroegen really were still alive, he and Kattalin would surely have found him. And so, he had grown unsure of what they should do.

"Could the river have carried him even farther south?" asked Kattalin. "I think Adroegen would have washed ashore by now."

"I agree," said Edelbir. "I begin to think that he is dead."

"I fear you may be right," said Kattalin. "But I do not want to stop searching until we know."

"Yes, I do not wish to stop searching either," said Edelbir. "By now, though, I cannot see any way that he could be alive. That was too great a fall to suffer, and Adroegen was already hurt as it was."

"What do we do now?" said Kattalin. "Do we end our search for him? What if Adroegen is still alive?"

Edelbir watched the river flow south, wondering if he might be wrong, and if Adroegen might just be farther down the river. Edelbir looked north again, towards the mountains in the distance that the company had been traveling towards before being split. He and Kattalin had a difficult choice to make.

"Gleowan and Vaenn are somewhere north and west of here," said Edelbir. "They have one task, which is to find Caitren and save her. We, however, have two tasks. One is to search for our friend Adroegen. The other is a task that Adroegen himself told us we had to succeed in. That is to reach the mountains and find the hidden kingdom of dwarves, and hope they might aid in the war against Vyroun, a war that we know from the goblins will come soon. The farther down this river we search, the more we distance ourselves from that kingdom. I do not believe Adroegen would have wanted this."

"I do not want to end our search," said Kattalin. "And yet, I believe you might be right. Perhaps Adroegen would have wanted us to make for the dwarves instead of searching for him."

"A terrible choice this is," said Edelbir. "But the more I think of it, the more I begin to believe that the worst has come of our friend. I do not believe Adroegen would want us to search for him any longer. I believe he would wish for us to seek aid for the north before war comes. And since war is not far away, I know not how much time we have to find the dwarves. But we may now be wasting that time, something that Adroegen would not want of us."

Night was starting to fall, and goblins were soon going to be out, even though the pack seemed to be a good distance north. Gleowan and Vaenn, wherever they were by then, were likely in greater danger. Hopefully they were faring better in their search for Caitren, because Edelbir and Kattalin had no luck in their search for Adroegen.

"I think you are right," said Kattalin. "Adroegen would want us to search for the dwarven kingdom. The longer we wait, the more that time will be against us in seeking aid from the dwarves."

"It is decided, then," said Edelbir with much regret. "When dawn arrives, we turn and move north for the mountains."

The two of them stopped for the night. Both were very demoralized and did not want to change course. But they had another task that Adroegen told them was of great importance. War was coming, and all aid would be needed.

Edelbir and Kattalin did not wish to enter a war, but with one friend in their company likely dead, another taken, and the remaining two separated, they simply could not turn their backs to the storm that was stirring.

Kattalin came out of the river one final time, and was very cold, as she always was when leaving the water. She quickly changed into the spare dress, which she had kept dry until it was time to leave the river for good. Though Kattalin was cold right away, after some time she was fine again. It was quite strange though how no cold had bitten her while in the river. Kattalin, however, had greater concerns, thus her mind did not dwell on it.

When dawn came, Edelbir and Kattalin turned to go back north. They worried that Adroegen was only a little farther down the river, and that they were turning back too soon. Kattalin felt awful, even cross with herself for agreeing to end the search, and she tried not to cry as they turned back. There was no way of knowing, though, how close or how far away Adroegen was, or if he still lived. And so, with time passing, it was time to end their search and make for the mountains to find the hidden door.

Though Edelbir and Kattalin had spent four days making their way south, it did not take as long to cover all of that ground on their way back north, since they could travel quickly and did not need to search the river and shores anymore. They did keep their eyes open, in case by some chance they might suddenly find Adroegen somewhere. Edelbir and Kattalin, however, did not find their friend. It took only two days for them to be back to where they first began searching, and from there they went back up the cliff and made their way north through the Dead Forest.

Once Edelbir and Kattalin were back in the forest, they had to be wary of goblins again. It was difficult to tell where the goblins were and what they were up to. Somewhere in that forest, Gleowan and Vaenn were searching for Caitren. Edelbir and Kattalin could only hope Caitren was all right, and that Gleowan and Vaenn were having better luck in finding her.

For the first couple of nights, the wolves were howling. However, they seemed to be at some distance. Kattalin hoped they were not wrong in their tracking of the hunters, for they were without Adroegen, who was always able to track the goblin pack's whereabouts rather well. It appeared, though, that the two of them had passed beyond the pack's sight, or rather, I should say, beyond the wolves' smell.

Because there were only two of them instead of the full company of six, they did not stop as often, and so Edelbir and Kattalin were able to travel a greater distance each day. I daresay that not having the wounded Adroegen with them also helped, although Edelbir and Kattalin much preferred that he was with them. For even if they covered less ground each day, Adroegen still knew where the door into the dwarf kingdom was. Edelbir and Kattalin knew only to reach the wall of the mountains, turn east, and then search for a hammer striking an anvil drawn upon the rock. They did not know how easy or difficult this door would be to spot though, nor how far they would have to go before finding it.

Though it seemed that the pack did not know of their whereabouts when reentering the Dead Forest, after three days the wolves were beginning to grow louder in the night. Edelbir and Kattalin were not sure if the goblins had picked up their scent, or if some members of the pack were farther north and the wolves grew louder because the two of them were hastily traveling in that very direction. If Adroegen were there with them, he would likely have known better where the goblins were within that forest, as well as whether the wolves were picking up their scent. The two of them had learned much from Adroegen during their venture, yet they felt quite lost once on their own. I could not begin to tell how much they anguished over having to leave Adroegen and presume him to be dead, wherever he was by then.

Edelbir and Kattalin had been heading north for eight days since deciding to end their search for Adroegen. The two of them were very close to reaching the mountains. The trees thinned as that day went on. All was quiet during the day, but they knew that at nightfall the goblins would be out. Edelbir and Kattalin ran north as swiftly as they could in hopes of reaching the mountains before the pack would be out and searching.

It was late in the afternoon when the two of them finally reached the wall of the Silver Mountains. The fells were steep, and their rock glittered a little in the sunlight. There was not very much sunlight, though, because they were drawing closer to the dark kingdom farther to the north. Night was soon going to fall, as well. Kattalin hoped the door was close, and that they would be able to find it quickly.

"How long do we have until nightfall?" said Kattalin as she and Edelbir began to search the mountain wall.

"I would think another hour, perhaps two," said Edelbir. "We do not have long before our enemies will search for us."

"I think we best search into the night," said Kattalin, who was uneasy about doing so. "Though I worry that in the dark we might pass the door. Yet if we linger and rest here, then it might be easier for the goblins to find us. And if the door is close, then we could find it and hopefully be safe from the pack."

"I must agree," said Edelbir. "I fear that in the night, this door might be difficult to find. Careful we must be, and very keen eyes we must have."

"Let us hope that we find it easily," said Kattalin. "For you are right, I think. And not only that, but we must hope that if we do enter the mountains, no goblins will see, nor know that we entered. For Adroegen has told us that these dwarves are a force Vyroun knows not of. I know nothing of war, and thus I know not what advantage these dwarves might be. But these kingdoms in the north, Gundmar and the Woodlands, surely would have a greater chance with help at their side."

"We must not fail in this," said Edelbir.

The two of them then turned east and began to search along the mountain wall. They were very careful. Even though there was need to move swiftly, Edelbir and Kattalin did not want to pass the door and miss it. Nightfall was coming, and soon the goblins would be out. The two of them searched but thus far did not find a hammer striking an anvil. They wished they had asked Adroegen for further detail on the door, as to how far east it was, how easy it would be to spot, and how large or small it was. Edelbir and Kattalin were unsure whether the door was simply farther down the mountain wall and they simply needed to keep going east, or if the door had been within their sight and they had missed it.

The sun soon set. It had been growing more and more difficult to see, and so Edelbir and Kattalin could not move as swiftly as before. Though the Silver Mountains glittered in sunlight, in the night those fells became dark. Edelbir and Kattalin needed to look very closely for the door in the night. Before long the two of them thought it best to put their hands on the walls, as the door, according to Adroegen, would simply open if one who was a friend to the dwarves, or one who did not mean ill, touched the hammer and anvil. To the two of them, such magic seemed difficult to imagine, but they trusted what Adroegen had told them. If Edelbir and Kattalin had difficulty seeing the mountain wall closely in the dark, then perhaps if they simply kept their hands on the wall as they moved eastward, then at some point a door might open.

It did not take long before wolves began howling in the night. They were not very far away too. Edelbir and Kattalin needed to hurry, and yet at the same time they needed to be silent, for they did not want the pack to hear them. They were moving a little more slowly and keeping watch behind them in case the pack was getting close.

"The wolves are growing louder," said Edelbir. "They are close. I am sure that they have caught our scent."

"I hope the door is close," said Kattalin, who was growing worried as she looked carefully along the mountain wall. "If the pack comes near, then we will have to find a place to hide."

The two of them had been searching for hours. It was uncertain whether or not they were going to find the door that night, and the two of them feared that the pack was so close that the goblins would find them first. Kattalin was searching, while Edelbir was beginning to look into the woods, watching and listening for the pack. It did not take very long before Kattalin heard him grow fearful.

"Oh no," said Edelbir. Kattalin soon heard not only the wolves, but the approaching goblins shouting to each other. They had to have been very close. She searched faster along the mountain wall and hoped that the door was close.

"We have to hurry," said Kattalin, who searched as Edelbir kept watch. The goblins' voices were faint at first, but they slowly became clearer. There were several small ridges along the mountain wall that were tall enough that Edelbir and Kattalin could hide behind them. The two of them began passing from one ridge to another while trying not to be seen, and at the same time searching for the door.

"These wolves are on to something!" Kattalin heard one goblin shout. The voice was faint, but she was able to discern it.

"I do not see them yet," whispered Edelbir to Kattalin.

"They're here somewhere," said another goblin. "But where on earth are those scum heading? I don't see nothing! There's no city nearby or anything!"

Edelbir and Kattalin hurried in their search. The pack was very close to catching them. Kattalin was looking in haste for the door as Edelbir searched for a place they could hide. It was still early in the night, and morning was far away.

"I see some of them now," whispered Edelbir, peeking over the rock. The goblins were still a short way away but within sight. "It does not appear that they see us. We need to find a place to hide. In the morning we can search any places along the wall that we missed."

"But first we need to make it to morning," said Kattalin. The two of them quietly ran east along the mountains. Fortunately, the woods were thicker there, and so the goblins had to look through many trees, making it easier for Edelbir and Kattalin to run without being seen. Several boulders sat upon the ground and many ridges formed from the mountain wall where Edelbir and Kattalin could hide. The pack did not find them, though the goblins stayed on their trail. The two of them found a place to hide, at least for a time, behind a larger ridge along the mountain wall. They listened for the pack. Edelbir and Kattalin could still hear the goblins, and their voices were growing louder.

"It looks like they're going east. Our wolves appear to have picked something up!" said one goblin. Edelbir and Kattalin heard more goblins approaching.

They could not linger, otherwise Edelbir and Kattalin were only waiting to be found. The two of them ran farther. Wolves howled loudly behind them. The goblins had not spotted them, but were getting closer. Edelbir and Kattalin quietly made for the next ridge and quickly hid behind it.

"I think I hear running!" said a goblin. "Someone is close. Maybe we best just run along these mountains and then we'll find them!"

"They are going to find us," said Edelbir. Kattalin worried that they would have to fight. Edelbir had his hand on his sword, ready to draw it. Kattalin was about to draw hers, too. She and Edelbir peeked over the rock. There was a good score of goblins on wolves, and they were slowly approaching their hiding spot. Soon they were only a few dozen strides away. Kattalin crouched behind the ridge again and turned towards the mountain wall.

About a dozen strides ahead was another ridge jutting out from the mountain wall, forming a half circle. As Kattalin faced the mountain wall, her eye caught something odd. She looked closer, and could faintly see chiseled into the stone a hammer striking an anvil. Kattalin's heart lifted. The drawing was difficult to see in the dark, and if Kattalin did not look closely, she would not have seen it.

"Edelbir!" whispered Kattalin, tugging on Edelbir's cloak with great urgency.

"Quiet!" whispered Edelbir, turning to her. Kattalin pointed to the drawing on the mountain wall. Though it took a moment, Edelbir lit up, and Kattalin knew that he too had spotted the door.

Kattalin's spirits lifted, though the goblins were still approaching. Their voices grew loud, and it would surely be mere moments before the pack found them.

"They are almost here," whispered Edelbir. "Go now and make for it!"

The two of them rose and ran for the hammer and anvil upon the mountain wall. Behind them, the goblins approached. "I hear running! And close, too!"

Edelbir and Kattalin, however, did not look behind them. They had to run about a dozen strides to reach where the hammer and anvil were chiseled into the rock. Edelbir and Kattalin were not sure if a door would open with but a simple touch of their hands, as such magic seemed difficult to imagine, and they only hoped that Adroegen was correct and that they would be able to slip into the mountains. The two of them reached out and immediately touched the hammer and anvil. The mountain wall swung inward, so suddenly that Edelbir and Kattalin nearly fell. They ran inside the mountain and then the door swung shut behind them.

All was silent. Edelbir and Kattalin could no longer hear the goblins, who were somewhere just outside the mountain wall, likely mere feet away from where they were standing. The two of them feared that the door might open for the goblins also, but it did not.

It was dark inside the mountains, though there was a little light coming from somewhere behind them. It did not take very long before Edelbir and Kattalin were discovered.

"Welcome, friends!" said a very hearty voice behind them. Both of them were frightened by the sudden greeting, but it was clear by the sound of the voice that it was not a goblin, nor any other foul creature.

Chapter Three; Miners at Work

Edelbir and Kattalin were given quite a surprise, I daresay, for mere moments before, they had been running from a pack of goblins along the mountains and were about to be found. Suddenly, instead, they were safe from their hunters, and almost immediately upon entering the mountains, someone appeared to have given them a warm welcome. Edelbir and Kattalin though did not settle their wariness, as they had not before met whoever it was that greeted them, thus the two of them did not yet know with certainty that he was a friend.

They turned around to see who had bid them welcome. Just a short way up a long stairway were two dwarves, both appearing quite jolly. To each side of the stairs were stone walls that held several torches, all of which were lit, though even then it was still dim inside the mountain. In the distance, Edelbir and Kattalin could hear faint sounds of metal striking upon metal, and roaring fires.

Both dwarves were quite ugly-looking. Although I would say that dwarves were not ugly like goblins, nor were they as ill as goblins. Dwarves were mostly friendlier, even if they oft kept to themselves, digging beneath the earth. The faces of these two dwarves were wrinkled, even though they were rather young for dwarves. They were almost as wide as they were tall. The dwarves had very long beards, one red, and the other orange. Both wore thick gambesons, each matching the color of the dwarf's beard. They also had wide belts with large buckles, and tall, thick boots over dark pants.

"Welcome!" said the red-bearded dwarf, a little more loudly the second time. Edelbir and Kattalin realized that they needed to speak, even though they were still looking about to see where they had found themselves.

"Hello to you," said Edelbir, not knowing what else to say. Though Edelbir and Kattalin were quite bemused at receiving what seemed to be a warm welcome from these strangers, the two dwarves had looks of equal bemusement upon their own faces, as if they had not been expecting Edelbir or Kattalin to enter their home.

"You must forgive us," began Kattalin. "For we have not before ventured to your kingdom, and as strangers we were surprised to be found so quickly and given such a warm welcome from you."

"Well of course we would give you a warm welcome!" said the orange-bearded dwarf with enthusiasm. "For you are friends of ours! You are of good rather than of ill. Otherwise you would not have been able to open the door into our home. And I would say that we are far more surprised than you are, for we oft stand guard upon the southern door of our home, though this door rarely opens, except by one other man who discovered us here."

Edelbir and Kattalin were surprised by how quickly the dwarves accepted them as friends. Though they had heard from Adroegen that the dwarves were allies, a worry still lingered that they would not be. I daresay that this was simply because Edelbir and Kattalin had only just met the dwarves and thus did not know them yet. But nonetheless, if the dwarves already considered them friends, Edelbir and Kattalin would take it. This was far easier than when Adroegen had to talk the company's way out of trouble with the eagles some time before.

"And what might your names be?" asked the orange-bearded dwarf.

"I am Edelbir," said Edelbir.

"A good and strong name," said the red-bearded dwarf. "And my fair lady, what name are you known by?"

"And I am Kattalin," said Kattalin. "We came from farther south, being chased and hunted by a pack of goblins since summer."

"Well, you shall be safe from them here!" said the red-bearded dwarf. "I am Kari."

"And I am Koli," said the orange-bearded dwarf. "A pack of goblins, you say? Well, a good thing it is that you found this place! What luck!"

"I must agree," said Kattalin. "We were searching for the door into your kingdom, and were fortunate to find it right before the goblins found us."

"I say, how did you know that we were hidden in these mountains?" asked Koli with a great deal of curiosity. "And what led you to search for us?"

"We and our company were making our way here," said Edelbir. "You say that one other man has discovered you here. Do you speak of Adroegen, by any chance?"

"Yes! It is Adroegen who discovered us here," said Kari. "A few summers ago, he stumbled upon our door. I suppose he was just venturing along these mountains aimlessly. We were standing watch here, though there never seemed any sense in doing so. But that day it was not the case, and we were surprised to find the door open, just as we did now when you entered."

"It seems to me that you know him," said Koli.

"Yes," said Kattalin. "Our home was razed to the ground by goblins and it was he who led us away from danger for the past several months."

"And where is he now, might I ask?" said Kari. "He has been a good friend to Koli and I, one who would visit on occasion. Though our king wanted him to keep our home secret."

Edelbir and Kattalin looked to each other. Kattalin did not have the heart to tell of Adroegen's falling. She was still filled with grief, and it hurt her greatly that the two of them had given up in searching for Adroegen, even if they felt he would have wanted them to find the dwarves.

And Edelbir, too, did not want to speak of what became of their friend. However, he had no choice. For the very dwarves asking what had become of Adroegen were the same dwarves Edelbir and Kattalin hoped would lend their help against Vyroun. If Adroegen was their friend also, then perhaps the news of his probable death might help bring the dwarves out of the mountains and into the coming war, though Edelbir, if he could choose, would much prefer Adroegen were there, speaking with the dwarves himself. For that matter, Edelbir preferred that all from the company were there with them.

"What became of Adroegen?" said Koli with concern in his voice. "You say that he has led you away from peril since summer, and yet he is not here with you now. I would have you speak of what has become of him."

"He fell over a cliff several days ago," said Edelbir. Kattalin was trying not to let any tears fall from her eyes.

Kari and Koli both looked very stunned.

"He is gone?" asked Kari.

"The goblins pursued us through the Dead Forest for the past many days," said Edelbir, who then told the dwarves about how the company was cornered by goblins, and how Adroegen had already been hurt by the goblin chief. "One in our company, Caitren, was taken captive by the pack. Adroegen was pushed over the cliff by the goblins. The other two amongst our company, Gleowan and Vaenn their names are, set out in search of Caitren."

"Edelbir and I spent days searching for Adroegen," said Kattalin, who spoke of their search at the bottom of the cliff and the river. "After four days we found not a sign of him. Then we decided he is likely dead and that we could not delay. For Adroegen wanted us to find this kingdom."

"What made him wish for you to reach us?" asked Kari.

Edelbir and Kattalin were both unsure of what to say, for they knew from Adroegen that the king wanted to keep his kingdom a secret, and that the two of them were there to try and persuade the king to enter the war in the north, and in doing so break that very intent. And so, the act of persuading the king needed to be done rather carefully. Edelbir in particular did not want to simply ask straightaway for aid, even if the matter was urgent, for he worried that pushing upon the king such a choice of entering war and coming out of hiding would lead the king to refuse their request. They needed to speak with the king, though Edelbir was a little unsure how best to go about it. "Where is your king? We hoped to speak with him."

"We may take you to him," said Koli. "Though I would

warn that it shall be quite a walk."

"Not to worry," said Edelbir. "We have grown quite used to long walks since leaving home."

Kari and Koli led Edelbir and Kattalin up the stairs and deeper into the mountains. Faint sounds of metal clanking and fires roaring slowly grew louder. After Edelbir and Kattalin made their way up the stairs, they were taken through many tunnels and passages. After some time, the sounds of metal and fires grew louder, and the two of them were led past mines where many dwarves were digging for what treasures lay in the deep.

Hundreds of dwarves were mining. They all were shorter than goblins, reaching only a little above Edelbir's and Kattalin's waists. All were dressed very warmly, as the air was cold within the mine. There was no fire there, so not only was it cold but also dark, although the rock itself did glitter a little, which helped the dwarves see. Although they contained gems and other precious metals, you might guess that in the Silver Mountains, silver was by far the most common treasure. And if you did have such a hunch, I would say that you were quite right. The rock glittered with silver.

Edelbir and Kattalin walked along a causeway. Beneath was a deep abyss that they could see no end to, and dwarves climbed down on ropes with hammers and chisels. Kattalin thought it was a good thing that Vaenn was not there, as Vaenn did not love heights. The sight of the abyss made even Edelbir and Kattalin a little anxious to go near the edge.

The two of them shivered as they walked through the mines, for it was quite cold in there. Some dwarves noticed them, and though Edelbir and Kattalin might just look like regular folk to you or me, to the dwarves they were quite discernible, as the two of them were very tall in comparison. A few of them gave Edelbir and Kattalin rather concerned looks, but most of the dwarves appeared friendly. They had a clear love for what they did, and this was something Edelbir could not help but admire, as he was one who loved to work. Edelbir would not have minded living and working in a place like the dwarven kingdom, though the only trouble was that he preferred to be out in the sun rather than surrounded by walls of stone. The dwarves had their own song to keep themselves cheerful:

> *Deep within the rock and stone,*
> *That is where the miners roam,*
> *Beneath the earth we make our home,*
> *Finding wealth before unknown.*
>
> *Fear not! The dwarves do you find,*
> *Digging for metals deep in the mine,*
> *Dark it may seem down in the deep,*
> *Til gold and jewels are found to shine.*

After walking for perhaps an hour and passing a few mines, Edelbir and Kattalin found themselves being led through dark tunnels again. They heard fires roaring and hammers striking against metal and stone. The air was getting hotter. The tunnels were dark, save for torches giving enough light to see, but soon it was very bright ahead. The mines by then were well behind them.

Kari and Koli led them into a great forge. There had been a forge back in Edelbir and Kattalin's village before it was destroyed, though only Edelbir made anything there, on occasion, and all he forged were horseshoes and farming tools. It was far beyond little in comparison to the forge the dwarves worked in.

"My goodness! I have worked in a small forge back at our home, but it was nowhere near this size," said Edelbir. He was most fascinated watching the dwarves crafting. Edelbir and Kattalin were in a gigantic hall, with many more dwarves forging coins, goblets, weapons, and armor. There were great furnaces, much taller than the two of them, making the room so hot that one might faint were they not careful. These flames were fanned by bellows the size of trolls, and they made the fires burn much hotter. From what Edelbir could see, barrels were endlessly wheeled in with what the miners had been able to find, and then some forgers appeared to inspect what metals they were given to work with before deciding what they would craft with them.

Elsewhere in the forge, Edelbir and Kattalin heard hammer strokes falling. Smiths were forging weapons of all kinds: swords, axes, hammers, and shields. Lying around was armor that looked thick and very heavy. Seeing this made Edelbir and Kattalin feel hopeful that perhaps the dwarves might have already been preparing for war, and that perhaps they knew of what troubles were taking place outside of their home, though they still heeded Adroegen's words, that the king wanted his kingdom kept a secret and did not want to join in any conflicts. Not only did armor lie about though, but also all kinds of coins, mostly silver, and other gems and treasures, thus Edelbir and Kattalin could not tell if they were readying for battle.

"Could they be preparing for war?" whispered Kattalin. She was hopeful that it may have been so, and that perhaps their task of seeking aid might be easier than they thought. Kattalin wondered if Edelbir thought the same.

"This cannot be a bad sign," said Edelbir. "In the least, the dwarves would be prepared for battle, if they are in fact going to enter. That is, in the end, what we do not know with any certainty."

Edelbir and Kattalin were led then to another hall, where they found the largest treasure that either of them had ever looked upon in their lives. (Although I must say that coming from a simple village, the two of them had never really looked upon any treasure at all.) There were all kinds of gems and silver coins lying about in the forge, but that was only a small portion of the wealth and treasure that the dwarves had unearthed. And they were working hard at unearthing even more. Most of the treasure was silver, and it shined and glittered immensely throughout the hall.

Kattalin thought the gems looked quite dazzling, but she and Edelbir, being simple folk, did not see much use in this sort of wealth, and had their friends been with them, they certainly would not have seen much use for it either, even if Gleowan's and Vaenn's eyes might have widened a little. Oh, how they missed their friends. It did not at all feel right being separated from the others of the company. Edelbir and Kattalin were led along a very long causeway that took them over a great hall of treasure, and to their sides there were dwarves wheeling barrels of gems and coins and then dumping them over the causeway, adding to what was already an enormous treasure.

It took quite some time before Edelbir and Kattalin reached the end of the hall. Then they were led back through long and endless tunnels, up and down many stairs. The air grew quite cold again, almost as cold as winter. The two of them were not sure how long they had been walking at that point. It must have been a good few hours since Edelbir and Kattalin first entered the mountains. They were not at all sure what time of day it was, or what time of night, as it was in the night when they first found the door.

After walking through some tunnels, Edelbir and Kattalin were led into an enormous dining hall. In there, hundreds of dwarves were feasting at long tables. From what Edelbir and Kattalin saw, the dwarves ate meat and almost nothing else. The two of them were not sure precisely where the dwarves found so much food, but then again, they had never lived in mountains, thus they knew nothing of what food might be found there. Great pillars many feet wide went to the ceiling, although the ceiling was so high it could not be seen. Several fires roared and made the room warmer.

It appeared that they had reached the end of their long walk. Kari and Koli had slowed down and appeared to be looking for someone, perhaps the king. Edelbir and Kattalin, of course, did not know which of the many dwarves was their king. As Kari and Koli led them through the hall, several dwarves quickly turned their attention to Edelbir and Kattalin, just as many in the mines and the forge had done, for they were probably not used to seeing such tall folk within their kingdom.

"Aki must be in the throne hall," said Koli, finally. The two dwarves had been quiet for some time while leading

Edelbir and Kattalin deeper and deeper into the mountains.

Before long they reached the end of the hall and were walking up many stairs through another tunnel. It was dark but there was some light ahead, and it was not firelight. Edelbir and Kattalin were not sure how high they had climbed, but finally they reached another hall, one smaller than the hall where many dwarves were feasting.

In this hall it was not nearly as crowded. There were only about a dozen dwarves or so. Edelbir and Kattalin were likely high up in the mountains. The hall had many windows, and if one were to look out from any one of them, they would see the whole kingdom at work, mining and crafting and adding to their treasure. It soon became clear that the night had lifted, and that it was at least sometime in the morning. Though the ceiling was high and hard to see, there was unmistakably sunlight coming in. Somewhere the dwarves had dug a small hole from the ceiling, and from some distance away the sun's light made its way in and shined directly onto a great throne carved of rock. The throne itself was dark but had strange writing carved in silver, which glittered where the sunlight touched it.

Sitting upon the throne was a dwarf that was a little taller than the others, though certainly not as tall as Edelbir or Kattalin. He had a gold crown, which was rather strange, being that the dwarves were living in mountains rank with far more silver than gold. Some dwarves around the king were clad in heavy armor, though the king himself wore only a red gambeson, which closely matched his red beard, although there was a little bit of grey within that long beard. Though he was as wide as the other dwarves, Aki looked strong and burly. He wore a wide belt with a large iron buckle, and on his feet were thick boots. The king was speaking with some of his guards.

Beside Aki was another dwarf who looked much the same but younger. He wore his own crown, but his was of silver. This dwarf was instead in armor that looked almost impenetrable. If the goblin pack had encountered him, Edelbir and Kattalin were not sure that any of them would have been able to draw blood from him. Yet this dwarf appeared friendly, and he walked over to Kari and Koli and Edelbir and Kattalin once they entered.

"You look as bored as ever, Lofar," said Kari to this dwarf. "And the king appears equally so."

"There is no fooling you, as I have found, cousin," said Lofar to Kari. "My father is thinking of digging a little farther down the mountains in time, though there is little else we are talking about."

Edelbir and Kattalin were surprised, as Kari and Koli made no mention that they were relatives to the king and the king's son, and Lofar then introduced himself to the two of them as he spoke to Kari and Koli. "I see you have not been bored, Kari and Koli. The door to the south has been discovered again, I see. I am Lofar, son of Aki."

Edelbir and Kattalin both introduced themselves. Edelbir spoke. "We are friends of Adroegen, and we wanted to speak with your king."

"This way," said Lofar. He led them to the throne, where Aki was speaking to some of his guards. He did not seem to notice Edelbir and Kattalin when they entered, but they had his attention before long.

"Who are these two that have discovered our kingdom?" said Aki.

Edelbir and Kattalin introduced themselves. Though the king looked upon them rather intently, he was still friendly.

"Welcome to our kingdom," said Aki. "You are not the first to have discovered us here, although there is only one other that knows of our existence within these mountains. Where do you come from, and how did you come to discover us, may I ask?"

"We come from far south of here," said Edelbir, who told of how he and Kattalin came to be where they were now, how they were attacked by the goblin chief and his pack, who razed their homes and killed all of the villagers, save for them and their friends. Edelbir spoke of how Vyroun commanded the goblin chief to recover the Night's Jewel, which Adroegen took from the goblin chief years before. He told of how they had been on the run since, fleeing from a pack of goblins, and how there were six in their company, though they had been separated when the pack found them again after the goblin chief's defeat, with Caitren being taken captive and Gleowan and Vaenn searching for her, and Adroegen falling over a cliff and into the ravine below, where Edelbir and Kattalin, after searching for four days, could not find him.

The king listened quietly, and his son appeared to show much sympathy for them. When mention of Adroegen's fall was made, Aki and particularly Lofar appeared stunned. The two looked at each other, and then Aki spoke. "And is he gone? We have grown familiar with Adroegen since he discovered us. He has met his end?"

"Edelbir and I searched for days for him," said Kattalin. "However, when we looked, we found not a sign of him. We believe he must have met his end."

"You were friends of Adroegen, who discovered us in the mountains?" asked the king, who appeared saddened to hear their troubles, but also curious. "He must have told you of our kingdom, did he not?"

"Yes, we have been friends with him," said Kattalin, answering the first question from Aki. She was nervous though to answer the second, for Adroegen told them that the king wanted his kingdom kept secret, and she feared that Aki would grow angry with them if she answered yes. "He wandered to our village by chance years ago, and we have been friends ever since, though it would seem that he is gone now."

"Yes, I am sorry to hear this," said Aki. "We had grown friendly with him since he found our kingdom a few years ago, a kingdom that you, after being led north by him, also found. He told you of us, there is no denying it. And you must have had a reason for coming here."

Kattalin worried that the king was not happy with them. Aki showed sympathy, but she could also sense anger beneath his voice. She was certain the king knew that Adroegen had told her and Edelbir of the hidden kingdom, and that he was not pleased about it. Though the two of them needed to request help against Vyroun, they worried that pushing the king straightaway into coming out of hiding, which Adroegen told them the king did not want to do, would lead to Aki refusing them. However, it appeared that Aki was very keen to the fact that the two them had a specific reason to enter his kingdom.

"Adroegen was leading our company here before we were separated," said Edelbir. "When Adroegen was wounded in the middle of the Dead Forest, we needed to take him someplace safe. The closest places for him were either the kingdom of Gundmar, which is a distance west of here, or to this kingdom, where he felt we might be safe from our hunters."

"Indeed, you shall be safe from them here," said Aki. "Though I am very curious. I have been told that Adroegen has fallen, or at least you are certain of it. That would take away any reason for you to find this kingdom, and yet you still came here and sought us. There must be another reason you are here. You say that one in your company has been taken captive, and yet after giving up in your search for Adroegen, believing him to be gone, you did not join your friends in search of her. You came to our kingdom. Your friend that is captive, where is she being taken?"

"Caitren is being taken to Vyroun's kingdom," said Kattalin, who was quite worried, as the king was pressing them and beginning to sound a little hostile. "The pack took her away west and to Mûrondûn in the north. Though we know not precisely where in Vyroun's kingdom."

"Mûrondûn, yes, once a dwarven kingdom thousands of years ago," said Aki. "Until Vyroun drove us dwarves east and took all that we mined in those mountains ages ago, and he has held dominion over what were once dwarven lands, and we dwarves have not returned there since. To the north that kingdom lies, and to go there the pack must surely first head west around these mountains. Yet you did not track them and seek out your friend. From what you have told me, I do not doubt the bond that all in your company share, so I cannot see why you would come here instead of searching for your friend, when Adroegen himself is gone. There is another reason for you to come here. Adroegen told you of this door. I cannot doubt it. Did he want you to come here, and if indeed he did, why?"

Edelbir and Kattalin looked to each other. It was clear to Kattalin that the king was not at all a fool. He clearly knew that there was some purpose why Edelbir and Kattalin came there, and perhaps he knew they were there to ask for aid against the north. It was vital, from what Adroegen told them, that they get help from the dwarves against Vyroun, as his forces were strong, and all help was needed. Kattalin knew that they were about to learn whether the dwarves might be of help to them, or how strong of a will the king had towards remaining hidden.

"Adroegen wanted us to reach this place," said Edelbir. "He told us that it was important that we find you. For these past months, our company has heard word from the goblins that war will soon come. Vyroun will soon launch an assault upon the northern kingdoms of these lands. The night Adroegen fell, we were told by one of the goblins that Vyroun would wage war very soon. He wanted Adroegen killed, and the rest of us brought before him. The goblins hunting us were to return swiftly to not be absent from the storm that is brewing."

"And why did Adroegen want you to find us?" asked the king.

Kattalin spoke, though she was certain that the king already knew the answer. "Adroegen told us you dwarves are a strong force," she said. "Not only that, but you are a kingdom in these lands that Vyroun knows not of, and so he has not faced you before. If you could aid us in this coming war, it would give the north an advantage, though I know not how much so, for I myself have never seen war."

"Adroegen wanted your help," said Edelbir. "He hoped we would reach your kingdom, in hopes of persuading you into helping face the evil growing in the north, evil that Kattalin and I have seen much of already. We know it will not cease, and it will not disappear if we but ignore it or hide from it. As our company learned in our recent journey, the only way to lift darkness is by facing it."

"I see," said Aki with a deep sigh of displeasure. The king slumped in his chair and planted his forehead in the palm of his hand. "So, you have come here for our help."

"Adroegen wanted to seek your aid in war, yes," said Edelbir. Aki looked to his son. Lofar appeared to show much sympathy for Edelbir and Kattalin, however, the king's son was not the one who would choose their course of action.

"Our battalions are prepared to fight," said Lofar. Edelbir and Kattalin's hopes rose, as the other dwarves seemed as if they wanted to fight and aid those in the north. But again, I daresay that it was the king's choice that mattered. Aki rose and went to one of the windows to look about at the many dwarves mining, crafting, or stowing away treasures.

"We have not been in these mountains for long," said Aki to the dwarves. "Some time ago we fled our home. Oh, Keldagull, how I long to look upon the Gold Fountain again. But it is lost. We have been driven away from our home, into these mountains, where we have built a new home. Our dwarves are still at work, but what a kingdom we have now! After we were driven away, I remembered what my duty as king of Keldagull's people was, more clearly than ever."

Aki then spoke a verse:

From this fountain shall wealth forever flow,
But our greatest treasure shall never be gold.

"Father," began Lofar, as if he were trying to reason with the king.

"I will not forget what my greatest duty is as king," said Aki. "And that is the well-being of my people. I have already seen many of us die in the past. I will not have it happen again. We are safe in these mountains, hidden from any enemy that might seek to harm us."

"Father, we cannot stand down when evil is legion," said Lofar. "It shall only surround us and then find us again in time, and we shall be driven from here as we were from Keldagull."

"Enough!" said the king, who then turned to Edelbir and Kattalin. "I am sorry to hear of the loss of Adroegen, I truly am. You may remain within this kingdom for as long as you wish. Safe shall both of you be here. If such peril is coming as you say, then I would advise that you remain here! However, I cannot give you what you seek. I have brought death upon my people before. I will not do it again. We shall not aid you, nor any kingdoms in the north in this war against Vyroun."

Aki then left the hall, perhaps to go to his chambers. Edelbir and Kattalin looked to each other and knew not what to do, nor if there was any hope of being able to persuade the king into helping the north. They could only wonder if they should have approached Aki differently. Edelbir and Kattalin worried that they had already failed greatly in their quest. Meanwhile, Lofar appeared to feel very sorry for the two of them. Kari and Koli looked no different.

"Let him be for now," said Lofar to Kari and Koli, who then signaled for Edelbir and Kattalin to follow them out of the throne hall and back into the kingdom the king wanted to keep hidden.

Chapter Four;
The Guard of the North

Fifteen days had passed since Gleowan and Vaenn parted with their friends, although I would say that by then they were not at all sure how many days they had spent on the run searching for Caitren. They had been heading west, chasing the goblins that had taken her captive. There was no time for rest, because if the two of them did so, they feared their friend might be taken well beyond their reach. Caitren, however, might have already been gone. Gleowan and Vaenn were not sure, and thus they could only keep searching in hopes that they might find her.

The two of them were very tired each day, out of breath, and growing hungry. There were some nuts for food in the Dead Forest, but not a lot. They hardly slept each night, worrying that they would fall farther behind the pack. The goblins were on wolves while Gleowan and Vaenn were on foot, thus there was already little hope as it was. The only chance they had was if the goblins rested during each day, allowing the two to them to gain and catch up. For this to happen, though, Gleowan and Vaenn needed to run swiftly not only during the day but also in the night.

Luck had not been on their side. Each night, Gleowan and Vaenn would hear wolves, though they were always faint, coming from somewhere to the west. The two of them would always run after the sounds of the howling. This was their only possible way of finding Caitren. Gleowan and Vaenn were not the most skilled in finding tracks on the ground to follow, nor any other signs of the goblins. If only Adroegen were with them, they could not help but think, for he would have known far better how to track the pack. Both Gleowan and Vaenn were feeling more and more hopeless, as the sounds of the wolves' howling seemed more and more distant with each passing night. Even though the two of them ran during the night as well as the day, it did not appear to be enough for them to gain any ground on the wolves the goblins rode. After several days, Gleowan and Vaenn no longer heard wolves in the night.

The two of them were not running along the very edge of the Silver Mountains, but close enough that the mountains towered over them. It was midday. Gleowan and Vaenn were near the western edge of the Dead Forest. The trees bore no leaves, and thus the two of them were able to see well ahead. Soon they saw the end of those eerie woods, and made it there. Ahead, they knew, was the kingdom of Gundmar.

Before the two of them was not another forest, nor was it a great field like the one they saw in the Southern Fold when the company made their way to the Fornwood months before. Instead a great garden lay ahead, one that went as far as the eye could see. There were few to no trees, but instead all kinds of thickets and shrubs and other sorts of bushes. It was not the Dead Forest, although being what would have been late November, by your calendar, nothing was bearing any leaves.

"It has been several days and we have not found Caitren," said Vaenn, catching her breath, feeling hopeless. "I do not think we have any chance now."

Gleowan and Vaenn looked to the north. Vyroun's kingdom was still far away, but the dark clouds were much closer and larger. The two of them were getting closer to what looked like a dark, empty void in the north. Gleowan spoke. "For all we know, Caitren is already in Mûrondûn, and who knows what has happened to her. If this is so, then we have failed."

"I do not want to give up, in case she can still be found," said Vaenn. "But I think we have lost the pack. We no longer hear wolves in the night, and no matter how little rest we take, we cannot gain on them."

"I, too, think we have lost them," said Gleowan. "Why do we still fight when hope is gone? Perhaps because we cannot know that it truly is. We must move north now, and hope that there is still a chance to find her."

Gleowan and Vaenn went into the great garden of Gundmar and turned north. There were several thickets to go around, but the garden had few enough obstacles for them to run at a good speed. It was daytime, so the two of them were not going to find any goblins or hear any wolves howling. Before long, though, Gleowan and Vaenn began to hear horses running, which meant men must have been close by. If so, Vaenn wondered if these men might know the whereabouts of the goblin pack.

"Are those soldiers of Gundmar?" said Vaenn, trying to listen. "If they are, then perhaps they might have found the pack, and therefore Caitren!"

"If they are Gundmar soldiers, that is," said Gleowan. "I do not wish to bring my hopes up. However, you could be right. We must keep hidden and find these men on horseback and see if they may be friends."

The two of them went on with their run but kept hidden in the thickets. The sounds of horses came from somewhere to the west. Not only that, but the horses seemed to be getting nearer. Gleowan and Vaenn climbed a tall hill and stayed low to hide, and to keep a lookout. There were soldiers riding not too far away, and these soldiers were heading in their direction.

"They must be soldiers of Gundmar," said Gleowan. "For they are all armored, and bear no resemblance to the wicked men we saw at the Gap of Gundmar this past summer. If so, then they are not foes of ours."

Vaenn began to feel hopeful, at least that the two of them might be able to find some clues or answers, if nothing else. "They might know something, or they might be able to help us. We cannot let these soldiers ride by us!"

Gleowan and Vaenn ran for the riders. The rumble in the earth grew louder as the horses drew closer. The two of them could not let the riders pass by, in case they might be able to help Gleowan and Vaenn in finding Caitren.

"Here! Here!" shouted Gleowan and Vaenn. They called for the riders, and to their fortune, the riders noticed them. Though the horsemen at first appeared as if they were about to ride by Gleowan and Vaenn, they soon turned and rode directly towards them. Vaenn began to feel some hope. The riders, however, did not ride towards them and say good afternoon. Instead they circled around Gleowan and Vaenn, surrounding them.

There were around a hundred riders in total. Every

one of them was clad in armor. Not one soldier was without a helm. Each wore a layer of chainmail beneath a green chest plate of scales. In the center of each chest plate was a symbol of a great sun surrounded by eight rays of light. Each ray was four-pointed, looking like they could also be stars, with the one at the very top being the tallest and largest. Within the sun was the head of a horse, and then a hawk, whose wings were spread. The soldiers bore green flags with the very same symbol. Gleowan and Vaenn thought it was likely the emblem of Gundmar, but were not certain. They only knew that the soldiers were not giving them any kind of warm welcome. They were all armed with spears, which they pointed at Gleowan and Vaenn. The two of them could only raise their hands in surrender. Vaenn was growing nervous that these soldiers were not going to be so friendly.

"Who are you, and what business do you have within the Kaelunen of Gundmar?" said one soldier. "Make haste with your words!"

"I am Gleowan, and this is Vaenn," said Gleowan. "We are but simple folk from the south, far south of your kingdom."

"Are you?" said the leader of the horsemen. "And if so, then why do you come this far north, and so armed?"

"We have been running from a pack of goblins since last summer," said Vaenn. "A pack under the command of Vyroun, hunting our friend Adroegen, and this hunt we were caught in."

"Adroegen? Never heard of him," said the soldier. "And where precisely did you come from in the south? Speak swiftly!"

Vaenn was hesitant to answer, wondering if they should tell of their hidden village, even though it was destroyed. Gleowan spoke. "Our home was hidden, though the goblin chief one night razed it this past summer and then hunted our company, until our friend slayed him recently."

"None have managed to slay the goblin chief," said the soldier. "I am not sure I can believe you. What might the leader of the goblins be doing so far south when war is coming? And we soldiers come from the Southern Fold of Gundmar, thus we know of the lands beneath our borders. Yet you cannot tell us precisely where you are from? Both of you sound very suspicious. Perhaps you are spies?"

"We search for our friend, who has been taken captive," said Vaenn, hoping they might be able to help, though she grew doubtful, as the soldiers clearly did not trust them.

"A pack of goblins took her and will bring her before Vyroun," said Gleowan. "We must find her before she is taken to his kingdom."

"And so now you are hunting a pack of goblins rather than running from them?" said the soldier. "Only a fool would hunt them on foot. You would have no hope of catching them. And if your friend was taken, you would know that there is no hope of saving her."

"We are not giving up hope," said Vaenn. "Though we are unsure of where she is now. Have you seen a goblin pack about?"

"All forces have gathered in the north," said the soldier. "And all our forces are retreating to Bared Nar. You make your way north to Vyroun's kingdom, saying that you search for a friend of yours. Maybe you are truthful, or maybe you are not. Perhaps you go north to serve the lord of the dark land, who will soon assault us all."

"We are not goblins," said Gleowan. "You must trust that we are your friends, not your enemies."

"Goblins are not the only creatures that serve Vyroun," said the soldier. Vaenn was growing uneasy, as the soldiers had not lowered their spears. The leader of the horsemen spoke on. "There are monsters behind the walls of that dark kingdom that are far more terrible. I know not what your loyalties are. Bind their hands, and take them with us to Bared Nar!"

"But we are not your enemies!" said Gleowan. Vaenn tried desperately to think of anything she could say or do that might help them.

"Even men have come to serve Mûrondûn," said the soldier, as Gleowan and Vaenn's weapons were taken and their hands were being bound.

"But I am not a man, I am a woman!" said Vaenn, who was not seeking to act amusingly but could think of nothing else to say. But that, I am afraid, did not work. The two of them had their weapons taken away.

"Well, that was worth a try," said Gleowan, thinking that what she said was rather humorous. Even though the two of them were in a most dire situation, Gleowan was still able to find some amusement. But that amusement lasted only a moment, because the two of them were then put onto horses and taken away.

The horsemen rode for many hours. Gleowan and Vaenn tried to pay attention to where they were and where they were going, but with their hands bound, the two of them had a more immediate concern, which was to hold on and make sure they did not fall off their horses. Fortunately, the horses did not seem to run as quickly as they could, as they were in the great garden of Gundmar, thus there were thickets to weave around. Gleowan and Vaenn grew hungry, but were not able to go into their food, and the soldiers did not give them anything. The two of them needed to be patient. It was not until evening when the soldiers arrived at Bared Nar, the great city of Gundmar.

When Gleowan and Vaenn first saw the city, they could not help but marvel at its magnificence. They were at the very end of the Silver Mountains, the same mountains in which Edelbir and Kattalin had found the hidden dwarven kingdom much farther to the east. There were two great peaks at the very end of the mountains, and they were far apart, as if the mountains broke into two separate paths just before they ended. Reaching to the tops of both peaks was a tower with a tall, glimmering spire, from which the banner of Gundmar blew in a strong breeze. Soldiers there kept watch. There was a valley between these mountains with a wide field.

The city wall was like a horseshoe, beginning at the northern peak and circuiting along the mountain edge, and then ending at the southern peak. The gate into Bared Nar was at the end of the great field, at the city wall's center, facing directly westward. Farther above was another tower at the center of the city. The whole city glittered in silver as the setting sun shone through the clouds.

"Oh! My hair is a mess and I can do nothing with my hands bound!" said Vaenn.

"And I would love to smoke a pipe very badly," said Gleowan. "But I cannot do so, either."

Though the two spoke quietly to each other, some of the soldiers appeared to have heard Gleowan and Vaenn. Gleowan was given a few looks of annoyance, and he remembered quickly that he and Vaenn were captive.

"What is this place?" said Gleowan, as the soldiers reached a road that would take them to the gate.

"Bared Nar," answered one of the soldiers proudly. "The Guard of the North, as those that know the tongue of Aundorin would say."

The soldiers rode for the main gate, which took about a dozen men on the other side to pull open. Once inside, the riders needed to be slow, as there were many people there. Just ahead was a courtyard with two great statues of men on horses, both holding swords. Surrounding the statues was a pool that some people took water from. Once in the city, the horsemen turned south and rode along the wall.

"Oh, what delight it brings me to return to the silver city," said the same soldier. "Seldom do I get to look upon the spires that reach to the clouds. I would be honored to give my life defending her charm and her beauty, as so many of my ancestors have. That time I think may soon come. Evil grows beyond this land. I will not let this kingdom fall as others have to darkness."

Gleowan and Vaenn turned to him, as this soldier seemed far less hostile than the one who had ordered them to be taken captive. Vaenn spoke as they rode south along the wall. "You have been here your whole life?"

"And I will remain here in this kingdom," said the soldier with a smile. "I do not grow tired of guarding this land."

The soldier then spoke a verse:

> *Oh, the sun shines upon endless hills of plain,*
> *From forest to forest, mountain to mountain,*
> *Oh, Esmael's home is not dampened by rain.*
>
> *Oh, between two rivers a great garden lies,*
> *Lords reside at the foot of the stream's fountain,*
> *Oh, to the stars do the silver towers rise.*

"Gundmar, one of the eight kingdoms of men," said the soldier. "The kingdom of Esmael, son of Aberran, who led men in the Goblin War of the Second Age."

"Aberran? A name I have never before heard," said Vaenn. Even though she and Gleowan were rank with concern, as they were captive and needed to find Caitren, they could not check their interest.

The soldier spoke another verse:

> Long ago when the earth was younger,
> Evil was born in chasms under,
> Of all foul things sprung from dark lords,
> Goblins, trolls, to match elves and dwarves.
>
> Assaulted they were by all things vile,
> Stunned were many by evil's arrival,
> The dark creatures they could not defeat,
> Elves and dwarves could only retreat.
>
> Aid was needed as light darkened,
> To their call Enilundar harkened,
> Greater and greater grew the goblin storm,
> Thus, a new race was ordered to take form.
>
> Men were then made, mortal and strong,
> Growing swiftly to many a throng,
> To match goblins, men were brute,
> Once their race had taken root.
>
> The might of men grew in number,
> And light had woke from its slumber,
> Through the War of the Second Age,
> Came Aberran leading men's rage.
>
> The greatest from the race of men,
> Aberran and all his children,
> Fiercely did he and his eight sons fight,
> Against ill did they harness men's might.

Across the lands did the enemies flee,
For Aberran's kin marched without mercy,
Against the darkness was victory,
As lands were rid of the enemy.

For their courage was Aberran's kin famed,
And they settled in the lands reclaimed,
His children went to spread men's reign,
From them eight kingdoms of men came.

"The eight kingdoms of men, whose lines of kings all descend from Aberran himself," said the soldier. "Though some of those kingdoms since have fallen."

"You seem to be well versed," said Gleowan. "What is your name, might I ask?"

"Eamon am I, son of Eadwine," said the soldier. "From the Southern Fold of Gundmar do I hail. And that is my home to guard. War comes, and this is my oath, my calling, my purpose, to guard the beauty of this land."

Vaenn found Eamon to be rather friendly, and yet she and Gleowan were still captive. She could not help but wonder what the soldiers thought of the two of them, if they thought the same as their captain. "Do you think us to be enemies?"

"Well, to me you do not seem to be," said Eamon. "Though I know not with certainty. The king, surely, will know, that is, if he is well enough, for he has grown sick of late from what I hear, thus his son has acted in his stead."

The riders by then had made it to the southern peak, where there was another gate that faced half-north and half-west, which would take them to the second level of the city. Then once they were on the second level, the horsemen had to follow along the wall as it circuited inward and then back out at the northern peak. If one wanted to see the king immediately, I am afraid there was no shortcut to the throne. The gate to the second level was at the southern peak, then the gate to the third level was all the way up at the northern peak, facing south. Then the gate to take the riders to the throne was at the center of the horseshoe-shaped wall, just like the main gate at the bottom level to go in and out of the city. It must have taken at least a good hour from when Gleowan and Vaenn first entered the city of Bared Nar to the point where they finally reached the top level, where the king's throne was.

Upon passing through the final gate, Gleowan and Vaenn were in a great courtyard with a line of trees to each side, though none bore flowers anymore, as summer had passed. Guards, all in armor, were standing watch along the trees. While the horsemen wore green armor of scales, the high guards of the king were clad in silver from helm to boot. Their chest plates were without scales, but were etched with the emblem of Gundmar. They all held shields in one hand, and in the other, spears that bore the banner of their kingdom. The horsemen stopped once they entered the courtyard, and each of them dismounted from their horses. Gleowan and Vaenn were brought off from their horses also. They looked about to find that they were quite high above the valley below, where they had entered the city. It was windy up at the top level of the city. There was no time to look around, though, as a few soldiers immediately moved Gleowan and Vaenn towards the throne room ahead.

Before long the two of them reached the door to the throne room, which was dug into the mountain itself. Two guards opened the door for them to enter. Gleowan and Vaenn then found themselves in a great silver hall of stone and marble. To each side were statues of the great kings of Gundmar's past. (Gundmar, however, was a kingdom thousands of years old, and thus there are far too many kings for me to name for you.) There were several more guards lined up, and a few more ahead, where the throne stood. A long table sat to the right of the throne, where a few men were gathered, all looking rather distressed. I would not blame them though, for they knew that a storm was coming from the north.

"And there stand the son and daughter of the king. Their father has fallen ill, I am afraid," said Eamon quietly to Gleowan and Vaenn, who were taken directly to the throne ahead, by which stood a man and a woman, both young but unmistakably older than Gleowan or Vaenn. The king's son and daughter awaited the soldiers. Of the two of them, the king's son appeared to be the older. He was tall, about as tall as Edelbir, and looked very strong. Long brown hair fell from his head, and a short beard covered his chin. The king's son was not wearing the crown, as his father was the king, at least for the time being, though he had grown sick. He wore a fine silver gambeson with gold and green trimmings, and strong iron boots covered his feet. He did not look completely suited for battle, but appeared as if he was preparing for one. Vaenn noticed the king's daughter quickly, though, for as strong and rugged as the king's son appeared, the king's daughter looked equally beautiful and graceful. Brown hair fell from her head, and she wore a green dress with gold trimmings, with a girdle of silver at her waist. On her head was a silver headpiece, and around her neck was a necklace with a purple jewel.

"Oh, what I would do to have a dress like she has," whispered Vaenn. "Never have I looked upon such splendid garb."

Gleowan looked to Vaenn amusedly, and then his gaze went to the king's daughter and the attire that drew Vaenn's attention. "I am afraid I cannot help you with that. The spinning wheel is not a tool that I am at all skilled with."

The king's daughter looked at them for a moment, and Gleowan and Vaenn wondered if she had heard them.

"Hail Cenric, son of Cyneric, prince of Gundmar," said the leader of the horsemen, who had ordered Gleowan and Vaenn to be taken captive. "And Aldreda, oh the honor to be in the company of the fair lady of Gundmar again."

"You have made it, Athelstan," said Cenric as Aldreda gave a bow. "Has the Southern Fold emptied, and all people have retreated here?"

"Some soldiers remain at Cornaylon, but they will ride here soon," said Athelstan. "All soldiers will be mustered before we come under siege."

"We await word of scouts in the North Fold watching for an army coming out from the Black Mountains," said Cenric. "It appears that all our women and children have made it here."

"Some have made for the Woodlands," said Athelstan. "I am quite sure that they have reached there."

"Very good," said Cenric. "The Woodlands have been watching beyond their borders, and Itilikin is mustering their army. We will surely need all help there is."

"Are there any other places that could help us?" asked Aldreda.

"I am afraid not," said Cenric, pacing about the throne. Gleowan and Vaenn were quiet. Vaenn could have told them of the hidden dwarven kingdom and the Fornwood, but it was better not to, as she was not sure if either would help. Only Edelbir and Kattalin might have known if the king of the dwarves was willing to aid Gundmar. The Fornwood needed to deal with their own troubles to their southern borders from when last the company was there, and perhaps they might join in northern conflicts afterwards, but their own borders were their first concern.

"Gundmar and Itilikin will fight this war alone," said Cenric. "And I know not what numbers the kingdom of the Woodlands has after we fought Vyroun a decade ago. Our armies have been weakened since then. Vaolnor has long since fallen. Hailnor, too, fell an age ago. Bornaren is too far south of here. And Rhunaur has never fought alongside us. We have not been allies, going back to before our kingdoms were born from Aberran's greatest sons, Esmael and Iosog. Rhunaur is leaderless, their king and queen ambushed years ago, and their line of kings gone. There are no other allies to help us."

As Cenric was in the midst of a small spell of desperation, his eyes suddenly met Gleowan and Vaenn standing with Athelstan, Eamon, and the other soldiers. The two of them were quiet, and not sure if they should try to relieve Cenric's desperation with what allies they knew of that he did not.

"Who are these two? And why are their hands bound?" said Cenric. Aldreda, too, looked upon them with interest.

"We found them in the Kaelunen," said Athelstan. "I

know that several amongst men have fallen to darkness, to serve Vyroun. These two looked like strange folk to us, and their tale to me seemed suspicious, thus we suspected they might be spies and took no chance."

"Tell me your tale," said the king's son to Gleowan and Vaenn. The two of them retold their tale, starting from the past summer. From the very beginning, Cenric was very curious.

"Our friend Adroegen led us and our friends away from the goblin chief," said Vaenn at one point.

"Adroegen? We have met him before," said Aldreda, as Cenric nodded.

"I would not say I am a close friend to him," said Cenric. "But from what acquaintances I have with him, we have been friendly."

Vaenn felt very relieved to hear this, and she and Gleowan went on. They told of how the hunt took them from their home all the way north to the Dead Forest, where they had a final meeting with the goblin chief.

"The goblin chief is dead?" said Cenric with surprise. All the soldiers in the hall appeared surprised also. "Who was able to kill the worst of the goblins? No soldier of Gundmar has managed to defeat that treacherous foe. Even with the sun's aid, that would still take a strong swordsman."

"It was our friend Edelbir," said Vaenn. "He was able to defeat the one that hunted Adroegen the past many months."

"Edelbir? Edelbir is his name?" said the king's son. "A mighty man he must be, from what I imagine."

"Yes," said Gleowan. "He was able to thwart the goblin chief from killing Adroegen, though Adroegen was wounded greatly."

"I am thankful to your friend," said Cenric. "And where is Edelbir now?"

Gleowan and Vaenn were unsure of what to say. It was likely not best to say that their friends were searching for a hidden dwarven kingdom in hopes of finding help for Gundmar, for they knew not if the dwarves would come or not. Fortunately, there was another answer that Gleowan and Vaenn could give, where they were not lying to Cenric, but simply not telling the full truth. Though for the two of them, this truth was still difficult to tell.

"Edelbir and Kattalin went searching for Adroegen," said Gleowan. "Vaenn and I have been searching for Caitren."

"Searching for Adroegen?" said Cenric. "What do you mean? What happened to him?"

"The pack retreated for a few days after the goblin chief's defeat," said Gleowan. "But they regrouped and came back after us. We were cornered one night against a cliff. Adroegen fell over. We searched but could not find him. Our friends remained to search for him, though I know not if they have found our friend. At the same time, another in our company, Caitren, was taken captive by the pack, thus Vaenn and I went west in search of her."

"We do not know what became of Adroegen," said Vaenn. "But we believe that he has met his end."

Cenric and Aldreda looked to each other and appeared saddened. Cenric spoke. "I am sorry to hear that you have lost your friend. Perhaps hope remains, but from what you say, it does not seem there is much hope that he lives."

"We hope that Caitren still lives," said Vaenn. "However, we have spent days searching for her, and we have found no sign. We fear that she is now in Vyroun's kingdom, awaiting a terrible fate."

All were silent for a short time. Aldreda looked at both Gleowan and Vaenn, then to her brother Cenric, before speaking. "I do not think they are enemies of ours."

"Neither do I," said Cenric, who then looked to Athelstan and the soldiers who had taken Gleowan and Vaenn captive. "You may release them."

Gleowan and Vaenn put their hands forward so that the soldiers could release them. Athelstan appeared reluctant but did as ordered. There was some relief as their bonds were cut, as Gleowan and Vaenn no longer needed to worry about the soldiers of Gundmar thinking them to be enemies. That, however, did not end all of their worries. They still wanted to find their friend, wherever Caitren was. By now, they were not sure if there was any chance of finding her.

"You must forgive us for taking you captive," said Cenric. "Many amongst the race of men have fallen to serve Vyroun, more than in the past, thus of late we have been untrusting of folk unfamiliar to us. You may go now and do whatever you must, or if you wish to remain here, you may do so, for this city is safe, though soon we shall be under siege."

"We must look for our friend Caitren," said Vaenn. "For we know not where she is now, and we are losing hope."

"When last did you see your friend?" asked the king's son.

"In the Dead Forest, when the pack cornered us," said Gleowan. "We heard one goblin say that Vyroun wanted Adroegen to be killed and the rest of us taken prisoner.

They took Caitren, while the other four of us escaped them. We must find her, though, for we know not where precisely she is, nor what fate awaits her."

Cenric looked to the north, and he had a look of great sympathy for Gleowan and Vaenn. "Gulgurod. The mouth of Mûrondûn, where all prisoners are taken. There will your friend be."

"Then we must go there! For time was already against us," said Vaenn, with much haste, to Gleowan. Cenric's sympathy seemed only to deepen.

"She is far beyond your reach," said the king's son. "Your friend is already in Gulgurod, I am sure, many leagues north of here. You would not reach her in time. In fact, it is likely already too late, I am afraid. Even if you did go there, the fortress of Gulgurod is not one that you can simply enter unseen. You, too, would be taken captive, and you would find far worse than death within those walls. I am sorry, but there is no hope of saving your friend."

Vaenn was devastated but did not want to simply give up. "But we have seen hope come to us before. We have been searching tirelessly for her."

"You never had a chance of catching the pack," said the king's son, who appeared deeply sorry for her and Gleowan. "On foot, you cannot hope to catch wolves. I would remain here, for this city is well guarded. Bared Nar shall be under attack soon, though we know not precisely when. Vyroun has long desired to raze this city to the ground. He managed to take it an age ago, only to lose it soon after. He tried to take our city again a decade ago and failed. Now he shall siege us again. And I worry, for we do not have the forces on our side that we had last time."

Gleowan and Vaenn turned and left the throne room.

Neither was at all sure what to do next. They could only stand in the courtyard, feeling very disheartened. Gleowan and Vaenn were all but certain they had lost Adroegen. It appeared that Caitren, too, was lost. They were unsure of where their friends Edelbir and Kattalin were. For all they knew, Edelbir and Kattalin had met a terrible fate also.

"How did this come to be? How did we make it to where we are now?" said Vaenn, beginning to weep. They wanted to find Caitren, but hope appeared to be gone. The two of them looked out into Bared Nar and saw soldiers preparing their defenses.

Chapter Five; The Tempter

Caitren was not at all certain of where she was, nor of how many days and nights she had been with the goblin pack. She had been unconscious for some time before finally waking up, only to find herself mounted on a wolf, tied up and unable to move, with a goblin behind her holding her captive. The wolves ran swiftly during the night. During the day, the goblins found caves to hide in, although the farther north they went, the less afraid they appeared to be of sunlight, for great dark clouds were ahead to the north.

It was very difficult for Caitren to sit upright as she rode. She felt very weak and was both starving and parched with thirst. The goblins on rare occasion would give her a little water and food, but it was not close to quenching or nourishing. Caitren was not treated well at all by the pack, although she did not expect to be. Whenever the goblins stopped for the day, she would be snatched and thrown to the ground, and when it was time to ride north again, the goblins would grab her and heave her back onto the wolf. Caitren was aching greatly, as she had been tied up for days, unable to move her hands or arms. She stood no chance of escape, for she would have had to cut all her bonds somehow without any goblins noticing, and then slip away unseen. With little strength, no weapon, and no horse, there would be no hope of making it very far.

On that night, the pack was riding through a great field. It appeared that she was the only member of the company who was taken captive, as Caitren at no point saw any of her friends amongst the pack. The goblins spoke little about the fate of her friends, and she worried greatly over what had happened to them. Caitren also wondered where her father was, though it had been a long time since she had any clue of his whereabouts. The farther north Caitren was taken, the more she feared that she might never see him again. The goblins were not far from Vyroun's kingdom, from what it seemed. Caitren was shivering with cold, as winter was not far. Her cloak was gone, and all she had was her blue dress, which had grown very worn, ragged, and ripped in some places. That, however, was not Caitren's greatest worry.

Though it was dark, Caitren could see tall, dark mountains not far ahead. These were the Black Mountains, or the Daur Igina, as they were known in the old tongue of Aundorin. The pack rode over one last great hill, and then once they reached the top, Caitren's worry grew.

Ahead was an opening in the mountains, and at this break was a black fortress. Two towers stood to each side, both nearly as tall as the mountains themselves. A wall stood between these towers. There were two gates into the fortress, one on each side at the foot of the towers.

"Oh no," said Caitren quietly to herself as the goblins rode onward. She was very afraid, for Caitren knew not what awaited within those dark walls. Caitren turned around and looked to the south, but was not able to look for long.

"Don't think you're getting away!" said the goblin behind her. Caitren promptly faced forward again. There were stars in the sky to the south, however, to the north all light was veiled. In the moonlight Caitren noticed a river ahead that was flowing swiftly. There was a short cliff, and this river flowed somewhere to the west. The goblins rode for a great bridge over the river, and before her stood one of the gates into the dark fortress. The gates opened, and Caitren shook as she waited to be taken inside. She was met with a feeling of doom, and Caitren felt as if she would not ever again look upon any decent places, nor upon her friends or her father.

It was quite noisy within the fortress. Caitren could not see very much, but from all around she could hear many beasts roaring. Some were unmistakably goblins, and there were certainly some trolls also. However, Caitren could hear other creatures that she knew not of. Wolves were growling and fighting each other, from what it seemed, though she could not tell. There were other terrible creatures, one making more of a screeching, screaming sort of sound. There seemed to be a great gathering. Vyroun's full strength was within that fortress, and soon it would surely be unleashed upon Gundmar.

There was almost no light within the walls of Gulgurod. Caitren was taken through a dark tunnel. Beyond a few torches, only the glitter and glow of the heaps of treasure within provided any kind of light. There were several goblins searching through piles of gold. Some fought each other over nothing more than a golden goblet, a gem, or a few coins. Caitren was not sure where the dungeons were, though she was sure that was where the pack was taking her. She remembered Adroegen saying that he was once taken prisoner, and she wondered if he had been within the very walls that she found herself in.

It took some time, but the pack eventually broke off. A few goblins, including the goblin lieutenant, went with Caitren. Before long they reached some large doors, which were opened by a pair of trolls that stood there. Caitren was taken in. Upon entering the prison, she was immediately brought off of the wolf she rode, and then the goblins pushed her to the ground. Caitren hit her elbow, though she had far greater worries.

The prison was large. There were some small slits in the wall, and Caitren immediately went over to one to look out. She was just inside the south wall of the west tower. The prison was not very high up, and the river outside was flowing almost right beneath where Caitren was standing. There was no hope of being able to leave, though, for the slit was far too small for Caitren to fit through. Even if she could climb out, the river would have been quite a jump, though it did look like one that she might have been able to make.

"Get away from there!" said a goblin, who then grabbed Caitren and shoved her away from the wall. "You're not going anywhere!"

Caitren was on the ground again. She found that she was not alone in that dark prison. Scores of prisoners were with her. Nearly every prisoner that Caitren saw was trembling in fear. None of them spoke to her. They only watched for the door and cowered anytime someone entered. Caitren, too, was very afraid. There was no way out of that fortress from what she saw, and even if there was, she was far too weak from hunger and thirst to be able to get far.

Caitren waited in that prison for what must have been a few hours. She could hear the sounds of beasts growling and roaring from somewhere else in the great fortress. "Doom! Doom!" chanted many goblins. There were not only the sounds of monsters, though. Drums were beating loudly. An army was gathered. There was no mistaking it, even if Caitren herself had not seen war. She could hear someone, likely a goblin, shouting to the creatures and beasts gathered there, and the army chanted in unison. The drums did not end.

Then Caitren heard the winds of a hurricane coming from beyond the walls. She had heard these winds before, during the company's journey, back when they were in the Dwimor Fells and when they crossed the Moor Glen. Ligwyrm had arrived. Soon the walls shook as thunderous footsteps landed upon the fortress. The floor beneath Caitren began to shake. Before long, she heard Ligwyrm's voice outside the walls. All of it made her tremble in fear and want to be with her father, or somewhere back in the wild, or anywhere else for that matter. Caitren found that place terrifying already, and I daresay that she still had much more to overcome.

Some goblins entered the dungeon. Prisoners retreated. Caitren heard one goblin shout, "Your master is coming!"

Some prisoners screamed, and others cowered. Caitren was already frightened greatly, and her fear grew yet higher. The goblin lieutenant was there, and soon Caitren heard loud footsteps that sounded like iron clashing against rock. It did not take long before someone else entered. Caitren had seen goblins, trolls, Ligwyrm, and great spiders, however, none of those things were nearly as frightening as the lord of Mûrondûn. Caitren knew it was Vyroun the moment she laid eyes upon him.

In the doorway stood someone covered completely in armor. There was no weakness to be seen. Tall was he who commanded legions of dark creatures and foul beasts, much taller than the goblin chief. Caitren was not sure what was beneath the heavy armor. Smoke rose from any chink in the iron. There were two slits for eyes, but no other openings in the armor. Caitren could not see a face, as the whole head was covered in iron, save the eyes, which glowed red. She wondered if there really was someone under all that iron, or if instead a fire was burning beneath. Spikes rose from the shoulders, the hands, and from the crown of the head. If any were to fight this lord, they would stand no chance. Caitren had never seen anyone so frightening in her life. She trembled in fear with the other prisoners.

"We have returned with one prisoner," said the goblin lieutenant to Vyroun. "She lies just over there."

Caitren stepped back as the goblin lieutenant pointed to her, and the red eyes of the lord of Mûrondûn looked her way. Caitren was given a fright, as she was met with a blinding light when Vyroun's eyes turned to her, and she had to shield her eyes. She then thought that she could hear a roaring fire inside her head, which grew loud enough that Caitren soon tried to cover her ears. It was to no avail, though, as her hands were bound.

"The others are still out there," the goblin lieutenant went on. "But we will find all of them in time."

Vyroun looked upon Caitren without moving. Caitren could not bear to look back, for his eyes were blinding to her own. She could only crouch down on the floor and try to both shield her eyes and cover hear ears from the roaring fire that sounded in her head.

"The vagabond you have sought is dead," said the goblin lieutenant. A great despair come over Caitren.

"That cannot be true," she whispered to herself.

"We pushed him over a cliff," said the goblin lieutenant. "He was already wounded and could hardly walk, so finishing him was easy!"

"No!" said Caitren, and tears began to fall from her eyes. She could not believe what she was hearing. Adroegen was too strong-willed to have perished.

"Quiet, you!" said the goblin lieutenant, moving towards Caitren. She, however, only cried more. Caitren cared not that she was before Vyroun and all his forces, and that her hands were bound and she was without a weapon. Her heart felt broken, and Caitren wept before all the evil gathered there.

Her crying did not last for long, though. Suddenly Caitren was lifted from her feet and thrown back against the wall. It was as if she were jerked from her shoulders, and yet no one had grabbed her. Caitren was moved several strides through the air and her shoulder collided with the stone wall. It hurt greatly, but Caitren could do nothing. She was completely restrained against the wall, a few feet above the ground. Yet nothing bound her there and nothing kept her from falling. She looked around to see who had done this to her, but all Caitren saw before her were two blinding eyes of red looking at her. Caitren could only close her eyes. Her hands could not shield them.

"The hunters will find the vagabond's body," said one goblin, who appeared to be speaking to Vyroun. "Fear not, master, we will bring his head to you, and you will see with your own eyes that he is no more."

"Our forces are ready," said the goblin lieutenant. "There are fewer here than what we had hoped for. The goblin chief sought the trolls from the south, but this girl and her friends killed their king. Fewer trolls have come than we wanted. The pack thought the spiders down there might have been allies, but they, too, betrayed us because of those scum. The goblin chief was a strong servant, but they have defeated him also, along with much of his pack. The jewel you sought has been lost. If we had it, we would be far more powerful. But no matter. Our army will not fall. Gundmar is not as strong as they were in our last battle. They and the Woodlands have not great enough numbers to match us this time!"

Vyroun turned to the goblin lieutenant. Caitren would never have thought she and her friends, mere simple folk from far to the south, might be such a nuisance to an evil lord in a dark kingdom far away to the north, and yet it appeared to be so. It also seemed that Vyroun greatly wanted Adroegen dead. The goblin lieutenant spoke to him as if they were having an exchange, and yet Caitren heard not a word from Vyroun himself. Caitren was not sure if Vyroun was speaking to him or simply listening to the goblin lieutenant. Moments later, though, some goblins departed and orders were shouted. "March!"

The army within the fortress roared. Caitren heard the drums beating, then moments later the sounds of many legions marching. Caitren was again suddenly jerked from her shoulders, undoubtedly by some dark magic, and she was thrown towards the slit in the wall that she had looked through when first entering the prison. Her head was forced to turn and look out. It was not yet morning, but the night appeared to be starting to lift far to the south. Both gates of Gulgurod had opened. There were goblins marching, but also many more creatures. Caitren saw trolls, men, and then another monster nearly as large as a troll, but more hideous and hairy. Several wore shields over their heads, which Caitren could only assume was to protect them from the sun when it rose again. She also saw a dark and sheer mist moving about. Caitren knew not what it was, but she could hear screeching from within it. Then the winds of a hurricane descended, and the fiery serpent of the west that had been summoned for war was flying south.

Before Caitren could think anything of the marching army, she was turned again to face Vyroun. Caitren was then released from whatever had bound her to the wall and she fell to the floor. A stone lay there and she hurt her leg on it, but Caitren could not tend to the pain. She tried to sit up, but whenever she looked up her eyes were again blinded. The roar of fire sounded within her head, thus while Caitren had to keep her eyes closed, she also needed to try and cover her ears. At one point her eyes opened and she found the iron boots of the lord of Mûrondûn only a few strides before her, though Caitren could not look up any higher, for the eyes of the dark lord were unbearable to meet.

"Strong and resilient hast thou been. No greater an ally do I desire," said a menacing voice inside Caitren's head. The voice did not shout, but it was so loud that Caitren screamed in pain. She had grown certain that her end had come. Her pain was too great and she only wanted it to end, and at that moment, even death itself was a tempting offer.

"Yield, and wealth shall be ushered unto thee," said the voice. This time the other prisoners screamed as Caitren did. Though the voice was in her head, it seemed the others were hearing it also.

Caitren's eyes were suddenly forced shut. She then saw herself in a great room of treasure. Vyroun stood at her side and gently offered to take her hand. Before her was water, and Caitren looked to find her reflection in it. She was no longer wearing the worn, ragged, and ripped blue dress, but instead Caitren was clothed in the most beautiful dress she had ever looked upon. It was of white silk. A girdle of jewels was around her waist. Her hair was combed and braided. A circlet went around her head, bearing a white jewel. Caitren put her hands on her neck, where a gold necklace with ruby jewels hung. She held the necklace, unsure if it, or everything else she wore, was real.

When Caitren turned, she found that Vyroun still stood there, offering to take her hand. Caitren looked into the fiery eyes of the lord of Mûrondûn, and suddenly they were not so blinding that she could not bear to look at them. She put her hand on her shoulder, and then her leg, which she had hurt upon hitting the wall and falling to the ground. Caitren was also no longer in any pain. She looked back at her reflection, and Caitren could not believe how beautiful she looked.

Caitren heard footsteps behind, and soon a shadow loomed over her. She looked again upon her reflection in the water and found that Vyroun stood right behind her. Caitren put her hands on the necklace she wore, and then she was given a scare as she felt iron hands upon her shoulders. "My queen could I make thee, with beauty unrivaled by any upon this earth. Thou shall rule at my side. All shall belong to thee, if thou but yield before me."

Caitren huddled her shoulders, for Vyroun's hands of iron felt very cold against them. She also felt a shadow over her, and in her head, Caitren still heard the sound of a roaring fire. She remembered her friends, and her father. Caitren's memory of being raised as simple folk entered her mind. She had never valued gold, or gems, or any other riches. They were dazzling to her, but even though all that Vyroun offered her was tempting, in the end she was resilient to it.

"I have no need for treasure," said Caitren. "For it is not riches, nor power, that support me. It has never been treasure that nourishes me!"

Caitren opened her eyes, and suddenly her leg and shoulder hurt again. The moment her eyes opened, they met the eyes of Vyroun, and she was forced to look away and shield her eyes. The fire roared louder in her head. Around her, she could hear other prisoners.

"I yield! I yield!" some of them said. Caitren was able to see some goblins cutting their bonds, and those prisoners bowed before Vyroun. The lord of Mûrondûn, however, seemed fixed upon Caitren.

"Yield, and thou shalt be quenched and nourished," said the voice in Caitren's head. Caitren was feeling very hungry and very thirsty, but suddenly those feelings grew considerably. She could see some prisoners being freed from the dungeon, and Caitren greatly wished to leave herself, but she was still trapped before Vyroun.

Caitren's eyes were forced shut again. When she opened them, she was in a great hall and sitting at a long table. Caitren was not wearing the white silk dress like before, but this time a red dress that she nonetheless thought was still quite beautiful. Like before, Caitren was wearing a jeweled necklace, and this time a gold bracelet also. The pain in her shoulder and her leg was gone, however, not all discomforts had ceased. Caitren's hunger and thirst were still great.

Seated next to her was Vyroun, and his eyes were no longer blinding to look upon. Vyroun did not offer to take Caitren by the hand this time, but his hand gently motioned towards the table. Caitren turned her gaze. Upon the table sat the greatest feast Caitren had ever seen. There was food of all kinds, and enough to feed dozens of folk. Ripe fruits that Caitren had never seen before lay on the table, and she could smell the warm, sweet bread. Drink, too, was endless. Caitren was surprised. She could not deny that she was very temped to accept Vyroun's offer, for she had hardly eaten in the past several days, and she was parched with thirst. All of it looked very delectable, and she reached out her hand without hesitation.

But as Caitren was about to take some food and drink, which she greatly yearned for, something stayed her hand. To the side of the hall was a roaring fire, and she could hear it inside her head. Caitren's hand slowly went back. She badly wanted to eat, however, she could not help but think of at what cost it would come. Caitren might be nourished and her thirst quenched, but she feared that she would forever be Vyroun's thrall in exchange. She felt certain that she would not leave Vyroun's captivity if she did accept.

"It is not food alone that nourishes me," Caitren said.

"But rather it is the light that shines within my heart."

Caitren opened her eyes, and the feelings of thirst and hunger grew greater. The pain had returned, and it had become worse than before. She cowered on the ground and would not face Vyroun, who still stood before her. The roar of fire sounded louder in her head. At the same time, Caitren heard more prisoners yielding. She could see little because her eyes were being blinded, however, Caitren was able to notice that the dungeon was emptying.

All became rather silent, but soon Caitren heard screeching coming from outside the dungeon. It went on for some time, and grew louder. Caitren knew not what was coming. Vyroun stepped aside and no longer looked upon her. A dark and sheer mist approached, and within it Caitren saw creatures enter the dungeon that looked far more frightening than goblins.

These creatures were black with red eyes. They had horns growing from their heads. Their faces appeared human, and yet the creatures had the teeth of animals and roared like beasts. They had claws on their hands and feet, and though they did have some hair, they had no fur coat like that which a wolf possessed. Caitren soon noticed that she could see right through these creatures, as if they were ghosts. One of them looked at her and let out a loud screech, and Caitren tried to cover her ears.

This creature then approached Caitren, who cowered. Vyroun faced her again and Caitren needed to shield her eyes. She was able to see, though, that the creature was running towards her and roaring. Caitren tried to retreat and avoid the creature, but she could not. The closer it came, the clearer it was to Caitren that this creature was some kind of ghost or spirit. The creature lunged straight at her, and for a brief moment Caitren thought it went right through her like a ghost.

But a moment later Caitren was screaming on the ground, writhing in pain. The creature was inside of her. She could hear its roars and screeches in her head. Caitren fought with all her strength, as the creature tried to take possession of her. The fiend tried to make Caitren's body kneel before Vyroun, and Caitren made great effort not to. This fight, however, was far worse than any she had ever been in. Caitren could not be still at all. She did not know how to end the torment that she was in.

"Yield, and thine agony shall cease," Caitren heard in her head. This time, Caitren was very tempted to accept, for the torment was unbearable. Yet somehow Caitren did not cease to fight it.

Caitren was not sure what might happen if she did yield. This was Vyroun, lord of Mûrondûn, after all. She wanted her torment to end and she wished to escape that dark dungeon. However, there seemed to be no way out. She was growing certain her end was at hand, and that it might not be long. Caitren was already weak and growing weaker, and she knew she would not to be able to fight forever against whatever creature was taking possession of her. Perhaps it was better to refuse Vyroun's offers and end it once and for all. The creature inside of Caitren tried to force her to kneel and bow before Vyroun. Caitren spoke before it was able to make her do so.

"It is my heart that I will be judged by," Caitren struggled to say as she resisted bowing. "And it will not be yielded to evil."

The agony rose a little higher, and Caitren gave out a scream. She writhed in pain again on the floor before

Vyroun. For a brief moment Caitren was able to notice that she was the only prisoner remaining in the dungeon. It appeared that all the others had yielded, though Caitren did not know what had become of them. She wondered for a moment if they were being given food and other comforts that she did not have, or if perhaps all was a ruse, and they had been made thralls, or even slain. Caitren was afraid to find out her fate if she did yield to Vyroun, even if she was certain her death would come next, for with all the torment she was going through, Caitren would have been far more welcoming of death in that moment. But the end did not come.

"Yield, and thy father shall thou be taken to," said the voice in her head. Caitren stopped fighting for a moment, and suddenly she did not know at all what to choose. Upon being captured by the goblins several days earlier, Caitren had begun to think she would never see her father again. She was surprised that Vyroun knew exactly what she longed for and would offer it to her. Caitren wondered, as she endured great pain, if the lord of Mûrondûn really did know where her father was, and if he could really take her to Huldnar. It had been several months since she had seen her father, and Caitren did not know what had become of him after their home was destroyed. Caitren only knew in her heart that her father was still out there somewhere, searching for her, and that she badly wanted to find him. Caitren was about to accept Vyroun's offer, but she then wondered if he really was truthful.

"Where is my father now?" Caitren struggled to say.

"Yield," said the voice. There was no answer beyond that. Caitren grew wary. Vyroun offered her many great things and might have seemed like an angel for doing so, however, I would say that even servants of darkness may disguise themselves in light and fool those susceptible enough to fall for such spells of temptation. Caitren thought of her father and how much she wanted to see him again, and though she knew that it was Vyroun, the dark lord of Mûrondûn, who was offering, she wondered if Vyroun really could bring her to her father. Yet the fire roared in Caitren's head, and her agony at Vyroun's hands did not cease. She knew that the tempter was not a friend of hers. Caitren could not trust any ally of evil.

"You will not take me to him," said Caitren with much difficulty. "You may cloak yourself in light, but I know precisely what you truly are. You are a demon! A servant of evil! You are not my ally. For you are only a tempter, a liar, a deceiver! All that you offer me shall never be mine! All that you offer shall never nourish my heart! How dare you have such audacity to tempt me so. Offer me all the gold on this earth and I shall still refuse, for what I must give in return weighs far more. You shall never gain my loyalty, demon of darkness! Tempt me no more!"

Caitren expected that either her end would come or her agony would grow. Neither happened, though. Suddenly the creature that tried to possess her left, as if it were expelled from her body. The pain from the creature's possession was gone. A thunderous roar sounded, and Caitren heard goblins screaming. She was not sure what had happened, but the creature appeared to have hit the ceiling of the dungeon. The ceiling collapsed, and Caitren quickly retreated towards the wall to shelter herself. She was able to avoid the falling rubble, though many of the goblins did not and met their deaths. Not only that, but Caitren found that morning had come. Though dark clouds were above, the sun shined brightly from the south, and its light reached the prison. The goblins that still lived cowered and shielded their eyes. Vyroun himself had retreated also, though he was not cowering like his servants. Much rubble separated Caitren from the evil servants and their master. She saw an axe lying on the ground, and behind her was a hole in the wall large enough to escape through.

"Find and seize her!" shouted one of the goblins. Caitren did not know what she had just done, nor why the creature seemed to be so suddenly expelled from her, causing the tower to crumble and break a hole in the wall. There was not time though for her to figure it out, for Caitren had a chance to escape that frightful place, and the servants of Vyroun were coming after her. Caitren swiftly went to the axe and cut her bonds. Then she made for the opening in the fortress wall. Though Caitren had grown weak from hunger and thirst, suddenly she found strength upon gaining hope of escaping the fate she had seemed doomed to meet.

Caitren had no time to linger, as she found wicked men trying to make their way around the rubble. In front of her was a treacherous, rocky hill. Descending it would be dangerous, but Caitren did not hesitate. It was a long way to climb down, and before long Caitren saw men who had become servants of Vyroun at the top of the wall. Caitren was not sure where Vyroun himself was, and she feared that the dark lord would pull her back into the dungeon. Strangely though, it did not take place. She looked ahead to find that she had climbed down as far as she could. Caitren was at the very edge of a short cliff, and at the bottom was a river whose water flowed swiftly.

Caitren was afraid to jump, as it was a rather long way. Ahead, though, she heard the winds of a hurricane, and with fear she saw the fiery serpent being summoned back to the fortress. Caitren knew that Ligwyrm was coming for her. Not only that, but it appeared that Ligwyrm knew not that she was to be seized and not killed. "Oh, here is a peasant cornered again! You are alone this time! No wizard to save you! No friends to help you! There is no luck on your side now. Only a furnace awaits you!"

Ligwyrm was about to conjure his inferno, and Caitren knew she had no choice but to jump into the river. Upon leaping over the edge, Caitren saw a great fire approaching her, but she fell before it met her. Her dress caught fire, however, there was no need to pat any flames, for Caitren fell deep into the river. Caitren had no choice but to endure the chill of the water. She was not as great a swimmer as Kattalin, but adequate enough. Caitren rose to the surface to catch her breath, but had no time to linger.

Men were soon running along the shores trying to catch her. Meanwhile, Ligwyrm flew above, and his fiery breath was about to strike. Caitren swam as swiftly as she could. Fortunately, the river flowed swiftly to the west, and it carried her quickly. Wicked men carried nets hoping to catch her. Caitren's best hope of escaping was to stay in the river and away from the shores, even though the water was cold and deep.

Soon Caitren heard roaring flames, and she knew to hold her breath and dive beneath the water. Though Caitren felt the heat of the fire, she was beneath the water, and so the flames did not burn her. The water became much warmer, even hot after the breath of Ligwyrm, and at least there was one stroke of fortune for Caitren, that she no longer had to endure the water's cold. She soon was running out of breath, and fortunately the flames stopped, so she rose above the water to catch her breath. Caitren, though, found men on horses riding along the river. Behind her the fortress of Gulgurod was getting farther and farther away.

The fires of Ligwyrm descended upon Caitren again, and she was forced to shelter herself beneath the water. The water grew hotter than before, almost to the point of burning her. Caitren swam as quickly as she could with the current. She then needed to catch her breath and rose to the surface. To her relief, the servants were beginning to fall behind. The river was helping Caitren distance herself from the wicked men that were after her. Ligwyrm, though, conjured his inferno again, and Caitren was not able to catch her breath for long.

Caitren decided that it might be best to stay submerged in the water for as long as she could. She held her breath and went below. Caitren swam as far down as she could to avoid being burned by the water to the top. Towards the bottom of the river the water was warm, but not hot. And hopefully, swimming beneath the surface might help her stay hidden from those chasing her. Caitren could see the riverbed quickly passing beneath her. But soon she needed air again and was forced to swim back to the surface.

No flames chased her this time. Caitren made sure only her head was above the water, so as to stay hidden. She saw the men riding behind her, but they were a good distance away and they clearly did not see her. Ligwyrm flew above but did not unleash his fiery breath, as it did not appear that he could see her either. Gulgurod was barely in sight, but Caitren was not at all relieved yet, as she was still being pursued by the dragon and the wicked men.

By then, Caitren had never felt so weak and exhausted. Yet Caitren would not dare be still, like a beast running from its hunter, and she would not dare make for the shore to take a rest, for she worried that if she did, Ligwyrm would find her, or the wicked men would catch her and take her back to that terrible dungeon. Caitren was very hungry, although at the very least, being that she was in a river, her thirst soon ceased.

And so Caitren swam onward. Soon the hurricane winds of the serpent grew faint. There were no longer men on horses within her sight. The river carried her quickly. Caitren kept diving beneath the water, afraid that Ligwyrm might find her, but after diving a few times, she no longer heard Ligwyrm flying. Not only that, but the dark fortress was out of sight.

She was not at all sure what time of day it was when she escaped. Several hours passed by, and all was quiet. The water had been very warm from the dragon's fire for quite some time, but by now it was beginning to grow cold again. Caitren looked to the sky and found it was evening. She was growing very tired and cold, and Caitren began to worry that she might grow sick and catch a fever. Caitren thought that the first few days of following Adroegen after her home was destroyed were difficult. She, however, would have been joyful to have only such troubles in that moment. The Black Mountains were still looming to the north, but they grew more and more distant.

The night soon came, and the air grew a little colder. Caitren began to shiver. She was still swimming, which only made her colder. Caitren was still afraid to leave the river, which continued to carry her away from the mouth into the dark kingdom. By then she had almost no strength left, but as the night fell, Caitren worried that goblins might be out searching for her.

After an hour or so in the dark, something finally caught Caitren's eye. Some light was ahead. The river carried her towards the light, and soon Caitren saw a great forest not far away. She made for it, though Caitren was afraid, as she knew not what resided within those woods. The river flowed into the forest, and Caitren allowed it to carry her there. Before long, she had entered the woods.

Suddenly, the water and the air grew warmer, as if it were summer. Though it was night, Caitren saw much light within the forest. Several fireflies flew about, but it was not only fireflies making the light, though Caitren was not able to see what else brightened those woods. The trees themselves were much larger than any she had seen in the forests to the south or within the Fornwood. Caitren was soon not shivering as she had been earlier. However, I would say that Caitren may have been weary, but she was also wary. She felt it might be safe to finally rest, but still worried that enemies might be lurking. Caitren swam until she was well into the woods, and before long she heard faint voices singing.

Come along! Come along! Be not afraid!
For your worries here are not dire nor grave!

Within these trees do the wood nymphs dwell,
Stand watch we do for things ill or fell.

Come along! Come along! Be not afraid!
Into the Woodlands your feet have strayed!

Beneath these trees may you safely rest,
For this realm welcomes you as guest.

"The Woodlands," said Caitren to herself. She remembered when Adroegen tried to lead her and her friends there, only to be forced to change course when Ligwyrm found them in the Dwimor Fells. Caitren felt a little relief, but she was still very much afraid after being imprisoned by Vyroun. She went to the shore and left the river. Caitren was very sore, and still in great pain from what she had endured within the dungeons of Gulgurod. She had no more strength, and lay there at the shore of the river.

"Welcome, Caitren," said a voice inside her head. Caitren screamed in fright upon hearing it and immediately covered her ears. However, it was not the loud and menacing voice she had heard back in the dungeon. Instead it was the soft voice of a woman, whispering to her. Caitren looked about and saw no one. She knew not who spoke to her, but the voice whispered on.

"Do not be afraid," whispered the voice. "Sleep now, Caitren. For you have entered the Woodlands. You are weary, and have endured much. There is no longer need for worry. No enemies of yours lurk here. Sleep, Caitren."

Calm began to overtake Caitren. She had been greatly worried the past many hours, but that wariness left her now. Within moments after hearing the whispers, Caitren was still and asleep beneath the trees of the Woodlands.

Chapter Six: Elves and Fairies

When Caitren woke, she found herself lying in a very soft bed. She had not slept in a bed in several months, and so Caitren was quite comfortable. Her clothes had been changed, too. She was wearing a white sleeping gown, which also felt very soft and comfortable. Caitren was not at all sure where she was. She was resting in a room of wood walls. A window was right behind her, but with no glass, and a gentle breeze blew into the room. Ahead was an open door. A small table was to her side, and on it was a cup of tea, pine, and honey, and because it sat right next to her, Caitren felt certain it was put there for her. She could not help but drink some. There was very little worry within her that the tea was poisoned, as the voice that had spoken to Caitren, whoever this woman was, had all but alleviated any wariness Caitren had. And the tea itself was wonderful, tasting of pine and honey. She had not had such comforts since before her home was destroyed the past summer.

Though Caitren was still sore and tired, she was greatly curious and rose to her feet. Caitren knew that she was in the Woodlands, but she knew not precisely where, nor whose house she rested in. She looked out the window behind her. Caitren was in the trunk of a great tree, very high above the ground. She heard birds singing and saw dragonflies flying all about. All was very quiet and peaceful, which Caitren was happy of after being in the dungeon of Gulgurod. She could not believe she had been able to escape that terrible place, and that she was somewhere far better.

Caitren was unsure how long she had slept. It appeared to be late in the morning. There was no one to be seen nor heard. She left her room to search for anyone. Upon leaving, Caitren found stairs ahead, which she went down.

After going down several stairs, Caitren found herself in a dining room, with many candles and enough well-carved chairs for a dozen folk. She did not see anyone there, but before long a woman came up the stairs to find her.

"Ah, you have awakened," said the woman with a gentle smile. She had brown hair and wore a dark green dress. Caitren in particular noticed that she was quite pale, and not only that, but her ears were pointed. At first Caitren was not sure why, but then realized that she looked upon an elf. She had heard of them, being most fair in appearance, but Caitren had never seen one before.

"Where am I?" asked Caitren.

"You are in the house of Dalgarinan and Mairawin," said the elf. "Lord and lady of the Woodlands. You are in very good hands here, for we shall tend to you after what torment you have endured. It was Mairawin who knew you were coming and housed you here."

The elf then spoke a verse:

The lady of the Woodlands, standing tall,
Her raven hair, so graceful does it fall.

Fair and kind, with wisdom unending,
Against ill she is fierce and unbending.

Upon the branches of her forest crown,
Sits a jewel whose twin could never be found.

Given to her from the stars themselves,
Granting wisdom to guide the Woodland elves.

"You are elves," said Caitren in wonder. "I never thought I might see one."

"Yes, although I would say there are not many of us," said the elf. "We are not great in number like men, or dwarves, or giants."

Caitren's mind was overrun with all kinds of questions. She was trying to figure out where she was, what might have happened to her friends, whom she had not seen in some time, and what took place beyond the woods, as she remembered that an army had begun to march south. She spoke to the elf. "Where are the lord and lady now?"

"Follow the stairs back up," said the elf. "They are above where you rested, in the canopy, gazing about to the north."

"Forgive me, but I have not asked your name," said Caitren.

"Navena, maiden of the elves am I," said Navena. "Worry not, for you will see me much. Go on and find Mairawin. She will give you many of the answers that you seek."

Caitren went back up the stairs and passed her room. She climbed farther up until the stairs ended, and she was as high in the great tree as she could be. Caitren found herself walking along a very wide and strong branch. A path appeared to be carved directly into the branch. The bark rose to each side as if to prevent anyone from falling, and fall a great distance they would if they were not careful! For Caitren was hundreds of feet high in the tree. Caitren followed the path, and before long she found that many branches of both that tree and other trees nearby intertwined. Several did so just ahead to form a very sturdy dais to stand, and there Caitren found two more elves, one a man and one a woman, waiting for her.

"Welcome, Caitren, daughter of Huldnar," said Dalgarinan. The lord of the Woodlands had long golden hair, and to Caitren he looked quite like her father. Dalgarinan wore a long brown tunic with gold leaves trimmed around all the edges.

"You have endured much torment, and you have grown quite weary," said Mairawin. Upon hearing the lady of the Woodlands speak, Caitren immediately knew who had whispered to her upon entering the Woodlands the previous night. Caitren found that there was quite a beauty about her, and yet Caitren sensed something strange about Mairawin that she could not explain. The lady of the Woodlands wore a green dress that looked like hundreds of leaves sewn together. A circlet was upon her head, one of small, woven gold and wood twigs, and at the center of Mairawin's forehead was an ornament. It had a seven-lobed leaf of red, and then a five-lobed golden leaf, and then a round twig forming a ring. Then at the center was a white jewel that glowed greatly in the sunlight. The lady of the Woodlands spoke on.

"There is much unrest within your mind," said Mairawin. "Your father is beyond your sight. You and your friends have faced many perils together, and now all of you are separated, and you worry greatly."

"I am unsure of where they are now," said Caitren. "The goblins in the terrible dungeon I was captive in told Vyroun that they are searching for my friends. But I also heard from them that Adroegen, our guide, has fallen."

"He has fallen?" asked Dalgarinan with a worried look. He turned to Mairawin. "Is this true? What do your eyes see?"

Mairawin closed her eyes, and the white jewel upon her circlet glowed brighter. Caitren grew with worry that the worst had happened. After all the fortune she and her friends had during their venture, Caitren did not want to believe that luck would turn so terribly against them.

"Tell us that it is not so. He was once here in our home, and is deserving of a better fate," said Dalgarinan. Mairawin opened her eyes finally, and looked to the distance, as if she were deep within thought.

"He has fallen," said the lady of the Woodlands. Caitren was devastated to hear this. Dalgarinan appeared calm, and yet Caitren could see in his eyes that he was stunned. Mairawin spoke on. "The goblins spoke the truth."

Caitren began to cry, for she could not believe it. Adroegen seemed far too strong to fall, and he had guided her and her friends quite far out of peril. Caitren felt alone suddenly.

"He is dead then? Has Adroegen met his end?" said Dalgarinan. Mairawin still gazed without blinking, as if she were seeing more.

"Much is clouded. He has fallen and has suffered greatly," said the lady of the Woodlands. "The fate of Adroegen I cannot see in full, but he has been hurt beyond what many could live to tell of. I know not if there is any hope for him. However, if there is, it is all but gone."

Caitren had never felt so saddened before, and she knew not what words to utter.

"Your heart is a heavy one to carry, Caitren, and you do not hide it from those who meet you," said the lady of the Woodlands. "I may possess the gift of seeing what you and others cannot, but I do not know with certainty that you have reason for sorrow, for there is much I cannot see, and I find that the veil can oft have purpose for clouding my sight."

Caitren still carried grief, but a peculiar hope overtook her. There was something strange about what had just been uttered to her, as if something else had become of Adroegen. And so, a suspicion crept over Caitren, and her heart could not help but tell her that she had not lost him, even if hope was very small, if not gone already. If that were so, though, Caitren knew not what could have taken place with Adroegen, nor her other friends for that matter. "I hope that there is a chance Adroegen lives, even if it is small. And oh, how I want to know what has become of my friends. Please, say not that hope is gone!"

"I do not know his fate with certainty, nor can I say what has become of your friends," said the lady of the Woodlands. "You must rest, Caitren. For you are burdened with much, and some pain must still heal."

"You may remain here for as long as you must," said Dalgarinan. Caitren was grateful, but still overcome with sadness. She was still hurting from what she endured in Gulgurod, also.

Caitren returned to her room within that great tree. She was still very tired but also sought some solitude. Caitren wept quietly, for she knew not what she must do. Her guide, and the company's guide, might have been gone, and yet her heart would not let Caitren be so sure. Caitren wished to find her father, and yet she felt a need to find her friends first, for they were likely in grave danger somewhere. Caitren sat in her bed to rest, overcome with sadness. Yet her heart strangely would not give up hope.

As she sat, Caitren placed her hand upon her leg and felt a great pain. Upon lifting the skirt of her sleeping gown, Caitren found a great bruise on her upper leg. She also found another great bruise behind her shoulder, which she had hurt back in the dungeon. Both hurt greatly when she put her hands on them. Caitren soon found though that she was no longer alone. At the door was Mairawin, and Navena was behind, carrying a few things, though Caitren was not able to see what.

"The nymphs of the Woodlands will now tend to you," said Mairawin, who went to the window behind Caitren. "They are coming here now."

Caitren waited, and before long there were creatures flying in from the window. At first Caitren thought they might have been birds, or large dragonflies, but there were no wings fluttering. Instead, to her wonder, Caitren found that they were fairies. They looked about as young as she was, however, these fairies were much smaller, just a little bigger than the size of Caitren's hand. Both flew before Caitren and looked upon her either with curiosity or annoyance. Caitren held out her hand for one fairy to stand, but instead the fairy kicked Caitren's hand away. The other fairy folded her arms and turned her back. Both appeared quite annoyed with the fact that they had to see Caitren.

"Now, now," said Mairawin to the fairies, smiling and speaking with calm in her voice. "Caitren here has pain to mend. She would be quite grateful for your help."

Caitren gazed upon the fairies and found them quite enchanting, even if they were rather rude to her. They wore little, with each having only a leaf wrapped and sewn around their body to form a small dress. Neither wore any kind of shoes or cloak. The fairies danced rather than walked, and they flew without wings.

"Come now, it will not take very long at all," said Mairawin. After being rather stubborn, one fairy flew to the bruise on Caitren's leg as the other flew to the back of her shoulder.

Caitren was not sure what they were going to do. One fairy then placed both of her hands upon the great bruise Caitren had on her leg, while the other placed both of her hands upon the back of Caitren's shoulder. The two of them then began to rub their hands upon the great bruises. The fairies' hands were surprisingly rough, and it did hurt at first. Then Caitren began to see that there was something they were rubbing onto her. She was not sure what it was. Perhaps it was either sand or dust. The fairies did this for some time, and at first, it hurt. However, after some time the pain began to lessen, and before long Caitren no longer felt any pain at all. The two fairies then flew back before Caitren, looking quite annoyed for helping her.

"There, that did not take long. And Caitren is very grateful," said Mairawin to the fairies. Caitren looked at her leg and had never been in awe as she was then. Her leg looked and felt as if it had never been hurt. She looked behind her shoulder and found the same, that the great bruise there was gone. She quickly looked back upon the fairies and could not help but be fascinated with them.

"Oh, thank you!" said Caitren. The fairies, however, only gave her looks of irritation in return and promptly flew away. Mairawin had a pleasant smile upon her face as they left.

"The fairies are truly fascinating," said the lady of the Woodlands. "These northern woods are filled with them. For we reside near the Fairywater, a great lake where they reside. The river that carried you here flows into it. Beyond this forest is the dawn of winter, but within these woods, winter's chill never bites so long as the fairies reside here."

"It looks as if I were never hurt at all," said Caitren, looking back upon her leg.

"Yes, they have the power to heal," said Mairawin. "Your friend Adroegen was once in this very room, like yourself, after being captive in the dark prison of Gulgurod. He was in much greater pain, and yet when I brought the fairies in to tend to him, he refused their aid. So much hate ran in his veins then, and so much anger was in Adroegen's heart. It was saddening, what he went through there."

"Yes, I heard his tale once," said Caitren, remembering Adroegen telling of watching his mother being fed to wolves. "I never thought that he would meet the fate I fear has taken him."

"This jewel allows me to see much that others cannot," said the lady of the Woodlands. "It is a magic jewel fallen from the stars themselves in the first age of this world, and it grants me sight that others do not have. However, I am not bidden to see all that is in motion. I cannot tell you all truth of what has become of him, nor am I certain what has become of your friends."

"Then I will not ask it of you," said Caitren, who then looked out the window behind her. She saw dozens of fairies flying about, and many dragonflies and white moths. The sight was most wondrous, and though Caitren had felt very saddened, suddenly some happiness found her.

"You may wander about as you wish," said Mairawin. "I would encourage it of you. Though I must warn you, even though the fairies are quite fascinating, they can also be quite cheeky and mischievous. They are not harmful, but at times they might also not quite be friendly, as you have already seen. You must be careful around them."

"I will be careful, then," said Caitren, who was undeniably eager to look about that forest, which appeared just as wondrous as the Fornwood, though in a much different way. For the Fornwood was filled with friendly animals and trees that could speak and walk. In the Woodlands, from what Caitren had found thus far, the trees were far bigger and no chill of winter appeared to enter within its borders. And fairies and elves dwelt there, from what Caitren had come to know. Navena then stepped forward, and she was holding a few things that appeared to be for Caitren.

"Before you wander about, we have some gifts for you that I must ask you to accept," said Mairawin as Navena walked over. Mairawin first took a small wooden box and opened it. Inside was a beautiful silver necklace. It held a jewel that was blue, and yet when Caitren looked closely, she found that at the center was what looked like a star in a night sky. It looked noticeably similar to the jewel that Mairawin wore, accept the jewel she wore was white.

Mairawin took the necklace and put it around Caitren's neck. Caitren gently took the jewel and held it. She could not have been more dazzled by it. Caitren looked to Mairawin and Navena. "This is absolutely beautiful. Thank you."

"That is no mere gem that you now possess, for it, too, is a magic jewel, one of the jewels known as the Galesirs," said Mairawin. "This jewel may help protect you from what perils you still have to face, and in time you will find

it may provide many other uses to you, though you will have to find all of its uses out for yourself as you venture onward. And there is another gift that I ask you to accept, that Navena here made for you."

Navena laid on Caitren's bed what must have been the most beautiful dress that she had ever seen. Mairawin and Navena told her to put it on. Caitren rose to her feet and hardly hesitated. It took a little time, but before long Caitren was wearing a new dress that looked as if it were made from the forest itself. She could not help but gaze down at it.

There was a girdle of red flowers around Caitren's waist. Beneath her waist the dress had what must have been hundreds of leaves sewn together. Then above her waist there was bark that was quite tough and yet still bendable. The dress did not have sleeves. Instead there were some vines of green ivy that went off Caitren's shoulders. Caitren was absolutely astonished at the dress. Mairawin and Navena appeared equally astonished at how Caitren looked.

"You look wonderful," said Navena. Caitren gently took the skirt of her dress and could not help but twirl around with it. Mairawin gave a smile.

"I must agree, Navena," said the lady of the Woodlands. Caitren smiled and was unable to take her eyes off her new dress.

"Thank you," Caitren said as she marveled at her new garb. "I have never seen such a beautiful dress before."

Caitren then wandered about the great Woodlands. The forest was unlike the others she had traveled through. The Fornwood was equal in wonder, however, the two forests were very different. The trees within the Woodlands were far taller. Their trunks were large enough that someone like her could live in them. Upon leaving the house of Dalgarinan and Mairawin, Caitren found that the door was just a hole in the tree, and that the windows like the one in the room where she slept were also just holes in the tree's trunk. The branches were wide and strong enough that one could easily walk within any tree's canopy.

Some animals wandered about, though not as many as within the great Fornwood. The Woodlands was filled with fireflies, butterflies, dragonflies, and fairies. Bumblebees, too, buzzed about. Caitren quickly found that she needed to be careful what she touched, as many bushes, thickets, small fallen branches, and large mushrooms were homes to the fairies. Caitren put her hand out to smell a large flower, only to have a fairy angrily fly out at her. Even then, Caitren was still very fascinated by them. She did find a flower or two to pick and put in her hair.

Later that evening she reached the Fairywater, the lake where the fairies resided, and the water felt warm against Caitren's feet. The lake itself glittered, and many fairies flew above. She found that not a single fairy wore shoes. The fairies, like the two that had tended to Caitren earlier, wore no more than a leaf sewn around their bodies to form a rather short and small dress, and Caitren found that some fairies simply went about naked. Caitren sat there until the night fell, and when night came, she found there was no need to carry any candle or torch. There were many fireflies about, and the fairies themselves also gave off light. Caitren noticed that the necklace she wore was quite radiant, glowing and glittering white in the dark.

In the night, there was a full moon, and Caitren saw a most dazzling display. The fairies all flew and danced in the moonlight. There was light glowing all above the Fairywater, and when Caitren looked up to the moon, she saw the shadows of many fairies dancing and flying across it. Upon seeing the fairies dance, Caitren could not help but dance with them in the moonlight. Caitren had endured much since having to leave her home, but that night she felt happy again that she was on that venture. The fairies made their own beautiful song, and Caitren had never heard such enchanting music. Caitren loved to dance, and she found quickly that there was perhaps nothing she enjoyed more than to dance among the fairies in the moonlight.

Each night Caitren slept quite well, although I daresay that each morning when she woke, she always found her hair tangled into a great mess. She first thought she must have slept in an odd manner. However, Caitren woke up in the middle of one night and found that the same two fairies that had tended to her were trying to tangle and mess her hair as much as they could as she slept! It took some time for her to brush her hair, though Navena was always happy to help her.

Caitren also ate quite well in the Woodlands. Each day there was soft bread and stew with mushrooms, and Caitren was happy, as she had been quite hungry when the goblins had taken her prisoner. It had not been since the past summer, before her home was destroyed and she and her friends were forced to go on a long journey, that Caitren had eaten good food rather than food from the wild.

As peaceful as Caitren felt in the Woodlands, though, she still worried about where her friends were, and a lingering torment rested within her mind about Adroegen's possible end. Caitren also feared the army marching, that it would bring much death. Dalgarinan told her that scouts of the Woodlands had confirmed that an army marched for Bared Nar, the great city of Gundmar. The kingdom of Itilikin, a kingdom of men that resided within the Woodlands, was preparing for war and would ride out soon to face Vyroun's forces. Dalgarinan heard that the army marched slowly, as there were many goblins and trolls, which were quite vulnerable in the sunlight. And so, the army marched only in the night, and the trolls needed to take shelter in the daylight, or else they would turn to stone. That gave them time. Soon the lord and lady of the Woodlands would ride south, before the army of Itilikin would ride off. Caitren wanted to go with them to see if she might be able to find any clue as to where her friends or her father might be.

One day as Caitren was in the house of Dalgarinan and Mairawin, she came across one room she had not found before. It was some kind of study. There were shelves with books, a telescope that looked out the window, and several tapestries. Some tables and desks held maps of places that Caitren was not familiar with. There was one tapestry hanging from the wall that caught her eye, though. Caitren went for a better look.

Upon this tapestry was the entire earth itself. At the very top of the round earth was a great tree, whose roots were planted within the earth. Atop the tree there were many branches, and from them hung stars rather than leaves. From the bottom branch to the right, or to the east, there hung the sun. Then from the bottom branch to the left, or the west, there hung the moon. Upon the top of the tree's trunk, which was about as tall as the width of the earth itself, Caitren saw a light, and when she looked closely, Caitren could see it shining from atop a white tower in a great city of white stone.

"Elunbelan," said a voice that scared Caitren. Dalgarinan was standing at the doorway. "You have found my study, I see."

"Forgive me, I can leave immediately if you wish," said Caitren, thinking she should not have entered.

"No, no. Feel free to have a look around," said Dalgarinan, walking in. "It is Elunbelan upon the tapestry that has caught your eye."

"Elunbelan?" said Caitren. She had not heard of this place before.

"Its roots hold the earth together," said Dalgarinan. "From its branches hang the sun and the moon and all the stars in the sky. And within its canopy do all the dead rest. That is the place where the Rhykwen will usher us in death. And upon the trunk is an endless city, and within this city is the very throne of Enilundar himself, watching over all the earth and blind to nothing."

"An enormous tree that must be!" said Caitren.

"Larger than any in this world," said Dalgarinan. "And the jewel that the lady of the Woodlands wears upon her forehead came from the tree of Elunbelan. It is one of the Galesirs, the jewels of the stars. Each of the first children of Enilundar cut one star from the tree of Elunbelan during the First Age of this world, and they fell to the earth in the form of a jewel, each possessing its own kind of magic. For Mairawin, that gift is sight, to see what many others cannot. Navena has her own jewel, and I, too, possess one of these Galesirs, one that allows me to see things from the distant past, though I am not able to see all. And now you, too, possess one of these jewels."

"My jewel was once a star?" said Caitren in surprise as Dalgarinan held out his hand. Upon it was a ring holding a great jewel, the same size as the one Caitren wore around her neck. It was white like Mairawin's jewel, and there was a small glow coming from it.

"It still is a star, and one day it will return amongst the stars, when its work upon this earth is complete," said Dalgarinan. Caitren was filled with wonder that she was wearing a star around her neck, and that it was not just any mere jewel.

Caitren gazed again upon the tapestry of Elunbelan, but soon another tapestry drew her eyes. On this tapestry were five warriors, each wreathed in blue flame. To the very right was a man with a large beard wielding a great hammer. Next to him was a lady who stood in water and held a trident. To the center was a man with long dark hair but no beard, wielding a sword. Then another woman stood in a forest shooting a bow whose arrow burned blue flame. Then finally to the very left was a man who held a mace, but this mace gave off a great light, as if it were also a torch. Each of them looked quite fierce, and Caitren's gaze soon could drift nowhere else.

"Who are they upon this tapestry?" said Caitren.

"They are the very greatest servants of Enilundar, the

greatest being of this earth," said Dalgarinan. "The Vistivar and their weapons forged by Enilundar himself. Dutharion and his hammer. Algarmaira wielding her trident. Rhunwin and the bow she was given. Celandorn and his mace. And Buludin, wielding the greatest sword to reside upon this earth."

"I heard of the Vistivar once," said Caitren, remembering when Ganglere the wizard told her and her friends of the servants to Enilundar, and the legend of Buludin. She looked upon the five servants. "They are all wreathed in flame, a great blue flame."

"Enilundar's fire," said Dalgarinan. "It is the greatest means of knowing they are the true Vistivar, and that their weapons are the true weapons forged by Enilundar himself. A roaring blue flame, and great light to dispel what darkness meets them."

"Light and blue flame," said Caitren to herself. She remembered Ganglere speaking of such things when describing Enilundar.

"Each was born during the Second Age of this world," said Dalgarinan. "And they were sent from Elunbelan to face Dorgelung and cast him into the Chasm, or Magordath, as elves call it, whereupon being cast there, one cannot be brought back to this earth. Dorgelung, the dark lord of that age, with his servant Melkroth, and his hordes of fell creatures he had spawned overran these lands. The race of men, after being created by the dwarves on Enilundar's orders, was beginning to multiply at that time. Upon Dorgelung's defeat, the Vistivar were called back to Elunbelan until being sent back in the Third Age of this world during the reign of he who was once Dorgelung's servant."

"I believe I have heard a little of this tale," said Caitren. "The Vistivar were sent to defeat different evils that were about an age ago, as I remember."

"Each was sent here an age ago with their own task," said Dalgarinan. "For there was much evil at the time. The Woodlands faced Vyroun in the north, although I would say that there was another foe to the west we had to face. One without any army, one without any dark kingdom. The Phantomwraith, whose power equaled Vyroun's own."

"The Phantomwraith?" said Caitren curiously. "I have not heard of this foe."

"The kingdom of Vaolnor, which once lay west of these woods, was brought to ruin singlehandedly by him," said Dalgarinan, who then spoke a verse.

> At eventide there awakens
>> A black malice that does not sleep.
> The reaper has come to harvest,
>> The chasm's host shall take his guests,
> He comes in the witching hour,
>> He smells fear like a beast smells blood.
> The bringer of fright, and nightmares
>> That none shall be awoken from,
> Before what none who live escape.
>> The breathful become the breathless,
> Yet their taker grants them no rest.
>> In death cursed spirits are born,
> They only know fear, see only
>> A faceless demon in their gaze,
> One so sinister and evil,
>> Even darkness itself fears him.

Caitren knew nothing of this Phantomwraith but found him quite frightening. Dalgarinan spoke on. "In the night did he snatch the spirits of people in Vaolnor one by one, until all in that kingdom were gone. It was not until Enilundar sent Celandorn that this evil ended."

"A frightening tale that is," said Caitren. "I have encountered Vyroun himself and never hope to again. Nor any other evil like that of which you tell."

"And to the north the Woodlands faced Vyroun himself," said Dalgarinan. "Until Enilundar sent Buludin to face him. Vyroun vanished for an age but only returned."

Caitren remembered hearing this tale. "I have been told that Buludin passed, and that the power of the Vistivar rested within his sword, until his heir would come and gain his might."

"The sword of Buludin, or the tempter's bane, as some know it," said Dalgarinan. "Vanquishing Vyroun when he but touched it an age ago to wield against its master. You have heard of this tale? And who uttered it to you? Was it Adroegen?"

"Actually, Ganglere, the wizard to the south, told of it," said Caitren. "Adroegen believed the tale to be rubbish. Do you believe it is?"

"Yes, he did not believe this tale was real," said Dalgarinan. "What do I say? I cannot tell you. It is one of the greatest secrets of this earth, and among the mysteries from long ago that I have not the ability to see."

"I have heard that there is no knowledge of an heir to Buludin," said Caitren, gazing upon the man wielding a sword in the tapestry. She knew the tale might have little chance of being true, if there was no known heir, and if none knew where the sword was. Yet Caitren could not help but think the tale would not have come into being if it were false. "And his sword has long since been lost. And yet Ganglere uttered that legends are not made for no reason."

"The only knowledge I can give is that we had a wizard in these lands, Ciarvur," said Dalgarinan. "He went to Buludin before the Vistivar passed, and the sword was not seen since, and then this tale rose."

"Perhaps that wizard might have taken the sword?" said Caitren. That was the only hunch her mind could conjure, and if there indeed was an heir, Buludin would have to have told the secret to Ciarvur, a wizard and another servant of Enilundar. "And Buludin must have uttered of a child to him? That is what I must guess, if this tale is true."

"As would I," said Dalgarinan. "However, that wizard passed a decade ago, giving his life to thwart Vyroun himself in battle, and thus there is no other tracing that can be done."

"If Ciarvur kept the sword of Buludin, then where might he have left it?" wondered Caitren.

"That is a mystery," said Dalgarinan. "But the tempter's bane is still somewhere upon this earth, you can be sure of it."

Caitren remained with Dalgarinan and Mairawin for two more days before it was time for them to make south. She was very saddened to leave their home. Caitren would miss the fairies greatly, and was quite enchanted by them and how they danced and flew about, even though the fairies did not seem to like her and tangled her hair each night. She greatly preferred being among the fairies to being before Vyroun. Perhaps that was why she did not mind their mischief so much. However, Caitren's friends were somewhere outside of those woods, likely in danger, and she deeply wished to find them. Perhaps traveling south with the lord and lady of the Woodlands might lead her to finding help, or any clue of what had become of her friends.

The travel itself was going to be easier, as they had horses and would not need to walk. Caitren had grown quite used to having to walk after Adroegen led her and her friends away from the goblin chief. It was November the Twenty-sixth, if we were to follow your calendar. And yet even though it was the beginning of winter, within those woods the air was warm like summer. Dalgarinan and Mairawin would make south for Itilikin with Caitren, however, Navena would remain and maintain their home. Caitren grew quite saddened to bid Navena goodbye.

"I will be forever indebted to you," said Caitren to Navena as the two of them were in Caitren's room.

"You have tasks that you seek to fulfill," said Navena. "Your friends are out there somewhere, and you must find them. Here it is peaceful, but danger grows beyond these woods."

"I was once in Vyroun's prison," said Caitren. "Never have I been so horrified before, and I thought that perhaps I would never find joy after, and yet I have done so here. But now I must leave here and go back into that which I fear greatly."

"You must promise me one thing before we part, Caitren," said Navena. "I have found such a beauty about you, such as I have never seen before. You look very beautiful, but it is not only that. It is your heart and your innocent spirit that I see such beauty in. There is much evil beyond these woods. Promise me that whatever foes you might encounter, you will not let them take that beauty which you possess away from you."

"I have always wanted to see the wonders of this world," began Caitren. "But then when I finally left home, it was not in the manner I had hoped. It was trying, and at the beginning there was one feeling I am not sure I had ever felt before. Anger had never before met my heart, but I felt it when leaving home. Then in time I grew used to the outside world, and then all seemed to become wondrous again. But I felt a fear, that the joy I always possessed might one day be overcome with anger, sadness, and a feeling of doom."

"The world seeks to steal your innocence," said Navena. "It already has tried, from what you say, and with your wondrous beauty, that is the struggle you face. You must fight, but not all fights are with swords. No, you must fight to keep the heart that you have always possessed, and to not let the ill of this world corrupt it, nor take it from you."

Navena gently put her hand on the jewel that Mairawin had given to Caitren, which rested right over Caitren's heart. Caitren felt very moved by Navena's words. "I promise you that they will not."

"I fear for you," said Navena. "And yet I do not. For who could take your heart from you if Vyroun himself could not?"

Caitren and Navena embraced one final time. Then Caitren left. She could not help but have a few tears in her eyes. Caitren had never had a mother, and thus she knew not the feeling of having one. But as Caitren parted from Navena, it felt as if she were leaving a mother who was saddened to watch her child go.

I would say, though, that this deep sadness that suddenly overtook Caitren would not last for very long. As she was about to make her way down the stairs of that great tree, she found both Dalgarinan and Mairawin waiting for her.

"We will depart very soon," said Mairawin. "However, a traveler arrived here not long ago."

"What could they have sought you out for?" asked Caitren.

"Oh, no," said Dalgarinan. "He who arrived did not come seeking us, but rather he came seeking you. You will find him waiting just outside."

Caitren grew very curious, for she was not sure who might know she was there. Dalgarinan and Mairawin stepped aside for Caitren to make her way down the stairs. Caitren went down and soon was outside. When she left the house and saw who awaited her, Caitren was overcome with joy and disbelief. A man with long golden hair but no beard and wearing a cloak stood before her. Caitren could not believe that her father had somehow found her.

"Caitren, I have found you," said Huldnar, who was clearly also overcome with joy.

"Father!" said Caitren. She ran for Huldnar and the two embraced. "I knew I would see you again!"

"I worried greatly," said Huldnar. "For I heard word from a traveler that an attack was coming upon our home to the south, and upon returning there I found our home razed, but I did not find you, nor Edelbir, or Kattalin, or

Gleowan, or Vaenn. I felt that you must have been somewhere, and I searched about these lands."

Caitren briefly retold of how Adroegen was hunted by Vyroun and the goblin chief, and how for months he had led them on the run away from the goblin pack. Caitren then told of how the goblin chief was defeated, and how shortly after she was taken captive, but escaped the dungeon of Gulgurod and reached the Woodlands.

"Well it appears that my tracking of you and your friends was quite behind," said Huldnar. "For I tracked your company as best I could, and the most recent news I received from this traveler was that you were making for the Woodlands. Though that was months ago, and I did not know that you turned course for the Fornwood near the end of summer. And yet, by the time I entered the Woodlands not long ago, you had found yourself here nonetheless, though the rest of your friends, I do not know where they are."

Caitren could not believe she had found her father again, and at such an unexpected time, too. The horses were ready, and Dalgarinan and Mairawin stepped out. Mairawin addressed Huldnar.

"We now will go south to the kingdom of Itilikin," said the lady of the Woodlands. "There we will bid farewell to the Itilikin army before it rides out to war. The army of Mûrondûn marches slowly for Bared Nar. We have time, but haste is still needed. Worry not, though, for the two of you will have time to retell all that you have been through as we ride."

Caitren mounted her horse. She was not the greatest rider, but she had ridden on occasion back at her old home. She, her father, and the lord and the lady of the Woodlands then made their way south. Caitren looked back upon the house of Dalgarinan and Mairawin. She saw Navena waving goodbye, and Caitren felt quite saddened to leave her. Caitren's heart also was burdened that Adroegen may have been lost, and that her friends were somewhere beyond her sight. However, when Caitren turned to look upon the road ahead, she saw her father, whom she had known she would see again, and some joy filled her heart also.

Chapter Seven; The Tree Kingdom

Caitren rode along with her father, Mairawin, and Dalgarinan down a small road that made south. They rode with some haste, though not quickly enough that Caitren could not recount what she had gone through to her father. Huldnar told her that he had spent the past several months searching for her and the others of the company, though he uttered little of where precisely that path led him, nor whom he spoke to. Caitren retold far more.

"I was taken captive by the goblins," said Caitren. "I know not the fates of all my friends, though I have learned that Adroegen has fallen. The others of our company are far beyond my sight. I know not where they are, but I hope to find them."

"Adroegen has fallen?" said Huldnar. He appeared aghast upon hearing this and turned to the elves. "He is dead?"

"All else is clouded to my sight," said Mairawin. "His fate in full I know not. There may have never been hope after what he suffered, and yet I know not with certainty what has become of him. I am unable to see his true fate."

"Could there be hope for him, then?" said Huldnar. "Could Adroegen still live?"

"His fate, as far as I have seen, is a terrible one," said

Mairawin. "None would suffer as he has and still live. And yet I cannot see any more. Something strange clouds my sight from him, but I cannot tell you who or what, nor why."

Caitren's heart felt saddened in reminder that Adroegen had suffered greatly, so much so that none else would live, yet her heart would not give up hope.

"We cannot search for him," said Mairawin. "For Adroegen is far beyond our sight and reach. It is the others of your company, Caitren, that you must seek out."

"I must find them," said Caitren. "For I know not what danger they might be in."

"I have found you, and I am joyful," said Huldnar. "As for your friends, they are the only folk from our home that still lived after it was razed, and so we will search for them in time. Do you know of their whereabouts now?"

"No, I know nothing," said Caitren. "For I was taken prisoner and separated from them. I was brought before Vyroun himself not long ago. Never have I had such a nightmare."

"I cannot believe that you somehow escaped," said Huldnar in surprise. "For that is an enemy that few, if any, could hope to defeat, or even encounter and come out alive. How precisely did you escape from the dungeon to the north?"

"I cannot say with any certainty," said Caitren, trying to recall what had happened, however, she was still very mystified at how she managed to thwart the creature that possessed her and escape the dungeon. "Vyroun offered many things to me. I was offered wealth, but I have never had use for it. He offered me food, but I knew not at what cost it might come. But then a strange creature entered, one I had never before looked upon. Some devilry it was, and this creature might have been some kind of ghost, for it entered me, as if it were trying to possess or control me."

"A deofol," said Dalgarinan. "Vyroun's most terrible of servants, for there are many deoflas that he has bent to his will."

"What are they?" asked Caitren.

"Those creatures were once amongst the race of men," said Dalgarinan. "But then at some point in life, they chose to reject Enilundar and serve evil. And men who choose to serve evil will in death become these demons. They cannot be killed, for such demons have passed already. Deoflas on their own are weak and in an agony that is eternal. They will oft try to ease their pain by possessing the living. A dark power such as Vyroun, though, can bend these creatures to his will, giving strength to them."

"Vyroun offered to end the agony I was in," said Caitren. "However, I would have had to yield to him for it to end, and I knew not if such agony would actually cease. And then Vyroun offered to take me to my father, and I wondered if he spoke the truth. However, in the end I did not trust him, and refused. And then suddenly the deofol left me, as if it were forced out, and the dungeon caved in, and there was a hole in the wall for me to escape, and I found a river to dive into that led me to the Woodlands."

"A total rejection of evil," said Dalgarinan. "A deofol, they say, can be repelled through a complete rejection of evil, through a heart that is pure and harbors none. Very few possess such courage that you showed, Caitren. I believe you possess a powerful weapon. No, it is not a sword, nor any other weapon wielded in war, but rather it is your heart. For it showed impeccable resilience to great evil, and this was why that monster was expelled from you."

Caitren noticed that Huldnar appeared to be holding tears back. He did not appear overcome with grief though, but rather joy, and Caitren had never seen him show such a look of pride.

"That is one of the few ways to repel a deofol," said Dalgarinan. "They, like goblins, trolls, and other foul creatures, cannot stand the light of day. After that, servants of Enilundar himself, the Vistivar or the wizards, can fend off these creatures, though the deoflas cannot truly be defeated, only rendered powerless by destroying their master. We had a wizard in these northern lands, Ciarvur, but his end came a decade ago. And so now the north is without a wizard to repel these deoflas. Vyroun has many of these creatures under his command, and he will unleash them when the army reaches Bared Nar. With no wizard, these devilish monsters will be unchallenged."

Caitren grew fearful upon hearing this. She knew of one wizard to the south, one the company had met during their venture, who could have been of help, however, when last they met, Ganglere was mustering the birds to face what foul things were gathering in the ruins of Hailnor to the south. Caitren knew not what had become of Ganglere. Had Caitren known these deoflas were going to attack the great city of Gundmar, she would have searched for the wizard for help. However, Caitren had not even known of such fiendish creatures until her imprisonment in Gulgurod, and by then the wizard was beyond her sight or reach. With Vyroun's army approaching Bared Nar, there was no time to search for Ganglere.

"You say that deoflas are men who reject Enilundar for evil," said Caitren. "They are only amongst the race of men?"

"Only amongst the race of men, yes," said Dalgarinan.

"If only men become such creatures, then what might become of an elf who makes such a choice?" asked Caitren. Dalgarinan looked to Mairawin, who had been silent.

"Something far worse becomes of us," said Mairawin, looking to the north, where the dark kingdom stood. "For Vyroun himself was once an elf, like us. But at some point, he chose to serve evil, and now he is a dark lord and a pawn of darkness. There were a few elves who once made such a choice to reject Enilundar long ago, beginning with Daugor and Nelor, then their son Dorgelung, his once-servant Melkroth, and other evils like Vyroun himself. There is no light in a lord like Vyroun. He is filled only with malice."

"If I might ask," began Huldnar. "Can one who has made such a choice come back from being so evil? Could a lord such as Vyroun, or any of the other elves who rejected light for darkness, somehow find redemption in the eyes of Enilundar?"

"That question is one of this world's greatest mysteries," said Mairawin. "It is far beyond my own wisdom to answer."

The four of them after some time reached a river. This was the Nordura, or the northern river, and to the other side of this river was a greater road that went directly south to the kingdom of Itilikin. The four of them rode along the Elven Road south. It took a few nights on horseback to reach this kingdom of men that lay within the Woodlands. The trees were as large and tall as they were in the north where Caitren had rested upon first entering. The Woodlands were quite quiet, though on occasion Caitren did see some folk living within the great trees. When the four of them drew close to the kingdom of Itilikin, Caitren began to see far more folk. After a few days since leaving the house of Dalgarinan and Mairawin, Caitren was looking upon the kingdom of Itilikin, and it was another wondrous sight.

All the trees within the Woodlands were very tall. Most Woodland trees were wide enough and had holes in them where one could take shelter within their trunks. It appeared that some folk even lived and slept in the canopies of the trees. There was one tree ahead that was not quite as tall as most of the others, however, it was much wider. It was wide enough to house many men rather than just a few. There was a great wooden gate ahead, and several folk were walking in and out. The trunk of the tree had scores of windows. It was the canopy of the tree, though, that Caitren was quite astonished by. There were several towers and turrets of stone built within the tree's canopy. A castle was built within the tree, as stone and wood were in unison. This tree castle was tall but short enough to still be beneath the other trees of the Woodlands.

Around this great tree was a city within the forest. There was not a single home built throughout the forest, or at least not a home like the one Caitren had grown up in. Instead, every tree was a home. Caitren saw holes for windows in some of the trees, and light was shining out from them. Never had Caitren seen such a city before.

"Itilikin, the tree kingdom," said Dalgarinan. "Here rules Badarion, the king, with whom we shall speak."

"This world never ceases to surprise me," said Caitren, looking upon the tree castle ahead. "The wonders that I find here seem endless."

"The army of Itilikin is gathered here," said Dalgarinan. "King Badarion greatly values the wisdom of Mairawin, lady of the Woodlands, and he sent for us seeking it. Itilikin is the only kingdom of men to be ruled by an elf. One of Badarion's ancestors instead fell in love with an elf, as did many children in the line after, and so the line over time changed into one with far more elven blood than blood of men. Though worry not, for elves and men are companions, not enemies."

The four of them rode for the gate to the castle. There was a drawbridge and a river that flowed out from under the great tree. Two guards were standing at the gate. Both were in gold armor, though their armor bore no banner. They wore helms with wings crafted to each side. Caitren noticed that the same ornament Mairawin wore on her circlet was also on the Itilikin armor, as a clasp for their green capes and on their helms covering each ear.

Once the four of them entered the castle, they dismounted from their horses, and more guards were there to take their horses to a stable. Inside there was some sunlight coming in from above, though some torches were still lit on the walls. Caitren found the castle to look the same as the house where Dalgarinan and Mairawin resided, though much larger.

The four of them were in a great mead hall, with several long tables where men were sitting, drinking, and laughing. Along the wall to the side sat large barrels from which men were getting drinks. Caitren could not help but think that if Gleowan were there, he would have very much liked that hall, though that depended upon what drinks they had and how good they were. Some music was playing, and Caitren saw some women dancing. She would have loved to join in, and Caitren was certain that if Vaenn were there, she would be dancing without hesitation. Caitren was not sure at all what had become of her friends, though. She desperately needed to find them, wherever they were.

There was a great green carpet that led ahead to some circular stairs, which Caitren and Huldnar followed Dalgarinan and Mairawin towards. This carpet led them over a small bridge, and Caitren looked down to see the river flowing. The water was underneath the floor that they stood on, and some men were laughing and fishing there.

As Caitren reached and ascended the stairs, she found that the walls of the castle were sometimes of wood from the tree and sometimes of stone. Soon she was walking through a stone tower, and then before long Caitren was back within the trunk of the tree. Soon the four of them reached another stairway that led them to the top of the tree's trunk and into a long, narrow hall. Ahead was another short stairway, and at the top was a man sitting upon a carved wooden throne, who Caitren was certain must have been the king.

Badarion was tall and had long golden hair. He wore a crown of twigs and green leaves. The king of Itilikin was cloaked in a long green tunic with a cape of much darker green. He was as stoic in appearance as the lord and the lady of the Woodlands. Badarion, upon seeing them approach, stepped down from his throne that stood in the canopy of the great tree.

"It has been some time since last we have spoken," said Mairawin. "Not since the last time your army rode off to war."

"And no passage of time changes the beauty of the lady of the Woodlands," said the king of Itilikin. Mairawin bowed and Badarion spoke on. "Welcome, Dalgarinan. I have hoped to seek out your counsel. The soldiers of the Woodlands have been gathering, and we must soon ride for war. I had hoped for greater numbers, though. We have only ten thousand riders, less than half of what we once had. Scouts say that Vyroun's army approaches Bared Nar. I hope there is still more time, and that we may gather more soldiers, though I know not how many more would come."

"Vyroun's armies seem only to grow," said Dalgarinan. "If this war is to be won, I fear there will be much more help needed than just Itilikin and Gundmar."

"There may be other forces at work," said Mairawin, as the jewel upon her forehead glowed in what sunlight made its way into the canopy of the tree. "But Vyroun's army is drawing closer to Bared Nar, and so time is not on your side."

Caitren thought immediately of the friends she had met during the company's venture from the past few months, and of how they could surely be of great help. However, the Fornwood was far away, and Caitren would never make it in time. The dwarves, too, were a distance away, and even then, Caitren would have to find the door and persuade their king to help. Ganglere was somewhere to the south, and Caitren knew not where to search. She could not help but feel quite helpless, or rather that there was help out there she could not reach.

"You have one night, and then you must ride at dawn," said Mairawin. "Time is against you. I am afraid there is no time to call for the aid of any other forces that might be out there. Instead we can only hope that help might join us from somewhere unknown, though we cannot count on it. If you wait any longer, Gundmar will be alone and fall before you reach them."

"I will heed your words and ride at dawn," said Badarion. The king of Itilikin then turned to Caitren and her father. "Huldnar returns, and I see that you have found your daughter."

"I have," said Huldnar.

"There is no greater treasure to a mother or father than a child," said the king of Itilikin. "And there is nothing more terrible to lose. Welcome, Caitren. The lord and lady of the Woodlands sent me word of your dealings in the dark fortress of Gulgurod. A great resilience you possess towards evil."

"I hope I never have to go through such a nightmare again," said Caitren. "But my friends that I ventured with north I have been separated from, and I must find them."

"I know not of your friends' dealings," said Badarion. "I can only hope that you have luck in finding them. Meanwhile, I welcome you to remain here. The army of Itilikin will ride for Bared Nar tomorrow at dawn. Our women and children shall be safe here, while the men ride north in hope to protect them from any evil descending upon us. A feast will be held tonight before the army rides out, and the women and children shall bid the soldiers farewell. A most terrible thing is war, for many men shall not return. If the war is not won, then our women and children may meet the same fate. That is what we soldiers fear above all else, and that is why we ride into peril."

Caitren stayed in Itilikin that day. She was in one of the towers that was built in the great tree, and her father stayed with her. The lord and the lady of the Woodlands, for much of the day, counseled the king. Huldnar sought what word he could find of the rest of the company, however, it was to no avail. Edelbir, Kattalin, Gleowan, and Vaenn were beyond their sight or tracking.

"We will remain here in Itilikin for right now," said Huldnar. "There is a war coming, and when it is over, we will find your friends."

"Wait until after the war?" said Caitren. "I believe they may be in that battle, if they are anywhere. I must find them there!"

"We will search for your friends," said her father. "But it will be very unsafe to search amidst a field of battle, and you may not come out alive. Believe me, we must find them, and we will, Caitren. But it will be far safer to search after."

"But it might be too late by then. We cannot wait," said Caitren. Caitren wanted to remain there, as the Woodlands was a most wondrous place, however, she felt she could not. For Caitren's bond with the others of the company was strong, and she felt a great need to find them. Caitren had no love of fighting, but the company had agreed after the goblin chief's defeat that they did not want to hide from the evil they had discovered was growing. Thus, Caitren felt certain that if her friends were anywhere, the coming battle would be the most likely place. And so, she worried greatly about waiting to search for her friends. If she could not convince her father to leave straightaway, then Caitren was not sure if she might have to leave on her own to seek her friends.

That night there was a great party held in the hall where Caitren had first entered the tree kingdom. The soldiers were being bid farewell before riding off to war. The hall held hundreds of soldiers and maidens of the Woodlands. Music was playing and many of the folk danced. Others drank and laughed. It was, in ways, like a party held back at what was once Caitren's home, when all the folk finished a day's work. But Caitren was now in a hall filled with folk who to her were strangers. The lord and lady of the Woodlands were elsewhere, likely speaking with the king. Caitren was not sure where her father was, either.

As Caitren watched folk dance and listened to the music, she could not help but wonder what fun the night might have been if there were no war coming, and even more so, if the whole company were there with her. Gleowan would have been drinking while Vaenn would have tried to drag him into a dance. Edelbir and Kattalin would likely have watched Gleowan and Vaenn with amusement. And Caitren missed Adroegen the most, as he was likely gone. Caitren would have loved to dance with the others there, but instead she stood against the wall, feeling very much alone and thinking only of her friends.

Though Caitren stood alone for some time, I would say that she was not unaccompanied for long. Many folk were walking around and laughing. Several were near Caitren, and then suddenly one man, who was young but a little older than her, approached Caitren and surprised her very suddenly, putting an arm around her and being quite loud and boisterous.

"My! Never have I looked upon a fair lady with such

beauty as yourself!" said the man, who then took Caitren by the hand. He was about as tall as Gleowan, and even looked a little like him. This man had golden hair and no beard, and wore a yellow tunic with green leggings. He went on. "If I were to meet my death in battle, it would not be so terrible if I were to first have a dance with a woman so beautiful as you."

Caitren felt flattered, though she did not know this man, and the mere surprise of him approaching her had made Caitren recoil. The man let go of her hand. "Oh, where are my manners? Come and sit."

The man gestured to the nearest table and pulled a chair out for her to sit. Caitren was still a little taken aback. He went to get a pair of drinks and then sat across from her, and suddenly the rather boisterous manner in which he spoke ceased.

"I heard about you," said the man. "Your name is Caitren, from what I have learned, is it not?"

Caitren was surprised that he knew her name. She nodded in return.

"My name is Gamenan," said the man. "I have heard of your story, or at least much of it. I am told that you were a friend to Adroegen."

Caitren felt surprised that he knew what he did about her, and she was quite saddened upon hearing Gamenan speak of Adroegen.

"I have learned that he has fallen," said Gamenan. "Sorry am I to hear of this. He was a friend of mine also. He was friendly, but I found that he was always sad and burdened with a heavy heart. And though he lived here for some time as a child, he soon left, after Vyroun vanished a decade ago. I could not blame him for always being filled with sadness, though, for there might never be a more saddening tale than that which he had been forced to live through."

Caitren remembered the tale of Adroegen and remembered how sad it was. She was filled with sorrow. "I have learned he fell, though I know not that he is gone. In my mind I cannot see how he might still live, and yet my heart will not give up hope."

"You know not with certainty," said Gamenan. "Then do not give up hope. Sorrow is a terrible burden to carry, and it can kill any who allow it to. I do not know you, Caitren, but you have a wonderful spirit, from what I see."

"I know not what I will do if Adroegen or my friends are gone," said Caitren. "The pain of war is not one I had felt before, until my friends and I were chased from our home."

"I would say that all in the north have been through such pain at some time," said Gamenan. "Look about this hall. All here appear joyful, but I will tell you that none of us truly are. For we all know what abyss awaits. We know all too well that some of us will not return. For all in this hall have seen it before. No one here has made it this far without losing someone to the sword within their own kin."

Caitren might still have been taken aback a little at how boisterous Gamenan had been upon first approaching her, but she was starting to find that he had quite a heart to him. She was also growing curious. "And what of you? You have also lost members of your own family?"

"I have," said Gamenan. "Though it was years ago now, and so the pain has passed. I was a very young child at the time, thus I remember not all that took place. My kin were ambushed, from what I understand, and goblins took my mother and father from me. I was told that I had a brother, younger than I, but from what I have been told, he was thrown into a river and carried away, and that he is gone now."

"I had not been through such horrors when I was a child," said Caitren. "Then last summer, my home was burned, and all I knew was suddenly gone. I always wanted to leave home and venture about, but when finally doing so, I immediately longed to have my old home back."

"Yes, you have now seen such horrors as we have, though I would have you never see such sadness if I could," said Gamenan. "Recently you had a taste of what is here in the north. You are like us now, I think, in that you also have seen evil take place. Though even then I could still tell upon seeing you that you were not one from these Woodlands, and that you came from elsewhere."

Gamenan smiled, and a little of his boisterous manner returned. "I knew because if a lady as beautiful as yourself had resided here for some time, you would have caught my eye long before now. I know not where your path shall take you, but I hope greater days are ahead for you, Caitren. For you have the heart and beauty of a princess, and I would have your heart not be filled with grief if I could, for you are not deserving of it."

Caitren felt quite flattered and tried not to cry, and she found that even though Gamenan might have been boisterous, he was also a good man. "And I would hate for someone like you to meet such a terrible fate also," said Caitren. "I only wish Adroegen were here and had better fortune, and I hope my friends have had luck on their side also."

"Yes," said Gamenan. "I do not know your friends, though I hope their fates are better than Adroegen's. I, too, hope that fortune will smile upon me, though we will see what happens upon riding for battle."

Gamenan's eye then turned and looked to the party. Suddenly his boisterousness returned. Gamenan pointed to someone who was dancing. "Although I will say, that lady over there, an elf wearing a dress of purple, her eyes have been fixed upon me this whole night. She might think that I have not noticed, but oh! She is mistaken!"

Caitren turned, and indeed she found an elf amongst the folk dancing, one she found quite fair and beautiful in appearance, with brown hair and a dress of purple. And this elf was looking her way, or I should say, she was looking Gamenan's way.

"What a quest that would be to fulfill," said Gamenan with his eye fixed upon her. "To have a dance with one of the fair elves and to receive a kiss from her after. I would have tried in this quest earlier, but you see, I was not drunk enough yet. But now, I am drunk and ready! There is no escaping the charm of Gamenan now!"

Gamenan quickly finished the rest of his drink and forcefully placed it back upon the table. He then rose to his feet and made his way for the elf. Caitren turned to see what luck Gamenan might have, and she did so with much amusement. As he reached the elf, he bowed and took her hand, and Caitren watched the elf give him a dance. Caitren could not help but laugh, and after Gamenan and the elf danced, sure enough, the elf did give him a kiss on his cheek. Caitren was quite amused. Though she had been saddened for the past several days, Caitren did feel happy right then.

That night Caitren returned to her room with her father. Caitren was not sure what she was to do next. Her friends were somewhere, and Caitren wanted to find them. Perhaps they were dead, but Caitren had not confirmed the worst, even in the case of Adroegen. Caitren's heart told her that Edelbir, Kattalin, Gleowan, and Vaenn were still somewhere beyond the Woodlands. Also, there was a war coming, and the whole company had decided after the goblin chief's defeat that they could not ignore what evil was ascending. Caitren thought that if her friends were alive, they would likely be in Bared Nar. And so Caitren knew what she needed to do, and that was to ride out and find them straightaway. Her father, though, had other plans.

"We will remain here for some time," said Huldnar. "Then we will search for your friends."

"I do not wish to wait," said Caitren. "If they will be anywhere, they will be at the battle that will take place at Bared Nar. I must ride off and find my friends straightaway."

"No, not if there is war," said Huldnar. "You are safe here. I will not have you go back into danger. We will search after, if all ends well."

"But my friends are in danger!" said Caitren. "I would be ashamed if they are in peril and I do nothing to help them."

"We will seek out your friends," said Huldnar. "For I believe it is important also. But I nearly lost you last summer, and from what I hear about these past months, there have been many times where you could have easily met your end. You have shown courage far beyond what anyone as young as you would fathom, but I would not have you show it again, for the next time, fortune might not be on your side."

"I might lose my friends," said Caitren. "They are surely going to be in peril and I must find them! I do not want to wait to seek them, even if war is coming."

"I will say no more," said Huldnar, who then left for his chambers. Caitren was quite unhappy, though she could not blame her father for his thinking. Caitren went to her chambers and thought of what she should do.

The hours of the night passed and Caitren did not sleep. She was deeply troubled. Edelbir, Kattalin, Gleowan, and Vaenn were out there somewhere beyond the Woodlands. Caitren was sure of it. The trouble was that Caitren knew not with certainty where they were, and in leaving the Woodlands, she would be leaving her father. Caitren was most overjoyed to be with Huldnar again, but mere moments after finding him, Caitren was already considering parting with him. And so, I would say that she was very much unsure of what she must do.

With this conflict in her mind, what Caitren could not get over was that she would not want to remain there in comfort if her friends were in peril. The guilt would forever burden her. And so Caitren very quietly snuck out of her chambers. Her father would not allow her to leave, and so Caitren would have to do so against his will. Caitren felt that if she simply found a horse and rode off, her father might find and stop her. However, an army was going to depart in a matter of hours, and if Caitren could sneak into some armor, she might be able to blend in among the soldiers and ride away with them to find her friends. Caitren left and went down the tower in search of the armory. She tried her best not to cry, as Caitren did not want to leave her father.

It was quite late in the night, and Caitren knew not how much time she had. She made her way to the great hall where the party had been held earlier. A few folk were in there. Some were asleep, and some of the others gave Caitren a look but then went back to their business. Caitren looked around to see where she might find some armor, weapons, and a horse.

Before long Caitren saw a pair of soldiers entering the hall from a doorway that she had not yet ventured through. Both were in armor, so Caitren had a hunch that they might have come from an armory. Caitren had to make sure she was not seen, as the soldiers surely would not want a lady to ride into war and be harmed. Caitren herself did not want to ride into war either, for even though she was able to fight, Caitren had no love of it at all. She waited until they left, and when it seemed no one was watching her, Caitren made for this doorway. She had to go down a stone hall, but then Caitren soon found precisely what she had been searching for.

There was a forge ahead and many sets of armor, several swords, shields, and spears. Caitren looked to make sure that she was alone. She heard not a sound. I would say that all the Itilikin soldiers already had their armor and weapons, and thus Caitren had been given a stroke of luck. She quickly searched about for some armor that she could wear.

Caitren found some trouble right away, though. All the armor was made for men, so everything she found at first was far too big. Caitren looked for the smallest set of armor that she could find. Outside the armory, she heard a few folk gathering, thus Caitren needed to hurry. After some time, she finally found the smallest armor that was there.

In all her anxiousness of the past few hours, Caitren had forgotten that she was still wearing her dress, which was not suitable garb for war. She quickly changed out of it and into the armor, which Caitren found took some time. She had donned long chainmail, then a chest plate, which took some time to fasten. Then Caitren put on some greaves and leg guards, as well as boots. Caitren found some armored sleeves, and she made sure to wear a helm, as she did not want anyone to recognize her. Finally, Caitren found gloves and a cloak. By the time she managed to put all the armor on, morning was not far away. She had only just put the armor on, and already did Caitren loathe what she wore.

"Oh, how I hate armor," said Caitren. "For it is heavy, uncomfortable, and harder to move in. I would rather be wearing my dress."

Caitren looked down at her dress that Navena made, which was lying on a chair. She wanted to wear her dress, for it was much lighter, softer, more comfortable, and far more beautiful than the armor. But I am afraid that a dress is not the best choice to wear when entering war. Caitren quickly found a place to hide her dress, gently burying it under some armor. She was quite saddened and began to cry quietly, as she loved that dress very much and was sure that she would never find and wear it again. But Caitren had friends to search for, and the war was the best place to begin her search.

Caitren began to hear shouts in the hall. The army was about to ride off. Caitren ran out of the armory and found many soldiers hastily gathering to leave. It was quite difficult to run and move in the armor. Caitren tried her best to cover her face and not look directly at any other soldiers, worrying that someone might discover she was a lady and not allow her to come along. She found soldiers making for some stables to get their horses. Caitren followed. There were several horses to choose from, and one was quickly given to her. Caitren climbed on the horse.

"Ride for Gundmar!" shouted one of the captains. She rode out with the other soldiers. Many women and children watched the soldiers ride off, and several wept. Caitren could not stop herself from crying, too. She saw her father amongst the crowd, who appeared to be searching in haste for her. I would say that it pained Caitren very much to leave her father right after finding him again, but she did not turn back. Caitren rode off with the army to war, and to find her friends.

Chapter Eight:
A Collector of the Dead

Adroegen woke to find himself washed ashore, quite cold, and in considerable pain. He was surprised to be alive after taking such a fall. All was quiet, save for the river flowing. Adroegen was not at all sure of where he was, other than somewhere far down the river along the cliffs. Not only that, but he knew not for how long he had been unconscious. It was daytime, although Adroegen knew not precisely which day it was.

Immediately Adroegen tried to rise to his feet. When he did, though, he gave out a scream and fell. He had never felt so much pain before, and Adroegen did not realize how hurt he was until then. Both of his legs were badly wounded, one from his meeting with the goblin chief, days earlier, and the other from falling over the cliff. Adroegen could not put weight on either foot. His ribs were badly bruised. Not only that, but his right shoulder was also wounded, and his chest, and his left arm. The pain he felt was almost unbearable. He was weak, too, and thought he might have caught a fever from being in the water.

Adroegen tried to bandage what wounds he had, though there were several. He soon found that he could not walk, and even standing was difficult. Adroegen had to crawl and roll away from the shore of the river and find a place to sit. Once he sat and settled a little, Adroegen tried to figure out where he was and what had happened.

"How is it that I still live?" Adroegen asked himself. He looked upon the sun, which not long ago had helped him and his friends escape the goblin chief when hope seemed lost. However, Adroegen began to feel betrayed and tormented by the day's light.

Adroegen listened for his friends but heard nothing. There were no sounds of battle. The fight had likely ended, as it was day and the goblins were creatures of the night. Adroegen, however, did not know where his friends were, nor how they were faring. He remembered that Caitren had been taken captive and that he was unable to save her. After falling, Adroegen had become helpless, and he could not help his friends in what troubles they might be in.

He was unsure of where he was. It seemed the river had taken Adroegen quite a way before washing him ashore, for he could not see nor hear any sign of his friends. He did realize that he was at the Shrouded Cliffs within the Dead Forest, though now at the bottom rather than on the level of the woods. Adroegen wanted to travel upriver, but he was not sure how far he would be able to go, as he could not stand nor walk. And so, he sat there and rested for the time being, and tried to settle from all the pain.

As Adroegen tried to figure out many different things, from where his friends were, to what he must do next, he thought he heard faint laughter. He listened, and soon Adroegen found that his ears were not cheating him. A cackling laughter was coming from just a little farther down the river. Adroegen found it quite queer, for he did not know of anyone who resided within the Dead Forest. He was not sure who it was, or if it was friend or foe. Before long the laughter grew louder, and soon Adroegen saw someone approaching him in the mist.

It was an old woman, cloaked in black. She was quite ugly. Adroegen knew not who she was. He tried to retreat, but upon doing so he only grimaced. This woman did not look friendly, for there was something rather unsettling about her. Adroegen, though, could neither run nor hide.

"Oh, what have I found?" said the woman, who then spoke a mocking verse.

> *Young Adroegen has washed ashore,*
> *He cannot stand anymore,*
> *His friends are all beyond his sight,*
> *A fall nearly ended his life.*

"Who are you?" asked Adroegen.

The woman approached Adroegen with a smile. "I have seen all of your dealings within this forest," she said. "For I reside here, and I see all that takes place within my home."

"You reside here? And you see all?" said Adroegen.

"Oh yes, maimed one," she said. "I watched a goblin pack wait for you, and I watched you take their bait and suffer in result. I have seen you fall and this river carry you to me. I have also seen what has become of your friends."

Adroegen desperately wanted to know where all his friends were. Yet he did not trust this old woman, whomever she was. "Tell me how you have seen all my dealings. What are you?"

"My skill in witchcraft allows me to see things that are

not in front of me," said the old woman. "I may show you, if you wish."

"You are a witch?" said Adroegen. He retreated upon hearing this, for Adroegen had heard of witches before, though there were said to be very few of them. They were not friends, as he understood. The witch only laughed when Adroegen drew back.

"Are you afraid of me?" the witch said mockingly. "Well, you can flee from me if you wish, but look at how wounded you are. I can only fathom how far you would make it. You may also wonder endlessly of the fate of your friends, or you can simply allow me to show you."

"How do I know that you are not an enemy of mine?" asked Adroegen. He was reluctant to seek the witch's help. Yet he also thought she might be able to answer some questions as to what became of his friends. "And how do I know that you speak the truth?"

"Oh, you will know that I do not lie to you," said the witch. "If you wish to know the fate of your friends, follow me. Or you may remain here and wonder endlessly until your agony takes you."

The witch laughed as she turned to walk away. Adroegen was not sure if he should follow her. From what little he had heard of witches, they were not to be trusted. And yet, Adroegen saw no other way of finding out where his friends were, nor where he was. Adroegen was very reluctant, but being as wounded as he was, if any enemy found him, he would stand no chance. If the witch wanted to kill him, she likely would have done so already. After hesitation, Adroegen struggled and crawled as best as he could along the river shore to follow the witch.

The witch walked slowly along the shore, and yet

Adroegen had quite some trouble keeping up with her. He crawled and pulled himself along like a maimed dog, but he could not do so without great pain. The witch never looked back. Adroegen could hear her cackling to herself, though. It took some time before Adroegen saw the witch approach a small cave beneath the cliff.

The cave itself was most unsettling. Inside, some skulls lay on the ground. There were bats and crows sitting inside, though some were dead. At the center of the cave was a black cauldron over a fire. The witch stood before the cauldron, then finally turned to look upon Adroegen.

"Oh, what a pity I see," said the witch. Adroegen pulled himself into the cave and sat in front of the cauldron, and the witch stood on the other side.

"You can show me what became of my friends?" asked Adroegen. "I must know where they are."

"I do require payment," said the witch, taking out a dagger. Adroegen retreated and put his hand on Endonhil. The witch laughed. "Oh, indeed you are afraid! I only need some of your blood. Wait, how silly of me! You are already wounded! I suppose that I do not need this dagger at all."

The witch quickly walked to Adroegen, and before he could do anything, she ripped off a bandage on his shoulder and held out a cup. She then squeezed Adroegen's shoulder, and Adroegen nearly screamed in pain. Some blood dripped out and the witch collected it.

"Now, now, that was all I needed," said the witch, pouring Adroegen's blood into the cauldron. She then walked over to the river, fetched some water, and poured it into the cauldron also. After stirring the pot for a short time, the witch signaled for Adroegen to have a look. Adroegen needed to get onto his knees in order to be able to see what was inside the cauldron, and staying on his knees was quite a struggle for him.

Adroegen looked into the water. At first, he saw only blood and water, but before long the water began to reflect, and Adroegen soon saw himself and his friends in the cauldron all together. They were searching the ground in the night, somewhere in the Dead Forest. Adroegen then realized that he was watching himself and his friends as they were seeking out the goblin chief many days earlier, just before entering a trap and being surrounded by the pack.

Some wind blew, and after the water settled, it showed Adroegen and Caitren standing against the edge of the Shrouded Cliffs, cornered by the pack. He and Caitren fought for their lives. Adroegen saw himself turn to face the east. It must have been when he realized that morning was not far, and that hope of escaping the pack remained if they could hold just a little longer.

The water stirred again, and then Adroegen saw himself on the ground, wounded, with Caitren tending to him. He was looking further into the woods, where Edelbir cut the head off the goblin chief. Adroegen was watching everything from the venture precisely as it took place. He quickly grew to trust that the witch would show him the truth. Adroegen then saw himself on his knees, looking to the morning sunrise, with all of his friends behind him.

Then Adroegen saw the whole company cornered again and the goblin lieutenant giving orders. He knew this was the night Caitren was taken captive, and the night that he fell. And indeed, Adroegen next watched Caitren being taken away by the goblin pack, and then he watched himself being knocked over the cliff, all precisely as it took place, however long ago it was by now. Adroegen grew very nervous, as he knew he would find out the fate of his friends next.

Adroegen then saw Edelbir, Kattalin, Gleowan, and Vaenn fighting together in the Dead Forest, surrounded by dozens of goblins. They were struggling greatly. Adroegen grew with worry and quietly uttered to himself, "No. Say not that this is their end."

But Adroegen then saw Gleowan impaled through the chest by a goblin sword. Vaenn ran to him, but then another goblin swung his sword and cut Vaenn. Both of them fell. Kattalin next was knocked over the cliff, just as Adroegen had been, and he watched her drown in the river. Back at the top of the cliff, Adroegen watched Edelbir fight alone, but before long his head was cut, and Edelbir was killed in the same manner in which he had killed the goblin chief.

"No!" said Adroegen, overcome with grief. There was still more for him to see, though. Next Adroegen saw Caitren in the dungeon of Gulgurod, before Vyroun himself. Caitren was in agony, and Adroegen watched wolves close in on her. Adroegen could not bear to watch, as it looked all too similar to when he had watched his mother pass. "Caitren!"

But Caitren stood no chance. The wolves feasted on her as she lay in agony before Vyroun. Adroegen could not look any further, for it was all too horrifying to watch. He was overcome with grief and with tears upon learning that his new kin had already been taken from him. Adroegen backed away from the cauldron, and upon doing so he fell, and the pain from all his wounds hurt much worse than before. The witch, meanwhile, watched Adroegen's grief with a smile. She only laughed once Adroegen finally began to settle down.

"I cannot help but pity you," said the witch. She slowly approached Adroegen, and he became nervous. "You have seen all of your kin taken from you one by one. Then you were given new kin, only to see them taken from you also."

"Only to see them taken from me," Adroegen repeated. A sudden anger overtook him, and he felt alone and forsaken, feelings that he had felt nearly all his life. After the goblin chief's death, Adroegen began to feel as if he were not alone anymore, but now that feeling had returned.

"Worry not," said the witch. "You are in much pain, but I could end it very quickly for you."

Adroegen looked to the witch, who redrew the dagger and approached him with laughter. His feelings of anger were overcome by fear, and Adroegen tried to run. I am afraid, though, that he was greatly wounded. Adroegen could not stand, let alone run. When Adroegen tried to flee from the witch, he only fell and grimaced in pain.

"Oh, don't be afraid," said the witch. "It will all be over very soon, and then all your troubles will end."

"Stay away from me!" said Adroegen. The witch was walking towards him very slowly, and in a rather mocking manner, for Adroegen could not flee from her, no matter how much strength he mustered.

"It will not hurt. Or at least I do not think it will," said the witch.

"I said keep away!" said Adroegen, drawing his sword. The witch might have cowered for a moment, but then only mocked Adroegen more.

"Well, now you have made me afraid," said the witch.

She was only a few strides away from Adroegen, who was ready to fight, though the arm wielding Endonhil was wounded. As the witch approached, he swung his sword. I am afraid, though, that Adroegen was not able to fend for himself like he once could. His arm hurt too greatly, and Adroegen lost Endonhil, which fell right before the witch, just beyond his reach.

"Such a magnificent weapon," said the witch, looking down at Endonhil. "What better way for you to die than by your own sword."

Adroegen tried to reach Endonhil but could not. The witch grabbed the hilt to wield it against the weapon's master. Adroegen lay before the witch and was certain that his end had come.

However, a blinding light shined so suddenly that Adroegen needed to shield his eyes. He waited for the blade to end him, but it did not. Adroegen had trouble seeing but could discern just well enough what was taking place. The witch screamed in agony, and the great light overtook her. Then the witch burst and was gone. Adroegen's sword dropped to the ground before him. The light did not cease, but Adroegen was able to see better.

Another woman stood before him. She was wreathed in light, and looked more angelic in appearance than anyone Adroegen had ever looked upon. The woman was clothed in white, and had long golden hair. There was a beauty about her, and yet a fierceness also. Adroegen felt relieved but frightened at the same time, for he knew not who she was who had saved him from the witch, but he was certain that she was not human.

"Do not be afraid, Adroegen," said the woman. Adroegen settled a little, though his curiosity did not cease, and his gaze remained fixed upon her.

"Who are you?" asked Adroegen. He tried to sit but could not. This woman was very graceful and stoic.

"I have been sent to this earth from Elunbelan," said the woman. "For I am one who is sent to take those whose hour has come."

"Elunbelan?" said Adroegen. He had heard of this great tree where all the dead and Enilundar himself were said to reside.

"I come down to this earth when one's time here has ended," said the woman. "And that is why I am here."

"One whose time has come? You mean death itself?" said Adroegen. He was then stunned to find out who stood before him. She must have been one of the Rhykwen, angelic women who were said to come and take the dead away. A feeling of relief met Adroegen, as he felt certain that his time must be over if such an angel had come. Adroegen thought his suffering would continue even worse than before upon watching his friends die, however, the arrival of the Rhykwen, if indeed she was one, made him think that he might suffer no more, and suddenly he did not fear death as he had when the witch tried to kill him. "You are among the Rhykwen, the takers of the dead?"

"I am," said the Rhykwen. "One of the servants of Enilundar himself, who has sent me here."

"You are a servant of Enilundar?" said Adroegen. He had wondered for a long time if this being was real or not, but if indeed he was, then Adroegen did not believe Enilundar really was watching over him. "I have been told before that I was never alone upon this earth, that he is always with me, but nearly all my life I have felt so alone.

And I have never been sure if he really does watch over me or not. Enilundar is real, then? There is not any doubt?"

"He is as real as everything you see before you," said the Rhykwen.

Adroegen became very joyful after feeling so devastated upon finding that his friends were gone. He was afraid of the witch, and yet suddenly Adroegen was far more welcoming of death, as there seemed to be nothing left for him on that earth.

"You have come to take me?" said Adroegen. "My time has come? All of my suffering that I endured is now over?"

The Rhykwen was silent and reached her hand out. Adroegen was not sure what she was reaching for. He grew worried he was wrong, for the taker of the dead would not tell him that his time indeed had come. Adroegen could not help himself. "Is it not I that you have come for? Why else would you appear before me now?"

"It is not you whom I was sent here to collect," said the Rhykwen. Adroegen was suddenly devastated, and he could not understand why the Rhykwen had not come for him.

"Not for me? But then who did you come for?" asked Adroegen. The Rhykwen held out her other arm, and Adroegen saw a ghost or spirit appear. It was the witch he looked upon, or the ghost of the witch, and she lay in the Rhykwen's arm without moving. Adroegen was beginning to feel anger that despite all the pain he was in, he somehow still lived, and his time was not allowed to come. With the angelic Rhykwen there now instead of the witch, Adroegen was not fearful of death, and in fact he almost felt it as something he should have by right after all he had been through.

"I am greatly wounded," said Adroegen, almost pleading to the collector of the dead. "I cannot stand, let alone walk. Never have I felt so much pain. Anyone as maimed as I am would have met their death by now! And yet you tell me that it is not my time yet?"

"Your time has not come," said the Rhykwen. "For there are still many tasks you must face upon this earth."

"I must still wait for my death?" said Adroegen. Despair was overtaking him. "You say that there are still tasks for me to face. What precisely might these tasks be? I have seen no task or purpose in my life but to suffer!"

"It is not for me to tell what Enilundar himself wants from you," said the Rhykwen. "Even if I do know what path he has set."

"So, my purpose is indeed to suffer," said Adroegen. He saw no other reason, and felt very saddened. For the takers of the dead appeared, as he understood, only in the hour of death, and Adroegen knew not why he could see such an angel now if it were not his time, nor why he would suddenly see one during someone else's death when Adroegen had seen many die in his past, but never saw a Rhykwen in those instances. "Why else must I still live upon this earth. Answer this for me, great Rhykwen: I have never seen any of you until now, and yet you say to me that it is not my hour of death. Then why do you appear before me? I have seen many die in my life. Years ago, I saw my mother die, and yet I never saw any Rhykwen appear. Why is it that I have never seen you before, and why is it I see you now?"

"That is a question I may answer for you," said the Rhykwen. "However, I may not tell you all the truth. I may appear before you, and you may now see both I and other takers of the dead, but no others can. For we do not wish for humans of this earth to see us if their end is not near. But you, Adroegen, are now permitted by my master to look upon the collectors of the dead."

"I am permitted to look upon the collectors of the dead?" asked Adroegen. He found this very strange, and he could not figure out why he would be allowed by Enilundar himself to see the Rhykwen. "And why may I look upon the Rhykwen when others may not? Is it so I can envy the dead? If Enilundar is real, and I believe beyond any doubt that he is now, then does he seek to torment me, to fool me into thinking that my hour has finally come, only to find that death has been granted to someone else instead?"

"The reason is one that I may not answer to you," said the Rhykwen. "But worry not, for you will know in time."

"So, it must be to torture me," said Adroegen. "I have seen all my kin taken from me, and I have wondered whether Enilundar is real, if he exists and has forsaken me, or if he does watch over me and simply finds amusement in my unending suffering. I know not which is the reason. The first reason I do not think is so, for I look upon you, his servant, and now believe he is real. But of the other choices, either one is cruel. I should have allowed the witch to kill me! Enilundar must have sent you to defeat the witch and save me, and now, when the chance at death has slipped through my fingers, I see the cruel stroke that was dealt upon me."

"You are mistaken," said the Rhykwen. "I did not save you from the witch. For it was not I who defeated her when she was about to kill you."

Adroegen was surprised and knew not what words to

speak. He thought it had been the Rhykwen who saved him, and so when the collector of the dead uttered that it was not so, he was surprised. Adroegen knew not what could have killed the witch if it were not the Rhykwen. He thought of what had just happened to the witch, however, she had burst just when she took Adroegen's sword and was about to kill him with it, so quickly and without warning that Adroegen knew not what happened to her. Then Adroegen saw the Rhykwen there immediately after the witch's death, thus he knew not who else could have defeated the witch. "Then what was it that brought about the witch's end?"

"The answer you seek is right before you," said the Rhykwen. "The answer you have sought from my master all your life has been right before you all this time. However, your faithlessness has rendered you too blind to see it. But worry not. For Enilundar knows all that was, all that is, and all that has yet to be. He knows what choices you will soon make, and soon the veil shall cease to blind you."

The Rhykwen's light began to fade. She was departing. Adroegen desperately pleaded for her to stay. "Wait, what is it that has been right before me all this time? Don't go!"

It was no use, though. The light of the Rhykwen faded, and the servant of Enilundar was gone. Adroegen took back Endonhil. Upon sheathing his sword, Adroegen sat where he was, and he could not help but let tears fall. He had endured sadness and sorrow many a time, but such pain had grown worse than ever before. The witch showed Adroegen's memory of the goblin chief's defeat precisely as it had taken place many days earlier. And so, Adroegen felt quite certain the visions he saw of his friends dying were true. Adroegen had thought that after losing his kin, he might have been given new kin, but it did not take very long before they were taken from him also. His suffering seemed to have no end.

As Adroegen sat against a rock along the shore, his wounds hurt greatly. He should have been dead, and the Rhykwen should have come for him, but it seemed Adroegen would have to live in great pain for some time longer. Many a time had Adroegen wondered why he still lived, and that same question rested within his mind in that moment. He could only wonder why Enilundar would not allow for his time upon that earth to end.

And Adroegen could not help but feel anger and hatred towards Enilundar, whom he was certain by then to in fact be real. After the defeat of the goblin chief, Adroegen had briefly begun to think there was in fact a greater power watching over him. He felt even more certain now, after seeing the Rhykwen, but Adroegen now felt that Enilundar watched over him only to see him suffer. Adroegen had lost his friends, and he was wounded to the point that he should not have lived. And yet Adroegen still drew breath, and for some reason he still needed to live with all the pain he was enduring, both of wound and of sorrow at losing his new kin. And so Adroegen sat there along the shore, feeling very tempted to simply give up, and I would say that he felt more alone and forsaken than he had ever felt before.

Chapter Nine; A King Hiding

After the king of the dwarves initially refused Edelbir and Kattalin's request, the two of them stayed in the mountains for the next few days. Although, being in the mountains, no sunlight made its way through the rock, so it was quite difficult to tell when it was day and when it was night. The king had not spoken to the two of them since they had first met. Edelbir was not sure what to do, though he and Kattalin knew they still needed to try and change Aki's mind. I daresay, though, that finding what to say to the king was rather difficult, as was simply finding him at all. Kari and Koli did speak with Edelbir and Kattalin on occasion, though they only uttered that the king had not wavered. Edelbir did not ask, but he began to think that all the other dwarves were willing to fight, and that only the king was not.

Edelbir and Kattalin were given their own chamber during their time in the dwarven kingdom. They quickly learned to always have a fire burning within, for if they did not, the air would grow cold. Not only that, but without a fire it was very dark, and thus Edelbir made sure there were some torches lit as well. Everything within their chamber was made of stone, though there was a pair of soft beds. These beds though, I daresay, were made for dwarves instead of regular folk like Edelbir and Kattalin, and thus they were far too small. And so, Edelbir and Kattalin had to sleep on the floor in front of the fire, and though the rock was hard, it was better than sleeping out in the wild, as there were no roots, no flies, and especially no need to worry of goblins searching for them in the night. Both wondered how Adroegen slept when he was in the mountains, and they could only assume that he would have been on the floor also.

Whenever Edelbir and Kattalin wanted to eat, they would go the dining hall, where there were always hundreds of dwarves. The hall was very loud with cheer, and it was much like the hall of the hidden village before it was destroyed. The two of them wished that the rest of the company were there, but instead they were alone. There were several roaring fires, and so it was quite warm, though once Edelbir and Kattalin left the hall, they were immediately met with cold again, and so they oft stayed within the hall. The greater reason to remain there, however, was the hope of sighting the king, and seeing if they might have a chance to speak with him again. They spotted Aki on occasion, almost always accompanied by his son, Lofar. There were others with the king, and often Kari and Koli followed him also. It was difficult to tell, but to Edelbir, it seemed from afar that the king was arguing with the dwarves that counseled him.

It was uncertain where the dwarves found so much food. They were living in the mountains, after all! And yet every day there was a great feast. The dwarves ate almost entirely meat, though Edelbir and Kattalin were not at all sure what kind of meat it was. Regardless, it was very tender and came right off the bone. Edelbir liked the food.

Kattalin did also, though not quite so much as Edelbir. The two of them did find bread on occasion, though no fruit, nor anything green to eat. Kattalin after some time began to long for such food again, though she made no complaint. The drink was beer, and I will tell you, the dwarves drank a lot of it. Edelbir drank some and thought it was quite good, and that if Gleowan were there, he would perhaps have drunk a whole barrel in a day. Kattalin, however, was not one who liked beer, and only drank a little to be polite. After that, she searched for water.

I daresay that dwarves did not possess the greatest of manners when at a dining table. They were not at all careful not to get food on their shirts, gambesons, or tunics. And when a dwarf drank beer, he would not pause. The dwarves always spilled beer on themselves. They grabbed their food and shoved it into their mouths. And they always laughed at each other whenever they made messes. Edelbir laughed too, though he himself would never display such a lack of dinner manners. Kattalin, I would say, was quite revolted by it, though she did her best not to show any disgust. The dwarves were quite interested in the two of them, and they tried to have Edelbir join them in games where they would drink until only one was still standing, or eat until only one still had a belly with room for more food. He politely declined, though. Kattalin was never asked to join in their eating or drinking games, likely because she was a lady, and if that was the reason why, then I would say that Kattalin was very glad that she was a lady, because she found such games quite abhorrent. Do not misunderstand, Kattalin did not dislike the dwarves, and she, like Edelbir, hoped for their help in battle.

It took a few days before anything significant happened involving the king. If you want to know, it would have been November the Twenty-ninth. Edelbir was not sure if it was day or night. Both were in their chamber. Kattalin was cold and sitting by the fire trying to get warm. Edelbir had to wear his cloak also, as the air had a chill. The two were about to rest for the night, however, there was a sudden knock on their door. When Edelbir opened it, he found an unexpected visitor. Before Edelbir was Lofar, Aki's son.

"Kari and Koli told me that this was where the two of you were resting," said the king's son. "If I may enter."

"Of course," said Edelbir. Kattalin rose to her feet as Lofar entered, though she had a couple of blankets wrapped around her, so it took a moment.

"Oh, you must forgive us," said Lofar. "Even after your friend found us, we dwarves still never came around to making beds for folk of your size. I daresay that we dwarves never really expected to be found."

Kattalin was rather cold and shivering, and it did not go unnoticed by the king's son. The fire was rather small, and Lofar made for it. "Here, let me fix the fire."

Lofar found a fan and blew it on the fire. It took a little time, but soon the fire was large and roaring. The room grew much warmer, and Kattalin stopped shivering. Edelbir was not sure why Lofar was visiting, but it had to regard their request of the king. It appeared that he and Kattalin might finally get an answer as to what had been happening with Aki since he had refused them.

"I wanted to speak with both of you," began the king's son. "Our scouts have reported that an army has come out from Gulgurod, the mouth of Mûrondûn. It marches south as we speak. War is about to take place to the west of us. This army, our scouts say, is marching for Bared Nar, the great city of Gundmar, at the very end of these mountains."

Edelbir and Kattalin looked to each other. There was no time to lose. They needed to plead for the king's help. If Aki would not help them after hearing of this army marching, then there was surely no changing his mind.

"We must meet and face it," said Edelbir. "Otherwise northern lands will be ruined and many will die."

"Yes, many will die if we do not face this evil," said Lofar. "I know what you want from the king, and you are not alone. Many dwarves here are ready to fight. This news has reached the king. The army moves slowly, for it is of goblins, trolls, ogres, and other creatures. Because some of them cannot walk in the day, they must take shelter when the sun rises and wait until nightfall to march farther south. That gives us time. However, my father does not seek to meet this evil alongside other kingdoms nearby. He seeks to keep all of us safe within these mountains, where he is certain that no one will find us."

"We must still plead with him," said Kattalin. "For Edelbir and I have seen what terrible things Vyroun's forces can do."

"If I may ask, why does your father seek to hide from the world?" said Edelbir. "For I would never want to spent my life with walls circled around me."

"We dwarves have not resided within these mountains for very long, probably for only as long as the two of you have been alive," said Lofar. "Not long ago we lived to the east, in Keldagull, the Gold Fountain, as we know it. But there are other evils beyond Vyroun. We were driven from our kingdom and for a time were vagabonds, until we made a new home in these mountains."

"What forced you to come west?" asked Kattalin.

Lofar appeared hesitant to answer. "We do not speak her name," said the king's son. "For my father loathes to hear it. Amongst the dwarves, we know her as the Winter Witch. Beautiful and fair, and yet also terrifying in appearance. She had her own servants. And some folk, including several of us dwarves, fell under the spell of her beauty and became victim to the curse of her kiss. For she, too, could seduce good folk towards evil, just as Vyroun himself does. A burning desire runs through Aki's veins to reclaim Keldagull, and he still wears his gold crown from that kingdom. But he sees no chance to defeat the Winter Witch, and it pains him greatly."

"The Winter Witch," said Edelbir. "I have not heard of her. I am afraid I know only of Vyroun to the north."

"We dwarves are familiar with Vyroun," said Lofar. "I am far older than both of you, for the lives of dwarves and elves are far longer than those of men. If fact, it was we dwarves who created the race of men thousands of years ago, under command of this world's very maker himself. And men were the greatest forgery of the dwarves, as men were able to drive back legions of goblins and other foul spawns of Dorgelung in the Second Age of this world, before the sons of Aberran began the kingdoms of men. But we dwarves once lived in Mûrondûn long ago, long before I came to this world. Vyroun came and asked the dwarves to serve him, and the dwarves laughed. What need had they for a dark lord to provide them with wealth when they could dig and craft it themselves? But then he and his armies drove the dwarves east. And there to the east, the dwarves encountered the Winter Witch herself, who more recently drove Aki and his people back west. And now we are here, in these Silver Mountains, with our king hoping this home shall never be taken from us, and that no more of our people will die."

"So, he believes that his people will be safe from evil if they are hidden from it," said Edelbir. "And Aki would not hide if he believed these evils could be defeated."

"Aki has seen his people die before," said Lofar. "And he does not wish to look upon such a sight again. As king he seeks the safety of us all more than anything else after what happened to us in the east. We were forced to flee west after we were driven from our home, as Aki saw no chance of defeating the Winter Witch, for she was too powerful and had too many serving her. Here we see Vyroun to the north in Mûrondûn, a land in which we dwarves once ruled long ago. Aki sees too much evil about and does not believe it can be defeated by us on our own."

"He would not be alone," said Edelbir. "And Vyroun knows not that Aki's kingdom is hidden here, which gives us an advantage I should think."

"I believe the same," said Lofar. "Our unknown presence is an advantage. Also, while I believe we are safe here in these mountains, how long will it be before we are found? Evil spreads beyond these walls. It will find us in time, I am certain of it. The dwarves are ready to fight, however, it is the king who you must persuade, not us. And he does not seek to bring further death upon them, even though those he seeks to protect are unafraid to enter the battle."

Edelbir and Kattalin both knew a little about hiding from the outside world. However, their hidden village one day was found by someone who became a good friend. Then evil found its way there and burned their home. The dwarven kingdom, of course, was far safer, however, Edelbir and Kattalin knew not how powerful Vyroun was, and thus they were unsure if the lord of Mûrondûn would be unable to find the dwarves and break open the doors of their kingdom.

"So, what must we do?" asked Kattalin. Lofar appeared to want something from them.

"The king is being counseled about this army that marches south," said Lofar. "We have a few days before Vyroun's legions reach the great city of Gundmar. However, it will take the dwarves time to march west to the city also. And thus, if you are to change the king's mind, now is the time. You can wait no longer, mingling amongst the dwarves in hopes of finding him. For if we dwarves wait any longer to march, then we will arrive at Bared Nar too late, and then we ourselves will become far more vulnerable if our army is alone against that of Vyroun."

"Where is the king now?" said Edelbir with haste. Kattalin rose to her feet and readied to leave their chambers.

"Aki is in the hall where his throne rests," said Lofar. "Several dwarves are speaking with him. I will bring both of you before the king, and give you another chance to persuade him. We dwarves are doing the same."

"And this is our final chance to do so," said Kattalin.

"Indeed," said Lofar. "That is why I wanted to find both of you. We cannot linger any more. Follow me!"

Edelbir and Kattalin followed the king's son out of their chambers. They walked swiftly through halls, up and down stairs, and through tunnels. I daresay that it took quite some time to walk from one place to another within that kingdom, as they were in the mountains, after all. It was a good hour or so before Edelbir and Kattalin reached the great dining hall, where there were many dwarves feasting and laughing. The two of them were not concerned with such things, though. They followed Lofar to the stairs that led to the king's hall. When they arrived, Edelbir and Kattalin found the king speaking with several dwarves about the army that was on the move.

"I will not bring further death to my people," said the king to the dwarves.

"Your people do not fear death," said one dwarf.

Edelbir and Kattalin were noticed by the king and he was silent for but a moment. "I see you have returned here. Have you come to ask of me again what I have already refused?"

"If I may be allowed to speak," began Edelbir, trying not to be hasty with the king, but instead trying to reason with him. He deemed it best to not speak of what Lofar had told them, how the dwarves were once driven from their home by a sorceress to the east, for that might only remind the king of what terrible memories he had and further convince him not to help against Vyroun. But Edelbir found a way to reason with him without speaking of it.

"Speak," said Aki.

"Kattalin and I have been on the run since last summer," said Edelbir. "We were fleeing from the goblin chief. I will admit that we knew not how to fight when our venture began, and thus we sought to flee rather than fight, and reach a place where the goblin chief could not find us. We reached the Fornwood, and safe we were there, without worry of those who hunted us."

"Very good," said the king. "I would not have left there if I were you."

"However," began Edelbir. "The goblin chief did not cease in his hunt for us, even as we were safe from him. Though we would have had no worry if we stayed in that forest, our company would have been trapped there until the end of our days. We did not wish for that. One amongst our company, Caitren, was separated from her father and wished to find him. There would have been no hope of finding her father by hiding."

"And our hunt did not cease," said Kattalin. "Our enemies only watched the Fornwood borders. They did not forget us, nor did they give up and pass by us. I myself would love to one day explore the vast wonders of the sea, but I would not have been able to if I had remained in the Fornwood until the end of my days."

"There is one thing we have learned since being on the run," said Edelbir. "Our enemies will not cease. They will not stop solely because we have escaped them for the time being. There is only one way to truly be safe from evil, and that is by facing and defeating it."

"You have not seen the world as I have," said the king. "My people have faced evil, precisely as you have said. We were not able to defeat it. The darkness in the north, we dwarves will not be able to defeat it on our own."

"But you will not be on your own," said Edelbir. "There are other kingdoms in the north. You will have Gundmar, which your scouts say will soon come under attack, and the Woodlands, whose dwellers I am sure will fight."

"What do you know of these northern kingdoms?" asked the king. "Have you journeyed there before?"

"No," said Kattalin. "But we know they will be under attack. Your scouts have said so. If you abandon them now, your kingdom will be far more vulnerable when Vyroun finds you."

"He will not find us here," said Aki. "That is what you do not understand. We are hidden, well protected. Evil cannot enter these mountains. None even know that we are here."

"Would you leave allies against Vyroun to die?" asked Edelbir. The king was silent, and Edelbir spoke on. "Vyroun knows not of your presence here. I have not fought in war, but that would be a great advantage, would it not?"

"It would be," said Lofar, and the other dwarves agreed. "We can march secretly beneath the trees of the Kyrrwood, and he will not know what moves under his very nose."

"It matters not," said Aki. "What hope is there of defeating Vyroun's army? Even if there is great hope, how can we defeat Vyroun himself? There is no one amongst us who can! We are better off hiding than facing him. For while we are hidden here, Vyroun will never find us."

Edelbir and Kattalin saw their hopes fading. The king might have been willing to listen to calls for help, however, he did not appear willing to answer them. Edelbir could think of one last reason to aid Gundmar and the Woodlands rather than hide. He was certain that if this did not work, then there would be no persuading the king.

"Kattalin and I were once hidden," said Edelbir. "We

lived in a hidden village far to the south of here, one that was hidden from the outside world. Neither of us had seen what was beyond our home. We sought no trouble and never thought trouble would find us. But it was not so. A pack of goblins one night found our village and burned it to the ground, leaving none alive except for us and our friends. Kattalin and I were once hidden like you, and yet evil still found us. What reason is there to think that the same will not happen to this kingdom? And if you choose not to aid Gundmar and the Woodlands, and those kingdoms fall? What then? Vyroun would find you one day, and you will be alone. And in trying to protect your people, you would instead bring further death upon them."

The hall was silent. The king sat there on his throne, and appeared to be considering greatly what Edelbir had said to him. Edelbir and Kattalin, however, knew not what lingered within the king's mind. All awaited Aki's answer, and after several moments of silence, he finally spoke.

"And how was it that your village was found?" asked the king.

"They tracked our friend Adroegen as he made his way to our home," said Kattalin. "And then they razed it."

"So, it was your friend's fault that you were found," said the king. "It was not because evil sought you out, but rather because Adroegen brought it with him."

"Not intentionally," said Edelbir. "Adroegen knew not that he was being tracked, nor that Vyroun had returned. He told us the following morning that had he known, he would not have come to our home."

"Not intentionally, but nonetheless, he brought evil to your home," said Aki. "No, we will not be found here in such a manner. Our kingdom is well guarded, by the mountain walls themselves. We are out of evil's sight! I will not risk such by putting my people into open war. We shall remain here."

Edelbir had lost what hope he had of persuading the king. Lofar appeared very disappointed in his father, and the other dwarves, too, seemed to not agree with his decision. There was no way of changing Aki's mind, though, from what Edelbir saw. He turned to Kattalin, and she could tell that he had given up, even though he did not wish to. Kattalin, too, saw no chance to persuade the king at that point, and she decided that there was no sense in arguing further.

"We are in gratitude to you for sheltering us these past several days," said Edelbir. "We will burden you no more. Kattalin and I will depart and help the north in whatever way we can. Though I would say that finding you was the only way we could have truly helped in the war against Vyroun."

"I would suggest that you remain here," said the king. "For you will be safe here with us from what darkness is outside these walls."

"A kind offer you make," said Edelbir. "But we will not stand down when dark forces are on the move. I wish to look upon the sun again, and Kattalin wishes to look upon the wonders of the sea again one day. We will not find those things by trapping ourselves within these walls."

Aki appeared surprised that Edelbir and Kattalin would turn his offer down. "I very firmly believe it best that you remain here, especially if goblins were searching for you before you entered these mountains."

"No," said Edelbir, and Kattalin agreed. "We are not

going to be blind to what manifests outside these walls."

"Very well. I will not hold you here," said the king.

Edelbir and Kattalin turned to leave. Both were very disheartened, for they knew an army was marching, and that they had a great chance to find aid against it, aid that the enemy knew not of. But Edelbir and Kattalin had tried their best to get the king's help, and I daresay that sometimes there is a point where there is no sense in fighting any further. Aki's will was set, and there was no altering it, from what it seemed. As Edelbir and Kattalin left the hall, they could hear Lofar speaking to his father, and the king's son was quite angry. "These simple folk would leave to fight on their own against this evil, but you, with a battle-ready army, would not!"

Edelbir and Kattalin returned to their chambers and prepared to leave. They were quite saddened and unsure of what to do next. It did not take long to be ready to depart, as neither of them carried very much. Upon leaving their chambers, Kari and Koli took them to the dining hall, wanting them to have good food to carry as they traveled west. Then the dwarves who had greeted them upon entering the mountains led them to another door at the northern mountain wall. Edelbir and Kattalin would then say goodbye.

"I know not what we can say to you," said Kari. "You will enter peril next, and yet you do so willingly. We can only hope for the best of luck to you."

"What is it that you will do next?" asked Koli. "For you will soon be in war. And you are only two folk."

"I do not know what we can do," said Kattalin. "For we seek to find our friends, if they are still somewhere beyond the walls of these mountains. And we hope to defeat what forces march. But two can do very little on their own against many."

"We will help in what way we can," said Edelbir. "Though we were certain that the way to truly aid the north was through seeking help from your king. Without it, there is little now we can do. Perhaps we best simply seek out our friends, if they are somewhere out there still. If they live, I think we will most likely find them in the coming battle."

Kari and Koli had much sympathy. Edelbir and Kattalin were ready to enter danger again. The dwarves opened the northern door into their kingdom, and Edelbir and Kattalin walked out from the mountains. It was sometime during the night, and I must say that this was a good thing, for if it were day, the two of them might have been blinded by the sun's light after spending the past few days in the mountains. Edelbir and Kattalin turned back to look upon the dwarves before they closed the door to their kingdom.

"There are still a few goblins and foul things about," said Kari. "That is what our scouts have told us. However, there are fewer of them now. Some goblins are still to the south, searching the forest for you, from what it appears, and they have been searching thoroughly along the mountains. I wonder if they suspect there is a way into the mountains, but I cannot say."

"There should be few enemies in the Kyrrwood, though," said Koli. "If there are any at all."

"Goodbye," said Edelbir. "We will be saddened to leave the dwarves."

The door into the dwarven kingdom closed, and Edelbir and Kattalin soon saw only a mountain wall in front of them, with a carving of a hammer striking an anvil, just like what they had found on the mountains' southern wall in the Dead Forest. They turned to see their path. Ahead was a very dark forest. All was quiet, and the forest, in ways, appeared rather ominous. Edelbir and Kattalin, however, were not going to travel through the Kyrrwood. They were going to travel swiftly along the Silver Mountains to the west, until they found the city of Bared Nar, and war.

"And now we must help the north against these enemies," said Kattalin.

"Yes, we must, and equally important to us, we must find our friends," said Edelbir. The two of them began moving west. They would seek to fight what evil was marching, rather than hide from it. However, Edelbir could not help but think that even though he and Kattalin sought to fight alongside Gundmar and the Woodlands, they had already failed greatly in aiding those kingdoms.

Chapter Ten: A Roasting Spit

Edelbir and Kattalin made their way west as swiftly as they could, running throughout the day and covering much distance without delay. Neither was sure of how far Bared Nar was, nor how close the army was to reaching the city. There was not very much time, though, and thus they needed to be quick.

The Kyrrwood was a very dark forest, and the farther into it they looked, the darker it grew. They would not enter the woods, as the path along the Silver Mountains was the easiest and swiftest way to reach Bared Nar. However, I daresay that even if Edelbir and Kattalin needed to go through the Kyrrwood, there would have been much hesitation. The woods looked very unsettling. Though the forest was quiet, there were some animals and creatures farther in. Edelbir and Kattalin heard rustling throughout the day and night. Both of them wished that Adroegen were with them, as he knew more about the north than they did, although I am afraid that even if Adroegen were there with them, he had not ventured into the Kyrrwood before, either, and thus he, too, would have been unsure of what was within those woods.

Edelbir and Kattalin decided to travel during the night, as they wanted to cover much distance. The two would rest, though not for very long. They were hesitant to travel too much in the dark, though, as they knew goblins and other foul creatures came out in the night. They were not sure how many such creatures resided within the Kyrrwood, and they did not want to take their chances. Both of them had some trouble sleeping at night, as branches oft rustled and they could hear animals somewhere in the forest. It made them wary. Worst of all, Edelbir and Kattalin heard the faint thumping of footsteps, and they worried that trolls or some other creatures were nearby. Thus, sleeping was a very difficult task.

It was the second night since leaving the dwarven kingdom. Edelbir and Kattalin were readying to rest for the night. The day had ended a good few hours before. Both were restless, for it was quite difficult not to be restless within that dark forest. Owls were flying and hooting, though not the great owls like Huf or Ule that they had met months earlier, before entering the Dwimor Fells. Though the two of them were tired, neither could sleep. They had decided to make for the war, even though Aki would not help them, but Edelbir and Kattalin were very much in despair and knew not what to do. There was little that the two of them would be able to do by then.

"How far is the city, do you think?" asked Kattalin. She looked along the mountains, and they still went on for quite a distance. There was no sound of an army marching, and thus Edelbir and Kattalin knew not whether they were traveling swiftly enough to reach Bared Nar before the army would.

"I think we are still a few days or so away," said Edelbir. "Even though we are traveling very far each day."

"I can only hope that we reach the fight in time," said

Kattalin, who was feeling hopeless, as the two of them were not having any luck in their quests, and so she was uncertain that any path they take next would fare any better. "But even if we do make it to the battle, we are but two folk. Of what use can we be in this war on our own?"

"We have already failed in aiding the north," said Edelbir. "The dwarves will not help us. And so, there is very little we can do now."

"We had our chance to change the north's fortune in this coming war," said Kattalin, sighing. "I know not how much it would have changed, but we can be sure that the dwarven army would have helped greatly. But in the end, they are not going to help us, and now, we are alone. Our friends may be gone. Adroegen we have given up our search for. Caitren may have met a terrible fate, and we know not what has become of Gleowan and Vaenn. What must we do now?"

"We must find our friends, for I can think of no other task now," said Edelbir. "If they are still alive. It appears that Adroegen is gone. Caitren's fate is one I am unsure of, though I am fearful, much like yourself. I believe we must instead search for our friends, or what friends might still live."

"Gleowan and Vaenn may still be out there somewhere," said Kattalin. "But where do we begin in our search, and how do we go about finding them?"

"I believe we are making for them now," said Edelbir. "For Gleowan and Vaenn went west and north in search of Caitren. Something makes me believe we may not be far from them. But they are well beyond our sight at this point. Thus, where will we begin?"

"They might be at the battle that will soon take place,"

said Kattalin. "Though that depends on how their search for Caitren has fared. Do we enter it in hope that our friends might be there?"

"Do we enter a battle in which we have already failed in turning its tide?" said Edelbir. "Well, if our friends might be there by any chance, then we best reach the city before the army does."

Their words were cut short, though. There was rustling from the trees, and it was not from the wind, for there was no wind at all. Kattalin rose to her feet, and Edelbir put his hand on his sword. The rustling sounded right in front of them, not thirty feet away. Then they heard it again, but to their side.

"There is something in the woods," said Kattalin, who was very uneasy suddenly. She and Edelbir listened further.

Next they heard thumping, as if something large were walking through the woods. Whatever creature was there, it was drawing closer to Edelbir and Kattalin. Then they heard thumping again, though from somewhere just a little farther down the mountains from whence the two of them came. Edelbir drew his sword.

"We need to run," he said. Kattalin agreed, drawing her sword also. Something began to smell rather foul. Then they heard trees rustling from all directions, along with the thumping on the ground. Edelbir and Kattalin quickly took their things and made their way west down the mountains.

As the two of them quietly ran, something growled. Kattalin looked behind, and she saw the shadow of a large creature, the size of a troll, however, it was not a troll. Whatever the monster was, it was following her and

Edelbir. Kattalin though did not want to stay to find out what it was.

Upon looking back, the two of them ran into something and fell to the ground. Before them was another creature like the one behind. Though it was dark, the moonlight allowed Edelbir and Kattalin to see what they had encountered. Neither Edelbir nor Kattalin had ever seen such creatures before. Whatever they were, these things were foul and not friendly.

"Are these ogres?" said Kattalin quietly to Edelbir. She had heard of them, though she had never seen one.

"I think they are," said Edelbir, who could not be certain, however, from what he had heard of their appearance, the vile monsters before them could very well have been ogres.

"They are ogres," said Kattalin, looking closely. There were four in total. Ogres looked quite different from trolls, appearing much more human, though larger and far more hideous. Each of them wore a ragged shirt with equally ragged pants. They had beards that were dark in color, either brown or black, though in the night it was difficult to tell. In their large ears were gold earrings, and over their heads were long strings of hair. A couple of them had rings in their noses also. Ogres had teeth sticking out from their mouths, even when their mouths were closed, and you might guess that in result, drool often dripped from their mouths.

Ogres were much like trolls in that they would feed on human flesh when able, and these ogres looked as if they wanted to feast upon Edelbir and Kattalin. Ogres were known to try to snatch and feed on children in particular. Both Edelbir and Kattalin had their swords ready, though they were only two folk, surrounded by twice as many ogres, and an ogre was far stronger and more dangerous than any human. However, while they might not have been as dull as trolls, ogres were creatures that could be outwitted by a human, if that human had the chance.

"Well, what have we here?" said one of the ogres that stood in front of Kattalin. Both she and Edelbir were silent and tried to think of a way out of what trouble they had suddenly found themselves in.

"These are the first humans we've seen in these woods," said a second ogre, standing in front of Edelbir. "Do you think they might be the ones those goblins were searching for?"

Kattalin grew quite worried. At first, she thought these creatures were simply in the wild and had found humans to eat, but it appeared that they were instead working with the goblins. She and Edelbir had heard little of what became of their hunters since finding the dwarves, however, it grew clear that the pack had not at all forgotten them and their friends.

"I don't know," said the third ogre. "Those goblins told us they were searching along the south side of these mountains and were about to catch some humans, only for them to disappear. But that was to the south! Why do they have us keeping a lookout here, north of these mountains?"

"Don't be so sure these ain't them," said the first ogre. "That one goblin, he said he thinks they might have climbed over the mountains to this side. Or he suspects there was some kind of passage that they slipped into and escaped."

Edelbir and Kattalin were unsure if they should return

to the dwarves to warn them, as it appeared that the goblins suspected someone to be living within the mountains. But at least it did not seem that Vyroun's forces knew with certainty that a kingdom of dwarves was hidden there. There might not have been a point in returning, as Aki had chosen not to help the north, but the king's worst fear might have been realized, even if he had not known it, that enemies were close to discovering the dwarves' presence within the Silver Mountains. Perhaps it may have been a good idea to turn back and warn the dwarves. However, the king might grow very angry with the two of them and even blame them. In addition, if Edelbir and Kattalin wanted to turn back, they first would have to escape from the ogres.

"Hey, where did you two come from?" said the ogre in front of Edelbir. "And don't think that you can lie to us!"

Edelbir and Kattalin needed to quickly figure out an answer that might fool the ogres. Because the ogres had some allegiances with the goblin pack, they could not say they came from the south, as the ogres might suspect that the two of them were part of the company that the goblin chief hunted. And so, Edelbir and Kattalin needed to claim that they were from elsewhere, though the difficulty was that neither knew those lands beyond what was once their home, and thus they worried that the ogres would not be fooled by any explanation they conjured up.

"Well? What are you two waiting for? Speak!" said the ogre in front of Kattalin, and she spoke right away and made up an answer.

"We come from the east," said Kattalin. She would speak no further unless asked, and Edelbir nodded to the ogres. He hoped they would believe her, though Edelbir was not sure they would and worried that the ogres would catch them in a lie.

"East, eh?" said the fourth ogre. "And where exactly? East within these woods? East where the mountains are? Or far enough east to where the giants live?"

Kattalin and Edelbir were silent, though they were smart enough to know that if they did not answer quickly, then the ogres would suspect them to be lying, if they did not suspect so already! And both Edelbir and Kattalin could tell that the ogres were indeed suspicious. Kattalin knew nothing of lands far to the east, and she certainly knew nothing of giants. The same could be said for Edelbir, who swiftly spoke. "We are from the woods to the east of here."

"They're lying! I told you these are the humans we were searching for!" said the ogre in front of Kattalin. "We've lived in these woods and ain't never seen humans here! We've never seen any cottage in our woods anywhere."

"Perhaps you have never found it," said Kattalin, though she knew that there was probably no fooling the ogres now.

"And if you really live in these woods, then why are you suddenly making your way west?" said one ogre.

"Perhaps we are looking to trade with folk from the west," said Edelbir.

"You are traveling light for traders," said the ogre in front of him. "You're lying! You both are among those humans the goblins are after! We're going to take you to them! But first we want to know how you escaped the goblins in the forest south of these mountains. They were about to catch you and then you disappeared suddenly."

Edelbir and Kattalin did not know how to answer, and they did not want to speak of the dwarves hidden in the mountains. It was growing beyond any doubt that the enemy suspected something or someone to be hidden there, and if that was indeed so, then surely Vyroun's forces would find the dwarves in time.

"Alright, if they won't answer, then we'll make them speak!" said one ogre. Edelbir and Kattalin were suddenly grabbed by the ogres, disarmed, and then tied up. The ogres carried both of them into the Kyrrwood, though not very far into the forest. Even though the ogre carrying Kattalin had a tight grip, she was used to it from when the troll king held her months before. She and Edelbir had no chance to whisper to each other and find a way to escape, as Kattalin was carried by one ogre and Edelbir by another.

The two of them were not taken far. At the ogres' camp, there was a pile of firewood in the center beneath a cauldron. To the side were clubs, a spit, some knives, and smelly, rotten meat that the ogres were still eating, it appeared. The ogres threw Edelbir and Kattalin down. They finally could whisper to each other and find a way out of the trouble they were in.

"I cannot free myself from these ropes," said Kattalin. She thought she heard some rustling coming from the forest, somewhere east of where they were and not far from the mountains.

"If we can take one of those blades and free ourselves, perhaps we can surprise them," said Edelbir. "But there are two of us facing four of them, thus I know not if this will work. And we would need a chance to take a knife or dagger, which I know not that we will be able to get."

Though the two of them had managed to escape

troubles like this before when the company was together, this time, I am afraid, Edelbir and Kattalin would not be able to conjure a way to escape. Or rather, they would not be able to escape on their own. One ogre took out a spit, and the others immediately tied Edelbir and Kattalin to it. Kattalin wished they had more time to find a way out, but that would not be so. The two of them, tied to the spit, were then hung over the firepit, with Kattalin facing the sky and Edelbir facing the pile of firewood. The ogres began to ready a fire. Out of the corner of Kattalin's eye, she thought she saw something move within the forest, though she had little time to see what.

"Now, where did both of you come from?" asked one ogre. "This time, if you lie to us, we will roast you for dinner!"

"Are you saying we won't be eating them if they tell the truth?" asked another ogre. "I must admit, I would love to eat them. They look tasty, even if they don't have much meat on their bones!"

"Well he looks quite tall and strong for a man, so perhaps he might have a decent portion of meat on him," said a different ogre. "But she looks very slender! It doesn't look like there's much of any meat on her! But I will still take man flesh when I can. It can be quite a delicacy!"

Kattalin heard some quiet footsteps coming from within the woods. The ogres were all talking amongst themselves and did not hear that someone was nearby. Kattalin thought she saw something, or someone, hiding behind a thicket. Whatever it was, it appeared small, or short. However, there was not time to ponder, as the ogres appeared ready to feast on her and Edelbir.

"I cannot think of a way out of this," whispered

Edelbir. "Perhaps if we are truthful then they might not roast us. They might take us to Vyroun, but at least that would buy us some time to escape."

"Perhaps," whispered Kattalin, who was still looking out to the woods. Whatever she saw hiding, there were several of them. "Can you see anything out in the woods? I do not think we are alone."

"We could take them to the goblins, but what reward would we get?" said one ogre. "I think eating these two is a great reward!"

"Well, perhaps the goblins or their master will let us have them," said another ogre. "And maybe they will give us more in addition."

"We don't know that," said the first ogre. "And besides, why bother giving them these two when we could eat them right now?"

"That's a fair point. Very well, let's eat them now," said another ogre, about to make a fire. Edelbir and Kattalin knew that they had to do something fast.

"We are the folk the goblins wanted," said Kattalin quickly. But I am afraid it did not matter. The ogres had changed their minds, and no longer cared that the goblins wanted them.

"Oh, you are?" said the ogre. "Well, I am sure that even if they wanted to take you, in the end they will have wanted you dead either way. So, we will do that for them right now! We ogres have far greater use for you than those goblins, as we are certain that both of you will be very tasty to eat!"

The ogre began to light a fire, but then suddenly he was hit with something from behind. He let out a roar and turned around. There was a hatchet in the ogre's back.

"Hey, what games are you playing at? That hurts!"

"That wasn't us!" said the other ogres. "We don't know who threw that! It must have been someone in the woods!"

There was a small flame growing in the firepit, but the ogres paid no more attention to it. Suddenly several more axes were thrown at them, and the ogres screamed and roared in great pain. Kattalin then saw the ogres being attacked by the creatures hiding behind the thicket. There were dozens of them. She tried to figure out what they were, but Edelbir was first.

"The dwarves are here! How fortunate we are!" said Edelbir, but then he looked down to see a growing fire in the pit beneath him, and smoke rising, with a growing heat meeting his face. He suddenly did not feel so fortunate. "Although we are about to be roasted! I hope they can free us before that happens."

The ogres grabbed their weapons, but they were too late. Though an ogre was stronger than a dwarf, there were many dwarves and only four ogres. Not only that, but the dwarves were clad in heavy armor. The dwarves overwhelmed the ogres and soon defeated them, and then they moved to save Edelbir and Kattalin from being roasted on the spit. Edelbir was quite relieved as the dwarves put out the fire and moved the wood out of the way.

I would say that freeing Edelbir and Kattalin was actually more difficult for the dwarves than what you or I might expect. The spit was rather high off the ground, and of the dwarves' many strengths, height and reach were not among them. They first put the fire out, and then they needed to cut the beams that held the spit, which caused

Edelbir to fall face-first into the firepit with Kattalin right on top of him. Finally, the dwarves freed them from the spit. Edelbir and Kattalin were most grateful. When they rose to their feet, Lofar and Aki stood before them.

Aki stepped forward to speak, but he seemed to struggle to find what words to say. After a brief moment, he instead stepped aside, and from behind the trees and thickets of the Kyrrwood emerged thousands of dwarves as far as the eye could see, all armored and battle-ready. Neither Edelbir or Kattalin could see an end to the army.

Their armor was thick and appeared impenetrable. Their helms were square-shaped, and their breast plates were of silver and bore no emblem. Axes, swords, hammers, and shields were in hand. It was surprising that a whole army was nearby and neither Edelbir nor Kattalin had known it.

"After your departure, further word reached us of enemies searching along the mountain walls," said Aki. "Our scouts reported that goblins were suspicious that something was hidden within the mountains, and that while the goblins could not open it, they had found our door along the southern mountain wall."

"We never intended for them to find your kingdom," said Edelbir. "But we just learned that the ogres suspected someone or something was hidden in the mountains. They were going to try and force the truth out of us before deciding that their bellies mattered more and that they preferred to eat us."

"Our scouts have always seen some foul creatures outside our walls, both to the north and the south," said Aki. "Even if you had not found us, they likely would have in time. It seems there is no hiding from evil. There may be no use in hiding, for it seems that one way or another, evil will eventually find us."

"We once were hidden," said Edelbir. "In the end it was of no use to us, either. One day we were found and chased from our home."

"I know not if we can defeat what evil is coming," said Aki. "But my people are ready to fight, even if I am hesitant."

"You would have a greater chance of doing so with the other kingdoms of the north fighting with you," said Kattalin.

"If you are to face Vyroun's army, the two of you on your own will not fare well," said Aki. "There would be far greater luck if an army of battle-ready dwarves fought alongside you."

"We could not be more grateful to you," said Edelbir with a rekindled hope. The dwarves quietly made their way west under the dark of the Kyrrwood, hidden from Vyroun's sight.

Chapter Eleven; Siege

Gleowan and Vaenn remained in Bared Nar. Winter had begun, and the air had grown cold. Clouds began to cover the sky after several days. This was not a good sign, for the natural weather of the world was providing some cover for Vyroun's army. There was at least a little light that made its way through the clouds, though not very much.

Gleowan was tempted to give up on their friends, and Vaenn felt the same. She, too, was in despair. Caitren was far beyond their reach, and they had failed to save her from what fate she had met. In thinking that there was no saving their friend, the two of them saw no other choice but to stay in the city. Hopefully Edelbir and Kattalin were faring well, though by then, Gleowan and Vaenn did not know what had become of their friends.

The two of them were granted a place to stay on the second level of the city. Gleowan and Vaenn, however, spoke with almost no one in Bared Nar. Cenric was far too busy preparing the defenses of the city, as scouts had learned of an army marching their way. Aldreda, too, was elsewhere. The people of Gundmar were quite frightened. Soldiers gathered weapons, and rubble for their catapults, and strengthened the city gates. The women and children readied to find shelter for when the storm would arrive.

Only Eamon spoke with the two of them from time to time, though he readied the defenses with the other soldiers. It was he from whom Gleowan and Vaenn were able to learn any news of what took place beyond the city. Eamon was friendly to them. It seemed he had grown quite fond of Gleowan and Vaenn after they were first taken captive by the riders of Gundmar.

It would have been December the Fifth, if we were to follow your calendar. Gleowan and Vaenn had been in Bared Nar for fourteen days. They were just outside their chambers and looking out into the city. Soldiers moved about everywhere. A few snowflakes were beginning to fall. The north wind had not arrived yet but would surely descend upon them soon. Eamon then paid a short visit. He gave the two of them some news.

"The army of Mûrondûn shall arrive soon," said Eamon. "Either in the night or perhaps tomorrow morning. They travel slowly, as many of Vyroun's forces are creatures of the night and cannot walk in day, though clouds gather and veil much sunlight now. The north wind is coming. Vyroun's army must still use caution, though, for should any light cut through the sky's veil, then for some monsters it would be their end."

"Fortune does not seem to be on our side," said Gleowan. "We are now trapped here with no escape other than through our enemies."

"Curious," said Eamon. "Both of you have stayed here these past days, knowing that an army comes. You swore no oath to Gundmar, yet you do not flee. What stays your feet here?"

"Our company vowed to face this evil rather than hide

from it," said Vaenn. "Do not mistake me, for I fear greatly what will soon come. However, even if we were to run and hide, Vyroun would find us in time. I am afraid we must fight, even though I greatly wish not to."

"Yes," said Eamon. "I myself proudly swore an oath to protect this kingdom and its people. Though I, too, fear what will come, and I, too, fear that death might find me, I will be grateful if I were to fulfill my oath. This is my purpose upon this earth, and on this coming night I will fulfill it bravely and with honor, whether it end in death or not. Both of you must fulfill whatever task has been set for you, though I know not what it might be. What reason do you fight in this war, above all else?"

"To face what evil has gathered," said Gleowan.

"Yes, but there must be a purpose why you seek to face it," said Eamon. "What is it that you fight for?"

Gleowan thought about what Eamon had asked. There was one thing that he and Vaenn valued above all else since being chased from their home. "We fight for our friends. I know not what has become of them, however. For Adroegen and Caitren might be gone, and we are unsure where Edelbir and Kattalin are now."

"We may be the only two left of our company," said Vaenn, beginning to cry. "We live, but after all that our friends have been through, they may have met their ends."

"Perhaps. I cannot say," said Eamon. "But I can offer this comfort to you. Neither of you flee from what will come. Neither of you are giving up hope, even if it may be dim. Do you know what that tells me?"

"What does that tell you?" asked Vaenn.

"That deep in your hearts, both of you know that your friends still live," said Eamon. "Edelbir and Kattalin, they must be out there. And that is your task. I am sure of it. Both of you must fight for your friends, and you must fight in hopes that you will find them amidst this darkness. Your hearts tell you that you still have friends out somewhere beyond this city. I might meet my end on this night, for my reason to be upon this earth is to defend my kingdom. Yours, I am sure, is to find your friends, who are beyond the gates of Bared Nar. Thus, I do not believe either of you will meet the fate that I might."

Eamon departed to join the other soldiers. Gleowan could not help but feel that he was right. Edelbir and Kattalin were out there somewhere. Vaenn's heart lifted some, and she felt a renewed hope. Both prepared to fight, gathering arrows and swords, even though they were not part of the army. From the top of the wall on the second level of the city, they might have been a couple of furlongs above the field below, which an army would soon blanket. Thus, Gleowan and Vaenn would not be near the front line of war, though the two of them still sought to take part in what battle would come and help however they could.

Night soon fell. Gleowan and Vaenn were frightened, as were many people in the city. It did not take long before brazen drums sounded. They were faint, early in the night, but grew louder with each passing hour. Gleowan and Vaenn heard marching somewhere in the distance. There was no mistaking that an army was not far, though for much of the night the drums and marching remained faint.

The hours of the night passed by. It was not until the morning light began to rise that chanting sounded. The marching and the drums grew louder. Soon Gleowan and Vaenn could hear echoing drums and chants of "Doom!

Doom! Doom!"

Sometime shortly after the sun rose, a black sheet began to blanket the field before the city. Everywhere soldiers were running and shouting. No end to the army could be seen. It was somewhere beyond the towers of Bared Nar. Vyroun's forces were made of many creatures, from goblins, to trolls, to ogres, but those creatures appeared to be shielding themselves from the sun. The army could not shelter itself there in the valley of Bared Nar, however, and so they had to hold large, broad shields over their heads in order to veil themselves until night fell again.

Soon Eamon returned, though he could not speak with them for very long. "The army will not be as powerful in the day, but formidable nonetheless," said Eamon. Several siege towers were slowly moving towards the walls. The larger creatures, the trolls and the ogres, pushed the towers, though they moved slowly, giving the soldiers of Gundmar some time. Behind each tower was a roof sheltering from the sun the creatures that pushed it.

"That army is endless!" said Vaenn fearfully. "How might you hope to defeat it?"

"This is not Vyroun's full force," said Eamon. "There are more creatures that will take part, creatures that will appear only in the night. Whatever happens, the defenses must hold. We cannot allow these enemies into the city. They are far more harmful within our walls. The gate cannot be broken open, for if it is, then that might be the end of Gundmar."

"Does the daylight buy good time to wipe out much of the army?" said Vaenn.

"It may, but I know not how much so," said Eamon.

"The goblins fortunately are of little use until nightfall. Clouds are above us, but some rays of sun make it through the clouds, which may be a trouble to goblins and may turn some trolls to stone if the light meets them. The goblins cannot storm the lower wall, nor set foot upon its parapet in the day, as they may be blinded by the light, and their wrath might be hindered. Instead it will be wicked men who will try to storm the city in the day. And so there seems to be some fortune early on for Gundmar."

"Then I would think we must take out all forces we can now!" said Gleowan, remembering the goblin chief being blinded by sunlight before his death at the hand of Edelbir.

"To your posts! To your posts! Mûrondûn is upon us!" shouted one of the captains. Everywhere, armored boots clanked upon the bare rock of Bared Nar. Gleowan and Vaenn watched many soldiers running swiftly by them.

"You best take shelter now," said Eamon. "We must hope the enemy does not breach and storm the city, but I advise that you be ready to fight."

Eamon quickly departed to his post, which was somewhere on the first level. Around them, women and children were taking shelter. Gleowan in that moment wished that he and Vaenn had fled before the army arrived, and without any doubt Vaenn thought the same. It was too late, though, for they were cornered. Before them in the valley the drums beat loudly and the army's chants echoed. Catapults were loaded with rubble, both right by Gleowan and Vaenn on the second level of the city and within the army below.

The catapults from the army then volleyed. Though Gleowan and Vaenn had felt safe being on the second level of the city, the feeling disappeared quickly, for rubble was hailing upon them before long, thus they needed to be careful. The ground beneath their feet shook as great rocks hit the lower and middle levels of Bared Nar. Everywhere, women and children were screaming and trying to flee. Towers within the lower levels were quickly crumbling, and their stone hit the ground like thunder.

Within moments Bared Nar returned the volley upon Vyroun's forces. Gleowan and Vaenn carefully made for the parapet of the second level wall and saw rubble hailing upon the enemy. Arrows whistled from the lower level. Within the army, ranks were being hit by arrows and rubble. One of the enemy's catapults was destroyed, while a siege tower, too, was hit. The towers were moving closer to the walls, though still in range of the city's volleys. Soldiers among the enemy were being hit in the field below, and some trolls were hit with rubble and lost their shields. Upon dropping them, those trolls were turned to stone by a white beam of sunlight. The soldiers on their own could do little damage to Bared Nar, and thus it was their tools and engines of war, their catapults and siege towers, that needed to be taken out.

One great stone suddenly flew by Gleowan and Vaenn. There was a catapult nearby, sitting upon a small turret. The soldiers there were hit and fell, and the catapult became unmanned. Gleowan immediately knew how he and Vaenn could help.

"Here! Fire the catapult upon them!" shouted Gleowan to Vaenn, and the two swiftly made their way up the stairs of the small turret.

Gleowan and Vaenn reached the catapult, but I daresay neither had ever used such a weapon before. And thus, it took a short time to figure out how to. The frame was about twice as tall as either Gleowan or Vaenn, and it was weighted well to the floor beneath, though there were heavy wheels that one could turn with much effort. A strong beam held a sling with a pouch on one end and a heavy counterweight on the other. A winch held a rope to pull the end with the sling down, and near it was a lever to hold the beam in place until loaded to fire.

Gleowan and Vaenn swiftly turned the winch to pull the beam down and held it there. It was rather arduous, and the rope was stiff from pulling the counterweight. Already did the two of them begin to think they were not suited for such a great battle, and that they were not worthy of helping the battle-hardened soldiers of Gundmar. They did manage to pull the beam, though, and then it took both of them to lift a piece of rubble into the pouch. If only Edelbir, by far the strongest of their company, were there, then that task would have at least been easier. Gleowan pulled the lever to fire the catapult, and the two of them watched the rubble being flung upon the army in the valley below. It hit some enemy forces, though only a few of them. Gleowan wondered if there might be something better to target than the lines. A siege tower was being slowly pushed near the spot the two of them had just hit.

"Hitting their lines I think will not be of much use," said Gleowan. "Though I am not one with expertise in war. However, I should think that we must hit those towers and their catapults if we can, for those towers can be of damage to us should they reach the wall and their army sets foot in the city. Their own catapults, too, can be of threat to us from within that field below."

"Then we must aim for those towers and catapults!"

said Vaenn as the two of them pulled down the beam and readied it to fire again. Gleowan looked closely to where the first rubble they fired had hit. A tower was about to pass by.

Gleowan waited for the tower to move just a little farther. Once it was close enough, Gleowan pulled the lever to fire and the two of them watched. Moments later, the tower they targeted was hit and collapsed. Vaenn's morale had lifted, as the two of them began to think that they might have figured out this mighty engine of war.

"There are wheels at the bottom," said Vaenn. "Do you think we can turn this weapon? For there are other towers that we might be able to hit."

Together they tried to turn the catapult to adjust its aim. It took much strength, but finally they were able to slowly move it. Another tower was about to pass, and Gleowan needed to make sure that they hit it. They fired, but this time missed. The tower was moving towards their targeted spot, though, and so Gleowan and Vaenn quickly reloaded the weapon and fired again. The second time they did not miss, and another siege tower was destroyed. There were no other towers about to pass by, but another catapult was close that they thought they might be able to destroy, if they could adjust their own again.

"Oh, if only Edelbir were here," said Vaenn as she and Gleowan tried to turn the catapult, which took much effort. "This would go far swifter if he were turning this."

Both turned their weapon as quickly as they could, and then they reloaded and fired upon the enemy's catapult. They did not miss, and Vaenn was joyful. Gleowan was beginning to figure out how far the weapon would fire. The two of them did not bother targeting any creatures in the army, for without the towers and catapults, those enemies would not be able to enter the city.

Below were a few dozen siege towers, all of which were spread out, thus Gleowan and Vaenn could not hope to hit all of them. However, after firing several times, they did manage to destroy five more, which I would consider to be a significant number. They also hit three enemy catapults, and soon the volley upon the city lessened in force. Gleowan and Vaenn might have taken a little time, but they quickly learned good aim, and a few soldiers at nearby posts took notice. Some other siege towers were taken out by other soldiers, and soon there were only about a dozen remaining that were moving towards the wall.

"There are too few towers left for the army to manage to storm the wall now!" Gleowan heard a soldier shout from his nearby post. There was no time to relish in such praises though. Gleowan and Vaenn immediately loaded the catapult to fire again.

By then it was a midday. Though Bared Nar was holding rather well thus far, I am afraid that the full force of Vyroun's army had not yet been unleashed, and its deadliest servant would strike the city next. Gleowan and Vaenn had met this enemy before. Soon the winds of a hurricane descended upon Bared Nar. Mighty wings fluttered, and Gleowan and Vaenn knew who had come before he revealed himself.

"Dragon! Ligwyrm has come! Take shelter!" shouted several soldiers. People were screaming and running. Gleowan and Vaenn heard the growls of Ligwyrm and saw the dragon fly over. Soon the sky was raining fire. Gleowan and Vaenn had to retreat from their post as the serpent's breath came down upon them.

Gleowan and Vaenn jumped swiftly from the turret, though they only fell upon stairs a few feet below. The tail of the dragon, however, struck the turret, and the catapult the two of them were firing was destroyed in an instant. Stone fell as the turret, too, was destroyed, and Gleowan and Vaenn had to run in order to not be crushed by the falling rubble. They were then back upon the second level of the city.

Ligwyrm flew over the city without end, conjuring fire and crumbling turrets with his tail. The soldiers of Gundmar clearly had encountered this enemy before, as many held their shields up, sheltering themselves from the flames. However, Gleowan and Vaenn saw many soldiers and people of Gundmar dead and burning. All levels of Bared Nar were soon in flames, and suddenly Gundmar struggled against the army of Mûrondûn.

Gleowan and Vaenn saw no more use in their current post, for the catapult had been destroyed. They found that the remaining siege towers were about to reach the wall. And so, the two of them knew where to go next. Gleowan and Vaenn ran for the gate to the lower level. Ligwyrm still flew over the city, and so now and then Gleowan and Vaenn needed to take shelter. The soldiers fired many arrows at the serpent, however, Gleowan and Vaenn knew that those weapons would not pierce the armor of the dragon.

It took some time before they reached the gate to the lower level. Just as Gleowan and Vaenn passed through the gate, they found that a siege tower had reached the wall. A heavy drawbridge fell and crumbled the merlon, making a walkway to the parapet of the wall. Right away, several men in black armor charged out upon the soldiers of Gundmar.

"They will enter the city. We must help to stop them!" said Vaenn, and Gleowan agreed. Both of them drew their bows. They found a small tower nearby. It was not a great tower, however, it was tall enough that the two of them would have a high vantage point to look upon the storming soldiers. It was also close enough that they would be able to shoot any soldiers who set foot on the parapet.

"That tower will do, I think," said Gleowan. "We can shoot enemies from there, and that should help the swordsmen holding the wall."

Both quickly made for the tower and went to the top. They needed to be very careful, as Ligwyrm flew about putting the city in flames. Fortunately, the tower that Gleowan and Vaenn entered had walls and a roof, and thus they were sheltered quite well from the dragon. A couple of soldiers inside were burning and lying dead though, as it seemed the fires of the serpent had made it through the windows of the tower and met them before they could shelter themselves. Thus, there was still danger. Gleowan and Vaenn drew arrows and aimed through the windows to shoot any enemies that came out from the siege tower.

Though the swordsmen defending the wall had several enemies to fight, soon those enemies began to lessen. Gleowan and Vaenn were able to kill several wicked men before they were able to set foot at the top of the wall. The soldiers then had less trouble defeating the fewer enemies. Gleowan and Vaenn kept shooting, though Vaenn soon noticed something.

"Are those siege towers built from wood?" she said. "It appears to me that they are."

In his efforts to shoot enemies down, Gleowan did not notice that indeed the towers were built of wood. He also found that right beside him in the tower was a lit torch and oil. Vaenn looked upon the torch and oil also, and Gleowan was certain that she had the same idea that he had.

"I do say, they are made of wood, and we have fire in this tower as well as oil," said Gleowan, who dipped his next arrow in the oil, lit it with the flame from the torch, and then aimed it at the tower. "Well this seems like a clever idea to me, or at least I certainly hope that it is. They have used fire against us, and now we will try and use it against them."

Vaenn did the same. Both of them lit every arrow they fired, and each arrow appeared as if a wizard had cast some kind of spell upon it. Rather than aim for the enemy soldiers, they aimed for the siege tower. It took a few arrows, but a great fire soon sprouted from the enemy's tower, and after some time, the siege tower was in flames, and few enemies charged out. Gleowan and Vaenn shot what wicked men came out, and after some time the siege tower collapsed and no more enemies would storm the wall. A few soldiers cheered.

"I do think that we are on to something here," said Gleowan. "Shall we go on to the next tower and do the same?"

"Yes, I believe we must," said Vaenn. They took the torch and the oil in case there would be neither where the next siege tower had been set. They needed only to run a short distance in order to reach the next tower.

Several enemies had set foot upon the parapet. Gleowan and Vaenn searched for someplace high from where they might have clear shots at the siege tower. They had to shelter themselves briefly, as Ligwyrm flew over and flames descended upon the city. The two of them then found another small tower to climb their way up. This tower had some soldiers in it.

"What are you doing here?" said one of the archers. Two other archers there aimed at the enemies trying to storm the wall, however, another archer was doing precisely what Gleowan and Vaenn were doing, lighting arrows and aiming to burn the siege towers.

"Helping! In any manner we can," said Gleowan, and he and Vaenn were immediately lighting arrows and firing them. The soldiers did not force them out, as they were understandably paying greater attention to the enemies entering the city, though they certainly did not want Gleowan and Vaenn to get in their way.

"Gleowan! Vaenn! Take shelter! Flee to the upper level!" said one soldier. Gleowan and Vaenn were surprised to find Eamon there. They did not obey, though, and helped to fire upon the siege tower, which was soon in flames.

"Eamon, look! The tower is already burning!" said another soldier. Eamon turned, and Gleowan and Vaenn found that fewer enemies were storming the wall. After some time the tower collapsed, and some soldiers cheered.

"You seem quite wise in battle for simple folk from far to the south!" said Eamon. "And with great aim. Now take shelter! Go back to the second level!"

"We can help you!" said Vaenn.

"You have shown great worth already," said Eamon. "Far beyond what would be expected of folk who have taken no oaths to this land. But I beg you, take shelter."

Eamon left for the next post. Gleowan and Vaenn looked to each other. Neither sought to flee to the upper level, not when they had proven to be helpful. The two of them left to make for the next siege tower. However, by then it was late in the afternoon, and a new trouble had arisen.

"To the gate!" several soldiers shouted. Gleowan and Vaenn left the tower, as there was no longer a need to be there, and the two of them followed several soldiers making for the main gate, though I would say that Gleowan and Vaenn stayed out of their way. Then, upon reaching the courtyard behind the main gate, both of them looked for a place where they could climb and see from a higher point.

"Brace the gate! They will break through!" shouted one soldier. Several swordsmen made for the gate to try and hold it shut. Several archers stood at the top of the gatehouse, shooting at enemies below. Gleowan and Vaenn had difficulty trying to find a way to help. Soon there was a loud bang on the gate, which caused several soldiers to fall back before bracing the gate again.

"What can we do here?" said Gleowan. "For this is the front line now, and there is no place I see where we might be able to help them."

"Perhaps we should climb the wall and shoot from a distance away," said Vaenn.

Gleowan thought that she might be right, as the wall was curved like a horseshoe, thus they might be able to stand to the side of the gatehouse and shoot some enemies. "I think you are right. To the wall we go!"

The two of them made for the top of the wall, where some wicked men were fighting, though not many.

Gleowan and Vaenn simply shot these enemies before they came close to them. Then they looked to the gate.

The gate was a few hundred feet away. Several trolls and ogres were trying to break it open. There was a great battering ram made of iron, and above it was a roof to protect the ogres and especially the trolls from any sunlight that might make it through an opening in the clouds. Gleowan and Vaenn shot at the foul creatures.

"We still have oil, do we not?" said Vaenn, finding that the roof over the battering ram was also made of wood, like the siege towers. "Perhaps we might burn it like we did to destroy the siege towers."

"I can think of no better idea," said Gleowan. Despair came over him, though, for Gleowan could think of no clever manner in which to stop the enemy from breaking open the gate, or at least not in such a small amount of time. The enemies banged upon the gate again. Gleowan and Vaenn had to hurry. The roof upon the ram also made it difficult for the archers atop the gatehouse to shoot the enemies below, thus Gleowan and Vaenn may have had a better angle from where they were.

Both of them aimed for the roof with arrows of fire. They fired at will on it, and soon it was aflame. The roof was large, though, and Gleowan and Vaenn could hit only a small corner of it. They aimed for the trolls and ogres below, hoping to kill a few of them. Those creatures, however, took more than one arrow to slay. Gleowan found one advantage though. Upon shooting one troll, it recoiled and fell a few steps back, and in doing so had left the roof's shelter. A ray of sunlight met the troll, and the creature writhed in pain as if it were burning. Then moments later the troll became still and was turned to stone.

"There may be a way to stop them," said Gleowan. "If we can just collapse that roof, we might destroy their shelter, making the trolls vulnerable to any sunlight that makes it through these clouds and turn to stone."

"I think you are right," said Vaenn. "We must aim for the beams holding their shelter and burn them."

They immediately did so, but I am afraid that this time their idea would not work. For the next time the ram hammered the gates, Gleowan and Vaenn heard the gate start to break. The two of them managed to kill an ogre, but they were not able to hit the inner beams of the rooftop and burn it.

"The gate will soon open!" said Vaenn. "We must hurry!"

Gleowan fired as swiftly he could, and another troll was felled. However, there were too many creatures there for them to shoot in a short time. And time, I am afraid, was not on their side. Were there more if it, then perhaps the two of them would have been able to stop the gate from opening. However, they heard another loud bang, and this time the gate of Bared Nar opened, and wicked men began to storm the city.

Gleowan and Vaenn ran for the great courtyard behind the gate, and there they saw soldiers of Gundmar lined up with shields and spears, trying to stop Vyroun's forces from storming the city and overwhelming them. It appeared that the dragon had departed for the time being, but soon there would be many other forces Bared Nar would have to defend against. The attack was not too strong yet. However, Gleowan and Vaenn found that the sky was darkening. Night was near, and in the night, Vyroun's army would be a far more formidable force.

Chapter Twelve; A Sheer Mist

Gleowan and Vaenn shot what enemies they could that were charging into the courtyard. The two of them looked ahead, though, and saw endless legions readying to storm the city. It was not yet night, but beyond the gate of Bared Nar thousands of goblins, trolls, and ogres were waiting. They still shielded themselves from what sunlight remained, but it would not be much longer before there would be no need to. The wicked men attacked for the time being, though I would say those men were only a small portion of Vyroun's army.

The attack carried on for a short time as the day was grew darker. Gleowan and Vaenn were not sure where they should go, nor how best to help the soldiers. They found a tower to climb so that they could see the whole battle. Most of the army was not yet attacking, and until the night fell, they would not be as great a threat. It was best to slay as many creatures of the night as they could before the light faded.

"We must not worry ourselves with these men," said Gleowan. "For there are few of them now. It is the creatures of the night that we must defeat."

"A shadow is coming," said Vaenn. She had grown more afraid than she had ever been before. Ahead to the west the sun was setting. However, a shadow was spreading from the field, appearing like a sheer cloud of mist and slowly moving towards the wall. It was not the night falling though, for the shadow was coming from the west, where the sun was setting. Gleowan saw it also. Soon they began to hear what sounded like monstrous beasts, and it seemed like they were starving.

"We must retreat," said Gleowan. "I know not what this coming devilry is, and we cannot face such a phantom if we know not of its weakness."

"I am fearful," said Vaenn. "Though I wish to stand and fight, my courage seems to have abandoned me suddenly."

Gleowan and Vaenn left the tower, ran a little farther away from the battle, and found a high point where they could see what took place. The two of them were at a decent distance. Beyond the gate was a most frightening sight. All sorts of foul and dark creatures made for the gate. That was not all, though, I am afraid. The worst of it was the approaching mist that was covering the ground in darkness. Soon the soldiers in the battle noticed it also.

The battle ahead suddenly quieted. There was still fighting near the gate. However, many soldiers of Gundmar were fixed upon the dark and sheer mist. Gleowan and Vaenn saw to the west the final light of day fading. The night had fallen, and next the true force of Vyroun's army would be unleashed.

Suddenly the two of them heard many loud screams and screeches. The soldiers were retreating. As the mist drew closer, Gleowan and Vaenn found scores of creatures that they had not before looked upon. They were like demons, but also like ghosts. These monsters emerged from the sheer mist and began their assault upon the city.

"Deoflas! Retreat!" Gleowan and Vaenn heard soldiers shout. The two of them had never encountered a deofol before. Thus, they had never before been so frightened, and both trembled as they retreated. Neither knew how to defeat these monsters, nor if there even was a way to, for that matter.

As the deoflas stormed into Bared Nar, so did legions of goblins, ogres, and trolls. The soldiers of Gundmar stood no chance, I am afraid. Gleowan and Vaenn briefly observed the battle. The ghostlike creatures charged towards Gundmar's soldiers, but did not attack. Instead they entered the soldiers, and within moments the soldiers screeched and screamed like the monstrous creatures who were now controlling them. Gundmar's soldiers struggled to fight the fiends that possessed them and as a result were unable to fight like before. Once the soldiers came under this possession, goblins were able to kill them with ease. Other soldiers, upon being taken possession of, turned and fought their own brothers of Gundmar rather than Vyroun's forces. Gleowan and Vaenn saw no way of defeating what had come. The only person they thought of who might know how to defeat such creatures was Ganglere, the wizard, whom they found held much knowledge. However, he was not there with them. Neither knew precisely where Ganglere was, though both were quite certain that Ganglere was far away and beyond their reach.

"We need to run," said Gleowan. "There is no hope of defeating whatever these monsters are. Or at least, I know not of a way."

"Where can we run to?" said Vaenn in a sudden despair. The army of Mûrondûn was taking the gate and the courtyard with extraordinary swiftness. Soldiers of Gundmar were being slain everywhere the eye could see. Though Gleowan and Vaenn were a decent distance away from the battle, Vyroun's army was very quickly approaching the two of them.

"Retreat!" shouted one of the captains. "Retreat to the second level! Get the women and children out! Retreat!"

Gleowan and Vaenn made their way to the gate that would take them to the second level of the city. It did not take long, though, before the two of them saw enemies on their tail. Many soldiers of Gundmar were retreating alongside of them. Behind were enemies of all kinds, goblins and trolls and wicked men, as well as the swarm of deoflas that they had not before encountered.

Vaenn suddenly found one soldier to her side being attacked. It was one of the many wicked men that sought to slay this soldier. She could not bear to see the soldier fall and immediately took an arrow out to fire and save him. Vaenn shot the wicked man, however, when she watched his body fall, Vaenn found one of the demonic creatures standing in its place. The demon then made for and entered the body of the Gundmar soldier that Vaenn had tried to save. That soldier screeched, and his eyes became red. It was no longer a swordsman of Gundmar facing Gleowan and Vaenn, but instead a fiend looking back at them, and the soldier, under the control of this creature, charged at them.

Vaenn knew not what to do, therefore she and Gleowan ran. The soldier was on their tail. Gleowan and Vaenn could have killed the soldier, but in the end, they would have been killing a soldier of Gundmar, an ally of theirs. There seemed to be nothing to gain, and there seemed to be no way to win such a fight. Vaenn greatly wished that she and Gleowan were elsewhere, where there were no such terrible enemies. She felt helpless and vulnerable, as if standing before a ghost that no armor or wall could shelter her from.

"What can we do against such an evil?" said Vaenn desperately. "There seems to be no way of escaping!"

"I know of nothing that we can do," said Gleowan. "I think we have made a mistake in remaining here."

The two of them ran for the gate to the second level, but they were unsure if it would be of any use. The deoflas would likely find them all the same in the end. Those creatures, when not controlling soldiers of Gundmar, appeared to be ghosts, or some kind of demonic spirit. Vaenn was not sure if walls or gates would be any good in shielding from them. She knew not what would happen if she or Gleowan came under the possession of one of these creatures, and she hoped greatly that she would not have to find out. Vaenn had never felt so afraid and unsure of what she must do.

But soon came a small stroke of luck for the two of them. There were some catapults still firing rubble upon the city, and as Gleowan and Vaenn ran, a tower was hit right behind them and crumbled. The rubble separated the two of them from the Gundmar soldier, possessed by the deofol. But they could not feel relieved at all, as there were still enemies all around, and the two of them needed to keep running.

As Gleowan and Vaenn ran though, they saw some women and children also making for the gate. Several goblins jumped from the stone roofs and were about to attack them. The women and children, I am afraid, were unarmed and stood no chance against the oncoming goblins. Gleowan and Vaenn made their way to help them, but before they reached the women and children, another soldier came to their aid. Eamon fought fiercely, and his wrath was the death of many enemies.

"Run for the gate!" Eamon said to the women and children as he fought against the goblins. The women and children ran, and Eamon blocked the goblins from reaching them.

"Eamon!" shouted Vaenn. She and Gleowan ran to Eamon's aid. The son of Gundmar was facing a few dozen goblins on his own. Gleowan and Vaenn immediately drew arrows and shot what goblins they could. Vaenn saw the women and children make it to the gate to the second level, which was not too far away but was still a short run from where she was. Though she and Gleowan wanted to make for it also, they could not leave their friend Eamon, whom they had grown fond of while in Bared Nar, behind to die.

Eamon, however, was not able to defeat the goblins. Suddenly he was stuck with a goblin sword and he fell, and Gleowan and Vaenn were devastated. The two of them managed to defeat the remaining goblins before they could kill Eamon, however, it did not matter. Upon reaching Eamon, they found that he was fatally wounded. Eamon, however, looked at the two of them, and though he was clearly in great pain, the son of Gundmar looked to be at peace with what became of him.

"Leave me here," said Eamon. "There is nothing more that you can do. My hour has come."

Vaenn was crying. Several enemies were approaching, but Vaenn and Gleowan did not want to leave Eamon there to be dishonored or defiled in death.

"I have fulfilled my purpose here upon this earth," said Eamon. "It is an honor to die for this land and its people, as my fathers have. Gleowan, Vaenn, your time here is not over. I know it. You must now fulfill your purpose, just as I have mine. You cannot remain here and die as I will, for it is not time for either of you."

"We cannot leave you here!" said Vaenn. She and Gleowan wanted to carry Eamon to the gate. However, there were enemy forces coming, and thus there was not time.

"You will not be leaving me here," said Eamon. "For I see a Rhykwen now. She offers me her hand, to take me away from this world. I will now leave this land, and I will join the mighty and honorable company of my fathers in the halls of Elunbelan. No doom awaits me. Go now, Gleowan and Vaenn. My time on this earth is over, but you still have much here to do."

Eamon sighed his last breath and became breathless. Vaenn was crying, and Gleowan, too, was saddened. The two of them, however, had no time to grieve. They turned their attention to several approaching goblins. The gate was not far, though it would still be a run. Gleowan rose to his feet. "We can help him no more. Enemies approach, and if we do not reach the gate, we, too, will be left here to die."

Vaenn rose to her feet and the two began to run. Ahead were Gundmar soldiers holding the gate to the second level open, though they were readying to close it. Gleowan and Vaenn ran as swiftly as they could, though the goblins were very close behind.

A troll, however, had caught up to the two of them and

soon blocked their way. Gleowan and Vaenn had no choice but to fight. Vaenn was uncertain if there were any more people or soldiers of Gundmar still on the first level of the city. She saw only enemies behind, and to make matters worse, up ahead, the gate to the second level was being closed. The troll took one swing and his club hit the ground, and Gleowan and Vaenn were separated. Vaenn had a clear path to the gate, but Gleowan had a troll in his way. The troll was about to swing at her.

"Here!" said Gleowan to the troll, which immediately turned its attention to him. Gleowan then shouted to her. "Vaenn, run!"

"I am not leaving you here to die!" said Vaenn, who grew fearful that Gleowan might not try to make for the gate with her. Watching Eamon pass was terrible enough, but Vaenn could not bear at all to lose Gleowan, for if such came to be, half of her spirit would be ripped from her. She swiftly fired arrows at the troll as it swung at Gleowan, who had some relief from the troll's wrath.

"What are you doing? Go!" said Gleowan. The troll turned to Vaenn, and Gleowan fired arrows upon it, but soon his quiver was empty. He drew swords as the troll turned back to him, and Vaenn was as fearful as she had been when the two of them fought the mother of the spiders the previous summer. Soon Vaenn, too, ran out of arrows, and she was forced to draw her sword.

As the troll faced Vaenn again, Gleowan swung his swords at it. Fortunately by then, the troll had suffered several wounds, and so with but another strike or two, it fell. Gleowan made his way to Vaenn. "Well, I suppose Edelbir is right. We appear to be inseparable. Now let us make for the gate!"

Both made for the gate, but I am afraid that Gleowan and Vaenn were too late. The gatekeepers to the second level did not appear to know the two of them were close, and once Gleowan and Vaenn began to run, they found that the gate was being swung shut, and they were blocked from the second level.

"Oh no," said Vaenn. They were too far from the gate, and enemies were right on their tail. Within moments Gleowan and Vaenn needed to fight goblins and wicked men. They were able to slay a few enemies, however, I would say Vaenn was certain that it was of no use, for there was a whole army approaching and no longer any chance to escape them.

Gleowan and Vaenn were surrounded. There were trolls and ogres not far behind and deoflas approaching. Gleowan readied to fight. "I think this will be our end."

But it was not so. Just as the goblins and men were about to attack, suddenly they ceased. Gleowan and Vaenn were not sure why their enemies did not attack. Soon, though, they heard someone giving commands to the enemy soldiers. The goblins and other enemies were being ordered to stand down, at least from attacking Gleowan and Vaenn.

"Hold!" said a goblin who was trying to make his way to them from somewhere behind the lines. "Leave these two alive!"

Gleowan and Vaenn waited and were not certain why they were ordered to be kept alive. However, the goblin that ordered the soldiers to cease finally made his way to them, and suddenly Gleowan and Vaenn knew the meaning of it. The two of them looked upon a familiar enemy that they encountered back in the Dead Forest, just before the company was separated. The goblin lieutenant was in command of the army, and he looked back at Gleowan and Vaenn with a smile.

"Well, look what we have here, boys!" said the goblin lieutenant. Some of the goblins laughed as more enemy forces reached them and made for the gate to try and break it open. At first it appeared that the goblins were going to play with their food before eating it, however, Vaenn then remembered something from when the goblin lieutenant had encountered the company in the Dead Forest. He gave more specific orders to the pack when they cornered the company, to kill Adroegen and bring his friends before Vyroun himself. It appeared that those orders still stood.

"The last time I saw you, your friend took a tumble over a cliff!" said the goblin lieutenant.

Gleowan and Vaenn both wanted to attack the goblin lieutenant, but I am afraid that there was no chance for them to. There were far too many foul things surrounding them, and they were alone. There were no other soldiers of Gundmar to be seen, though they could be heard beyond the gate and upon the second level. Gleowan and Vaenn were saddened upon being reminded of Adroegen. They did, however, wonder if they might hear any news of Edelbir and Kattalin, though they worried that if they did, then the goblins might have caught their friends also.

"We have orders to leave these two alive and bring them before our master," said the goblin lieutenant. "He will then deal with them himself. This gives us two from their company of scum to take away. You won't be going to Gulgurod. We're taking you to our master's stronghold, in the very heart of his kingdom. You will have no chance of escaping there. Bind their hands! Take them back to our master at Norungad!"

Gleowan and Vaenn's swords were taken and their hands tied. At the very least they were used to it by now, as their hands had been bound when the riders of Gundmar took them captive. The two of them were then shoved along towards the main gate. All about Gleowan and Vaenn were vile creatures, from trolls and ogres, to goblins, to the demons that stormed the city at nightfall. They could have tried to escape, and I would say that would have been their best chance to do so before being taken into the heart of Mûrondûn. Escape, however, was impossible, for they were unarmed and overwhelmingly outnumbered.

The winds of a hurricane descended again upon the city, and the dragon returned. Ligwyrm stood upon the gatehouse, and as Gleowan and Vaenn drew nearer to the dragon, he appeared to smell that they were coming.

"Ah, I remember your scent as if I smelled it yesterday," said the dragon as Gleowan and Vaenn were brought before him. "You have been lucky enough to escape me before, but look at you now. Unarmed! Hands bound! Surrounded! Your friend might have managed to escape the prisons of Gulgurod, but you will not be taken there. No! I will take you into the very heart of the dark kingdom to the north. There will be no one to find you! No one to save you now!"

"Our friend escaped?" said Vaenn quietly to Gleowan. "Caitren is still alive?"

"If so, then I am grateful, though now we ourselves will be in such danger," said Gleowan. The two of them though had no time to ponder such news, as the claws of the dragon took both of them in a tight grip. Gleowan and Vaenn could only utter a few more words before Ligwyrm took flight.

"This is our end, it seems," said Vaenn in great despair.

"If a terrible fate meets us, then we will suffer it together," said Gleowan.

The dragon then flapped his wings, and Gleowan and Vaenn were lifted into the air. Smoke from the fires in Bared Nar met their noses at first, but before long the city was distant. Ahead was the dark kingdom, from which the two of them would very likely not escape. Gleowan and Vaenn were hopeful for their friend, as Caitren seemed to have escaped from Gulgurod. However, both were overcome with a feeling of doom, as they had now found themselves in the same situation. Gleowan and Vaenn knew not precisely where they were going, other than to a place called Norungad, which was somewhere deep in the dark kingdom, and to Vyroun himself.

Chapter Thirteen: Fire on Water

A few days had passed since Adroegen's encounter with the witch and the Rhykwen. He had been moving south, though he had not been able to go very far on his own. Adroegen encountered no one over the next few days. He was hoping to find someone who could help him, but was certain he would not. Even if he did, Adroegen worried that whomever he might encounter would not be a friend. The witch certainly was no friend to him.

Adroegen was also growing very weak from fever. He had run out of food and had hardly eaten in days, for he was far too weak to be able to search for and gather food. He could have tried fishing, but Adroegen had no bait nor rod nor net, and he was not sure if there were even any fish in that water. The river provided him water, but if there was food, it likely would have been somewhere up in the forest, and to get there Adroegen first needed to climb the cliff that he had been crawling along the foot of the past few days. Adroegen was skilled in climbing, but his wounds were too agonizing to be able to climb easily. And Adroegen was as hurt now as he was when he fell.

All was quite baffling to him, how he was enduring as much pain as he was and how he was still somehow alive. Adroegen was certain that he should have been dead, and yet upon meeting one of the takers of the dead, Adroegen was told that it was not time for him to leave that world. The Rhykwen had told Adroegen that he still had tasks to fulfill upon that earth, but whatever such tasks were, if he could not even walk, then Adroegen could not fulfill them. Anyone with the wounds Adroegen had suffered would have died by then, and yet he was not granted death by the Rhykwen or by her master. The only reason Adroegen was alive was because Enilundar himself would not allow him to die, and with all the pain and sorrow Adroegen had endured all his life, he felt certain that the reason he lived was that Enilundar must have found amusement in his torment.

"What is it that you want of me?" asked Adroegen as he looked upon the morning sun as it rose. "Why must I remain here when I cannot anymore fend for myself? What road can I walk when I am rendered maimed and weak?"

Adroegen had felt sorrow many a time in his life, though I would say that it had never been so strong as it was then. His friends appeared to be gone, and Adroegen was not sure what do to, nor where to go. "What reason do I have to fight onward? Everything I find is taken from me in time. My torment only worsens as I go on."

Not only had pain and sorrow overwhelmed Adroegen since his encounter with the witch and the Rhykwen, but also he had been overcome with an anger that he had not felt before. And I would say this anger was far stronger than his sadness. Adroegen, for but a short time, began to think a greater power might have been watching over him. However, once Adroegen thought that fortune had begun to shine upon him, his pain only grew greater than ever before. Adroegen sat with his eye fixed upon the morning sun, which at that moment were veiled by passing clouds.

"I have no hope anymore," said Adroegen. "For I am now but a candle whose wick is burned, yet my flame will not go out. What further road could be set for me? Wherever that road might lead, I cannot hope to walk it. Something will overtake me. Something must, whether by my body being broken or by fever or hunger. I cannot escape death for much longer, even if death seems to hide itself from me."

Adroegen was not certain what was left for him upon that earth, but I will tell you that much still remained for him. Both you and he will soon find out what.

As Adroegen sat there, a cloud passed over the sun. The light then shined upon him, and Adroegen had to shield his eyes and turn away. Upon doing so, he found a deep cave. Next to it was some jutting stone, which Adroegen thought he could use to climb up the cliff with his bare hands. Adroegen was a little amused.

"I once thought your light shined upon me," he said, looking back to the morning sun. "Why am I tempted to believe it again? Very well, I will make the climb, for either outcome will be good. Either I find food and help, or I fall to my death. Perhaps I am presented with a way out of my troubles. There might be some mercy within you, but I will see for myself. I have been fooled already by you."

Adroegen, with much effort, made his way to the cave. It took quite some time for him to crawl there. He then studied his obstacles before going through them. The bluff was about two hundred feet high. The ground before Adroegen sank into what was a small cave, though when Adroegen looked into the cave he saw no end. It looked more like a deep cavern. Adroegen, however, did not intend to enter the cave, and thus it mattered not. He made his way to climb up the wall of rock, though he needed to be very careful, as he could not climb like he once did.

Adroegen did his best to grab hold of any jutting rock and pull himself up. It was very difficult, though, for he could not stand upright with his legs wounded, and his shoulder hurt very much also. But Adroegen pressed onward, as torturous as it was. It took quite some time, as he moved most cautiously. He was able to make his way halfway up the cliff and was right above an overhang where the cave stood.

As Adroegen looked down, he began to think he might be able to make it up to the forest. He made his way higher, but bad luck found him. There was some rainwater upon the rock, and Adroegen's foot slipped. He was able to catch himself, but he had much trouble keeping himself from falling. Adroegen was beginning to regret taking the climb, and for good reason.

When Adroegen tried to regain his footing, he only slipped farther, and this time he was unable to hold himself. One tumble down a cliff was not enough, it would seem. Adroegen fell back down and hit the rocky foot of the cliff, and then he tumbled into the cave. It was some time before Adroegen finally stopped. The ground sank many strides down from the door into the cave, and Adroegen was soon lying a few steps from the shore of a small lake inside of a great cavern. He had never had to endure so much pain before.

At least a few bones had to have been broken. Adroegen could not even sit upright anymore, let alone stand on his feet. When Adroegen tried to crawl, he only grimaced and screamed in pain. Simply drawing breath hurt his ribs greatly. Adroegen was still for some time, and he knew that he had grown utterly helpless. He had no hope of fending for himself anymore. The end was surely near, and yet for Adroegen, death would still not come. He waited for a Rhykwen to return, but no angel of the dead came to take him.

"I am broken, spent," said Adroegen. "Now I cannot even move, let alone stand or walk. Yet where are you, Rhykwen? Why does your master not instruct you to come and take me away? Have I not suffered enough upon this wretched earth?"

All was silent, though Adroegen had not expected an answer to his plea, for he was alone. That appeared to always be his destiny, to be alone and filled with pain and sadness. Adroegen waited, yet he still would not be granted that which he desired so greatly. No taker of the dead would come, even though death should have met him by now. And after some time, Adroegen decided he would endure such torment no more.

"Very well," said Adroegen, with his hand upon Endonhil. "It grows clear to me that I will never be granted death, and that I am to remain here and suffer. I will no longer endure it, one way or another. Hear me, Enilundar. If you will not allow for me to gain relief from my suffering, if you will keep death hidden from me, then I will seek it out myself. My end has come, by your will or not."

Adroegen drew his sword. The hilt felt remarkably hot, which Adroegen found very peculiar, but he cared not for the pain, for it would soon end. Adroegen had nothing left upon that earth. His father and brother had been taken in battle, and Adroegen's mother was fed to wolves before his very eyes. And now his friends, which he had come to know as his new kin, had been taken from him, or he felt very certain of it. Adroegen could go no further, and yet no servant of Enilundar would come and take him away from that earth.

The hilt burned hotter as Adroegen prepared to make one final blow to end his time upon that earth. He spoke what he thought would be his final words. "I know not what awaits me, but I know what remains here for me now. Thus, I will happily take the path that many upon this earth fear. Here ends our friendship, Endonhil, greatest treasure I have had upon this earth. In your final act, I pray that my death be swift."

Adroegen tried to deal a final blow upon himself, but something odd happened. The hilt of Endonhil suddenly grew hot as flame, so much so that Adroegen's hand burned. He screamed in pain, though it did not deter him. Adroegen tried again to take his own life, but this time the sword burned so hot that he could not bear to hold it. Endonhil fell to the ground, and Adroegen's whole arm was in a great pain. He could not even hold his own sword in what Adroegen had hoped would be his final deed with it.

Adroegen tried to settle himself, though he looked upon his hand to find that it was black and burned. Endonhil lay before him, and though Adroegen found this to be very strange, he did not care very much to figure out why such a strange thing had taken place. Instead, Adroegen was filled with anger that he could be granted no peace or mercy of any kind. In a great rage, stronger than any that Adroegen had ever felt in his life, he quickly grabbed Endonhil again and cast it as hard as he could across the cavern. His sword clinked upon the rock and then fell into the shallow of the lake with a splash. It hurt greatly to make such a move, but Adroegen cared not, for wrath had overtaken him.

"Enilundar," said Adroegen, fighting tears. "Why is it that you hate me so? What have I done to deserve such torment from you? I learned to love as a child, but upon doing so, you took everything from me. Why do you take such joy in my suffering? Why?"

As Adroegen expected, there was no answer. He looked about the cavern, and all was dark and silent, save for his own voice. Adroegen noticed his sword glowing within the water near the shore several feet away, which must have been from what little light made it into the cavern. It mattered not, though. Adroegen shouted into the cave, even though he knew no one was there to hear him.

"You are cruel," said Adroegen to Enilundar. "I have been told that you watch over me! Where are you? Why did you allow my mother to die as she did? Where were you then? There is no love within your heart. None! You are as evil as Vyroun himself! And dark as all other lords that have walked this earth! Curse you! I shall spurn you from now until the end of my days! And I will renounce you further in death!"

In Adroegen's rage he had risen up, however, his agony forced him to fall again. Adroegen's whole body was in pain, and he could hardly bear it. He was then silent, for Adroegen had run out of words to say, and instead he lay there and wept. The anger had left him, and Adroegen was overcome with grief unlike any he had ever felt before. There was nothing else Adroegen could do besides linger within that cave and weep with sadness over all that he had loved and then lost during his life. He was certain that no one would find him there within that cave, not even death itself, even if Adroegen waited and starved there. Adroegen's back was turned to the lake where his sword lay, and for several moments he saw only darkness.

For a short time Adroegen lay there weeping, but soon he thought he heard what sounded like breath coming from somewhere behind him. He quieted but did not turn. It was uncertain at first whether his ears were playing tricks on him, but before long Adroegen found that they were not. A soft and gentle breeze met him, which was strange, as he was not sure where such wind might come from, for he was inside a great cavern. The breath slowly grew louder, and Adroegen began to hear a voice.

"Adroegen," whispered someone. A gentle breeze continued to reach him. Then the dark of the cavern lifted a little. A light was growing, one that came from somewhere behind him, where the lake was. His tears ceased, but Adroegen began to grow afraid. The voice whispered onward.

"Do not be afraid, Adroegen," he heard, but this time it was a different voice. Adroegen listened further.

"Who is it that speaks to me?" said Adroegen, whose back was still turned to the lake, and he was nervous to look.

"Turn to the lake, and we will show ourselves to you," said another voice. Adroegen was rather hesitant, but he did so. It was quite agonizing for him to move and face the lake, but soon Adroegen saw upon the water something most peculiar.

Upon the water there was a blue flame, burning very

quietly. It was strange, as fire could not burn upon water. Adroegen was certain that he was encountering some kind of magic, though he was not sure of what sort. Perhaps there was something within the cavern that he knew not of. Adroegen also noticed his sword was shining quite brightly beneath the water. The blue flame, meanwhile, grew in size, and the cavern was glowing with a very dim light.

"Who are you?" said Adroegen. He received no answer. The flame grew and spread across the lake. It then separated into five flames. Adroegen watched closely. People were taking shape in the flame, and soon there were five standing upon the water, though they were not of human flesh.

One man to the far right had a large, dark beard, and next to him stood a woman fair and angelic, with hair of golden brown. To the far left was a man of golden hair, and next to him a woman of brown hair. Then to the center stood a man with long dark hair but no beard. All of them were clothed in white, and the blue of the flame glowed about each of them. They appeared angelic, and yet there was also a fierceness about each of them. Adroegen was afraid, but with the agony he was already in, fear did not overwhelm him anymore.

"I am Dutharion," said the bearded man to the very right, who then gave Adroegen a small bow.

"Algarmaira am I," said the woman who stood beside Dutharion.

"And I am Celandorn," said the man who stood to the far left. Adroegen was most bewildered, for he was certain that he had heard these names before, but could not recall where. Then the woman who stood next to Celandorn spoke.

"Rhunwin am I," said the woman. The man to the center did not answer immediately. Instead they all approached Adroegen, and the man to the center went to Endonhil, which lay in the water. He reached into the lake and took Adroegen's sword, which glowed brightly.

"And I am Buludin," said the man holding Adroegen's sword. "We are the Vistivar, the very highest servants of Enilundar himself."

Adroegen was taken aback, and unsure of why they appeared before him. He first thought it could be because of his cursing of their master mere moments before, but Adroegen knew not with certainty. Adroegen cared little if they were angry towards him, for his heart was filled with too much pain and sorrow. "What is it that you want from me?"

"Enilundar has sent us unto you," said Buludin. "For he has watched over you very closely for all of your life. He has heard all of your cries to him, and he knows all of your pain."

"Does he now?" said Adroegen. "I have never seen any reason to believe that he is with me."

"You have followed the path that was set forth for you precisely as Enilundar had sought," said Algarmaira. "All has gone in motion as he has intended. But here and now, you have strayed from his path."

"Why do you curse our master so?" asked Celandorn. "And why do you seek to give up your life? Do you not know that Enilundar has always had a great path set before you?"

"Why do I curse him?" said Adroegen in anger. "Have you not seen all the suffering I have endured? All those I have come to love have been taken from me one by one. And your Enilundar, who is said to watch over all upon this earth, has done nothing to stop it. My father and brother are gone. I heard my mother scream and watched as her body was ripped apart. Where was your Enilundar then? And not so long ago I thought I had been given new kin, that perhaps your master had heard me, only to see them all taken soon after!"

"Not all is what it might seem," said Dutharion. "Are you so certain of the fates of your kin?"

"I have seen enough to know that no greater power watches over me," said Adroegen. "My mother, what cruel being would give her such a fate as that which she had to suffer?"

"We have seen your mother in Elunbelan," said Rhunwin. "She is at peace now, and she has been at peace since that day of which you speak. Your mother worried greatly for you as a Rhykwen took her away, but the Rhykwen told her that you will be well cared for, and that she need not worry. Your mother fulfilled her purpose upon this earth precisely as Enilundar intended. Mairenn, your mother, is at peace, and she watches over you with love."

Adroegen was overcome with tears upon hearing of his mother, for no day passed when he did not think of her, though he was still filled with great anger. "My mother fulfilled her purpose? Was that purpose to be the carnage of wolves?"

"Your mother died so that you could be saved from what fate she suffered," said Buludin. "For you have a great task set before you."

"I have learned enough of my purpose," said Adroegen.

"So, my mother was to die so that I could live on and be tormented further! Your Enilundar seems to take joy in my own agony!"

"A Rhykwen came before you and you did not heed her words," said Algarmaira. "The answer to what you have always sought has been before your very eyes. You have simply been blind to see it."

Buludin held up Adroegen's sword. "Endonhil has defended you many a time. A mighty weapon it is. Do you know the old tongue of Aundorin? Have you been told what is written upon your greatest heirloom?"

Adroegen grew nervous. He had always known of there being strange writing upon the blade of Endonhil, but Adroegen did not know the tongue of Aundorin. "No. I know not of what is written."

Rhunwin then spoke, but not in the common tongue that you or I know, but instead in the first tongue of Aundorin. "Ena on Endonhil, gaurnen na Enilundar. Enilundarim unath onkular fronin ena. Egi du lorn ongad galunwair. Rauk enruda fur nin tenad."

And as Rhunwin spoke in Aundorin, Buludin spoke in the common tongue. "I am Endonhil, forged by Enilundar. Enilundar's might is wielded through me. They with faith are not hopeless. Darkness will tremble at my sight."

Adroegen knew not what words to speak. He was quite surprised, though as Adroegen tried to lean forward to look upon his sword, his agony forced him back.

"This sword was given to me by Enilundar himself long ago," said Buludin. "And when my time had come it was taken by Ciarvur, who then passed it down to the end of my bloodline, when the time came for it to be wielded again. And he passed it down to its rightful owner. To you,

Adroegen, the heir to my bloodline. Now you are called upon by Enilundar to take my place among the Vistivar, to smite down those who will seek to veil this earth in darkness."

Adroegen had not words to speak. He was still filled with anger, though that anger was being overcome with disbelief. "But why do I not know until now? Why must I suffer so much before finally receiving such a blessing?"

"One cannot know what light is without also seeing darkness," said Buludin. "Those of good upon this earth are so because they have seen evil. And so, you have endured much. But let your heart not grow heavy, for you will one day again look upon your mother, and all others that you have lost."

Adroegen's anger grew hotter upon hearing this. "So, the fairy tale was true? You did leave your sword to an heir to wield?"

"All is true," said Buludin. "A great plan had been in motion for you since before you came into being. Whether by your knowing or not, whether by your will or not, much has been bestowed upon you."

Adroegen only laughed. He tried to sit up but could not. "I am very touched by your sentiment, I truly am. But have any of you looked upon me? Has your master seen me? I cannot stand, I cannot walk, and thus I cannot face Vyroun, nor fulfill any other tasks that your Enilundar might set for me. I am wounded more than any mortal man could fathom. You are far too late, I am afraid. Perhaps if you had come to me well before now, then I would have been able to fulfill whatever it is that you seek from me. But I am too broken to serve your master now! You have failed!"

A sudden strong wind blew towards Adroegen, and he fell back. He was forced to his side and was no longer facing the Vistivar upon the lake. Every wound Adroegen had suddenly hurt immensely, and he screamed in great pain. As he did so, a thunderous voice echoed in the cave. Adroegen thought it must have been Buludin, though he was not certain.

"And who made life and death? Who made joy and pain?" said the voice. Adroegen had never felt such pain before, and he could only lie there in tears, as if he no longer cared what might happen to him. The voice spoke on. "Was it not he, Enilundar? Is it not he who by will can give life and take it?"

Adroegen was in great pain, but suddenly his agony began to lessen. His screams ceased and soon he no longer felt any pain at all. Adroegen was able to sit up again. He felt no bruises, nor any broken bones. Adroegen seemed to be healed completely and was suddenly free to move as if he had never been hurt at all.

"Adroegen," said Buludin. "Harken and hither to me."

Adroegen grew very nervous and rose to his feet. No pain of any kind met him. Adroegen turned to face the five Vistivar, who still stood above the water of the lake. Buludin held Endonhil, and the sword glowed with a great light. Blue flame had engulfed it.

"It is time, Adroegen," said Buludin. "Time that you are hallowed as one of us. Here. No longer are you any mere man. You shall now become Adroegen, the Vistivar, highest servant of Enilundar. Wielder of Endonhil, the once sword of Buludin."

Adroegen made his way to the five Vistivar with hesitancy, for he knew not what would come. As Adroegen

walked towards Buludin, one of the other Vistivar spoke a
verse. Adroegen was not sure whether it was Rhunwin or
Algarmaira, as his eye was fixed upon Buludin and the
sword that both he and Adroegen had wielded.

> *Many a time you have called upon me,*
> *Never have I ignored your cries,*
> *You cannot know what I have in motion,*
> *Nor see yourself with my eyes.*
>
> *Never were you forsaken,*
> *I watched over you all this time,*
> *Never have you wandered alone,*
> *I have always been at your side.*
>
> *For I have always loved you,*
> *Long before ever you knew me,*
> *I hallowed you steward of nations,*
> *Long before you came to be.*
>
> *Fear not that you shall drift astray,*
> *For I have always been your guide,*
> *No darkness shall you need to fear,*
> *For I walk with you against the tide.*

Adroegen stood before Buludin and the other Vistivar.
Buludin held Endonhil out for Adroegen to take. "You have
wielded Endonhil many a time before, and it has always
defended you. Cast it not again from your side. Take my
weapon, and what has been your weapon. This time when
you wield it, you shall wield its full might."

Adroegen held out his hand, though I would say that

he was quite afraid. For he knew not what would happen upon grasping his sword again. Endonhil glowed of white, and blue flames burned upon the blade. Adroegen took the hilt of his sword and held it again.

When Adroegen held his sword again, he raised it, and upon doing so the light grew immensely and the flame roared. Great thunder sounded, and the fire spread throughout the whole cavern. The winds of a hurricane blew about, and never before had Adroegen been so startled.

Adroegen in surprise dropped Endonhil into the waters and he fell back. He had never been so overcome with so many feelings in his time upon that earth. Tears fell from his eyes. Adroegen in but a very short time had gone from giving up on his life to finding answers to everything he had maddeningly wondered before.

"That cannot be," said Adroegen, absolutely stunned. Endonhil shined bright enough that he could see it several feet below the water. "All this time?"

"All this time," said Buludin. "The shroud no longer veils your mind. That about which you have wondered all your life is answered. The signs have been always before your very eyes, but your anger towards Enilundar clouded your sight. But no longer. Know who you are now. You are of my bloodline, heir to the highest servants of Enilundar himself. Know that he has always watched over you, and that he has always had a magnificent path set for you."

Adroegen knew not what words to utter, for he realized then that there were signs throughout his life that he had overlooked. For Adroegen had heard the tale of Buludin, that his sword had not been seen since his battle with Vyroun an age ago. And a few thousand years later the wizard, Ciarvur, who had saved Adroegen from the prison of Gulgurod when he was a child, and the only one who could have had knowledge of whether or not there was an heir, and if so, whom, bestowed Endonhil upon Adroegen as a family heirloom for him to fight with. And after allowing Adroegen as a child to fight in battle, the wizard died to save him when Adroegen came face to face with Vyroun himself a few years later. Much had grown quite clear to Adroegen all of a sudden.

"Rise," said Buludin. Adroegen rose to his feet and stood before Buludin, who spoke again. "Enilundar has a command for you. Vyroun's evil is growing. Legions seek to raze these lands. You have Enilundar's might bestowed upon you. He commands that you strike down the dark lord that stirs in the north."

"The time for fleeing has ended," said Celandorn. "Vyroun will know that you are servant to Enilundar, wielder of his power, as you lay your vengeance upon him."

Adroegen looked down upon Endonhil, which lay beneath the water of the lake. "The sword of Buludin shall face Vyroun again."

"Your time upon this earth has not ended," said Rhunwin. "For there are many tasks for you to fulfill. No Rhykwen shall seek you out. The time for you to come to Enilundar is not now. When your work upon this earth is finished, then you will be called home."

"I have many tasks?" said Adroegen. "And what must I do beyond smiting down Vyroun? I must know what my road is if I am to walk it, otherwise I may wander off my path and fail in what is wanted of me."

"Your path will be made clear as you walk it," said

Dutharion. "Fear not, for you will always be guided along your way."

Algarmaira then spoke a verse:

> *You know not where you are going,*
> *But never shall I lead you astray,*
> *You shall walk your path without knowing,*
> *For I shall carry you the whole way.*

"Fear not," said Buludin. "For you will know in time all that Enilundar wants of you. But for now, your task is clear. Take my sword and wield it again, but this time wield its full might. He with the power to wield my sword is mightier than any army that walks this earth. But you have another foe to face, one who is not beneath you as goblins and other mindless creatures are. Enilundar orders you to smite down he who commands legions in the north."

"Take back Endonhil," said Celandorn. "The blessings of all Vistivar are upon you. The full might of the greatest sword upon this earth shall answer to you, and the weapons of all Vistivar shall answer to you should you ever have to find them in need."

"Take Endonhil now and wield it as I once did," said Buludin. "Cast it not aside again."

Adroegen went into the water to retrieve his sword. Endonhil lay at the bottom of the shallow water, but he needed to immerse himself completely in order to retrieve it. Endonhil glowed brightly, and Adroegen took it by the hilt. He then returned to the shore.

And when Adroegen rose from the water, he stood tall again. He had been reborn, in a way, for Adroegen had tumbled into the cave maimed to the point of utter helplessness and seeking to end his own life. Now he was healed, rekindled with resolve, and no longer simply Adroegen the wanderer or Adroegen the vagabond. No, he was now Adroegen, Vistivar, highest servant of Enilundar himself.

Adroegen turned to face the five Vistivar who stood upon the lake, but upon doing so, he found that they were gone. He thought he heard faint whispers echoing in the cavern, but soon all was silent. I cannot begin to tell you how overwhelmed Adroegen's mind had become. However, I will say that among his thoughts was a memory of when he had spoken to Caitren one night in the Moor Glen, where Adroegen told her he was not sure why he still lived, and Caitren uttered that perhaps there was some purpose for him. Adroegen at the time thought it foolish, but now Adroegen found that Caitren had been right about him. And with Adroegen's joy came also a sadness, for he greatly missed her and the others of the company, and Adroegen wondered what Caitren and the others might have said if they still lived and could see what had become of him.

Chapter Fourteen:
The Eagles' Ascension

Adroegen spent the next few days making his way south with all haste. He needed to return to the Fornwood and find the eagles of the forest, for Adroegen needed to reach Vyroun swiftly and face him, but his kingdom was a distance away on foot, and the eagles could take Adroegen there far quicker. Adroegen was very hungry, but he was able to find at least some fruit and nuts within the Dead Forest. The hunger though did not bother Adroegen too much, for such a trouble did not compare at all to what pain he once had when hurt. Adroegen was able to cover much distance each day, for he was on his own and did not need to stop very much, and he was a very hardy traveler.

Fortunately, the river Adroegen had fallen into had taken him a good distance south already, giving Adroegen a good head start. There were some signs of goblins farther north, but Adroegen, having been hallowed a Vistivar, now held power beyond any mere man, or even a wizard, and thus he had no need to fear a pack of goblins. However, he was certain that the pack thought he was dead, and if so, then Vyroun might think him dead also, and thus Adroegen did not want the enemy to know that he lived, as it could be an advantage when seeking to defeat the dark lord in the north. Adroegen now thought there must have been a greater reason he was hunted than just the Night's Jewel, as Vyroun must have somehow discovered, or at least suspected, that Adroegen was the heir of Buludin. He had wielded Endonhil when he last encountered Vyroun a decade earlier, and Adroegen felt quite certain that this must have made Vyroun suspicious.

After only a few days, Adroegen reached the Flotvatin, the rapid river that bordered the Fornwood and the Dead Forest. Adroegen hoped that his good friend Treeling, one of the great tree men and guardians of the Fornwood, might be there, though Adroegen did not expect him to be. Treeling, indeed, was not there, nor were any other tree men, and so Adroegen needed to cross the river himself. He had to run a small distance along the river before he finally found some stepping stones on which he could cross. The river was meandering a little, and at the place where Adroegen crossed, the river took a very sharp meander. Adroegen did step into the water twice, however, he was soon on the south bank of the river and back within the Fornwood.

The Fornwood, however, appeared very much different from when the company had last been within it. If you want to know why, I would say that fortunately it was not because the forest had been attacked, but rather simply because the north wind had come and brought winter with it. The leaves had fallen from the trees. Adroegen needed to find the eagles for help, though he was not sure if they were still in lands to the south, facing forces that had gathered within the old ruins of Hailnor, which Adroegen had heard when leaving the forest in search of the goblin chief. And so, Adroegen needed to speak with the trees that stood upon the northern border, as at least some of the trees within the Fornwood would know where the eagles were. The trouble, though, was that it was winter, and the trees of the Fornwood normally slept for the winter when the north wind came.

"Hello? Are any trees of the great Fornwood still awake?" asked Adroegen. Fortunately, at least some trees were not yet asleep, as Adroegen soon heard much groaning, and the nearest trees answered him.

"Still awake?" said the tree nearest to Adroegen, which was a willow tree right along the border, and because of the river's sharp curve, he was the only tree on the shore, and the other trees stood behind him. The willow tree spoke on. "It is well past time for us to sleep for the winter! But we have been told to remain awake! There is war in the north, and whomever is causing it, I would break their bones and rip them apart if I could, for they are causing me to lose my sleep!"

"Oh! Your manners!" said a pine tree right behind the willow tree. It was the only tree that still appeared green. "In my day we trees were not so fussy as some are now! I have been told of you, little Adroegen. You must forgive Willowtwig here. Pineleaf, at your service."

"Oh, you and your talk of manners. I, too, wish to sleep already," said a beech tree next to Pineleaf, sounding very groggy. Adroegen was quite amused, even though he needed to move with haste.

"You cannot sleep with war taking place beyond our borders, Beechbark!" said Pineleaf. "The tree men of this forest are now on the march! And so, we must remain awake to watch this forest until they return. And as we speak of it, Willowtwig, you are closest to the border.

Could you not tell the rest of us what has taken place beyond this forest?"

"Do not ask that of me again! Such inconsiderateness, and to think that you speak of manners!" said Willowtwig. Adroegen was quite entertained by these trees. He was always a good friend to Oaknut, the old and pleasant oak tree that stood nearby Adroegen's home. Oaknut had told him of several other Fornwood trees in the past, and Adroegen could not believe that Oaknut had not spoken of the trees Adroegen was talking to now. Willowtwig and Pineleaf argued for a few moments over Willowtwig being asked to watch beyond the borders, something he could not do very well. Willowtwig, you must understand, was a willow tree, and that meant that he had trouble seeing, as all of his branches hung low before his face and hindered his sight! And so, he grew quite cross when asked to tell what he could see beyond the Fornwood borders.

"If you do not like to be asked such things, then you should have made sure to rest each winter farther within the forest instead of on the border," said Pineleaf. "That way, when it was time for your roots to set hold in the earth, you would have been farther in the forest and thus not be asked to watch the border. Though at the very least, if you are rude to me, then I know what to say that will get under your bark! Now, little Adroegen, what is it that brings you to us?"

"Well, some of my questions you have already answered," said Adroegen. "I need to find Andor and the eagles, for I am in need of their help. I must be taken to him, although you have uttered that the tree men are marching to war. Where are the eagles now? Are they flying off now to the north?"

"I think not, actually," said Pineleaf. "Though I am not too sure. Hmmm. Well, Andor was going to meet with the other birds, somewhere within the forest, and then I heard that they would fly off to war."

Adroegen grew quite worried. If he were to make for Vyroun, he would need the help of the eagles, for Mûrondûn was too great a distance to walk to, and the eagles would be able to take him there swifter than anyone. "I must find the eagles. Could the forest find out if they are still within the Fornwood?"

"Why yes, we could," said Pineleaf. "Beechbark! Send word to the trees within the forest! Ask if Andor is still present within these woods. Little Adroegen is in need of him!"

"Hmph!" said Beechbark. "Typical evergreen! Always wanting others to do things!"

"Oh! Enough of your fuss!" said Pineleaf. Beechbark relayed the message to the trees behind him, and those trees carried the message to those behind them, and tree by tree Adroegen's call went farther and farther into the forest. Adroegen needed to be patient before he could find out if Andor was still there, as the trees kept relaying his message deeper into the Fornwood to see if any trees knew where the master of the eagles was. Meanwhile, he listened to Pineleaf, Beechbark, and Willowtwig quarrel on.

"Oh, the trees these days!" said Pineleaf. "The stubbornness! The ill manners! In my day we trees were most chivalrous and gallant!"

"You keep asking favors from us!" said Willowtwig. "Asking a willow tree to watch beyond the borders. Hmph!"

"Well, perhaps you might seek help and find someone to cut your branches," said Pineleaf.

"What? Cut my branches? Oh!" said Willowtwig. "I am not a pine tree like yourself, able to see far better."

"I do say, that makes me wonder," said Beechbark. "Pineleaf, why have you been given such a peculiar name?"

"Peculiar name? What do you mean by peculiar?" said Pineleaf. "How is my name strange to you?"

"Because your name is Pineleaf," said Beechbark. "But pine trees do not have leaves!"

"What? No leaves? Oh!" said Pineleaf, very cross. "The impertinence! The insolence! The impudence! The irreverence! Pines having no leaves. This is just as when poor Appleroot was inquired about his name, and then told that apples grow not in the ground. Oh, but I have not seen him in some time, for he is somewhere in the southern part of this forest."

Adroegen could have stood there and listened to the trees quarrel amongst themselves for hours, but before long Adroegen heard wings flapping. He was quite amazed at how swiftly word had reached the lord of the Fornwood that Adroegen had returned. Andor landed beside him.

"Thank you, Beechbark, for sending word to me," said Andor.

"Oh, how you receive thanks and not us!" Adroegen heard Pineleaf say to Beechbark, though after that he paid no attention. The master of the eagles had arrived to speak with him.

"You departed as six but you return here with only one," said Andor. "What has become of your friends?"

Adroegen grew quite saddened. "I am afraid they have

met their end. We defeated the goblin chief, however, the pack found us again days later. I fell into a river and was separated from them."

"I am very saddened if this is true," said Andor. "Did you see your friends die? Do you know beyond any doubt that they are gone?"

Adroegen had to think to himself before speaking, for a strange doubt came over him. Though he once believed what the witch showed him to be true, in the end Adroegen did not know with utmost certainty. "No. I do not know without any doubt that they are gone."

Andor inquired only a little further. "I can see what the forest might know of your friends' whereabouts. But in the meantime, you have arrived just in time, for the Fornwood will soon enter war. The great birds are gathered right now, at your very home! We have somewhat resolved the troubles in the southern lands, though I will say more when I return with you to the others. Climb up, and I will fly you to your home."

Adroegen climbed atop Andor and held on. Andor flapped his wings mightily, and before long Adroegen ascended high into the air. The air was very cold just several hundred feet above the ground, and it was much windier, too. Many snowflakes blew by Adroegen and Andor, and Adroegen found that some snow had fallen within the Fornwood. The forest looked far unlike it did when the company was there months before, for now it was grey and white.

It did not take long for Andor to reach the house of Adroegen. Though the Fornwood appeared very quiet and not crowded at all, as many of the animals were resting for the winter, there was quite a gathering at Adroegen's home. Orn was there, as well as many eagles. Adroegen soon found Huf and Ule, lord and lady of the owls, and the two of them were accompanied by many more owls. There were also some other birds though that Adroegen had not met before. He found two great ravens, several hawks, and scores of falcons. Adroegen saw quite a sight, as nature's forces had mustered. And then Adroegen found Ganglere speaking to all the birds.

Andor landed upon the ground and Adroegen got off. All the birds turned their attention to Adroegen and the master of the eagles. There were hundreds of great birds in total, each large enough to eat a man whole. Adroegen made his way first to Ganglere, as the wizard surely would have much news to give. Strangely, Andor, lord of the Fornwood and master of the eagles, did not join the other birds. Instead he made his way to Oaknut, who appeared quite drowsy but was still awake amidst the great gathering before him. It appeared that none of the trees of the Fornwood were asleep yet, but I can tell you that in a normal winter, they all would have been by then, were there no war taking place.

"Adroegen, our paths cross again, but this time at your home!" said Ganglere pleasantly, but then his look grew curious. "Where are your friends?"

"I was separated from my friends," said Adroegen. "And I fear they have met their end."

"And what makes you fear they are gone?" said Ganglere.

"I encountered a witch in the Dead Forest," said Adroegen. "And she showed me visions of things I have already endured, like the goblin chief's defeat, precisely as they took place. Then she showed me visions of each of my friends meeting their end one by one. I know not what level of deceit the witch possessed, but I watched the goblin chief's defeat precisely as it took place, and thus I worry that the fates of my friends are precisely as she showed me as well."

"We will see if we can discover whether this witch was truthful or filled with deceit," said the wizard. "Oaknut might be able to answer, however, it may take some time."

Ganglere went to join Andor and Oaknut. Adroegen did not want to follow, as he did not wish to grow hopeful only to be overcome with grief again if the witch in the end was truthful. He watched them, and though Oaknut's eyes were closed, he was not asleep. Oaknut was soon uttering to Andor, though Adroegen knew not what the old tree was saying. Andor and Ganglere, after listening to Oaknut speak, returned to Adroegen, and Orn, too, joined.

"My leg is far better now, Adroegen," said Orn. The bandage that Adroegen put on his leg the previous summer was no longer there. "Ganglere removed the bandage you put on me when we met in the ruins to the south."

"Very good," said Adroegen. "I am happy to know you are better now."

"The wizard and I returned from the ruins in the south," said Andor. "We eagles found a great gathering there, of goblins and other foul creatures. Strangely, it seemed they were waiting for a master to command them, but no master came. And so, many of the forces there have fled and are moving north as we speak. The trees of the Fornwood are facing them now and will next join the war north of here. What creatures that remained in the ruins, we defeated with ease."

"Igon Daugor, the hill of death," said Ganglere. "Once the stronghold of Threnidir, who commanded great evil and brought the kingdom of Hailnor into ruin. I was suspicious of evil about beyond Vyroun, and that Threnidir may have returned. However, no lord was found in the southern lands like in the north. Thus, I know not the truth of why foul things had been gathering there, if there was no dark power to draw them."

"Is that something you must find answers to?" asked Adroegen, who knew not of what brewed in the south like he did in the north.

"In time, yes," said the wizard as Huf, Ule, the two ravens, a great hawk, and a falcon joined them. "For I worry that evil might brew in the south like in the north. However, now is not the time, for we must worry of the evil in the north first."

"Words of your deeds and the deeds of your friends in the southern woods has reached us," spoke one of the ravens to Adroegen. He was covered entirely in black feathers, and though he looked frightening, the raven spoke in a friendly manner. "Crawa am I, lord of the ravens."

"And Crawe I am, lady of the ravens," said the other raven. She, too, was covered entirely in black feathers, and Adroegen had great trouble telling them apart. Huf and Ule differed in appearance, as Huf had feathers of black and brown while Ule had feathers of white, however, there was no difference in the ravens' appearances. Crawe spoke on. "We have heard that crows and ravens attacked you and your friends one night this past summer. Crawa and I must ask your forgiveness."

"I heard that you both have had trouble of late, as

many of your kin have become spies for evil," said Adroegen. A large hawk, with a golden beak, feathers of black, and a head and belly of red, spoke. The hawk's red eyes were as fierce as those of the eagles.

"Hafoc am I, lord of the hawks," said the hawk. "Word reaches us of great evil growing within these lands. We hawks have seen it, and so we fight alongside the other mighty birds of these forests. The birds have not entered the wars of humans in a very long time, not since the kingdoms of men formed, when the hawks held a bond with Esmael, the first king of Gundmar. We hawks know the lore of men quite well."

"I am grateful that you come to our aid," said Adroegen. "I was a child once living in Gundmar and knew not of a friendship among Gundmar and the hawks."

"And I am Feolsen, lord of the falcons," said a falcon with feathers of black, brown, and white. "Word reached me of the deeds of you and your friends, Adroegen, defeating the mother of the spiders and other enemies in the forests to the south, and for that I am most grateful."

Ganglere spoke after all had introduced themselves. "I think it is a good thing Adroegen is here, for he has seen the forces of the north before. The tree men march as we speak, and the birds must join them. First, however, we must decide how it is that we will face this army. What say you, Adroegen? What forces are we up against?"

Adroegen needed to think before answering, as there were many different creatures that served Vyroun. "Some of Vyroun's forces the forest can defeat with ease. Goblins, trolls, ogres, wolves. Though I would say that this will not be just a mere pack of hunters running about the woods. These monsters will be legion, and all battle-hardened.

There are some other creatures, though, that are of greater worry. Ligwyrm, the fiery serpent of the west, will surely be present. That is a foe formidable to even the great birds. And then there are Vyroun's most terrible servants, deoflas, the spirits of men that turned to evil in life. They are beyond any of you, save for Ganglere. Only a servant of Enilundar himself can repel such creatures. I think that each of you will have a task of your own upon this battlefield."

"There was once a wizard in the north, Ciarvur, who could repel these deoflas," said Ganglere. "However, he passed a decade ago. And so, these creatures are mine to face, I think."

"And of the dragon?" said Hafoc. "A most fearsome monster that is, one beyond any single one of us."

"The claws of the eagles are among the few things that can pierce the armor of a dragon," said Andor. "Though I will say that even then, a serpent's hide will still be difficult for us to penetrate. I believe that the eagles must face the dragon."

"Then that would leave the rest of us to face the army," said Ule. "There will be many of them, from what Adroegen says."

"It is decided, then," said Feolsen. "The trees are on the march. We must make haste and join them!'

"Not all is decided," said Ganglere, looking to Adroegen. "Where will Adroegen be in all of this?"

"I will not take part in this battle," said Adroegen. "For I have my own enemy to face. Andor, I will need you in my task. You must take me to Norungad, the very stronghold of Vyroun himself."

"That is a rather unexpected request," said Andor with

a curious look. Ganglere appeared renewed with hope, if not triumph. Adroegen had a strange feeling that Ganglere had known all that time that he was the heir to Buludin, but Adroegen could not think further. Andor spoke on. "Very well, Adroegen. If you must go there, then I will take you."

"We must go secretly, though," said Adroegen. "For I do not wish for Vyroun to know that I will seek to face him."

"There is nothing more to decide, then," said Hafoc. "Time it is for the hawks to defend Gundmar again, as they did long ago."

"We will all face great peril," said Huf. "Our strength must hold, but most of all, our courage must remain kindled. Take heart, all of you. For this will be a trial far beyond any we have encountered before, for the forests have not gone to war in a very long time. The best of qualities within all of us must prevail in this hour of need."

And the mighty birds of the Fornwood and the southern woods readied to fly off to war. Hafoc went to the hawks to give orders, while Feolsen made for the falcons to do the same. Huf and Ule made for what owls had accompanied them. Andor went back to Oaknut for a few words. Adroegen, before departing, was addressed by the wizard.

"You have discovered the truth, it appears," said Ganglere. "It was no fairy tale that I told to your friends when I hosted them this past summer."

Adroegen had not words to speak. It appeared Ganglere knew he was heir to Buludin all along. If indeed he did, then Adroegen knew not why he kept it a secret. "Did you know? All these years?"

"No. I did not know, actually," said Ganglere. "However, I was very suspicious that there was far more to you. One night, a few summers back, a young man found his way to my home by mere chance. I learned who you were and your tale, but what was strange was that I saw the sword you carried. And I began to think that there must have been some reason for chance to work as it did. I am servant to Enilundar, and I know all weapons of his servants. Upon your sword is a symbol of an eagle, wreathed in blue flame of five stems, and seven rays of light, for the five Vistivar, the seven wizards, and one Enilundar."

Adroegen looked upon Endonhil and saw that symbol he had never known the meaning of. Back when his friends first saw it, he told them that it may have been just a family crest. Adroegen was wrong in his guess, and yet he was also right, as he was of the bloodline of the one who first wielded that sword.

"All weapons of Enilundar bear that symbol," said Ganglere, showing his oak staff to Adroegen. Upon looking closely, Adroegen found a carving of the very same symbol upon the wizard's walking stick.

"And so, I knew right away that you carried the sword of Buludin," said Ganglere. "Yet I wondered how you came by it. And thus, I asked you, and learned that it was given to you by another wizard, Ciarvur, whom I learned died in order to save you from Vyroun. I knew the tale of Buludin, and that this same wizard was at Buludin's side when he passed, after which the sword was lost. Ciarvur must have known of an heir, if anyone knew of an heir, and some thousands of years later he bestowed that very weapon of Buludin onto your father, and then to you. But of course, being from lands to the south, I knew not of the north as folk from the north themselves might! And so, I was not entirely certain you were the heir of Buludin. All I could do was guess. However, there were many clues that I had seen, and other clues that I learned from you, which led me to suspect you were heir to the Vistivar."

Adroegen looked down upon his own weapon of Enilundar. He could not help but wonder if perhaps he should have known all that time that he was Buludin's heir. And yet, there may not have been any way of knowing, but only suspecting, as Ganglere said.

"And now you have your own enemy to face," said Ganglere. "One that you have wanted to face but always thought you could not hope to defeat. But you were wrong, Adroegen, and I am certain that you could not be happier to learn that you were so."

Adroegen laughed a little. "Well, I must say you are correct. I can face him, and I seek to lay my vengeance upon him. The Vistivar not long ago appeared before me and told me that Enilundar commands that I do precisely thus."

"Very good," said Ganglere. "Once you would have been fearful upon facing the dark lord of Mûrondûn. But now you will fight him without fear."

Andor had finished speaking with Oaknut and made his way to Adroegen. "I will take you to the stronghold of Vyroun, though you must lead me there, for it is a place I have not before ventured to. Before we leave, however, Oaknut wishes to speak with you."

"Very well," said Adroegen, who grew nervous, for he had nearly forgotten that Oaknut might be able to learn the true fates of his friends. He made his way to Oaknut.

The old oak tree appeared as if he would fall asleep at any moment, but Oaknut was quite awake.

"Now you listen here before you depart, little Adroegen," said Oaknut. "The north wind is upon us. Soon will I sleep for the winter, though war delays such slumber for these woods. The master of the eagles has just spoken to me. He uttered that you fear your friends are dead. I grew quite fond of them when they stayed within these woods."

"I fear they are gone," said Adroegen, who grew more nervous than he ever had before.

"I grew very fond of them," said Oaknut. "Now, my roots go deep into the earth, and they feel much. I came to know your friends quite well. In their time here, I came to recognize the soft and gentle footsteps of Caitren as they treaded upon the earth. I know the thumping step of Edelbir, and the light steps of Kattalin. And I know the swift, cheeky steps of Gleowan and Vaenn as they run."

"The sight of the trees does not cease to surprise me," said Adroegen.

"In particular, I know the soft step of Caitren better than any other," said Oaknut. "And I still feel her feet treading upon this earth. Caitren is not dead, Adroegen. My roots can feel it. She still walks these lands."

"Caitren is alive?" said Adroegen in surprise. He was overcome with joy, for he had once thought that Caitren was fed to wolves, just as his mother was.

"Her soft and gentle steps still tread this earth," said Oaknut. "And my roots can feel the footsteps of the rest of your friends, too. They are not all together, but soon I think they will be. Caitren is alone from the others. I feel the swift steps of Gleowan and Vaenn together, perhaps within a great city, among many folk. And elsewhere my roots can feel the light steps of Kattalin and the heavier steps of Edelbir. I believe they may be among an army, of folk small and yet heavy in steps. Your friends are all still alive. I know not how you came to believe them to be dead, but my roots tell me that you have been lied to."

"If so, then indeed I have been," said Adroegen as joy took him, though he did feel like a fool. He had at first trusted what the witch had showed him back along the river within the Dead Forest, but now he thought that perhaps he should have known not to. For she was a witch, and witches were deceitful, from what Adroegen had heard. And so, Adroegen came to realize he had not lost everything upon that earth, as he had been so sure of before he tried to bring about his own end within the cave.

"Yes, your friends all live," said Oaknut. "But heed my warning. My roots also feel great evil about, and this evil meets all of them. Your friends are in grave danger. They are all in peril or on the brink of peril, as are many folk north of here. And even then, I do not know the full danger, for even those of ill can cover their treading from my roots. Your hunters did so when you left this forest, thinking the goblin chief was alone, and I did not know he was not alone until it was too late. And so, I must warn you, Adroegen, that you may find need to save them."

"I will do so," said Adroegen, and his joy was then matched with great worry, for he did not want to learn that his friends still lived, only to then find them dead. "Though I must also defeat the leader of legions to the north of here. Doing so would be of great help in saving many in the north, including my friends."

"My roots feel that you may do both in one single

stroke," said Oaknut. "However, I know not with certainty. For there is much in motion. And so, it is clouded, what will soon take place."

Andor, after having words with the eagles, made his way to Adroegen. "All are ready. We must fly off to war."

Adroegen climbed atop Andor. As he did, he heard the owls all hooting. Then he heard the hawks. The falcons all croaked loudly, and then finally all the eagles screeched. The owls flew off, followed by the hawks and falcons, and then finally the eagles began flapping their wings. Adroegen saw Oaknut watch him depart. While Adroegen was joyful upon finding that his friends still lived, he worried of what danger they might soon be in and heeded Oaknut's words.

"When we reach the battle, you and I must stay out of sight," said Adroegen to Andor. Soon the Fornwood was below, and Adroegen's home was out of sight. Ever higher the eagles ascended, and upon their master was Adroegen, heir to Buludin, newly dubbed member of the Vistivar, who made his way north to smite down the lord of Mûrondûn under the command of Enilundar himself.

Chapter Fifteen: A Lost Disguise

The cold of winter met Caitren right away when she rode out with the army from the Woodlands. She already wished to be back where the air was warm like summer. To make matters worse, the army rode swiftly, and the wind blew at her face. The army traveled across the Southern Fold of Gundmar with little time for rest. The horses slowed at times but did not stop often. They followed the North Woodland Road, which went northeast and directly from Itilikin to the city of Bared Nar.

It was a five-day ride to the great city of Gundmar. In the Southern Fold, Caitren saw almost nothing but barren fields. On the second day, the army crossed a great river, and before long, they entered the Kaelunen. There Caitren saw the great garden of Gundmar. It was a fold of few trees but many thickets, though the army had no obstacle, as they simply stayed on the road north.

Each night, many tents were set up within the Kaelunen. Fires were made to stay warm, and being in a garden of many thickets, finding fuel was quite easy. It was not until they stopped that Caitren realized she had no tent and very little food. She watched the soldiers set up camp for the night and instead tended to her horse, trying to look busy. Caitren slept by her horse and remained in all her armor.

A few scouts were sent farther up the road to see how close the enemy was to reaching Bared Nar. The scouts, upon returning, reported that Vyroun's army was quickly approaching Bared Nar, and that the riders needed to hurry. The trouble was that even though the Woodland army wanted to reach Bared Nar in time, they also did not want to press their horses on without rest and have them reach battle without strength to face the enemy.

It was the fourth night since leaving the Woodlands. Caitren heard they would arrive at Bared Nar sometime the following night. She always kept her distance from the soldiers in hopes no one would find out that she had snuck into the army, and she tried her best to mind her own business. This worked well on the previous nights, but on that night, one soldier noticed that she was not joining in with any of the other soldiers there.

"Are you going to pitch your tent for the night?" asked the soldier. Caitren turned her head but tried to cover her face. She did not want to speak nor remove her helm, otherwise the soldiers would discover that a lady was amongst them, and they surely would not want her to go through the dangers of war. Caitren, too, did not want to enter a war, however, she needed to find her friends. Thinking quickly, Caitren began coughing so that she would be able to speak to the soldier.

"Well, we must not be sick on the eve of war!" said the soldier. Caitren was handed some water. She did not speak, but instead took it and patted the soldier on the shoulder in gratitude. Caitren was then surprised to find it was Gamenan standing before her. For a moment she was petrified, thinking that he might recognize her, and

Caitren put her arm over her mouth to cover what could be seen of her face. Gamenan, however, motioned towards a company of soldiers at a fire nearby.

"Come and sit by the fire with the rest of us!" said Gamenan. She was nervous, but did not want to appear too suspicious. Caitren hesitantly made her way to the other soldiers with Gamenan. However, she made sure to keep to the back of the group. Some were still wearing their helms, likely because of the cold, so fortunately Caitren did not stand out by keeping her own helm on.

Some soldiers were laughing, though it was not as lively as the party within the hall of Itilikin. Caitren could sense a feeling of doom amongst several of them. Gamenan was among the loudest of the soldiers jesting to each other.

"I will revel in this coming day," said Gamenan. "For after my heroics, I can tell all the fair maidens in Itilikin of my deeds!"

"That is if you live," said one soldier as some others laughed. "You cannot take a woman's hand if you are dead!"

"Oh no," said Gamenan. "I will find one after this battle. Fear not! For if upon the battlefield you see a lady more beautiful than you could ever dream of, then you have met a Rhykwen, as your death has come. She will take me by the hand, and what a gift that would be!"

"I am not so sure, Gamenan," said another soldier. "For we have not seen you have such luck with ladies before."

"You are mistaken, for the night before we rode off, I received a dance and a kiss from not just any lady, but a beautiful elven woman," said Gamenan. The soldiers did not appear to believe him, though Caitren had seen it and knew Gamenan to be truthful. Gamenan spoke on. "I will have the hand of a fair lady, no matter what becomes of me upon the field of battle. And I say take heart to all of you, for this coming battle is where you win a fair maiden's heart!"

The soldiers eventually went to sleep for the night. Caitren kept her distance from the other soldiers and did not speak to any of them. She returned to her horse and slept out in the cold, though Caitren had enough blankets and coverlets to keep warm. Still, she was not able to sleep very well. She could not remove any of her armor before sleeping, because it would risk her being discovered, and also because back in the armory in Itilikin Caitren had much trouble putting all the armor on by herself, and she would not have the time to put it all back on in the morning when the army would ride swiftly to war. It was uncomfortable to sleep in all the armor, but Caitren made no fuss. She was overcome with fear about the coming battle, but was certain that she would find some answer there as to what had become of her friends, though she knew not what that answer would be.

"Oh, I hope my friends are all well," said Caitren quietly to herself. "They must be alive, for my heart tells me that they are."

The hours passed, and soon dawn arrived. Soldiers were rising and readying to leave. Suddenly, however, several scouts arrived with much haste and began shouting to the army.

"Ride now! The army is reaching Bared Nar!" shouted the scouts. "Gundmar shall be under siege! Make haste, men!"

"Time turns out to be far against us," said one of the soldiers to Gamenan as they ran by Caitren. Caitren moved in haste, as did the other soldiers. She kept her eye on Gamenan and tried to remain close by, as there was at least one soldier within the army that she had grown familiar with. Soldiers were hurrying to put on their armor, put out their fires, and ready their horses. Tents were pitched everywhere, but no one bothered to take them down, for there was not time. Soon all soldiers were on their horses and riding off again.

"How great are Vyroun's forces in this battle?" said one of the soldiers near Caitren as they rode.

"Scouts say well over one hundred thousand strong," said another soldier.

"One hundred thousand?" said Gamenan. "If it is all goblins, then we might handle it, but greater creatures like trolls are far more formidable."

"No," answered the soldier. "It is an army with not a few, but legions, of trolls, ogres, the dragon, and surely deoflas when the night falls."

"Our horses can ride through mindless goblins with ease," said Gamenan. All his boisterousness had gone. "But trolls and ogres will surely not be so simple. I know not what hope we have on our own."

"Had we departed earlier, we could have met them before they reach the city," said another soldier.

"Nay, but our full forces had not yet gathered by then," said the first soldier. "But even with our full strength, I do not think we can defeat them."

Caitren trembled. Though she had fought a pack of goblins before with her friends, Caitren had never entered a war with a great army of fell things. She rode quickly with the rest of the army, but Caitren wished that she were back at the house of Dalgarinan and Mairawin, exploring the woods and dancing among the fairies in the moonlight. I daresay that she felt regret upon sneaking into the army, but at the same time, Caitren greatly sought to find her friends, and her heart told her that she would find them in the battle. And that was what stayed Caitren's feet from turning back, afraid as she was.

The army rode on without break, for there was no time. Caitren saw the end of a mountain range ahead, and from what she had heard, the city of Bared Nar lay at the very end of it. She knew they were getting close. The hours passed, and soon it was afternoon. Because Caitren was among many soldiers, she was able to hear word of what was taking place in Bared Nar.

"The city is now in flames!" Caitren overheard. "Ligwyrm has come. The lower level is being turned to rubble. Siege towers reach the walls and the army begins to storm the city!"

Caitren looked around her, and upon finding that Gamenan rode right beside her she covered her face, although Caitren was certain Gamenan did not know that it was her riding next to him. In fact, he looked to another fellow rider as he spoke. "If we can reach the city before nightfall, then our riders could defeat many forces with ease, I should think. However, I do not think we will be there until nightfall. What advantage can we gain against them in battle during the night?"

And Gamenan, though he was young like Caitren, only a little older, was absolutely right. The riders of the Woodlands would have a greater chance of defeating the forces of Mûrondûn if they were to meet in the daylight.

However, the soldiers could not wait until morning to fight, for the city was already under siege, and thus the riders needed to meet the enemy straight away, before the kingdom of Gundmar might fall.

When the light of day had waned, Caitren could see that several soldiers around her were in despair, as Vyroun's army was far more formidable in the night. Still, they rode onward, and before long they were close. The riders after some time emerged from the garden of the Kaelunen. They no longer rode in a file along the North Woodland Road, but instead gathered together. Caitren was not sure where the king was, though certainly somewhere to the front of the army. She stopped, and Gamenan was by her again.

Caitren grew very afraid as she waited. Of course, she was afraid throughout the entire ride, and I cannot blame her, but she was most fearful now that the army had arrived at the battle. She could hear the roar of another army somewhere not very far ahead. Drums echoed. Caitren and the soldiers took a short rest while the army gathered. She knew not what they would do next, other than ride off to war, of course. There was no speech given, though there were some riders, higher in rank within the army, that were riding around and giving direction to the many soldiers gathered.

"We will ride quietly into battle," said a passing rider. "If they do not know we are here, then we might be able to surprise them. No horn shall sound, no cry shall be screamed. We will ride immediately when all are gathered."

Caitren waited and her hands shook. Soon she would be in the middle of a great battle, a place she had no desire to be in. In the night, Caitren noticed something glowing under her very nose. She looked down to find that the necklace Mairawin had given her was shining brightly beneath her armor. Caitren quickly tried to conceal it, in case Gamenan might recognize it. Gamenan was next to her, but he did not appear to see the glow from her jewel, as he paid more notice to what lay ahead.

"The fire's glow can be seen from here," said Gamenan. Caitren could not yet see the city of Bared Nar, however, a great glow lit the night sky from what must have been many flames burning. There was no time to think, though, for the full army had gathered.

"Take courage! We ride now!" said a captain. The soldiers ahead began to ride forward. Caitren drew her sword, and her hand trembled as she held it. Soon it was time for her to go. Caitren, Gamenan, and the soldiers around them began to slowly ride forward. Before long, their horses began to pick up speed. Caitren was approaching the top of a hill, and when she reached it, she was able to see the city of Bared Nar, and the army that was laying siege to it.

Even though it was night, Caitren could see a black sheet covering the field before Bared Nar. It went into and covered the valley behind the north and south towers of the city, and the army ended somewhere beyond the north end of the mountains, along the edge of the Kyrrwood. Caitren could not see the end to this army. She grew quite frightened, for though Caitren had seen a pack of goblins and some trolls before, she had never before seen such an enormous and frightening gathering of enemies. Only her encounter with Vyroun himself was a greater nightmare.

At the moment, it did not appear that the army of

Mûrondûn had noticed the riders of Itilikin approaching. From what Caitren could see, they were not marching towards the attacking riders. As the horses rode more swiftly, the ground beneath her began to rumble. Soon Caitren was riding very swiftly with the other soldiers, and she looked ahead to see that it would not be long before she would be in the middle of a great battle.

Before long, Vyroun's army had taken notice of the riders approaching. Caitren soon heard arrows whistling, and a rider or two nearby were hit. Caitren grew even more frightened, but she would not run. Ahead, trolls and ogres were at the front of the lines, while behind were goblins arching and trying to shoot the riders Caitren rode with. They were not able to take out very many riders, though. The riders reached the enemy lines and rode through them.

Caitren could see the very first Itilikin soldiers meeting the enemy forces. The trolls and ogres held clubs and swung them at the horsemen. Some riders and horses went flying to their deaths, but fortunately there were far too many horsemen for the enemy to repel. Soon the vile creatures were struck and felled. It took a little time, but when Caitren reached the enemy lines, the army of Itilikin had broken through them. Her sword was in hand and ready, and as much as Caitren disliked wielding such a tool of war, she knew that she had no choice, for she was no longer in the peaceful Woodlands, but on a field of battle in search of her friends. If Caitren wanted to find her friends, she would have to take heart and fight what enemies stood between them.

Caitren rode onward. Now and then she needed to be careful not to ride too close to a troll or an ogre. She swung her sword and struck trolls whenever able, though it certainly took more than one strike to fell creatures of that size. But fortunately, Caitren was not the only rider facing them, as many Woodland soldiers too were striking the enemy forces. Soon Caitren was riding past many goblins and wicked men. Many times, such enemies were simply run over by the horses, and when they were not, the soldiers struck these enemies as they rode by. The riders soon had defeated a decent portion of Vyroun's army, but when looking ahead, Caitren still could see no end to the enemy forces.

The army of Itilikin made a very valiant charge and was able to drive through the front lines of Mûrondûn. However, the horses soon began to tire, and the soldiers from the Woodlands were forced to fight with swords against the fell creatures. The advantage of the horses was still great, but that advantage was growing smaller, as the riders became easier for the enemies to strike, and some were beginning to fall in battle.

Caitren struck what goblins were within her reach, though she tried not to ride near a troll or an ogre unless they had their back turned. Whenever Caitren was able to strike such a large creature, she aimed for either the head or the neck, as it appeared that striking them there would kill the creatures far more quickly. Caitren's horse soon stopped, and she had no enemies near her. She very quickly looked about the battlefield.

"Oh! I don't like fighting at all," she said to herself.

Some riders were making their way into the valley of Bared Nar. All three levels of the city were in flames. It appeared that the Gundmar soldiers had retreated to the third and final level. Caitren thought she saw a great shadow of black mist moving through Bared Nar. She also heard great screeches, and Caitren knew all too well what creatures were making such sounds, for she had been possessed by one of them in the dungeon of Gulgurod. Though Caitren was able to repel it through a total rejection of evil, she did not at all wish to encounter such a fiendish foe again.

Ahead to the north were many more legions, extending along the borders of the Kyrrwood. Many riders were making their way to meet those forces. Caitren saw Gamenan among them, and she decided to keep close to him. Gamenan did not appear to know that he was being followed by the lady he had met the night before riding to war. Soon Caitren met more goblins, and some were riding wolves, just as the pack had been when they were hunting Caitren and her friends the past summer.

The north tower of Bared Nar was to Caitren's right, and not far was the border of the Kyrrwood. Several goblins and some ogres were ahead. The soldiers rode and slayed many of them, but legions still remained. Caitren appeared to be among only perhaps a couple thousand soldiers from the Woodlands, though it was difficult to tell. She found that the horses were a good advantage on a field of battle, as Caitren could quickly ride by and strike an enemy, and the horse's swiftness made it difficult for enemies to strike her. Still, many of her fellow soldiers were being killed, and Caitren was not sure that there were enough left to defeat Vyroun's army on their own.

A part of Caitren wanted to ride for the city instead, as she wanted to find her friends above all else, and she felt that she might have a greater chance of finding them within Bared Nar. Too many riders were behind, though, for Caitren to be able to turn around, and so she could only go farther north. She struck one goblin, and then Caitren reached out with her sword to strike an ogre.

Suddenly, however, Caitren found a stroke of bad luck. There was a troll right in front of her, and Caitren did her best to turn and ride past it. When Caitren pulled the reins, however, the troll swung his club at her. Caitren's horse stood on his hind legs and was barely able to avoid the swinging club. However, Caitren was taken by surprise and fell backward off of her horse. To make matters worse, her horse fled, and Caitren's helm fell off. Caitren tried to retrieve it, but it was kicked away by another horse that was passing by.

The troll swung his club at Caitren, and she had to roll away to evade it. Not only that, but Caitren needed to be careful not to be trampled by any oncoming riders of Itilikin. She tried to get back on her feet but could not. After having to roll around some more, Caitren drew close, mere feet away from the troll, well within its reach. But Caitren then noticed that something was glowing very brightly in the night, and it was hanging from around her neck.

The troll was about to grab Caitren, but instead he suddenly needed to shield his eyes. Caitren looked down at the necklace Mairawin had given her, and she was most grateful to have it. The blue jewel glowed with great radiance and was blinding the troll. A few goblins came to attack, but they, too, needed to shield their eyes.

Useful as her necklace was, though, it did not make Caitren invulnerable to such enemies facing her. An ogre then swung his club from behind and Caitren was nearly struck by it. She needed to roll again, and then was able to rise to her feet. She attacked what goblins there were, and it was easier, as they were blinded by the jewel around her neck. The troll and the ogre, however, were still formidable foes. Before long, Caitren was knocked back to the ground by the arm of the ogre. Fortunately, she was fine, though Caitren might have been greatly hurt if she was not wearing armor. She was back on the ground though and had to evade both the swinging of the troll's club and the stomping of the ogre's feet.

Suddenly, however, Caitren was given a stroke of luck. A spear hit the ogre, and the foul creature was slain. Caitren had to get up and out of the ogre's way as it fell. When the troll tried to swing his club at Caitren, a rider from behind swung his sword and felled the troll. The rider then looked to Caitren.

"The most beautiful of angels has descended upon this field of battle!" said the rider with surprise, and yet also jest. It was Gamenan. "The Rhykwen is fairer than I could possibly have imagined! I hope my time has not ended yet, though, for I do enjoy this battle thus far. Surely my death cannot be so soon."

"Oh, how could anyone enjoy battle?" said Caitren.

Caitren could no longer pretend that she was one of the soldiers, for the secret had been discovered. Caitren did not worry very much, though, for she had made it all the way to the field of battle without any soldiers finding out. Gamenan appeared to be his boisterous self again, although there was no mistaking that they were in the midst of a war. And his outgoing manner changed very quickly, for a few goblins and an ogre made their way to attack Caitren. She stood ready to fight, but Caitren worried that she was quite overmatched.

Just before the goblins and the ogre reached Caitren, however, Gamenan rode over and held his hand out. "Here! Climb on!" said Gamenan. She took his hand straight away and climbed upon Gamenan's horse. Caitren was grateful that Gamenan had taken her, but she was still in the midst of a field of battle, and enemies were legion in every direction that Caitren's eye could see.

"Hold on tightly!" said Gamenan. "Something seemed strange about you back when we camped, but I did not know that it was the lady Caitren beneath that helm."

Gamenan held the reins, and Caitren was seated in front of him. She needed to hold on with one hand, as Caitren did not want to fall off a horse for a second time, and she swung her sword at whatever foe they rode by with the other.

"A fair lady who loves to fight!" said Gamenan after Caitren swung her sword to slay a goblin. "I like you more and more, Caitren. A woman who enjoys fighting as much as we men do! If any man ever has your hand, he will hold the jealousy of many fellow men."

"No! I do not like to fight at all!" said Caitren. "For it is brute and barbaric."

"Are you sure?" said Gamenan, cleaving a goblin. "You seem quite good at fighting to me."

"That does not mean I enjoy it," said Caitren. "Dancing about the Woodlands and picking flowers is far better."

"Well, if you do not enjoy fighting then what on earth are you doing here?" said Gamenan.

"I am here to find my friends," said Caitren. "For they are surely going to be somewhere here. I know it!"

"I do not think you will find your friends in the middle of a field filled with goblins and other foul things," said

Gamenan. "Unless any of these trolls here are your friends, though I am doubtful."

"They are somewhere close," said Caitren. "My heart tells me that they are here, and I must see them again. And so, I came here with the army.

"Well," said Gamenan. "I must say again that I doubt your friends will be on this field of battle, nor in the city, and thus I know not where we might search. But you are in the midst of a war, and there is no escaping it now. We can search for your friends."

Gamenan and Caitren rode onward, though not as quickly as the other soldiers. Caitren struck what fell things she could, while Gamenan did the same. At one point the two of them rode by a troll who was about to swing his mace, but Caitren's jewel glowed and blinded the troll enough that it needed to shield its eyes, and Gamenan struck the foul creature. It was not felled, but at least she and Gamenan were able to escape the vile creature's reach.

"I say, what is that thing around your neck?" said Gamenan. "Back in the hall, I thought it was just a mere lady's trinket, but there seems to be much more to it than I first thought."

"Mairawin, the lady of the Woodlands, gave it to me," said Caitren.

"Did she?" said Gamenan. "Then it is surely of far greater use than what might first meet your eye. It appears to help protect you from enemies, though I know not how protective it truly is. Quite an advantage it is over these creatures of the night, for enemies are shielding their eyes when we meet them, and I am finding the task of felling them quite easy!"

"I am finding that to be so, also," said Caitren. She and Gamenan had ridden past the northern edge of the Silver Mountains, and the northern tower was behind them. The moon was out, and it shined brightly. When Caitren's jewel was in the moonlight, its glow grew stronger.

Caitren turned then towards the Kyrrwood to the east. It was very difficult to notice in the dark, but Caitren thought she saw some creatures coming out from the woods. She could not look for long, though, for they were in a battle, after all. She and Gamenan were forced to fight and slay a couple of nearby goblins. Then Caitren looked again to the Kyrrwood, and she found that her eyes were not cheating her. There were what appeared to be many men, though shorter and wider than a normal man. Not only that, but from what Caitren could see, they were also very heavily armored.

"What is in those woods over there?" said Caitren, pointing to the Kyrrwood and turning to see if Gamenan noticed them also. Gamenan's gaze also turned to the woods, and he had a very curious look upon his face.

"I say," said Gamenan. "Though I myself have never met any dwarves before, I am fairly certain that an army of them is coming out from the Kyrrwood. Strange this is, for I have not known of any dwarves living within these lands."

Caitren's spirits lifted and she rejoiced greatly. The hidden dwarven kingdom within the mountains had come to enter the war against Vyroun. Though the Woodland soldiers might not have been enough to defeat Vyroun's army, it appeared that they were no longer fighting alone. Sure enough, the dwarves began their attack upon the army of Mûrondûn.

"The dwarves have come! The dwarves have come!" said Caitren. "We are not alone! Another army has come to help us!"

The goblins and the other foul creatures soon took notice of another army entering the battle, and Caitren could tell that it was not a force they had been expecting to face. The enemy scrambled to fight this new army. However, Caitren found that the dwarves were very strong and quickly slayed one foe after another.

"I say, how did you know that an army of dwarves was coming to help us?" said Gamenan, who appeared quite baffled. "For that matter, how did you even know of an army of dwarves in these lands? To my knowledge, there are no dwarves in these lands."

"There is a hidden dwarven kingdom farther down these mountains," said Caitren. "One Adroegen found one time while wandering about, and he was leading me and my friends there in hopes of seeking their help in this war, before we were separated. And indeed, they have come to help!"

Another thought entered Caitren's mind, in regard to her friends. If only Adroegen and the rest of the company knew of the dwarves, and the dwarves had come to help in the war against Vyroun, then perhaps there was a good chance that Caitren's friends, or at least some of them, had made it to the dwarven kingdom and persuaded them to aid the north. Caitren grew certain that if she were to find her friends anywhere, they would surely be amongst the dwarves. And so, Caitren immediately knew where she needed to go.

"Gamenan, take me to the dwarves!" said Caitren. "For I wish to find my friends, and I am certain that if they are anywhere, they will be there."

"Very well. If you feel so sure, then I shall take you there," said Gamenan. And the two of them rode for the dwarves. Caitren had a renewed sense of hope, both that the army of Vyroun could be defeated, and that she would look upon her friends again.

Chapter Sixteen: Taken North

After marching with the dwarven army for five days, Edelbir and Kattalin had reached the end of the Silver Mountains, and the city of Bared Nar. The dwarves had been remarkably quiet during their march beneath the Kyrrwood, for they were clad in clinking armor and marched with clanking iron boots, oft on bare rock against the edge of the mountains.

The dwarves reached Bared Nar in the middle of the night, the very same night the army from Itilikin had reached the battle. Edelbir and Kattalin could hear the roar of Vyroun's army and the sounds of battle taking place ahead. The two of them were not anywhere near the front line of the dwarven army. However, being that Edelbir and Kattalin were normal folk while the soldiers around them were dwarves, who were much shorter, it was quite easy for the two of them to see what was ahead. Soon the dwarves had reached the very edge of the forest, and those in the front line had begun their attack.

"I hope they do not have warning that we were coming," said Kattalin as she looked ahead and saw quite a massive army of foul creatures. It would surely take a great force to defeat it, or if not that, then the advantage of surprise, which the dwarves hopefully had.

"And I hope we will find Gleowan and Vaenn somewhere," said Edelbir. "I know not what has become of our friends, and thus, I can only hope they are well."

The two of them looked ahead. It did not appear that Vyroun's forces had known of the dwarves, for Edelbir and Kattalin saw enemies being slain with haste, and no dwarves being felled. The dwarves advanced into the battle swiftly, and very soon, Edelbir and Kattalin would be in the midst of a war.

"We must remain together," said Kattalin. "I do not at all want to fight in a battle, for I would much prefer to swim about beyond the shores of the sea, but I am not going to turn back. Whatever it is that we are to face, you and I must stay alongside one another."

"I, too, do not wish to fight in a war," said Edelbir. "For I would rather be farming in a great open field. But I am ready to face what evil is ahead. And you and I must find our friends, and if we do, then we must fight alongside them."

Edelbir and Kattalin were soon at the edge of the Kyrrwood. The northern tower of Bared Nar stood tall in the mountain next to them. They could not see the flames in the city, but Edelbir and Kattalin could see a great red glow from the top of the mountain, and much smoke was rising. Legions of goblins and other foul things were ahead, though farther away they did see another army of horsemen fighting them. Edelbir and Kattalin thought that they must have come from the Woodlands. The dwarves that were lined in front of Edelbir and Kattalin charged to attack, and it was now time for the two of them to enter the battle also.

Both of them then charged at the enemy. I would say,

though, that Edelbir and Kattalin did not have too many foes to defeat, at least not right away. The dwarves had taken the enemy by surprise and were quickly slaying one foul creature after another. Goblins were being killed with ease. Trolls and ogres, even though they were much larger than dwarves, were not able to harm the dwarves with the thick armor they wore.

"Dwarves!" shouted many of the goblins. "Another army is upon us! Kill those ground-dwelling maggots!"

"Where on earth did dwarves come from?" said another goblin. "I ain't seen no dwarves in these lands before!"

"Goblins! How I hate the obverse of dwarves," said Lofar, who was fighting nearby Edelbir and Kattalin. "For while we dwarves will mine our own treasures and forge them ourselves, goblins will seek to take them from us. They are thieves! Foul and evil! Looters! Slay them all!"

And Edelbir and Kattalin fought in a battle greater than they had ever taken part in. Kattalin saw no end to the enemies ahead of her. Though she and Edelbir had fought against a pack of goblins before, this battle had so many thousands of foul things that Kattalin thought there might never be an end to it. She and Edelbir fought close by to Lofar, and they had to defeat a few goblins that reached them. The dwarves advanced farther into the field of battle, though there were still many foul things to the north.

"Where is it that we must go now?" said Kattalin to Edelbir. She wondered if they should make for the city, in case anyone from the company might be there, though there was still a distance to go to enter Bared Nar, and many enemies stood in their way. Even if she and Edelbir made it into the city of Gundmar, Bared Nar was a large city, thus finding their friends would be difficult, and that was if Gleowan and Vaenn were even in the city at all.

"I think we can only fight for now," said Edelbir. "Hopefully we can defeat all of these forces, and maybe then we can search for our friends."

It was sometime in the night, though they knew not precisely how close morning was. Edelbir remembered his fight with the goblin chief, and how the morning had turned the tide. Morning, however, appeared to be several hours away. Vyroun's army was still formidable, but at least more help had come, as the dwarves had joined the battle, giving the northern kingdoms a greater chance of victory. Edelbir and Kattalin felt they had succeeded in aiding the north and had fulfilled the task that Adroegen thought to be vital in defeating Vyroun's forces.

On the field, Caitren was riding with Gamenan and making for the dwarves. They needed to ride by some enemies and strike them as they passed. Caitren tried to keep her eye fixed upon the dwarves that had come out from the forest. They were fighting fiercely, and it was quite difficult to pierce a dwarf's armor. They were clearly very good craftsmen. Gamenan and Caitren drew closer to the dwarves, and Caitren searched for any members of her company.

"My friends must be among them. I know it!" said Caitren. She could not see her friends, but Caitren was in the midst of a great battle, thus it was surely going to take some time to find them, if they were there.

The two of them had reached the dwarves, although there were many of them. "Do you see your friends anywhere here?" asked Gamenan. Caitren thought that it should not be difficult to find her friends, if they were amongst the dwarves, for the dwarves were much shorter than any normal man or woman. And so, if any of Caitren's friends were there, they would surely be easy to spot.

"I cannot see them yet," said Caitren. There were too many trolls and ogres in the way, hindering her sight. She and Gamenan rode onward, having to strike a couple of ogres as they went.

Caitren's eye turned towards the border of the Kyrrwood. She soon saw two folk there, both in cloaks rather than the heavy armor that the dwarves wore. Also, the two of them were far taller than the dwarves, being as tall as any normal man or woman would be. Caitren could not yet tell who they were, as they were a small distance away and it was hard to see in the night, but one appeared to be a man of dark hair who was quite tall and looked strong, while the other appeared to be a fair lady of red hair. A great hope rose within Caitren's heart, for she might have found two members of her company.

"There are two folk amongst the dwarves over there!" said Caitren, pointing. "Near the edge of the forest. I cannot know with certainly, but they may be Edelbir and Kattalin from my company. Let us ride to meet them!"

"Then that is where I shall take you," said Gamenan. "And then I can meet your friends, if they are who you believe them to be."

They both rode for the two folk that fought amongst the dwarves. Caitren could not recognize them with certainly in the dark, but if they were indeed Edelbir and Kattalin, then they would surely recognize Caitren, as the jewel she wore glowed and illuminated her face. They both fought amongst the dwarves and felled what goblins came to them as Caitren and Gamenan drew closer. Caitren's heart then rejoiced, as she soon recognized with certainty that the man was indeed Edelbir and the lady was Kattalin. When the two finally noticed her, Caitren knew straight away that their hearts lifted also.

"Caitren!" said Kattalin. "Is that really you? We worried you had met your end!"

"Edelbir! Kattalin!" said Caitren, getting off the horse. Gamenan remained with her and her friends. "Both of you are alive! My heart knew it! Once I saw the dwarves arrive, I was sure that it must have been my friends who had brought them here!"

"This is a great surprise," said Edelbir. "We have found you, and we were not expecting to! Gleowan and Vaenn were looking for you, though. Now we just need to find the both of them."

"Gleowan and Vaenn are not here with you?" asked Caitren with a sudden unease. "If they are not with you, then where might they be?"

Edelbir and Kattalin quickly retold their tale to Caitren, starting with Adroegen falling off the cliff, which Caitren had already known of, as the lady of the Woodlands had told her back when Caitren stayed in her home. Kattalin spoke as the dwarves slayed a small group of goblins near them. "We chose to split, with Edelbir and I searching for Adroegen, and then looking for the hidden kingdom of the dwarves. After searching for days, we found no sign of Adroegen, and we are certain that he is gone. It hurt greatly to end our search for him, but we were certain he would have wanted us to find the dwarves.

Gleowan and Vaenn went searching for you, hoping to save you from whatever torment awaited you."

"Gleowan and Vaenn never found me. Oh, I hope they are all right," said Caitren, who then told her own tale of being brought before Vyroun himself, and how great a nightmare it was, and then escaping and reaching the Woodlands. "I miss the Woodlands, for it is such a magical and enchanting place. But I needed to find my friends. And so, I snuck into the army and rode here, thinking that I might find you, and I did! Oh! You must meet my newest friend, Gamenan of the Itilikin army!"

"Edelbir am I, and most pleased I am to meet you," said Edelbir.

"Thankful I am that you brought so much help here," said Gamenan. "For this might turn the tide in this war. Never before have I met you, Edelbir, but know that I now consider you to be the highest of friends."

"And I am Kattalin," said Kattalin.

"I find another lady so fair and beautiful upon this field of battle!" said Gamenan. "And I, too, consider you now to be the highest of friends, for the aid you have brought here. I and the Woodland soldiers could not be more grateful. And let me say what a delight it is to look upon the fair lady Kattalin, whose face is pale as pearls and whose hair is as red as coral beneath the sea. A rare and unique beauty do you possess, one that I could not be more fortunate to see."

"You are most charming, Gamenan," said Kattalin, as Gamenan took a bow. Caitren quietly laughed to herself, as she had been quite certain that Gamenan would give Kattalin such flattery upon seeing her, as he had with her when they first met. Kattalin smiled and gave a small bow.

The four of them then rejoined the fight, although they did not go far onto the battlefield. The dwarves had given the north a great deal of help. At the very least, it seemed that there was now enough strength, between the dwarves and the Woodland riders, to challenge Vyroun's forces, although there were still other creatures that were not on the field of battle, but in the city itself. Vyroun's army was still much greater in number than the northern forces, even with the dwarves. However, the surprise was an advantage, at least for now.

Soon, though, the winds of a hurricane descended upon the battlefield. Caitren looked to the north and spotted a familiar and fearsome foe. Ligwyrm was coming from the north, it appeared, and he was entering the battle. Caitren knew from her imprisonment in Gulgurod that Ligwyrm would be with the army, and so she wondered why the dragon had been absent from the battle since she arrived. Caitren had no time to wonder though, for a dragon was coming, and such a creature was far more formidable than any pack of goblins, or trolls, or ogres.

"Oh, no," said Caitren. The dragon was flying in their direction, though it appeared Ligwyrm did not notice them amongst the many fighting soldiers.

As the dragon drew nearer, however, Caitren noticed something else that was quite peculiar. The moon was behind her, and in the moonlight, Caitren thought that she saw something else fluttering and flapping. Caitren was certain that it could not have been the dragon, but she had no time to look and see what it was, for Ligwyrm was approaching. She retreated, as did Edelbir and Kattalin.

As they did, something swiftly flew over them.

Ligwyrm's fiery breath had been unleashed, however, it was not aimed for the soldiers on the ground, but rather at whatever creature had flown past Caitren and her friends. More of such creatures immediately followed. Though it was difficult to tell in the dark what they were, these creatures flew swiftly for the dragon and began attacking him. Caitren then heard the sounds of eagles.

She turned to the south, and Caitren's spirits lifted higher. Caitren, Edelbir, and Kattalin had seen a few of the great birds of the forests, but never so many as they did now. Many eagles faced Ligwyrm. Huf and Ule were soon there, accompanied by several owls. Scores of falcons and hawks arrived soon after. Then farther to the south, Caitren could barely see many tree men stomping upon goblins and fighting trolls and ogres.

"The Fornwood has come!" said Caitren. Ligwyrm tried to burn the eagles, but they were swift and strong in flight, and so the dragon had trouble defeating so many of them all at once. Caitren soon saw Orn flying above, with the other eagles. She remembered the wound he had suffered when the company first met him, but now he appeared to be healed. Caitren also looked for Andor, but strangely she could not see the lord of the Fornwood anywhere.

While Caitren, Edelbir, and Kattalin were on the battlefield, Adroegen rode upon Andor towards Bared Nar. They were high in the air, near the clouds, hoping to keep out of sight. Adroegen could see a great army upon the ground, and flames engulfing the city. A sheer black mist moved about Bared Nar, however, that was not for Adroegen to worry about. The wizard instead would be the one to face Vyroun's most terrible of servants, the swarm of deoflas that had overwhelmed the city of Bared Nar. Adroegen had a much greater foe to defeat.

"Keep out of sight," said Adroegen to Andor. Flying beside him was Ganglere, upon Crawa, but before long they had reached the city, and it was time for Ganglere's task of repelling the fiendish demons there. Adroegen watched Ganglere and Crawa fly lower towards the great shadow. He was barely able to see Ganglere leap from the lord of the ravens and land within the city. Adroegen then heard a thunderous voice echo through the city, and a blinding light shined from the oak staff of the wizard. Then many loud screeches and screams sounded, and Adroegen heard what sounded like the steaming of kettles and the sizzling of flesh upon a frying pan. The deoflas were a very formidable foe, but Ganglere appeared more than equal to them. Adroegen watched many ghostlike creatures try to flee, and the shadow began to slowly thin out, though Ganglere had a great swarm of such devilish creatures to face, thus Adroegen was sure it would take time to entirely rid Bared Nar of the frightening creatures.

Andor flew onward north, and once they had made it past the smoke coming from the fires within Bared Nar, Adroegen looked upon the great field in the valley of the city. The falcons and the owls were striking the enemy forces and felling many of them. Thousands of tree men of the Fornwood were advancing north, stomping and crushing goblins and ripping trolls and ogres apart. Vyroun's army was still massive, but they appeared taken by surprise and soon it seemed that they were beginning to retreat. The war though was not won yet, for many enemies still remained, and much strength was needed to drive them away.

Ahead, the fiery serpent faced the great eagles. Ligwyrm was conjuring his inferno, and Adroegen saw a few eagles falling to the ground in flames. The eagles, however, were many. One after another, they readied their claws and speared the belly of the serpent. Before long Ligwyrm roared and recoiled, and then he lost his balance in the air. The mighty birds persisted in their attack, and soon the dragon was cast down to the earth. But the serpent was not dead, for he was a great beast of evil, and one who could not so easily be done away with.

"My eagle eyes are very keen," said Andor to Adroegen. "Though we are at a distance, I see three of your friends who came to my home, Caitren, Edelbir, and Kattalin, beside the dragon where he has fallen. They will surely be in grave danger."

Adroegen looked to where the dragon had fallen. Though his eyes were not as keen as those of an eagle, nor the other great birds, Adroegen thought he could see some of his friends there also. His spirits lifted upon discovering for himself that some members of his company lived, but Adroegen also felt a great worry come over him, for a dragon was at their side, a creature whose armor was impenetrable by the swords or spears of men. Though Adroegen and his friends had escaped Ligwyrm before, he feared that such luck might not hold this time, and he wondered if he should save his friends first. Being a Vistivar now, Adroegen could have defeated the dragon with ease. However, he also did not want word to reach the enemy that the heir of Buludin had emerged, for the secrecy could be an advantage. There was, however, no other kin that Adroegen had in that world, and even if

Vyroun learned that he was coming to face him, Adroegen had the strength now to defeat him.

"Make for the dragon. If I must defeat him myself, I hope to do so swiftly, without drawing attention to myself," said Adroegen. He and Andor though were a distance away, and Adroegen's friends may have been too far away to be able to reach and save them from what danger they were now in.

"The eagles are making for another attack on the dragon now," said Andor.

On the field of battle, the dragon fell down to the earth, and Caitren, Edelbir, and Kattalin had to run out of the way, otherwise the dragon would have fallen on top of them. They were just able to avoid being squashed by the falling Ligwyrm, who landed right beside them. Caitren and her friends backed away as swiftly as they could. Though there were many eagles that could match this terrible foe, to Caitren and her friends, who were mere humans, that foe was still very deadly.

The eagles flew at the dragon and attacked again. Ligwyrm, however, was on his belly, and so the eagles were not able to hurt him as they had before. The dragon took some time to regain his balance, and then he rose back to his feet while flapping his wings to wave the eagles away. Ligwyrm appeared to be hurt, though not greatly. The dragon was just about to release his fiery breath upon the eagles and fly off, but then his gaze for but a moment reached Caitren, Edelbir, and Kattalin. Ligwyrm's eyes remained fixed upon them, and they grew quite worried that he recognized them.

The dragon's eyes widened upon seeing them, and he

let out a great roar and began to approach them. It was quite clear that Ligwyrm had recognized the three of them from past encounters with him, where they and the rest of the company were lucky to escape. Caitren grew quite scared, for she expected that the dragon would conjure his fiery breath, and Caitren fled with Edelbir and Kattalin.

The dragon, however, did not unleash his breath upon the three of them, even though Caitren, Edelbir, and Kattalin were all certain that he would. Ligwyrm instead gave chase as they ran from him. Several eagles attacked the serpent, but they were unable to hinder Ligwyrm as he made for Caitren and her friends. His wings did take flight, but he stayed very low to the ground, and thus the eagles had great difficulty flying below and clawing at the belly of the serpent, which was the most vulnerable place for the claws of the eagles to strike the beast.

"Run as swiftly as you can!" said his thunderous voice behind them. "You will not escape me this time!"

Caitren looked back, and the dragon was quickly catching up with her, Edelbir, and Kattalin. The dwarves threw axes and the Woodland soldiers threw spears at the fiery serpent, but no weapon made by man could pierce the armor of a dragon. Eagles flew in to try and attack, but none were able to hinder Ligwyrm. Caitren found it strange that the fiery breath had not been unleashed upon her and her friends, but she soon found out the reason.

"The lord of the north seeks you, and I will take you to him," said the dragon. Caitren then remembered that she and her friends were to be brought before Vyroun himself, and a great fear came over her, for she had already been taken to the lord of the dark kingdom, and never before had she been through such a terrible nightmare. Caitren ran as swiftly as she could, for she did not want to be imprisoned again, as Caitren was unsure of what Vyroun might do after she was taken to him before, refused to serve him, and in the end escaped the dark lord.

The eagles did not cease in their attack upon the fiery serpent, however, they were unable to hinder the dragon. Though Caitren, Edelbir, and Kattalin all ran swiftly, and though they had been lucky to escape the fiery serpent of the west before, this time they would have no such luck. The shadow of the dragon soon was upon them, and Caitren was grabbed by the claws of Ligwyrm. Edelbir and Kattalin, too, were scooped up in the dragon's other foot, and then the three of them were taken into the air.

"Oh, the grip of a dragon is far worse than that of a troll," said Kattalin. The claws squeezed tightly around Caitren, and she was about to cry, for she did not want to return to Vyroun. Edelbir and Kattalin were being squeezed together, and neither was able to move. Edelbir tried to find a way to escape, but soon there was no chance. Before long they were far above the ground, and so even if they were to somehow escape the dragon's grip, they would only fall a great distance to their deaths. Caitren, Edelbir, and Kattalin felt very helpless.

"I have taken your friends to the dark lord of the north, and now I will take you also!" said Ligwyrm as he flew them away from the battle.

"Taken our friends?" said Caitren to herself as they flew farther north. She grew even more afraid. Caitren, Edelbir, and Kattalin were unsure of what had become of Gleowan and Vaenn, and she feared greatly that the dragon had taken them to Vyroun, and that they too would meet a terrible fate, if they had not suffered one already.

Caitren had worried that the two of them had already met their end, but if they had indeed been taken to Vyroun, then it would seem that the company was about to be reunited, save for Adroegen. Caitren saw the Black Mountains ahead, but the dragon was not taking them to Gulgurod, where she was once imprisoned, but instead he appeared to be taking them deeper into Vyroun's kingdom. Caitren did not want to give up hope, but she was beginning to be overtaken by despair. She had been able to escape from Gulgurod, whether by great resilience or by sheer luck, but Caitren could not see any hope of escaping from the heart of Mûrondûn.

Adroegen, from farther behind, watched as his friends were taken away by Ligwyrm. He wanted to save his friends, but at the same time he did not want to reveal to the enemy that the heir to Buludin was coming to challenge him. And so, Adroegen faced a difficult choice.

"The dragon has your friends," said Andor. "If the eagles attack Ligwyrm now, they would surely fall to their deaths."

"Do not attack the serpent," said Adroegen, with his eye fixed upon Ligwyrm. "For he retreats from the battle, thus there is no need to fight him now."

"Will Ligwyrm kill them?" asked Andor. "Must we save your friends before making for Vyroun's stronghold?"

Adroegen looked upon the dragon as he flew north. He grew very certain that if Ligwyrm were going to kill Caitren, Edelbir, and Kattalin, the serpent would have easily done so already. Adroegen then remembered that in the Dead Forest the goblin lieutenant had ordered the pack to take his friends to Vyroun himself. He felt certain that there was time still to save them, although Adroegen did worry that he might be wrong.

"The dragon will take them to Norungad, the stronghold of Vyroun himself," said Adroegen. "They must be going there, or else the dragon would surely have killed them rather than take them captive. The goblin pack was ordered to take my friends captive back when we were last together. And so, we need not stray from our task, for the dragon takes them to the very place that we ourselves make for."

"Your company must have been troublesome when they were hunted," said Andor.

"Indeed," said Adroegen. "For I cast away the Night's Jewel, which the enemy sought greatly, and some creatures that Vyroun hoped would serve him we defeated. My friends were told when last together that Vyroun admires how long they have lasted, and that he would offer them one chance for clemency, if they would agree to serve him. But I am certain they will refuse. We must hurry, or else their fates will be terrible to behold."

"Very well," said the lord of the Fornwood. "If they are to be brought before the lord of Mûrondûn, then we best follow Ligwyrm. For wherever they are taken, the dark lord will surely be."

"Have a few eagles follow," said Adroegen. "For we will need a few more eagles to get my friends out of that dark kingdom. But they must also keep out of sight. I do not wish for Vyroun to know that I come to face him."

Andor made the scream of an eagle. It took some time, but soon a few other eagles were following behind. Andor spoke to them. "Follow that dragon, and keep out of sight! Do not attack, for Ligwyrm holds three friends captive!"

The eagles flew closely together, and Adroegen found Orn to be among them. He looked behind, and the city of Bared Nar was now far away. The sounds of battle grew faint. The eagles were swift in flight and covered a great distance in little time. Adroegen's eye then turned back to the dragon. The walls of the dark kingdom were ahead. A great distance away to the west, Adroegen could see Gulgurod, the mouth of Mûrondûn. Ligwyrm, however, did not make for that fortress, but instead flew towards the very heart of Vyroun's kingdom.

"All takes place as I thought. Ligwyrm is not making for Gulgurod," said Adroegen. "He is taking them to Norungad, the very stronghold of Vyroun in the heart of his kingdom, precisely the place that I first wished for you to take me."

"We will follow him there," said Andor. "Though we must hide behind the many mountains in that dark land, for if we do not, then Vyroun will surely see us coming. The eagles must reach the stronghold of Norungad unseen, and then we must find your friends and get them out of the dark place they will soon enter."

"And I will seek to defeat he who will hold them captive," said Adroegen. "We will do both tasks in but one single stroke."

Adroegen remembered the words of Oaknut, that all of his friends still lived, but that the old oak tree sensed grave danger. The tree was right, that Adroegen might need to face and defeat Vyroun while saving his friends all at once. Andor and the other eagles passed over the wall into Vyroun's kingdom. Adroegen and his friends were no longer in decent places. A very dark fortress was ahead, with a great tower at its center. Ligwyrm soon reached

Norungad, the fortress and stronghold of Vyroun himself. Adroegen, upon Andor, made his way there, weaving around and hiding behind many scattered and dark mountains within the black land that was Mûrondûn. Above, all the stars were veiled, and if it were day, no sunlight would have made its way into Vyroun's kingdom.

Chapter Seventeen:
A Jewel from the Stars

Caitren did not want to see any more of the dreadful place that was Vyroun's kingdom, for she had seen enough when captive in Gulgurod. The dragon flew around one mountain after another. Occasionally, Caitren could see doors into the mountains, with heaps of treasure lying at the doorsteps. Beneath her was a black and barren land. There was no one to be seen on the ground within the dark kingdom, as the kingdom had emptied and was on the field before Bared Nar. That battle, however, was now far away, and Caitren looked ahead to see where they were being taken. She, Edelbir, and Kattalin were flown just a little farther.

Ahead was a great fortress of black stone. The walls were very tall, perhaps double the height of the walls of Bared Nar. Norungad was a circular stronghold, appearing to be around three furlongs wide. Six turrets projected from the outer wall, all looking very ominous and evil in shape. Caitren saw some goblins and other creatures standing guard upon the battlements and along the wall's parapet, though there seemed to be no need for the stronghold to be well guarded, for in order to reach it, an army would first need to enter the kingdom of Mûrondûn itself, either by climbing over the Daur Igina, the Black Mountains that bordered the land, or by breaking through the fortress of Gulgurod at the mouth of Vyroun's kingdom. A great gate lay to the front of Vyroun's lair, and to the center of the circle formed by the outside walls was a great tower. At the top Caitren saw a black window, but inside it was dark.

Ligwyrm before long passed over the wall of Norungad, and behind the wall was a great ward. The dragon swooped close to the ground and then he suddenly loosened his grip upon Caitren, Edelbir, and Kattalin, who were dropped into the ward. Caitren took a tumble, which hurt a good deal, though she did not expect to be treated with any kind of mercy by their enemies. Edelbir and Kattalin were both alright and rose to their feet. Behind them was the gate into the stronghold, and ahead was another gate leading to the keep, which was about four fathoms high, and at the heart of the keep was the great tower that was most frightening to look upon. Several goblins then made their way to them and took away their weapons. The goblins pointed their swords at Caitren, Edelbir, and Kattalin, making them close ranks. Caitren's necklace though was glowing quite brightly, and in result, many goblins were being blinded by its light and needed to cover their eyes.

"Dim that light!" said one goblin as he held his hand over his eyes. Another grabbed Caitren and tried to take her necklace away, but he was unable to. The goblin instead appeared to burn his hand when it got too close to the jewel around Caitren's neck.

"Ouch! What on earth is this trinket?" said the goblin. Caitren knew that it was a Galesir, coming from the stars themselves, but she knew not its full magic. However, she was indeed finding the jewel to be quite useful, just as Mairawin told her she would.

"Bind her hands! She might be up to something with that jewel!" said one goblin. Edelbir and Kattalin's hands were bound, but when the goblins tried to tie Caitren's hands, they had to shield their eyes from the jewel's light, and so binding her hands took quite some time.

"No matter," said the first goblin. "Our master will destroy it, and then he will destroy you!"

"This is where you will die!" said another goblin. "You don't have any chance of escaping here!"

The three of them were kept there for a short time. Before long, however, there came a somewhat pleasant surprise. Well, perhaps I should not say pleasant, as the company was trapped in Vyroun's fortress with no way to escape, but goblins soon brought out two more prisoners. Gleowan and Vaenn were alright, although both of them appeared to be quite afraid. Upon being reunited though, Caitren was happy, though I daresay only for about a brief moment.

"You're alive!" said Edelbir. Gleowan and Vaenn took a moment to answer. Both were looking upon the keep and the tower.

"I suppose that we are," said Gleowan. "I see you have made it this far also, though I am not sure of how much longer we will go."

"What happened to both of you?" asked Caitren. Gleowan and Vaenn quickly retold their tale, of how they went after Caitren and the goblins that held her captive, only to be captured themselves by riders of Gundmar and taken to Bared Nar, where during the battle they were taken by the goblins.

"Ligwyrm carried us here," said Vaenn. "We did not arrive long before you three."

"Is Vyroun within this fortress?" asked Kattalin. "I grow quite worried, for that tower is a most frightening sight to look upon."

"The goblins say that we will be at his mercy soon," said Gleowan. "Thus far we have not seen their master, though we are certain that he is within that tower before us."

"I have already encountered him," said Caitren, who was the most fearful of them, as she knew what was likely to come. The jewel on Caitren's necklace was very radiant and lit up her face. Caitren strangely sensed that the jewel itself might have known danger was near.

"What is that necklace you wear?" asked Kattalin. "That is no mere jewel around your neck, from what it seems."

"It was given to me back in the Woodlands," said Caitren, who began to feel uneasy. She looked ahead to the keep to find a dark and growing mist. Soon there was a score of deoflas approaching them, and Caitren trembled.

"Is Vyroun here?" said Edelbir, looking at the deoflas. They were not coming to attack, though the score of Vyroun's worst servants surrounded the company. Edelbir and Kattalin, having been with the army of dwarves during the battle, had not encountered those dark and demonic creatures.

"What are these things?" said Kattalin, trembling. The five of them closed their ranks, and Edelbir stood in front to try and shield the others.

"Deoflas," said Caitren. The others were quite curious,

though also unmistakably afraid, as none of them were certain of what surrounded them. Caitren knew quite well by now what those creatures were, and she trembled as she spoke. "The most frightening creature I have seen in this venture. They will enter your body and try to control you, and a painful fight it is just to keep them from possessing you fully. I encountered them when Vyroun first stood before me."

"We saw them in Bared Nar," said Vaenn. "When night fell, these creatures appeared and moved like a great shadow, and the guards of Gundmar stood no chance against them. We knew not how to fight them, and we still know not how to defeat such creatures."

"I do not think that we are going to escape this dark place," said Caitren. "My heart hurts greatly to utter such words, but I have encountered these frightening things before. Only a true rejection of evil expelled one from me, and then I was lucky that a way out of the fortress at the mouth of this kingdom presented itself to me. We are in the middle of Mûrondûn. The borders of this land are far too many leagues away. No light shall meet us. I do not see any way for us to escape."

"I will not give up hope," said Edelbir. "But should we meet our ends here, our bond with each other shall be immortal. Honored I am to die beside all of you."

An echo sounded, and a gate opened somewhere in the keep of Vyroun's stronghold. Caitren could hear footsteps that sounded like iron clashing upon rock, and by now she knew all too well who made them. The company did not notice that Ligwyrm was still there until the dragon's head coiled around the tower to look upon someone within the keep. Caitren was the most fearful of all of them, for she had encountered Vyroun before, though I can tell you that the others were all very afraid also.

"He is coming," said Caitren. She was very certain of it, even though the dark lord had not yet appeared before them. Soon, however, someone who was very tall and covered entirely in armor entered the ward. Caitren knew that this was the dark lord of Mûrondûn, and she knew not to look into the glowing red eyes of Vyroun. The others, however, did not, and soon each of them cowered and shielded their eyes. Caitren retreated but could not escape.

Vyroun stood before and looked down upon the five of them. All in the company could feel his eyes upon them, but they could not look back at the dark lord, for the gaze of Vyroun was unbearable. Edelbir, Kattalin, Gleowan, and Vaenn soon tried to cover their ears, and Caitren immediately knew that they could hear the roaring fire inside their heads. Vaenn then began to scream. Caitren, however, strangely did not hear a roaring fire. Though the others were cowering, it did not seem to Caitren that Vyroun was paying as much attention to them. She would not look into the eyes of the dark lord, and yet Caitren could sense that his eyes were fixed upon her more than the others. She waited for his voice to speak inside her head, and Caitren expected that she would have to try and cover her ears like her friends.

"You cannot flee," said the voice inside Caitren's head, and she knew that her friends heard it also. Edelbir, Kattalin, Gleowan, and Vaenn screamed and covered their ears as best they could. Caitren tried to cover her ears also, expecting that the voice would also be loud inside of her head, however, to her surprise, it was not. The voice of

Vyroun instead came no louder than as if they were having a casual exchange. "Hitherto hast thou defied me. Yet even now, clemency may be granted. Strong art thou. Even now, I may welcome thee as my highest of servants.

"Yield, and no death shall meet thee," Caitren then heard in her head. She was not sure if the others were given the same offer or not.

Caitren knew not what to do. Vyroun had offered her very lavish things the last time she was before him, and Caitren had refused, as she had no need for wealth and would not become a thrall to such a dark lord. It seemed that Caitren was now being given one final offer, and if she did not yield now, she would die. But Caitren did not want to yield her heart to evil, and she greatly hoped for there to be a way to escape that dreadful place she and her friends had found themselves trapped in. Her friends, too, heard the voice of Vyroun in their heads, and though Caitren did not know precisely what was said to them, she felt certain that they were offered the very same things she was offered in the dungeons of Gulgurod.

"No matter how strong an ally I could be, I will not serve you," said Edelbir. "I have no use for gold or power, only for good tilled earth!"

"Offer me all the sea and I shall still not yield," said Kattalin. "Never to an evil like you."

"No amount of leaf and ale will gain my loyalty," said Gleowan.

"You need not give me beauty," said Vaenn. "For Gleowan knows all too well that I already possess it."

"Yield now, or death shall meet thee," said the voice in Caitren's head. She had no more time to hope for a way out of their trouble.

Strangely, even though Caitren could hear the voice in her head, she was not affected like the others. Edelbir, Kattalin, Gleowan, and Vaenn were desperately trying to cover their ears, and Vaenn was screaming. Caitren knew that Vyroun was speaking to them inside their heads, though she knew not was he was saying to them. The four of them soon all looked to her. Caitren's jewel upon her necklace glowed brightly in the face of the lord of Mûrondûn.

"We will not abandon Caitren," said Edelbir, who then stepped between Vyroun and Caitren. The others did the same. Edelbir, however, was immediately flung aside, although no one had grabbed him.

"Edelbir! No!" said Vaenn. Edelbir was hurt, but he was fortunately all right. Kattalin, Gleowan, and Vaenn were then thrown aside in the same manner. They, too, were not hurt badly, though Caitren was most afraid for them. Caitren now was all alone though, with Vyroun standing right before her. Elsewhere, her friends were held by goblins, and some deoflas approached her friends to possess them.

"No mercy shall find thee now," said a voice in Caitren's head. Caitren could only look up at Vyroun for but a brief moment before having to shield her eyes. However, she could see and sense a malice in the dark lord's eyes that had not been there when she was first brought before him. And yet, at the same time, the lord of Mûrondûn held up his hand, and it seemed that Vyroun was shielding his own eyes from Caitren's jewel.

Caitren was then thrown back, though not as hard as in the dark dungeon of Gulgurod. It seemed as if there was a struggle, as if Caitren were much heavier and far more difficult to heave during this meeting than when she was first brought before Vyroun. Caitren lay on her back, but she was soon pulled to her feet and then lifted a foot or so into the air. She then felt her eyes forced open, and her head was forced to look directly ahead into the blinding eyes of Vyroun.

Caitren expected her end to come, or at least that she would lose her sight. However, neither happened. The first thing that met Caitren's eyes was the glowing light from the jewel that hung around her neck, which grew more radiant than before. She could see the glowing red eyes of Vyroun, but the light from her jewel seemed to make the dark lord's eyes more bearable. Caitren was now able to meet the gaze of the lord of Mûrondûn without having to shield her eyes. However, even though she could bear his gaze, when she looked into Vyroun's eyes, Caitren saw a vengeful malice that she had not seen before. Caitren knew not what she might see if the helm of Vyroun were removed, though she did not want to, for even though his face was covered in armor, Caitren could sense that Vyroun was filled with a growing anger.

Vyroun extended his hand towards Caitren. She could then see black smoke seeping out from the chinks in his armored hand, and it swiftly blew towards her. Caitren could only hear the winds of a hurricane and roaring fire, but it was not inside her head. The smoke surrounded Caitren, though it did not touch her. She felt sure that this would be her end, but when her eyes drifted down for but a moment, she found that the jewel around her neck was protecting her from the wrath of Vyroun. A glowing light shined around Caitren and shielded the black smoke from taking her.

Soon black flame blew out from the hand of Vyroun, and when Caitren again looked into his eyes, she found them to be glowing brighter than before. Caitren was surrounded by black flame, and she could see nothing else but the eyes of the dark lord. Vyroun's eyes were starting to become unbearable to look back upon, but Caitren's gaze could turn nowhere else. A few screams sounded, and Caitren was certain that they were from her friends. Caitren could not see them through the smoke and flame, but she feared that they were all in great pain, and Caitren worried that they were being tormented by Vyroun's most terrible of servants. And yet at the same time Caitren worried that if her friends stopped screaming, then it might mean that they have all met their deaths.

Though Caitren could see nothing beyond the black smoke and flame, as well as the blinding eyes of Vyroun, the lord of Mûrondûn could not hinder her, even though Caitren was enduring extraordinary wrath from him. The jewel on Caitren's necklace did not yield in its light, and it did not allow the wrath of Vyroun to harm her. Caitren was very grateful to the lady of the Woodlands for giving it to her, and though Caitren feared that her end would come, she could not help but wonder if it might not be so. It began to seem as if Mairawin had known Caitren would be where she was now, and that the lady of the Woodlands gave her the jewel for that very purpose. However, even if Vyroun could not harm nor kill Caitren, she was still trapped within that dark stronghold. Caitren could not move, and though the jewel around her neck protected her, it did not give Caitren the power to vanquish the dark lord that sought her end. She was still in great need of help, as were her friends, who were far more vulnerable to Vyroun than she was, even though Caitren was facing the worst of his wrath.

The roaring flames and smoke, however, suddenly ceased. Caitren felt some relief, though she was not naïve enough to think this was the end of Vyroun's wrath. However, she was finally able to look to her friends. Though they were in a bad state, Edelbir, Kattalin, Gleowan, and Vaenn still lived. Each of them was on the ground and in great agony. Caitren knew that the deoflas were possessing them, and that her friends were fighting to keep these demons from controlling them.

Vyroun, however, did not turn to look upon Caitren's friends. His gaze remained on her. The eyes of Vyroun were almost unbearable, but Caitren's jewel did not yield at all, and it made the gaze of Vyroun endurable for her.

Caitren soon found, however, that Vyroun's eyes were not looking at her, but rather they were fixed upon the jewel that she wore. Though Caitren was already fearful, a worry crept over her. In the eyes of the dark lord, Caitren could see and sense an anger, but also a curiosity. Caitren knew little of the jewel that she wore, beyond that it was once a star. However, when she briefly looked into the eyes of Vyroun, she had a growing feeling that Vyroun recognized the jewel around her neck. And though Caitren was trapped and could not move, her body still trembled, for she knew not what rested within the dark lord's mind, nor what Vyroun might do next. The eyes of the dark lord then met Caitren's again, and his gaze grew more difficult to bear.

"Vinara," said the voice in Caitren's head. Caitren was most bemused. She knew not why Vyroun called her Vinara, for it was not her name, and she had never heard of the name Vinara before.

"No hope is there for thy friends," said the voice in Caitren's head. "They cannot escape from me. They cannot hinder me."

Caitren tried to move but could not. She could not bear to see her friends in what terrible agony they were in, an agony Caitren knew quite well, as she, too, had been possessed by a deofol before. She, with the jewel she wore, was much safer, but that jewel around her neck began to suddenly lift from her chest.

"Remove thy trinket, Vinara, and freed shall thy friends be," said the voice. The necklace grew heavy, as if it were clinging to Caitren and would not abandon her. She knew not why Vyroun wanted her jewel, whether it would be of use to him or if the dark lord simply wanted it out of his way so that he could kill her. For but a small moment, Caitren felt tempted to give him her necklace. However, Caitren knew that Vyroun was a servant of evil and could not be trusted. Caitren had also by then found that the jewel around her neck had protected her from the wrath of Vyroun, and if she were to lose it, then Caitren would surely become helpless to stop him from killing her. It was not Caitren's own suffering she worried about though, but rather that of her friends, whom Vyroun was using as a means of making her give up her trinket. Caitren did not want to see her friends in great agony, but she was unsure whether it would end if she yielded her jewel.

"You cannot tempt me," said Caitren. "I know you seek to deceive me. You will not set my friends free if I give you my trinket. You will only kill them all the same, and then you will kill me!"

Caitren worried that her friends would die, and that it

would be her own fault. However, Vyroun did not order them to be killed. The lord of Mûrondûn gently lifted his hand instead, signaling for his most evil of servants to give Caitren's friends clemency, and the deoflas possessing her friends departed from them. Her friends took a short time to regain themselves, and soon the four of them were on their knees and looking upon Caitren, who was still trapped by Vyroun. His hand was extended towards Caitren's jewel, which was being tugged towards him and looked as if it might break from Caitren's necklace at any moment. To Caitren, it felt as if the jewel were trying to resist the reach of Vyroun. The necklace seemed to desperately cling to the jewel, and Caitren could feel it pulling against her neck.

"Yield it now, and all shall be set free," said the voice in Caitren's head. "Defy me again, and thy friends shall suffer."

I cannot tell you how afraid Caitren felt, for she knew not what she needed to do. Caitren wanted her friends to be safe, but she did not trust the lord of Mûrondûn to keep his word. She also knew not what her own fate would be if she did choose to give up the gift that Mairawin had given her in the Woodlands. And poor Caitren could not move, let alone escape the trouble that she was in. Though the jewel might have protected her from being harmed by Vyroun, it did not protect her friends, nor did it give her any power to defeat him. If Vyroun could not be defeated, then surely it would be only a matter of time before Caitren would see her friends die, and then meet a terrible fate herself.

Chapter Eighteen; Hailing Fire

Adroegen and Andor could not land just outside the wall of Norungad, for goblins stood on guard, and though Adroegen could have taken care of them with the greatest of ease, he did not want any alarm sounded that he was there. Andor and the eagles quietly landed a short distance away from the gate, where no one could see them. There was one mountain peak, not far away, where no goblins could be seen. The eagles hid behind it, and Adroegen got off of Andor.

There was a field with a very rocky terrain before the walls of Norungad. This was good, as there were plenty of places for Adroegen to keep hidden as he crept his way to the stronghold. He needed to hurry, though, for his friends were all in there somewhere, and they were surely dealing with great torment.

"Keep yourselves hidden here," said Adroegen. "You cannot be found by the dragon. I must find my friends and save them from Vyroun. Await my signal to come and take them away."

"We will remain here," said Andor. "And very good luck do we wish upon you in this quest."

"Your friends have done many good deeds for my home to the south," said Orn. "We eagles will not abandon them to their deaths in this dreadful place."

Adroegen swiftly set out for the gate into Norungad. Guards kept watch, but their attention appeared to be fixed somewhere within the fortress. Adroegen was able to run and hide behind one boulder, and then he made his way to another. He did not want Vyroun to know that he was still alive, nor that he had found out the truth of his lineage, that he was heir to Buludin and had gained his power, for the secrecy might be an advantage in his fight with the dark lord.

Before long Adroegen was close to the gate. A few guards kept watch for anything beyond the wall, but Adroegen was very skilled in hiding and did not allow for them to see him. Before long he began to hear screaming within the walls. He was certain that it was his friends he heard, and so he needed to move with great haste. Soon he found a place to climb the wall where one of the turrets stood, and Adroegen hurried his way there and made the climb without hesitation. He made sure to keep to the other side of the turret from where some goblins were standing watch so that he would not be seen. After a short time, Adroegen found an embrasure to climb through, and then he stood at the top of the turret.

Immediately Adroegen made his way down. He could unmistakably hear his friends nearer to the gate. Once upon the parapet, Adroegen made sure no goblins could see him, and then he quietly leaped down from the wall. He still had a short distance to go in order to reach his friends. The ward behind the gate was ahead, though there was another wall running to the keep that separated Adroegen from it. A door was ahead that led to a tunnel within the stronghold's outer wall. Adroegen entered and made his way through the tunnel as it led him towards the gate.

Caitren's friends doubtlessly wanted to help her, but they stood no chance against the malice that held her captive. She held out for as long as she could, hoping to forgo having to make the choice of whether or not to give up her jewel. Caitren was certain that either outcome would end in death for her and her friends. However, Vyroun did just give her friends clemency, as his demonic servants were no longer possessing and tormenting them. Caitren wondered if perhaps Vyroun might keep his word and free her friends if she did yield her jewel. A fear came over her that if he was being truthful, and if she, out of distrust, refused to give up her jewel, then her friends would suffer, and that Caitren would be at fault for their torment.

As Caitren waited in fear, the necklace began to tug harder against her neck. Vyroun's hand was extended, and the jewel was being pulled towards him. Caitren looked down towards it, and the jewel was shaking, and Vyroun was trying with much might to take it from her.

"How do I know that you will free my friends?" said Caitren.

"Yield thy trinket, and they shall be free. Defy me again, and they shall be tormented," Caitren heard in her head. She was given no further answer. Caitren then grew certain that Vyroun would not release her friends, for Caitren had received the same answer in Gulgurod upon asking if Vyroun knew where her father was. She felt certain back in Gulgurod that Vyroun would not take her to her father, and indeed he was deceitful, as Caitren in the end found her father in the Woodlands not long after. And so, Caitren knew that Vyroun was not going to free her friends.

"You have tried to tempt me before," said Caitren. "My friends are still held captive. I do not believe you will release them. And I know that you will not release me."

"Thy friends shall be in anguish," said the voice. Caitren's head was forced back, and suddenly the necklace was being pulled against her neck much harder than before. Caitren was unable to turn her head and could hardly look upon Vyroun, who was unleashing his full might upon her. Caitren, however, was still not being harmed, even though she could not move nor escape.

"Caitren!" shouted Vaenn. Caitren's friends tried to help her, but I am afraid that four unarmed folk stood no chance against an evil lord like Vyroun.

"Vinara, thy trinket shall be taken, and thy companions shall suffer before thee," said the voice in Caitren's head. "Clemency is vanished. Only death awaits thee now."

And Caitren was forced to withstand Vyroun's wrath once more. The black smoke and fire surrounded her again, though it still did not touch her, and this time she was able to see her friends, who once again came under possession of Vyroun's most terrible of servants. The goblins could have easily killed them, however, their master seemed intent on making them suffer greatly, and on making Caitren watch. And as Caitren saw her friends in terrible agony, her heart hurt greatly, and she could do nothing to help them. She could only hope that in tormenting her friends, they would remain alive long enough that some kind of help might come. Caitren, however, could not see anyone being able to help her and her friends out of that terrible trouble they were in.

Caitren's jewel had not shattered, and her necklace had not broken from around her neck. She was, however, beginning to feel a considerable pain, for the necklace was being pulled with much force. Caitren was not sure that the jewel would protect her forever, and she feared that the gift from the lady of the Woodlands would be taken from her at any moment. If Caitren could not defeat Vyroun, and if she could not find a way to escape, then it would surely be only a matter of time before Vyroun would bring death upon her. Caitren was most desperate.

"Oh, if there is any way for me and my friends to escape this terrible fate, please let it be shown to us now," said Caitren. She could hear only the sounds of roaring fire and the screams of her friends. Caitren feared that her friends would die at any moment, but their torment went on. Caitren pleaded some more. She did not want to give up hope, but Caitren found it very difficult to see any chance of escaping that dark place. "Oh, please! There is always hope! But I cannot see it! Show us a way out of this fate!"

Caitren had to withstand the wrath of Vyroun for a little longer. The dark lord clenched his fist, and Caitren worried that her jewel would break. The smoke began to rise and engulf her again. However, something happened that Caitren did not expect. She heard a voice, thunderous and sounding strangely familiar. Caitren though could not tell at first who it was.

"Stay your malice from her!" said the voice. The black smoke ceased, and Caitren no longer felt her necklace being tugged against her neck. She still could not move, but Caitren at least had some relief, as Vyroun's attention had been drawn elsewhere.

"No command from he who hides in the shadows shall be met by me," said the voice in Caitren's head. Though Caitren could hear his voice, Vyroun this time was not speaking to her. Caitren was able to hear the exchange he had with whomever spoke from the shadows of that stronghold.

"No more evil shall you inflict upon them," said the strange voice. It grew louder, as if he who spoke was drawing closer to Caitren and her friends. Whoever spoke was not far from the gate, it appeared, though he would not reveal himself.

"No courage shall avail thee," Caitren heard in her head. She was unsure what was happening. A small gust of wind began to blow, and Caitren found it to be blowing towards the wall behind her, which was where the voice seemed to be coming from.

"You are mistaken," said the mysterious voice. As Caitren listened on, the voice was beginning to sound very familiar to her. It could have been the leader of their company, however, Caitren did not want to be fooled by false hope that Adroegen might have still lived. And yet, Caitren knew his voice, and her heart felt more and more certain it was Adroegen who was speaking. "Your end will soon come, by command of the true master of this earth, who bestows the privilege of defeating you unto me."

"No might shall end darkness," said the lord of the dark kingdom. "No man hidden from the dark shall lift it."

"Worry not," said the voice. "You will know precisely who I am. Oh yes. You will know who I am when my vengeance is laid upon you."

Edelbir, Kattalin, Gleowan, and Vaenn all appeared to notice the growing breeze also. The four of them were all on their knees with their hands bound, though Vyroun's most terrible of servants did relieve them of their agony for the time being. Caitren, however, worried that a sword might meet them at any moment, and that Vyroun might choose to heed the voice no more and order their deaths. However, Caitren found the voice to be quite thunderous, and that whoever spoke could not have been any mere man. And yet, to Caitren, it became more and more unmistakable that the voice sounded like the leader of their company, whom she once thought might have been dead.

Adroegen was still a short way away but drew closer to where the company was held captive, and soon he was within a few dozen strides. Adroegen found Caitren trapped in the air and unable to move, and the rest of his friends in positions that were not much better. Still, Adroegen was grateful that they had lived long enough for him to reach and save them. He knew already that Caitren, Edelbir, and Kattalin were alive after seeing them in the battle at Bared Nar, and now Adroegen had found Gleowan and Vaenn there. Oaknut had indeed been correct, both in that all of his friends still lived, and that Adroegen might have to both thwart Vyroun and save his friends in a single stroke

"Long have you hunted me without avail," said Adroegen, hidden in the tunnel within the wall and peeking through a small crack in the stone. He quietly drew his sword and was ready to unleash the true might of Endonhil. The sword began to glow dimly. He passed one small window but remained hidden. Adroegen could see his friends and though he was quite relieved that they lived, they were in a most dire of circumstance. Adroegen reached and climbed the stairs ahead that led to the stronghold gatehouse. "And your failure shall be your ruin here on this night."

"No more shall thou riddle me," said Vyroun.

In the ward, Caitren was taken by a terrifying surprise as the necklace suddenly yanked against her neck again. She heard the sound of a roaring fire and thought her jewel would break. However, it did not. Caitren saw goblins raising their swords. A despair came over her, as Caitren thought her friends would die, and that she would meet the same fate.

There was then a great boom of thunder, one louder than any Caitren had ever heard before. Caitren fell and hurt herself a little, but she was fine. The lord of Mûrondûn had been driven back, and Caitren could see rubble falling all about. She felt the winds of a hurricane, though these winds did not harm her nor her friends. Edelbir, Kattalin, Gleowan, and Vaenn all fell back in surprise. The goblins though still held them, and the deoflas still surrounded Caitren's friends.

Great balls of fire then hailed down from the sky. The fire though was blue rather than red. One goblin after another was felled once the flame hit them. The goblin that held Edelbir was hit and quickly dead. The same then happened to the goblins that held Kattalin, Gleowan, and Vaenn. Upon being freed, all of them regained themselves. Caitren and her friends heard the sound of an echoing fire, but it was not the flame that they heard inside their heads upon being brought before Vyroun. Caitren, upon turning around, found quite a sight.

Upon the gate wall stood a man with a sword in hand. Caitren and her friends though could not tell who he was, for the man appeared in the form of a blinding light, brighter than any they had ever looked upon. A blue flame was wreathed around him, and it roared louder than thunder. The ground shook and rumbled beneath their feet, and the winds of a hurricane descended upon the dark lord's stronghold. The fire before the company was greater than any they had ever looked upon, and from it many flames hailed down and felled one goblin after another.

Caitren had much difficulty seeing beyond the magnificent blue fire, however, she was barely able to notice some eagles a small distance away, making their way to the fortress. She had forgotten that Ligwyrm was there, and to her side, Caitren saw the dragon making for the eagles. The man wreathed in flame, however, made but a turn towards the dragon, and the winds blew upon Ligwyrm and cast him down with ease. The dragon made no further attempt to attack, and he retreated from that stronghold. The deoflas still surrounded Caitren's friends, however, the light suddenly grew far brighter. Caitren then heard screeches and what sounded like flesh on a frying pan, and then the worst of Vyroun's servants all disappeared in but an instant. Then as the light finally dimmed, Caitren and her friends were able to see who had conjured this magic and saved them, and they could not believe their eyes.

Before them stood a friend they had thought to be dead. Caitren had to look closely to be sure that it was in fact Adroegen, for it looked like the leader of their company, who had guided her and her friends away from the goblin chief the previous summer, and yet at the same time, in a way, Caitren did not recognize the man that stood before her and her friends. There was a fierceness in Adroegen's eyes that she had never seen before, and he had conjured magic Caitren had not known him to be able to conjure, thus Adroegen was somehow no longer just a mere man like any other. Caitren's heart leaped for joy in a way that it never had before.

"Adroegen still lives! Our friend did not die!" said Caitren as she rose to her feet. Her friends equally marveled at the sight of their friend. It was Adroegen who stood before them, and yet it was not. All were without words and shielded their eyes as the strong winds continued to blow down upon the fortress and the blue fire roared within their ears.

Though Caitren marveled at how Adroegen still lived, and how he was not the same as she had known him before, Adroegen showed no joy, nor did he speak to his friends about what had become of him since the company had split. He appeared to be filled with a sense of purpose, and to Caitren it seemed that Adroegen had far more pressing business. Adroegen turned around, and Caitren looked to find that the eagles were arriving. Andor landed beside Adroegen, and then Orn made his way beside the company. A few other eagles landed there, enough to take away all in the company, save for one.

"Andor! Orn!" said Caitren. Both the lord of the Fornwood and the great eagle of the southern woods bowed. There was no time though for any pleasantries. The eagles had come to fly the company out of that dark place.

"Take them away from here," said Adroegen. "Leave me."

"Adroegen!" said Caitren, walking towards him, though she did not walk too close to the leader of their company, for a great blue flame surrounded him. "Whatever has become of you?"

"Leave with Andor," said Adroegen to Caitren. "You have shown your worth in this fight. I am where I must be, for it is now time for my own task."

"But we do not want to leave our friend," said Caitren. "For we had thought you to be dead, and only now do we find such a joyous truth!"

"Go now! Leave this dark place!" said Adroegen. "This is not your fight, but rather my enemy to face."

"Come," said Andor to Caitren. "Adroegen is right. The ruler of this stronghold is a foe beyond you, Caitren. You have shown courage far beyond what any could fathom, but your part in this war has ended. And Adroegen's part in this fight has now begun."

Though Caitren did not want to leave, she climbed upon Andor. Kattalin sat upon Orn while Edelbir, Gleowan, and Vaenn all climbed upon the other eagles, ready to be flown away from that dark place. They all held on tight, and soon the eagles flapped their wings and rose into the sky. As they were flown away from Vyroun's stronghold, all Caitren and the others could do was look upon the leader of their company, who stood at the gate of the fortress, wreathed in a blue flame that roared like thunder. The hurricane winds blew the eagles away with a great speed, and soon the stronghold was out of sight.

"What has happened to our friend?" said Gleowan

loudly in the wind. "For we believed him dead, and now Adroegen not only lives, but it seems he is no longer human!"

Caitren remembered when she was at the house of Dalgarinan and Mairawin. When there, the lady of the Woodlands had said that she had seen Adroegen fall, but she could not see his fate in full. Mairawin also uttered that she found there was oft a reason why her sight was sometimes clouded. At one point, she had looked upon a tapestry of five warriors, all wreathed in a blue flame as Adroegen had just been. Caitren remembered a tale of one of Enilundar's highest servants, who began a mysterious bloodline and whose sword seemed to be lost. But it did not appear the sword of Buludin was lost at all. Caitren grew certain that it must have been in the hands of its rightful master all along.

And all had been answered for Caitren. It was curious that Mairawin could see that Adroegen fell but could not see his full fate for some strange reason. Caitren felt certain now that Mairawin's vision must have been veiled, because something great was being put in motion for Adroegen, something that a higher power did not want others to know of yet. She was joyful, for she had thought Adroegen was likely dead, and yet her heart had not given up hope that he still lived, and in the end her heart was right.

"All makes sense to me now. The tale is true!" said Caitren to her friends. "Buludin, the Vistivar, highest of the servants of Enilundar himself. The tale of his bloodline, and the legend of his sword being passed down to his heir. Adroegen thought it was only a foolish fairy tale, that there was no knowledge of an heir and that the sword had been lost. But he was wrong. The answer had always been under his very nose, before his very eyes. It was he who has been the heir to Buludin all this time! And the sword of Buludin has been in Adroegen's hand in battle without him knowing. Adroegen had wondered why he still walked this earth after all the pain he had been through, but it happens that he had a mighty path to walk. We have known our friend as merely Adroegen, the wanderer, the vagabond, leader of our company. But no longer! For he is now Adroegen, heir to Buludin, wielder of Endonhil, the greatest sword upon this earth! He is a Vistivar, high servant of Enilundar himself!"

Caitren was overcome with joy, and the others were in awe that the tale they had once heard was true. The eagles flew swiftly away, and soon they reached the Daur Igina, the mountains that bordered the dark kingdom. Caitren and her friends were flown out of that dreadful place. Their part to play in the war against Vyroun had ended. They had done all they could to aid the north, and I can tell you that they had done many great deeds for the northern kingdoms. But now it was time for the leader of their company to fulfill his own task.

Chapter Nineteen;
Thunder in the North

Adroegen watched the eagles carry his friends away from the dark place that was Vyroun's kingdom. It was quite a relief to him that they all still lived, for not too long ago Adroegen believed that his friends were all dead. But it was not so, and the resolve Adroegen lost after his tumble some time before was now restored. Soon the eagles were a distance away, and his new kin were no longer in danger. The newly hallowed Vistivar could now worry about his own task that Enilundar ordered him to fulfill, and nothing else.

Adroegen turned back to look upon the keep. Atop the wall stood Vyroun, and he was looking back at Adroegen. The eyes of the dark lord though did not blind Adroegen at all. He was not certain, but Adroegen thought that he could sense surprise, or even fear, within the enemy, even though that enemy was clad entirely in armor.

Adroegen held Endonhil in hand, forged by Enilundar and weapon of Buludin of the high Vistivar. Vyroun, too, had a weapon in hand, which was a great iron mace that was well-crafted and frightful in appearance. It was doubtless heavy to the point that no man would be able to wield it. If Adroegen's friends were still within that stronghold, they surely would have been fearful.

Adroegen, however, was unafraid, for he was a mere man no longer. Instead, a fire burned within his eyes and a desire for vengeance filled Adroegen's heart, and though this desire had corrupted him at times when leading his friends away from the goblin chief, on this night his vengeful desires were sharp and focused. He was acting to smite down the lord of the dark kingdom not of his own accord, but under order of Enilundar himself. And thus, now was the time for such desires to run through Adroegen's veins, for they strengthened both his courage and his ferocity. There were no friends to divert him in his task, for Adroegen and Vyroun were alone within that dark fortress.

And so Adroegen began approaching the keep, and Vyroun made his way down. It was very dark, but as Adroegen made his way to Vyroun, he began to see lights out of the corners of his eyes. They were moving about in the air and circling around the stronghold where very soon a great battle was going to take place.

Adroegen looked more closely at these lights that were encircling him and the dark lord, and he found that they were no mere lights. One flew close enough to him, and Adroegen found that it was a woman wreathed in bright light, who was angelic in appearance, and yet had a fierceness about her. She drew closer to Adroegen, and he was surprised to find that she was a Rhykwen, and not only a taker of the dead, but the very one whom he had met back in the Dead Forest after his encounter with the witch.

The Rhykwen, however, did not speak to Adroegen. Instead she merely circled around the battle that was about to begin. Adroegen saw several more women all clothed in white, looking beautiful and angelic but also fierce, all flying about the stronghold of Norungad. There were at least a score of takers of the dead, if not two scores. Adroegen then remembered what the Rhykwen had told him when he met her, how she uttered to him that he can see them when others cannot, and that they would appear when one's hour of death had come.

And so Adroegen grew quite certain that so many takers of the dead had gathered there because someone was about to meet their death, and that the Rhykwen were there to await whomever would fall and then take them away from that world. Adroegen also remembered the Rhykwen uttering to him that he still had many tasks to do, one of which he later discovered was to smite down Vyroun. And so, Adroegen grew certain that fate was on his side, that it would not be his end in that battle, but rather that it was Vyroun whom the takers of the dead had come to collect.

Vyroun had made his way down from the stairs of the keep, and Adroegen stood a dozen or so strides away from his enemy. The lord of the dark kingdom was engulfed in a black smoke, while the Vistivar was wreathed in a blue and roaring flame. As the two foes reached each other, the Rhykwen closed in on the battle that was about to begin.

"The takers of the dead fly about," said Adroegen. "Do you see them? Many have come, waiting as death draws near. Tonight, they come for you."

"Thou fool," said a voice, which this time was in Adroegen's head. "No angels come for me. Thy death shall thee find."

"Oh no," said Adroegen. "It is you who are mistaken.

For I have faced death many a time and have not suffered it. One amongst the Rhykwen have I met, and she has uttered to me that my time to leave this world is not now. For I have tasks left to fulfill upon this earth, and among them is to destroy you. My hour shall not come on this night, but rather yours."

"No fate shall avail thee," said the voice in Adroegen's head. "For no fate was availed before by thine ancestor."

"It will avail me," said Adroegen. "For you have sought my death before and have failed in finding it. Fate smiles upon me on this night."

The eyes of Vyroun were very bright, however, Adroegen was not blinded by them. Adroegen held his sword up, and the blade glowed brightly. "No darkness shall save you now. My wrath now descends upon you, and no mercy shall meet you. For the heir of Buludin arises. Many a time you have failed to bring about my end, and now I shall be your end."

Vyroun raised his mace, and black flame began to burn from the top, as if it were a dark torch. Then the dark fire roared its way towards Adroegen. No fear met Adroegen, however, for his heart was filled with a desire to destroy Vyroun. The blade of Endonhil shined brighter and the light shielded him from the dark flame. After Adroegen parried Vyroun's attack, he immediately advanced upon the enemy. There were then clashes of sword and mace, and flames roared as the ground rumbled.

And the Vistivar would fight with the lord of the dark kingdom in a battle worthy of those of old, when the earth was younger. A storm began brewing within the stronghold, as the dark fire collided with the purest of flame. Thunder sounded, coming from both the servant of

Enilundar and from the dark lord. Buludin's heir and Vyroun appeared equal in power, and for a time neither was able to find any advantage over their enemy. Adroegen thus far was not able to hinder the lord of Mûrondûn, but his will did not wane. All the while, the Rhykwen circled around the battle, awaiting the outcome.

"Thou fool," said the voice in Adroegen's head. "No master may give thee power to lift darkness."

Both fought for some time at the keep of the fortress. Adroegen attacked with much ferocity, for he held no fear, nor would he show mercy to his foe. He had been both commanded and given the power to destroy Vyroun, and Adroegen refused to fail in such a task. The lord of Mûrondûn was able to evade or parry each blow that Adroegen tried to deal upon him, however, Vyroun was soon retreating in the face of the Vistivar's wrath. Adroegen heeded no clemency. The dark lord was strong, do not misunderstand, but it appeared that he had not been expecting such a storm to rage upon him.

"No joy shalt thee find in victory," said the voice in Adroegen's head. Both of them entered the tower, and Vyroun retreated upward.

"You are mistaken," said Adroegen. "For I will find much joy in striking you down. Grateful am I that the task has been bestowed upon me."

"Thy mother shall not return to this earth," said the voice in Adroegen's head. Though Adroegen was filled with wrath, his attack weakened upon mention of his mother. A sudden sadness entered his heart, and Adroegen briefly thought of how much he wanted to look upon her again.

Thick smoke then emerged from within Vyroun's

armor, and it blew towards Adroegen. Endonhil's light grew brighter and shielded him, and the blue flame sent the winds of a hurricane to blow the smoke away. But Adroegen was on the defense now, and he fought to withstand the assault of the dark lord.

"Yield, and thou shall see thy mother again," said the voice of Vyroun. Adroegen, however, was not tempted, for he knew his mother was in Elunbelan, and at peace. He knew that Vyroun could not take him to his mother, and so Adroegen would not let Vyroun's temptation sway him at all.

"I shall never yield," said Adroegen. "You have tried to tempt me before and failed. And now shall you also fail. I know you will not lead me to my mother, for it was your very servants who brought about her death!"

Adroegen then turned the tide against Vyroun. The blue flame of Enilundar roared and descended upon the lord of Mûrondûn, and the dark lord retreated again. Some of the tower walls began to crumble, though the tower still stood.

"Thou knoweth not the power of the darkness," said the dark lord's voice in Adroegen's head.

"Oh, no. For I do know its power," said Adroegen. "There is no joy that evil can bring to me. Only anger has it brought me, only pain and sadness. For I have seen it all of my life. I have no use for evil's might."

"Yield, and thou shalt be taken to her," said the voice in Adroegen's head. But Adroegen was not fooled.

"I know where my mother is now," said Adroegen. "She resides within the halls of Elunbelan, and I will look upon her again when my tasks upon this earth are done."

"Death hast thou long wished for," said the voice in

Adroegen's head. "And death shall take thee to her."

"Your audacity knows no end," said Adroegen. "You are but a liar, a deceiver. For if I were to die now, before my tasks upon this earth are complete, then would I look upon my mother again? Would I be given such an honor in death? No. My master would not wish for me to leave this earth by such a choice."

The tower rumbled as the two foes fought. Dark was the lair of the lord of Mûrondûn, and within were many weapons and torturous devices that would frighten anyone. Up several stairs did Vyroun retreat, and Adroegen followed. He did not cease in his attack, though Vyroun was able to shield himself from the Vistivar's wrath. Adroegen, however, sensed that Vyroun was struggling, at least more so than Adroegen was. It also seemed Vyroun was trying to trick Adroegen into choosing not to defeat him, as if the dark lord were facing an adversary that he did not think he could defeat. Outside the windows, Adroegen could see the Rhykwen flying around the tower. There was no other light beyond that of Endonhil, which shined brightly as Adroegen wielded it.

After some time, the two foes reached the top of the tower. The battlement at the top was round, and in its center was a water-filled basin about as tall as one's waist. The water was as still as a sheet of glass, even as strong winds blew upon it and the tower shook. Adroegen drew close to it as he fought, and when looking into the basin, he caught his reflection as clear as anything around him. Vyroun though quickly forced Adroegen back from the well, and the two circled around the top of the tower.

"Why serve a master who brings only pain upon thee?" Adroegen heard inside his head. He looked briefly to the sky, and Adroegen found that all the Rhykwen had flown to the top of the tower.

"Only pain has been brought upon thee," said the voice in Adroegen's head. Adroegen remembered his hatred for Enilundar, and his uncertainty of whether he was even real. But that was no longer so. For there had always been a reason for his past to happen as it had, and there was always a purpose why Adroegen must go on, and it was because fate meant him to be standing where he was now.

"Only death has thee sought, but never been given," said the voice. Adroegen drew close to the lord of Mûrondûn, and Endonhil nearly struck the dark lord. Sword and mace were locked for but a brief moment.

"There was once a time where I hoped for death," said Adroegen, looking up at the many Rhykwen that flew about, awaiting the result of the battle. "Yes, there was a time. But no longer. I came to learn that it was not yet time for me to die. And that is why I know you will not defeat me on this night. For I have encountered the very takers of the dead that observe us now. And I have stood before the very servants of Enilundar not so long ago, among them Buludin, my ancestor, who once wielded this very sword against you. And that is why I no longer seek death as I once did. For I have been given the greatest of blessings, the most magnificent of purposes to fulfill."

Adroegen and Vyroun broke free, and the battle of dark lord and heir of Buludin went on. Beneath Adroegen the floor was shaking with much force. The tower walls were starting to crumble, and Adroegen was growing certain that the great tower of Norungad would soon fall. He had to be careful to keep his balance.

"Thy master has brought only agony upon thee, and

yet thou chose to serve him," said the voice in Adroegen's head.

The tower was beginning to totter back and forth, and so both Adroegen and Vyroun had need to be wary not only of the foe they were facing. Soon it seemed as if a lower level caved in upon itself, and Adroegen felt the floor beneath him dropping. He was able to maintain his balance upon the tower, but he was certain it would soon crumble.

Fires dark and pure collided, but this time Adroegen was finally able to overpower Vyroun in their battle. The flames of blue overcame those of black, and the dark lord fell. Adroegen heard a roar from the lord of that dark kingdom, and Vyroun seemed to be hindered. One final assault did Vyroun launch upon Adroegen, one that appeared to be sent in desperation, but Adroegen was able to withstand it. He could only laugh at the words that had just been uttered to him, that Enilundar was the one who had caused all of his pain. Adroegen could not believe that the lord of that dark kingdom would possess such audacity.

"Enilundar is the cause of my pain?" said Adroegen while struggling to keep his footing as the tower began shaking harder, though he would not cease in his fight. "I once believed such. Enilundar? Oh, no. It was not he that brought all of my suffering upon me. It was not Enilundar that filled me with sorrow all of my years."

The fortress was indeed crumbling, but the mighty tower of Norungad was not small, and thus it would take some time to fall completely to ruin. It was tilting one way and then another, and Adroegen had to make sure that his guard did not fall in his fight against Vyroun. However, the lord of Mûrondûn had even more trouble. Adroegen soon felt the tower tilt in his direction, and Vyroun fell forward, and Adroegen was close to being able to strike him.

"It was you who caused all of my suffering," said Adroegen. "For you are a servant of evil, and you will not deceive me so. It was you and your servants who have taken everything from me, not Enilundar! You will tempt me no more. I will not turn to evil. For I am a Vistivar, heir to Buludin, highest servant of Enilundar himself, and he has bestowed upon me the greatest of tasks, which I will now fulfill. Long have I sought to lay vengeance upon you, and now that time has come!"

Endonhil glowed as bright as it ever had before, and its blue flame roared all about the tower. Adroegen lunged his way towards his enemy, and as he did the tower again tilted his way, and Vyroun lost his balance for but a moment. It was all that Adroegen needed, though, for the dark lord was within reach and off guard, and quickly Adroegen thrust Endonhil into the head of Vyroun. To a normal weapon, the armor of Vyroun would have been impenetrable, but the weapon of Enilundar cut through it like a knife through bread. To Adroegen, it did not seem that there was a body beneath the armor of the dark lord, but instead there might have been a spirit of some kind filled with malice. There was no time to wonder, though, for the tower was falling, and Adroegen had to be careful as he fell with it.

There was a thunderous roar, one so loud that it might have been heard from the battle taking place in Gundmar. Adroegen looked upon his enemy, and the eyes of Vyroun had grown brighter than Adroegen had ever seen them, and he had to shield his eyes as the tower fell. The helm then shattered like glass, but Adroegen was not yet able to see the face that was beneath, for he first needed to be careful, as he was falling with the crumbling tower. Soon though, for but a moment, he was able to see the enemy that he defeated.

There was a blinding red light that looked like a fire, and then Adroegen's enemy burst into a flame that spread far and wide before it was gone. Its force threw down Adroegen and the remaining rubble from the tower that had not yet reached the bottom of the fortress. Adroegen took a tumble, though not a terrible one like the fall he took over the cliff in the Dead Forest. Noticeably, the rush and fright of a fall did not overcome him like it once did when he was a mere man. Adroegen soon rose to his feet and looked around. The stronghold was crumbling, and its walls were coming down. Soon Norungad was completely in ruin, with Adroegen being the only one left who was still alive.

Then Adroegen saw several lights rain down from the sky. They were only the Rhykwen, who had observed the entire battle and waited for it to be decided. Though only one had come to take the witch when Adroegen encountered it, this was not a mere witch. It was Vyroun this time that the Rhykwen had come to take away, and Adroegen could only think that such an evil spirit like Vyroun must have required far more than one taker of the dead to usher away.

The servants of Enilundar gathered in a circle, and soon Adroegen could see what looked like the spirit of a man forming before them. This man, however, was made of red flame, and Adroegen had to shield his eyes when looking upon he who was being taken away. Soon

Adroegen was able to discern that it was actually an elf who lay still before the takers of the dead. Adroegen thought that it must have been Vyroun, in what would have been his human appearance, from very long ago, perhaps not long after the earth first came into being, and maybe before he became the evil lord that Adroegen had just defeated.

The Rhykwen tied many chains made of silver light around this elf, though he did not move. The spirit of Vyroun appeared to be unconscious. The elf was tied and soon completely covered in silver chains, though those chains were not of the world Adroegen walked, but rather of the realm of the dead. Then the dozens of Rhykwen hoisted the elf and flew away with him. Adroegen watched the great light fly away south and into the distance.

One taker of the dead, however, remained with Adroegen as the others flew away with the spirit of Vyroun. It was the very same servant that Adroegen had encountered just after the witch was defeated. Though any Rhykwen had a rather fearsome appearance to go with their angelic beauty, during this exchange Adroegen was not fearful like he was the first time that he encountered her. The Rhykwen smiled upon Adroegen, and he could only think that he had done precisely what he had been tasked with. One time, Adroegen had a loathing for the Rhykwen's master, and now his master also. Now, however, Adroegen's loyalty was to Enilundar, who turned out to have a magnificent path set for him, one that thus far Adroegen was sure he was walking. She waited until the other servants were out of sight before speaking to Adroegen.

"I have not come here to take you," said the Rhykwen.

"For your time to leave this earth for Elunbelan has not yet come. Much is left here that you must do."

"Indeed, as I have come to learn since last I encountered you," said Adroegen with a smile. "Once I thought that there was nothing left for me upon this earth, but I have since found that to not be true."

Adroegen looked to the sky. The black clouds that covered the dark kingdom were beginning to clear. Morning had come, and to the east the sun was rising. Many clouds covered that land though, and so Adroegen thus far could only see the morning light to the south. That land had once belonged to dwarves, digging through many mountains and finding endless treasures. Adroegen was not sure what would become of Mûrondûn now that Vyroun had been defeated. Perhaps if there were more dwarves out there somewhere, then they might return to a land that was once theirs. That, however, was out of Adroegen's hands. For the time being, he was simply happy that the dark lord who long ago took that kingdom from the dwarves was gone. Mûrondûn, once a dark kingdom, would soon be dark no more.

"I have fulfilled a task that has been commanded of me," began Adroegen. "For I was instructed to strike down the lord of this evil place, and I have done so. Yet I was told by the Vistivar of long ago that I have many tasks to fulfill, and you come before me now to utter that my time still has not yet come. I can only think that this was but one deed, and my work is not complete. I know not though what remains, nor what more Enilundar wants from me."

"Now that you know who you are, I may utter more to you," said the Rhykwen. "Although there are some questions that Enilundar does not bid me to answer. For you might be a Vistivar now, highest servant of Enilundar, but you are also human and were born human, thus your road upon this earth will be walked as such. Not all answers may be simply given to you, for you must find those answers on your own."

"Very well," said Adroegen. "If that is how it must be upon this earth, then I will ask only that which you are permitted to answer to me."

"You speak that Vyroun is no more, and yet I say to you now that your time upon this earth is not finished," said the Rhykwen. "Yes, Enilundar bestows more tasks upon you to fulfill beyond simply defeating he who ruled over this dark kingdom. However, I am not bidden to utter what your next tasks are. For each man's path upon this earth is one they must discover as they walk it. I may utter to you, though, that Vyroun is not the only servant of evil who has walked this earth. And so, you have more tasks here, but as a human you will need to discover them for yourself."

"Very well," said Adroegen. "Although I will say that I know not where nor how I might discover what is wanted of me."

"Worry not," said the Rhykwen. "For your path will always present itself to you in time, wherever it will lead."

The Rhykwen then spoke a verse that Adroegen had heard back when he was in the cavern before the Vistivar:

You know not where you are going,
But never shall I lead you astray,
You shall walk your path without knowing,
For I shall carry you the whole way.

"That is the promise your master makes to you," said the Rhykwen. "For he will guide you wherever it is you must go. Fear not, Adroegen, heir to Buludin, for any shroud that veils your sight shall always lift when the time comes."

The sun was out by then, and the clouds had cleared even more. Mûrondûn was no longer a dark kingdom like when Adroegen and his friends first entered, for the day's light was making its way into the land. Adroegen no longer had need to wield Endonhil, and he sheathed his sword. The Rhykwen though looked upon what was once Buludin's weapon and had more words to speak.

"When last we met, you thought it was I who saved you from the witch that was about to kill you," said the Rhykwen. "And I uttered to you that it was not I who saved you. For all weapons forged by Enilundar himself cannot be wielded by those of ill, as the act of touching such a weapon shall be their ruin. That was what saved you from the witch, for she sought to end you with your own weapon, just as Vyroun did to Buludin long ago."

"I do remember," said Adroegen, whose mind had been overwhelmed since learning himself to be Buludin's heir, and thus he had forgotten the witch's odd and sudden death, and that the witch had indeed tried to take Adroegen's sword and kill him with it, just as Vyroun did when he faced Buludin long ago. The witch was dead upon the mere act of grabbing a weapon forged by Enilundar himself, though Adroegen did not realize at the time that the witch died upon taking his sword, nor that his sword might have once belonged to Buludin.

Adroegen though became very curious. "You say the witch's death came when she took my weapon.

Something, though, I find queer. For the legend of Buludin says that Vyroun once did the same. Vyroun himself, however, was not defeated upon taking a weapon of the Vistivar, for he returned an age later. I cannot help but wonder, why was he not defeated long ago, never to return, after taking Buludin's sword?"

"I may answer this," said the Rhykwen. "For a witch might be skilled in some magic, but a sorcerer such as Vyroun is far greater. And there are other evils equal to him, and even some far more powerful, who have walked this earth. Some ancient evils have been able to raise the dead, those that possessed the Galesir that was cut from the tree of Elunbelan by Daugor, the child of age and death, who was among the very first humans created by Enilundar himself long ago. It is a most arduous magic, one that takes many lives of men to achieve, but some evils have managed it."

Though Adroegen had heard of the Galesirs, magic jewels that were once stars from the tree of Elunbelan, he knew nothing of Daugor, nor that the Galesir of Daugor could raise the dead. He knew only of the Galesirs that Dalgarinan and Mairawin possessed. Adroegen grew very troubled, for he worried greatly that he might have defeated Vyroun only to perhaps see him return one day, and he did not want to allow such to take place. "If so, then have I truly done any good on this day?"

"You have done a great good," said the Rhykwen. "Some of the greatest evils to walk this earth have managed to raise the dead. And so, Vyroun could be brought back, many lives of men from now, should other evils raise him. But do not let your heart worry for now, Adroegen, for Vyroun's shadow no longer darkens these lands, and by your doing. I will only utter that your time upon this earth has not ended, for there is much Enilundar still wishes for you to fulfill."

"Much he still wishes me to fulfill," said Adroegen. "And what else must I do upon this earth? For I do not wish for a lord such as Vyroun to one day return."

"That is a question I am not bidden to answer to you," said the Rhykwen. "For that is something you must discover in your time upon this earth. And so, I must leave now, for soon you will no longer be alone here, and I may not show myself to anyone among the living who is not among Enilundar's servants. I will now return to Elunbelan, to the throne of Enilundar himself. Before I leave, I say this to you. I am bidden to tell you that it was I who took your mother when her time upon this earth had ended, and I am bidden to utter that she is at great peace now, and any pain in her heart has long since left her. One day you will look upon Mairenn again, though not now. Know, however, that there is not a day when she does not watch over you with great love."

"Thank you," said Adroegen, overcome with sadness and yet joy all at once, for he missed his mother greatly but was comforted that one day he would again look upon her. "I will await the day when I see her again. However, there is still much left for me upon this earth, as I have found since last we met."

"One day we will meet again, though I cannot utter when that day will come," said the Rhykwen. "I will, however, be there to take you from this earth, whether in death or when Enilundar calls you home."

The taker of the dead flew into the clouds and soon vanished in the sun's light. Adroegen looked to the south.

The light met him in that once dark place, and he was quite at peace. For there had been a time when he thought he had strayed into darkness and would never escape. Adroegen, however, found that he was wrong. He felt as if he could suddenly see after being blind all his life. All now made much greater sense to Adroegen as to why his past had happened as it did, and what purpose he had upon that earth. And as his eyes looked to the south, Adroegen found there were wings flapping in the sunlight. Adroegen looked more closely to find that Andor was making his way back into what was once Vyroun's kingdom, perhaps to investigate what had happened and to see if the battle had been decided. Adroegen stood upon the ruins of what was once Norungad, and Andor found him and took Adroegen out of that place.

Chapter Twenty: A Battle Won

Caitren and her friends were soon flying over the North Fold of Gundmar. For a while she did not see anything but endless fields beneath them, though the Silver Mountains before long were ahead. The night was beginning to lift, but it was still quite dark. Though the winds gusted loudly against the company as the eagles flew them, they soon were able to hear faint sounds of battle, both to the south in the distance and behind them in the dark kingdom.

"I see the army ahead," said Kattalin as the company was drawing near to Bared Nar.

The city was still a distance away, but the eagles were already flying over what remained of Vyroun's army. To Caitren, it seemed that they were retreating, with legions of goblins and other foul forces running north. From what it appeared, Vyroun's army had come close, but ultimately failed to take Bared Nar. A little farther south, the trees of the Fornwood were stomping on goblins and wicked men and tearing apart trolls and ogres with ease.

Some of the birds flew north to keep the enemies from escaping, though there were still foes near and within the city. Soon the company was flown over many other birds. Hawks, falcons, owls, and other eagles were clawing at the goblins and other creatures. Only the trolls were able to put up much of a fight against the great birds and the trees of the Fornwood, however, in the end they were no match against either. Caitren was quite happy to see that the battle was being won.

Soon Caitren was able to see the city of Gundmar and the battle that still raged there. All three levels were in flames, however, it did not appear that Vyroun's army had reached the very top of the city. They might have broken the gate to the third and final level of Bared Nar, though it was difficult to tell from her vantage point.

"Oh, good," said Vaenn. "I do not see such a shadow that spread through the city earlier. It appears that those frightening creatures we encountered may be gone."

"It seems to me as well that they have disappeared, Vaenn," said Gleowan. "I certainly hope that it is so, for we saw no manner of defeating them."

"Worry not, Gleowan and Vaenn," said Andor. "For your friend, the wizard Ganglere, was amongst the forces of the forests and made into the city to repel those devilish fiends. Only a wizard like him, or someone as powerful as Adroegen is now, could defeat them, and so that was Ganglere's one task upon entering the field of battle."

"Well, thank goodness!" said Vaenn. "For I never wish to look upon those frightening things again! And I thought the spiders scared me when we were in their nest this past summer! I am also fearful of heights, and yet after all of these frightful things we have encountered, I am suddenly far less afraid of flying upon an eagle than what I expected to be."

The eagles began to fly down into the field before Bared Nar. They were just outside the valley between the north and south towers, and thus Caitren could still see the dark kingdom to the north. The eagles soon landed amongst the trees of the Fornwood, and the company set foot upon the ground again. They were well behind the front lines of the battle, and no enemies were anywhere near them. There were still sounds of battle, however, they were quite faint.

"This is where we will leave you for now," said Andor. "There will be no more fighting for any of you upon this field of battle. The enemies are all much farther north, and they are retreating, for we have overwhelmed them."

"This, I think, is a wonderful sight," said Caitren, as the great battle was coming to an end. "My, have I come to loathe fighting! I never want to be in a battle again!"

Everywhere there were trolls, ogres, and goblins lying dead. Some of the birds were having a feast like they had never eaten before. For Caitren, it was most revolting to watch, but the birds did not appear to notice nor care. Orn, upon landing and letting Kattalin get off, immediately went to a nearby dead ogre and began feasting upon him. Caitren did her best to not look and turned to her friends, finding that Vaenn and Kattalin simply covered their eyes. Gleowan was able to bear to look, however, he, too, appeared sickened before long.

"My! I have never eaten such a feast before!" said Orn. Other eagles and a few hawks nearby agreed. "I am stuffed already, but there is so much food left, and I know not if I will find so much to eat in the southern woods during winter."

"I do not think I mind war so much," said a nearby hawk. "If this is the spoil of war, then I would seek to take part in any battle I am able to find!"

Before long some tree men walked by the company. Caitren looked for Treeling, but she saw no sign of him anywhere. I will tell you, however, that she would soon be in for quite a surprise.

The trees that slowly walked by were all very groggy and yawning. They appeared terribly tired to the point that they might doze off at any moment. But in fairness, I could not blame them, for the trees would normally be sleeping for the winter by now, however, they had been forced to remain awake for a few extra weeks beyond the end of autumn. I am not sure how much sleep they lost, but I can tell you that quite a few trees were not happy and wished that Vyroun would have either gone to war earlier or waited until spring, as it would have been far more convenient for them. But I am afraid that in a war, no enemy will accommodate its adversary. In fact, Vyroun and his forces seemed not to even know that the trees would enter the war.

Caitren was sure that Treeling was there somewhere. She approached the nearest tree to ask him where Treeling might be. "Excuse me, I am looking for Treeling. Might you know where he is?"

The tree, however, did not appear to notice Caitren. "Oh, I must sleep now. Most tired am I. I will not stay awake much longer."

Caitren thought it best to not bother the tree any further, as he was tired enough at it was. She went on and asked the same question to several others, but they responded the same. Finally, one of them yielded a better answer. "Why, little Caitren! At least I now have some reason to be a little less cross that I cannot sleep yet. And the rest of you are here, too, save for young Adroegen.

Hmmm, I know not where he might be, but he will surely appear somewhere. I only hope I can go back home soon!"

None in the company, however, were sure who this tree was. Gleowan spoke very politely, pretending to know this tree. "Good to see you also. We were just searching for you, and for Treeling also. Might you know where he is?"

"What? Where is Treeling?" said the tree. "Why, I am Treeling! Oho!"

All in the company were quite surprised, for the tree before them did not resemble Treeling at all. However, when they looked more closely, they found that it was in fact the same tree that had carried them both into and out of the Fornwood. The trouble, however, was that it was now winter, and so the leaves had all fallen, and the beard that Treeling had worn was no longer there. And so, I daresay that it was almost impossible for the company to recognize him.

"You do not know who I am?" said Treeling, sounding rather sad. "Have you already forgotten me after leaving my home?"

"No, no," said Vaenn quickly. "It was simply difficult to recognize you, for you look quite different now."

"Hmmm," said Treeling, who then made a long yawn. "Perhaps I am not as young as I was when last I saw you. That must be it, yes."

"No, you are not that much older," said Caitren, who then realized that because it was winter, many of the other trees did not have leaves either. "It is simply that the north wind has changed your appearance. Oh, it is so wonderful to see you again! How do you do, Treeling?"

"How am I? Oh!" said Treeling. "I have never felt so cross. Tired am I, far more so than I have ever been before.

By now I should be sleeping for the winter, as should all of us trees, and yet here we are upon this field far from home. Some of us had much difficulty remaining awake during this fight. I had to wake Mapleleaf a dozen times this past night, for he kept dozing off! Hmmm. Come to think of it, I must find him again, for I am certain that he will not be awake, wherever he is."

Treeling walked away, and the company was left alone. Before long, though, another bird found them, though none in the company was sure of who it was. This bird was a great raven, and sitting upon the raven was the wizard the company had met back in the southern woods the past summer. All were quite happy to be reunited with Ganglere.

"Ah, I thought our paths might cross again in time," said the wizard to the company as he got off of the raven. "Thank you, Crawa, for I am afraid that an old man like myself might not have the spring in my step to make it this far down from the city on my own."

"Worry not, for none of us mighty birds could have fended off those fiendish demons," said Crawa. "I must now find the lady of the ravens, though I am certain that Crawe is not far, amongst the owls I think."

Crawa flew away, and the company was able to speak to the wizard about what had become of them since last they met. They quickly found, however, that Ganglere already knew of some of their dealings, as he had met with Adroegen back in the Fornwood before the birds flew off to war.

"What were you up to within the city?" asked Caitren. "We were just imprisoned within the heart of Vyroun's kingdom! But we were not there for very long, as

Adroegen came and saved us, and the eagles took us away."

"I myself was in the city, for there were many terrible demons to thwart," said Ganglere. "The deoflas, if you are unfamiliar with what creatures I speak of. But they are gone now. We wizards do not seek to look upon ourselves with any lack of modesty, but I will say that only we, and the Vistivar themselves, are able to repel those terrible spirits, and so that was the first business I had to see to. But that is over now, and the birds and trees, along with the dwarves and Woodland soldiers, have forced the army into a retreat."

Their talk though did not last for long, for a great roar sounded, one so loud that even many miles away, Caitren and her friends had to cover their ears. They all looked to the north, and the ground began to shake. When the roar ceased, a sudden wave grew and made its way south. When it met the company, a strong gust of wind blew upon them, and they all fell back. The ground then began to calm, though none in the company were sure of what had taken place. Caitren rose back to her feet and looked to Ganglere, certain that the wizard would better know the meaning of it. He was looking to the north with what seemed to be a great deal of joy, and triumph.

"What is it that just happened?" said Caitren to Ganglere. She looked back to the north and thought she could hear the sounds of something crumbling, though she was not entirely sure.

"There is but one answer that I can give," said the wizard. "And that is that Adroegen has defeated Vyroun, and that his fortress crumbles as we speak."

Andor made his way back to the wizard and the

company. "My eyes are keener than those of a human. I am barely able to see fires of blue just beyond the mountaintops, and I know that such magic is that of our friend."

"It is, lord of the Fornwood," said Ganglere. "I am very certain that the dark lord to the north is gone, and that Adroegen has smote him, as were his orders from Enilundar himself. And so, this war has ended."

Soldiers of Gundmar cheered from the top of the north and south towers of Bared Nar. The birds from the south were flying high and looking to the north, and soon Caitren saw a pair of familiar owls make their way down to them. One was of snowy white feathers while the other was black and brown and white. The lord and lady of the owls both looked quite fierce, however, the company could also see that they looked very pleased also.

"We can see from high in the clouds," said Ule. "The stronghold in the very heart of the dark kingdom is in ruin. The great tower there has fallen, and but one man remains there, wreathed in blue flame."

"Not only that, but we see another fortress at the mouth of the kingdom, which has also crumbled," said Huf. Caitren knew that they were speaking of Gulgurod, the dreadful and frightening place in which she had been held captive and brought before Vyroun, what felt like quite a while ago by then.

"The news we had hoped to hear is confirmed, then!" said Ganglere. "Adroegen has indeed defeated Vyroun. And so now there is no longer need for worry on this day."

"There are still many forces remaining from Vyroun's army," said Huf. "They were all retreating north, but now they have changed course and are fleeing into the woods to the east."

"There is no longer a master to shelter them," said Ganglere. "And so they flee in despair to the nearest shelter they can find for now, which is the forest of the Kyrrwood."

"Someone must go and find our friend," said Caitren. "For he is there alone, if what you say is true. How will he make his way back to the rest of us?"

"Yes, Caitren is right," said Ganglere. "It would be quite a journey back here for Adroegen, even as the high servant he is now."

"I will go and find him," said Andor. "For it was I who took Adroegen to that stronghold when we followed the dragon, and so I will go to take him away from there."

Andor then flew away to the north. Caitren was joyful, as were the others, although she would await Adroegen's return with anxiousness, for only then would she truly know that he was fine, and that the dark lord who held the company captive was no more.

The company looked about the battlefield as they awaited Adroegen's return. Some of the dwarves were still on the battlefield, though they were farther north speaking with some Woodland soldiers. The two armies seemed to be meeting for the first time, and Woodland soldiers appeared to be expressing their gratitude.

In Bared Nar, fires still burned, and much smoke rose in the morning sunrise to the east. The city though was no longer under assault. It appeared that at least some of the flames were being put out. Some soldiers of the Woodlands were riding into the city, likely searching for any enemies that might have remained. Though the enemy failed to take the city, Bared Nar certainly had sustained much damage, and there would be much work to do and sorrow to be had, as many had died during the battle.

Caitren's eyes, however, were fixed upon the sky to the north as she awaited Andor's return with Adroegen. There was a time when she thought he might have been dead, and for that matter the others too thought the same. To their pleasant surprise, however, it was not so. Caitren was eager for all six members of the company to be reunited again after all of the different troubles that they had been through. Afterwards, Caitren would want to find her father after leaving him to enter the battle, and she would be most joyful to see him again. Caitren though first needed to see with her own eyes that the leader of their company was in fact all right. To the north the dark clouds were thinning. It seemed that all she had heard of Vyroun's defeat was true.

The company waited. Some birds flew about, though most were feasting on the trolls and the ogres, stuffing themselves with what they considered the spoils of war. After a long wait, the dark clouds above Vyroun's kingdom cleared, and in the light, Caitren saw an eagle flying towards them. As the eagle approached, Caitren found that it was indeed the lord of the Fornwood, with the leader of her company riding upon him.

"Adroegen has returned!" said Caitren.

Andor landed, and then Adroegen stepped down and thanked the master of the eagles for bringing him back to his friends. The master of the eagles then left to join the other birds in their wonderful feast. Caitren was the first to embrace Adroegen, and Edelbir, Kattalin, Gleowan, and Vaenn followed, one by one.

"I feared the worst had happened to you," said Caitren. "But it was not so!"

"Indeed," said Edelbir. "Kattalin and I searched for days after you fell, but we never found you and thought that you had met your end."

"And I thought all of you had met your ends also," said Adroegen. "But I then found that it was not true. As for me, well, I thought I should have been dead, but as it turned out, it was not my time to leave this earth. For there are still many things here I need to do, though one of those tasks I have just fulfilled."

The company all retold their stories of what had happened to them since being separated. Caitren had never been so merry. "My heart could not be more joyful that we all are together again. And with no worry anymore of foul things hunting us! Our troubles here are now over!"

All in the company were indeed very happy to be reunited after all the trials that they had been through. The battle had ended and Vyroun was gone, and so there were no more worries for them. All were joyful that they had made it through the battle, and that they were together again. Caitren had felt within her heart that she would see her friends again, and in the end her heart had been right.

Chapter Twenty-one: Many Reunions

The company stayed in Bared Nar for the next several days. All were merry. Some soldiers of Itilikin remained, however, a good part of the army returned home to the Woodlands. The dwarves stayed, including King Aki and his son, Lofar, as Cenric wanted to know who had led the army that none had expected to come to their aid. They made certain that Cenric knew it was Edelbir and Kattalin who had persuaded Aki to enter the war. Adroegen was quite pleased that his hope of the dwarves fighting had been fulfilled, and that his friends had made it so.

As for the Fornwood, I am afraid that it was well past time for the trees to sleep for the winter. The birds remained for just a little longer, as there was a great feast left over upon the battlefield. Andor, however, was hesitant to speak with any kings, I daresay, as his name was kept a secret to men as a test to discern who was a friend to the eagles, as there were those amongst men who hunted the great birds. Regardless, Cenric was grateful to all from the forest and the southern woods who had come to their aid. The trees returned to the Fornwood immediately, and the birds, after feasting upon all the carcasses they could, also departed south, save for the hawks, who had a history of companionship with the kingdom of Gundmar.

Gleowan and Vaenn went to Eamon, as the two of them wanted to bid the friend they had made in Bared Nar a more proper farewell. The soldiers who had died were all laid in a great tomb within the rock of the northern mountain, beneath the tower. Gleowan and Vaenn discovered that thousands of soldiers were buried there, some of whom had died in more recent years, while others had perished long ago.

Cyneric, the king of Gundmar, passed away shortly after the war was won. He was old and sick and his time had come. The news spread through the city of Bared Nar. Ganglere gave his own blessing upon Cyneric as he was laid to rest, that the king would join his ancestors who had ruled over the kingdom of Esmael, son of Aberran. The hawks were in attendance and gave their own salute to the dead king with a screech in unison. And then the king was sealed within a crypt behind the hall of the king, just within the mountain, where all of the kings were in tombs of silver marble. A statue of him would be built and placed within the hall where the king's throne was, though that would be at another time. And thus ended the reign of Cyneric.

A few days after Cenric's father was laid to rest, Cenric was crowned king. The company was in attendance. Along with them was Badarion, king of Itilikin, another one of the eight kingdoms of men, as well as Aki and Lofar of the dwarves. After Cenric was crowned, he made his way around to speak with many who were there. Aldreda followed, and the two of them eventually made their way to the company.

"A small company of friends," began Cenric to them.

"All separated but bound by a friendship that no evil can break. No oath did any of you swear to my kingdom. Never before had we met. For that matter, never before had you set foot within Gundmar's borders. And yet you all came to our aid in ways that as king I cannot hope to repay. Without your help, Gundmar surely would have fallen, and I would not be crowned king on this day."

"In the siege upon this city, you were of great help, with courage and cleverness beyond what we would expect from simple folk," said Athelstan, who had taken Gleowan and Vaenn to Bared Nar as captives, but now showed no hostility. "And yet perhaps simple folk as yourselves are full of far more surprises than soldiers in a great kingdom as ours might expect. You must forgive my taking of you as captives, for I knew not of your loyalties, and yet in a way I am glad I did so. Were you not within our city fighting with us when the army came, perhaps we would not have lasted the night, and Gundmar might have fallen before help arrived."

"We are quite pleased to have been of great use," said Gleowan.

"There are some gifts we hope you will accept, with our gratitude," said Aldreda. Behind her another soldier carried two chests, one larger than the other. Aldreda took the smaller one and gave it to Gleowan, who took it graciously and opened it.

Within it was a well-carved smoking pipe, and some of the finest leaf in the kingdom of Gundmar. Gleowan was uncertain of how they knew he liked to smoke a pipe, but nonetheless, he was eager to try the leaf. "How did you come to know that I love to smoke?"

"Athelstan heard you whisper such to Vaenn one

time," said Aldreda, and Gleowan was quite surprised. The soldier set the other chest on the ground before Vaenn, and Aldreda then addressed her. "And this gift is for you, Vaenn."

Vaenn opened the chest, and within was a most beautiful dress, one not entirely the same but quite close in appearance to the one Vaenn saw Aldreda wearing when she and Gleowan were first brought before the king's son and daughter. It was green with gold trimming that glittered in the sun, with a golden girdle around the waist. It looked quite like royal attire, and Vaenn was unable to take her eyes off of it. She was astonished, but I daresay that an embarrassment also came over her.

"This looks beautiful," said Vaenn. Aldreda gave her a smile, with a look of amusement that told Vaenn that she had heard her whispering to Gleowan, upon first seeing her, about how Vaenn wanted such a dress. Vaenn kept quiet, though, as she was blushing and did not want to ask. Aldreda bowed without a word, smiled, and walked on.

"I think she heard me," whispered Vaenn to Gleowan.

"It seems that way," said Gleowan, holding the pipe in one hand and some of the leaf in the other. He took a quick sniff of the leaf. Never had Gleowan smelled a leaf so good, and he impatiently wanted to smoke it. Vaenn's eyes gazed back upon her new dress.

"I need to wear this dress," said Vaenn. "If there is a party that we attend anytime soon, I must wear this dress and I must dance in it. For I will look so wonderful."

Gleowan's eyes for but a brief moment shifted to Vaenn's new dress, and then he looked at her. "Oh, I don't doubt that at all." He put his arm around Vaenn, but his eyes were then fixed again upon his own gifts. "But in the meantime, and more importantly, I need to smoke this leaf, for never have I smelled any so good as this."

Edelbir and Kattalin waited as the new king spoke to Gleowan and Vaenn, and before long Cenric addressed the two of them. "I gave my gratitude to King Aki of the dwarves for coming to our aid. However, he told me that it was the two of you who persuaded him to enter the battle. And thus, we will always be indebted to you, Edelbir and Kattalin."

"I would say that Edelbir did far more in nudging them to fight than I did," said Kattalin.

"We both worked in trying to recruit them," said Edelbir.

"I also heard from your friends that it was you who defeated the goblin chief," said Cenric to Edelbir. "A great deed that was, for many have failed to defeat that once-formidable foe."

"In truth, morning was of great help in that fight," said Edelbir.

"It matters not, for he is gone, and sometimes in war, luck can be quite an ally," said Cenric. "I say this to you, Edelbir. You came to my aid before ever you knew me, as did you, Kattalin. Edelbir, I know not where you come from, but from what I have heard about you, you possess both the strength and qualities of a king."

"I have no desire to be a king," said Edelbir with a smile. "For my love is of tilled earth and a life of simplicity, and it is one that I hope one day to return to."

"I shall wish the best upon you wherever you choose to go," said Cenric. "But know that you shall always be welcome here, and that I shall always be an ally to you, whenever you have need for me."

Cenric then turned to Kattalin. "And Kattalin, I have heard that you have a love for what lies beyond the shores. I know not where your path will take you, but I will hope you get to return to the sea, perhaps beyond the shores by ship or to the south where the mermaids are said to dwell. I wish the greatest of happiness upon you, wherever you go."

"I will hope for it as well," said Kattalin. It had been some time since the company journeyed to the Fosscove, and Kattalin longed to go there again, as well as many other wondrous places along the shores of the sea. That, however, would have to wait for later adventures.

After the crowning of Cenric, Adroegen bid farewell to Ganglere, who then returned to the south. The company was suddenly in a situation that they had not been at all used to during the previous several months. They were free to venture wherever they wanted. Caitren told Adroegen though that she wanted to return to the Woodlands to find her father again. Huldnar was nowhere to be seen in Bared Nar during the days after Vyroun's defeat. And so, the company decided to venture to the Woodlands next, and from there, none of the six of them knew what they would do after.

The company took one final look upon Bared Nar. The city had sustained much damage from the battle, however, the people of Gundmar were working on rebuilding what had been destroyed. The six of them then rode slowly down the North Woodland Road that Caitren had traveled along to reach the city. The road was not empty, as many soldiers were traveling. After two days, the company reached the place where the Itilikin army had camped on their way to war, and some soldiers were there cleaning up.

After a few more days, the company entered the great forest, and Edelbir, Kattalin, Gleowan, and Vaenn were all quite surprised to find the air grow much warmer upon entering. The six of them before long reached the kingdom of Itilikin, where Caitren thought she might find her father, though she did wonder if he might have left to find her after she snuck into the army.

When the company entered the great hall of the tree kingdom, they found that a magnificent party was being prepared for later. All kinds of barrels of ale, mead, and beer were brought into the hall, while food was being prepared. Edelbir went to sit. Kattalin walked over to the bridge and looked into the river flowing beneath. Gleowan took out his pipe to smoke the new leaf he was given, and then he went to find some ale. Vaenn, meanwhile, left to put on her new dress. Adroegen went with Caitren to search for her father and see if he was still in the tree kingdom.

"You are sure that he is here somewhere?" said Adroegen. He had not spoken with Huldnar since the past summer in the hidden village, hours before it was razed and the company was forced to set out on its long journey.

"I believe he is," said Caitren. "Perhaps we best start with what were our chambers when my father and I stayed here. If he is still here, then that will surely be where we find him."

Adroegen followed Caitren up some stairs until they reached Caitren and Huldnar's chambers. When they entered, Adroegen found that their search quickly ended.

"Father!" said Caitren. Huldnar turned around and was given a very pleasant surprise.

"Caitren? You have returned," said Huldnar as the two embraced. Adroegen stood at the door. He wondered if Caitren's father would by unhappy with her, as Caitren told him of how her father wanted her to remain in the Woodlands, and she instead decided to sneak into the army, but Huldnar did not appear so.

"I found my friends, and they are all here!" said Caitren. "I knew they would be in the battle somewhere."

"I worried that you had snuck into the army," said Huldnar. "Though as I searched for you, the lady of the Woodlands uttered to me that you were far safer than I thought. For she told me that she had given you a jewel, one that held great magic, that would help protect you from suffering great harm. And Mairawin told me I need not worry, that it was better if I remain here and wait for you. Curious, I thought, but I trusted her wisdom."

Adroegen grew curious about this jewel Caitren wore, as he remembered that Vyroun had not been able to harm her back in Norungad when the company was captive. Caitren looked down at her necklace and held the jewel that hung around her neck. "I was brought before Vyroun a second time, with my friends, and on that occasion, he tried to kill me. Yet this jewel protected me from his wrath, and though I could not face him, nor escape, he was not able to harm me. I could not be more grateful that the lady of the Woodlands gave it to me."

"Mairawin will surely be able to tell you more," said Caitren's father. "As it happens, she is here and wished to speak with you whenever you would return. I believe that she is merely down the hall. You best find her, and I wish to speak with Adroegen here."

Caitren went to search for the lady of the Woodlands,

and Adroegen was left alone with Huldnar. Adroegen was not quite sure what words to say to him. "Much has taken place since last we met."

"Yes," said Huldnar. "I remember leaving that village to find any news of the outside world, and what I found was that a pack of goblins were after a traveler, whom they had tracked to a hidden village, and when I made swiftly for home, I found the village razed and the villagers dead. But my daughter I did not find, nor the others of your company."

"I knew not that I was being tracked," said Adroegen. "For had I known, I would never have entered your home."

"It might be easy to feel at fault," said Huldnar. "However, there was nothing you could have done. What I know is that my daughter was in grave danger, as well as the others of your company, and you led them out of that peril against great odds. And for that, I am most grateful."

"We wanted to find you," said Adroegen. "However, I knew not of your whereabouts, and with the goblin chief hunting us, it was far too dangerous at the time to search for you."

"You did precisely the right thing," said Huldnar. "I would utter this. There is a traveler I have come to know, whom I speak to for news of the outside world. You have not spoken with him before, from what he tells me, however, he uttered to me that you have seen him, back in Lidborg. He is a spy within the goblin ranks, and I have sworn to keep him a secret. When I found him, I learned that Vyroun had ordered the goblins to hunt you. I was able to track the whereabouts of your company, at least for a time, until finally I found Caitren in the Woodlands and learned what had become of all of you. I was devastated to learn that you were likely dead, for this spy had told me the secret about you being heir to a bygone warrior. But it turned out to not be so, for you still live."

Adroegen was quite curious about this unnamed traveler Huldnar spoke of. Back in Lidborg, his friends, Arrow and Longshanks, told of one traveler they had seen before named Floin, whom Adroegen himself had also seen before in the north, and of how Floin had an exchange with a tall man of golden hair that the hunters overheard, about a coming attack on a hidden village, prompting this man to leave straightaway. He grew quite certain this spy Huldnar spoke of was Floin, but because Huldnar had sworn not to speak the traveler's name, Adroegen would not ask.

"This I also utter to you," said Huldnar. "I once worried that Caitren's venturous spirit would cause her to leave home, into the dangerous world. It became so. However, now that I know that a great warrior, a high servant of the earth's maker himself, ventures alongside her, I do not fear for my daughter as I once did."

Adroegen did not expect to hear this at all from Caitren's father. "If my company has more adventures to journey on, I will tell you now that I will let no harm meet your daughter, nor our friends."

"I know not where your paths will take you," said Huldnar. "But I cannot keep Caitren and her friends safe from the outside world anymore, for it has found them. But I would say that you have found them also, and for that I could not be more grateful to whatever fate or greater power made it so."

Caitren made her way down the hall. She had to search

for a short time, but Caitren soon found the lady of the Woodlands. Mairawin was waiting in another chamber, and the door was open. It appeared as if she had known Caitren was coming. When Caitren entered Mairawin's chamber, she was given a pleasant surprise. Navena had made her way down to Itilikin.

"You have come back," said Navena as the two embraced. "What a joy it is to see you again."

"And you have made your way south from the Fairywater," said Caitren. "I could not be happier that you are here!"

"I had learned that the evil to the north had been defeated, and that a magnificent celebration would be at hand, and thus I came down to Itilikin," said Navena, putting her hands on Caitren's face. "And you still have all the beauty that you had when last I saw you. I am so pleased to see that no one has taken it away."

"I was brought before Vyroun again," said Caitren to both Mairawin and Navena. "But this jewel kept him from harming me. I could not be more grateful that you have given it to me, for it saved my life."

"I have been given a gift of foresight," said Mairawin. "I am not permitted to say what your future holds, however, I will say that I knew you would still face much danger, and so I bestowed that jewel upon you."

"Vyroun wanted it after trying and failing to kill me," said Caitren.

"A Galesir is no mere trinket, Caitren," said Mairawin. "It is a magic jewel that was once a star hanging from Elunbelan, yours being cut by Vinara herself, the child of youth, beauty, and innocence. Among its many uses, the jewel may protect you against dark sorcery like that which

Vyroun possessed. You will not be totally invulnerable, however, those of the dark will have greater difficulty in harming you. I must advise that you never take it off, Caitren. For if you do so, then the jewel will not protect you as it does when you wear it around your neck."

"Vinara was the name of she who cut this star?" said Caitren, remembering Vyroun calling her such a name after looking upon her jewel. "I was called that very name by Vyroun himself, before he told me to remove the necklace."

"He clearly knew what trinket you wore," said Mairawin. "As well as who it came from."

"And Vyroun must have wanted it for that very reason!" said Caitren. "I shall never remove this jewel. For it has quickly become my most treasured possession. I would not stand here now without it."

"There are several Galesirs upon this earth," said Mairawin. "Mine grants me wisdom and foresight, and the ability to see things in motion that others cannot. Your jewel, Caitren, is one of purity and innocence, possessing great magic, though not power, like what Adroegen now possesses as a Vistivar. That jewel can be of use only to one with a pure and innocent heart, a heart as Vinara herself once possessed, free of hate and malice. I saw that you resisted Vyroun and his servants, and I saw that you possessed a wonderful spirit, and so I thought this jewel might help you. Vyroun would not have been able to use the jewel you wear, for he did not possess the innocent heart that you do. If he wanted the jewel, it surely would have been so that such a device could no longer be of nuisance to him. The jewel aided you, Caitren, which means your heart matches that which the jewel has sought. It has chosen you as its bearer, just as I had foreseen, and it will be of great value to you in your coming ventures."

Caitren was very surprised and knew not that she was worthy of wearing such a jewel when others were not. She looked down and held the jewel in her hand. It looked nothing short of enchanting, and Caitren was determined to always be worthy of wearing it. "Then I must never betray it."

"You have a most wonderful possession," said Navena. "Your greatest quality is your heart, which makes the jewel loyal to you. We do, however, have something else belonging to you here."

Navena briefly left the room. When she returned, she was carrying the dress that she had made for Caitren. When Caitren saw it, her heart was joyful. She had been certain, when sneaking into the army, that she would never see it again. Navena handed Caitren's dress back to her.

"You found my dress!" said Caitren. "Oh, I thought I would never wear it again! How did you find it?"

"Well, you disappeared the morning the army left, and your father worried that you had left to enter the war," said Mairawin. "I foresaw that you would search for your friends, and so I searched the armory, thinking you might have found armor and snuck into the army, and there I found it."

"I do not want to lose it again," said Caitren, holding her dress tightly. "I must put it back on!"

Caitren swiftly entered the chamber to put on her dress. She felt very happy to be wearing it again and not armor like when she was in battle. When she stepped out, she could not help but twirl around. Mairawin and Navena looked upon her with smiles, just as when Caitren had put it on for the first time.

"You are as beautiful as you have ever been," said Navena. "And your beauty never ceases in its enchantment."

"Thank you so much for finding it," said Caitren. "My, did I hate wearing armor, for it was heavy and hard to move in. I love wearing this dress far more, for it is so much lighter and far more wonderful than any suit of war."

"There is a great feast about to begin," said the lady of the Woodlands. "And I believe you are ready to attend it. I think you best make for the great hall now."

"Not yet," said Navena. "I must first brush and braid your hair. Then you will be ready."

Navena signaled for Caitren to sit, and she began to work on Caitren's hair. It took a little time, but not too long. Soon Navena had finished, and Caitren was able to see herself in a mirror. She could not believe how beautiful she looked. Caitren then turned to face Mairawin and Navena, who both appeared equally astonished.

"You look wonderful," said Navena. "What a pleasure it is to brush and braid the golden hair of Caitren, who looks like nothing less than an angel."

Caitren gave a small bow, and the lady of the Woodlands spoke. "You now have a great party to attend."

"I will!" said Caitren. She then quickly and happily made her way down the hall. Caitren soon reached her father's chambers. Adroegen was inside, speaking with him. Caitren quickly ended their exchange, for there was a great party to take part in.

"Come along, Adroegen!" said Caitren. "There is going to be a magnificent party now. We must attend it!"

In the hall, Gleowan made his way to the barrels, though he had to be careful, as food for a great feast was being brought out. He lit his new pipe and began to smoke as he searched for a good drink. Vaenn would be back quite soon, for she was putting on the dress that Aldreda had given her. Meanwhile, Gleowan was having a great dilemma, as he had never seen so many choices of ale, beer, mead, and other drinks before him. There were dozens of barrels, far too many different drinks for Gleowan to be able to taste in a single night!

"What have I done to be so lucky?" said Gleowan as he looked upon all the different drinks to choose from. "Never have I seen a sight so wondrous, and so beautiful. But I know not which to choose."

"I beg your pardon?" said Vaenn, who had made her way back and was wearing her new dress of green and gold. "Never before have you seen a sight so wondrous and so beautiful? Your gaze was not upon me when you uttered those words."

"Beyond you, of course," said Gleowan, quickly turning to Vaenn, whose frown then ceased, as she was much more satisfied after his clarification.

"Yes, so wondrous this is," said a young man next to Gleowan who was about as tall, with similar golden hair, but appeared just a little older than he. "There are as many drinks here tonight as there are pretty women! I would take the ale, and amongst the women, if I were you, I would not ask that elven lady by the musicians for a dance, for she gave me a kiss the night before I rode to battle, and

I can see her eyes fixed upon me again today."

"The ale, eh? Very well," said Gleowan, who took a pint and began to drink it, and his eyes widened, for never had he drunk such a good drink. "Well, you are now a greatest friend to me, whoever you are! For I have never tasted so good an ale!"

"Oh yes. It is the greatest upon this earth!" said the man. Gleowan did not at all know this man but liked him already, for he seemed quite alike to Gleowan in his taste for drink, and Gleowan immediately held the man in high regard for pointing him to the greatest ale that Gleowan had ever tasted.

"I am most fond of this place now," said Gleowan. "I do not wish to leave here, other than to go to Bared Nar for more leaf to smoke when I run out."

"Well, that may be a worthy reason, but no other," said the man. "For this place has the greatest of drink, and countless women! I should introduce you to each and every one of them, for every maiden here knows my name. I am very well-known amongst them."

"Oh no," said Gleowan. "For a lady has already claimed me as her own. Vaenn here is her name."

The man turned to look upon Vaenn, and she knew immediately that he was quite astonished at her beauty. "Well, how lucky a man you are to have a woman so beautiful as she! For you, my fair lady, are as gorgeous as an elven princess. Gamenan is my name."

Gamenan gave Vaenn a bow, and Vaenn was quite flattered by him. "Vaenn is my name. An honor it is to meet you."

"And Gleowan is my name," said Gleowan, who thought that Gamenan seemed incredibly alike to him.

"Might I say, fair Vaenn, that your dress is quite enchanting," said Gamenan. "And your beauty will cast a spell upon any man fortunate enough to look upon you."

"I can only agree," said Gleowan as he downed his first pint of ale of the night and immediately poured another. Vaenn was relishing the flattery she was receiving, but I am afraid that it ended rather abruptly, as Edelbir and Kattalin joined them.

"Ah, I have met both of you upon the field of battle, arriving with an army of dwarves," said Gamenan. "Edelbir and Kattalin, great it is to see both of you again. And Kattalin, you look fair and enchanting as ever."

"I am pleased to see that you have lived out the war," said Kattalin. "Well, there are only two of us missing. Adroegen and Caitren appear to be elsewhere."

Soon, though, the four of them caught sight of the remaining two members of their company. At the stairs, Adroegen was making his way back down to the great hall for the party, but it was not he who caught their eye. For beside Adroegen there stood an angel, or at least the four of them at first thought she was some kind of angel. However, as she drew closer, they found that it was Caitren, in the dress given to her by Navena. She was almost unrecognizable to them, and Vaenn, I daresay, felt a little jealous at how beautiful Caitren looked as she made her way down with Adroegen.

"She is lovely," said Vaenn. "What an astonishing beauty Caitren possesses."

"Indeed," said Gleowan. Vaenn then turned to him with a frown upon her face, and Gleowan swiftly went on. "But not as beautiful as you." Vaenn then looked back at Caitren, and her frown became a smile again.

Adroegen and Caitren joined the rest of the company, and they were all united again. Then Adroegen noticed Gamenan also amongst them, and he was quite glad to see that funny fellow again. Adroegen had known him from his time in the Woodlands when the two were lads.

"Gamenan! What has become of you since last we met?" said Adroegen as they embraced.

"An elven lady has fallen under my charm, I think," said Gamenan, pointing to the same lady that Caitren had watched him dance with and receive a kiss from the night before the army rode to battle. She appeared to be giving glances back at Gamenan from a distance.

"Well, that is quite an accomplishment! Well done!" said Adroegen, who knew that Gamenan spent much of his time trying to woo women. "What is her name, might I ask?"

Gamenan looked back at the elven lady and then turned to Adroegen. "She actually did not utter her name to me that night. Though I am certain still that she has a liking to me, for I have seen her eyes fixed upon me again on this day. First, I must drink, but then the charm of Gamenan will be at work again!"

Adroegen knew all too well of what splendid food was served in Itilikin. A magnificent feast was prepared. Upon the tables were soft breads with much jam and butter to spread. Countless meats were assembled, from roasted chicken and salted pork to all sorts of fish. There were fresh and ripe strawberries and other berries that were too many for me to count, along with all sorts of green foods. Large barrels held ale and other drinks, and there were several flagons sitting on the tables. And then finally there was a great assortment of cakes, all of which would have been very good, were you to try them!

Adroegen had a drink and was quite happy that his friends had not perished like he once thought. Caitren danced merrily, while Vaenn crossly tried to bring Gleowan up to dance also, though he was trying to please Vaenn, hold his pipe, and not let his drink spill. Kattalin sat on the small bridge over the river that flowed underneath the hall, and Edelbir sat and watched Gleowan and Vaenn with amusement. There was a time when looking upon the merriment of others only reminded Adroegen of the sadness of his past, however, on that night those feelings did not meet him.

After some time, Adroegen found he was being watched. Upon the stairs leading to the upper chambers stood Mairawin and Navena. Both of them appeared quite happy. Adroegen remembered meeting them after he had lost his mother in the dark dungeons of Vyroun's kingdom. Both had been very loving to him in that sorrowful time, and Adroegen felt a need to go to them. The lady of the Woodlands appeared half joyful and half proud when Adroegen reached her, whereas Navena appeared to be on the edge of crying, though from joy rather than sadness.

"I remember a time once," began Navena. "A young boy was brought to our home. One who had just lost his mother, who had been tormented beyond what anyone could imagine. He was filled with grief and anger, and he was confused about why he suffered so much. For he had been robbed of all joy and love, and this boy felt so empty that he wished for death itself.

"And it agonized me that I could not help the child, for no matter what I tried, there was nothing that could ease the terrible burden he carried. All I could do was hope with all of my heart that one day joy would find him again, after all that he had to go through. And I could only wish that this boy would one day find meaning and purpose, and that love would find him again."

Navena put her hands upon Adroegen's face, and tears fell from her eyes. "Look at you now."

Adroegen felt quite overcome with emotion, for he remembered everything that Navena spoke of. Adroegen had thought as a boy that joy was something that did not exist upon that earth. But now Adroegen had found it not to be so. "I lost my mother in what was a most tormenting memory, and I have lost all others of my kin. And I know I will not again see her upon this earth. But a veil that once blinded me has been lifted, for I know there is a purpose for me upon this earth. And above all else, I know my mother is at peace, and that I will one day again look upon her, however soon or far away it might be."

"She is not gone, for your mother has always been with you," said Navena, who then put her hand upon Adroegen's heart. "She is here, and she always will be."

"Let me say to you, Navena," said Adroegen, "that you are very much like her."

"I knew all this time that you had a great path set before you," said the lady of the Woodlands. "Ciarvur once told me so. I thought hope might have faded, for I had seen you fall in the Dead Forest. Yet I could not see your fate in full, and I had a feeling that it was because something extraordinary was being set in motion."

Their exchange, however, ended abruptly when Caitren appeared and took Adroegen by the hand. "Come along! The rest of us are waiting for you! We must all have a dance!"

Mairawin and Navena smiled at Adroegen and stepped back, and he quickly followed Caitren as she happily led him to the others of the company. Adroegen then had a dance with Caitren, while Gleowan had a dance with Vaenn, and Edelbir danced with Kattalin. Then Adroegen danced with Kattalin, and Caitren with Gleowan, and Edelbir with Vaenn, and so on. All were merry in a way they had not been in a long time, if ever at all.

"What shall we do after tonight?" asked Edelbir to the others as he danced with Caitren. "For there is no more evil to worry of. I do not fear the road now as I once did."

"I think it matters not to me," said Gleowan while dancing with Kattalin. "Although I would hate to leave here so soon, for the ale is a delicacy! Though I am sure we will find good drink in other corners of this world, if we venture out and find them."

"We have no home anymore," said Kattalin. "Except out there on the road, I think. In time I would not mind venturing about some more, especially if our road leads to the shores, for I would love to look upon the waters of the sea again."

"I would not mind another adventure," said Vaenn, who was dancing with Adroegen but then switched to dance with Gleowan. "But no more dangers! I do not want to run all day from a pack of goblins and then be tired and worried each night."

"I must agree," said Caitren, who danced with Edelbir but then switched to Adroegen again. "For I had always wanted to see what lay beyond the borders of our home, but when finally we left, it was not in the manner I had imagined. I would love another adventure, but one where there is far less worry. What do you say, Adroegen?"

Adroegen looked at Caitren with a smile. "I could do with another adventure. And perhaps we could drift about to a place that even I have not before seen."

All members of the company were merry. Adroegen danced with Caitren, and he had never been so overcome with happiness, a feeling that all his life he had not been used to having. For Adroegen had a new kin, one that he not so long before thought he had lost, but Adroegen found that it was not so. He had once believed there was nothing left for him upon that earth and that there was no purpose for him there, but Adroegen discovered the very opposite, and that much had been laid before his feet. And Adroegen once felt that he was all alone in the world. But I can tell you now that Adroegen knew beyond any doubt that he was not alone, and that he had never been alone either.

Acknowledgements

I wish to give a special thank you to the following people for their help in publishing what is now my second book:

To David and Justine Duhr of WriteByNight for their counsel and assistance in the process of consulting, critiquing, and editing.

To David Duhr and Brad Tyer of WriteByNight for their editing work.

To Nick Courtright and Cameron Finch of Atmosphere Press for their work in the publication of this book.

And finally, a special thank you to Tom Andes of WriteByNight, in listening, consulting, and critiquing this story for several month to help bring it to this point.

About Atmosphere Press

Atmosphere Press is an independent, full-service publisher for excellent books in all genres and for all audiences. Learn more about what we do at atmospherepress.com.

We encourage you to check out some of Atmosphere's latest releases, which are available at Amazon.com and via order from your local bookstore:

The Tattered Black Book, a novel by Lexy Duck
The Red Castle, a novel by Noah Verhoeff
American Genes, a novel by Kirby Nielsen
Newer Testaments, a novel by Philip Brunetti
All Things in Time, a novel by Sue Buyer
Hobson's Mischief, a novel by Caitlin Decatur
The Black-Marketer's Daughter, a novel by Suman Mallick
The Farthing Quest, a novel by Casey Bruce
This Side of Babylon, a novel by James Stoia
Within the Gray, a novel by Jenna Ashlyn
For a Better Life, a novel by Julia Reid Galosy
Where No Man Pursueth, a novel by Micheal E. Jimerson
Here's Waldo, a novel by Nick Olson
Tales of Little Egypt, a historical novel by James Gilbert
The Hidden Life, a novel by Robert Castle
Big Beasts, a novel by Patrick Scott
Alvarado, a novel by John W. Horton III
Nothing to Get Nostalgic About, a novel by Eddie Brophy
GROW: A Jack and Lake Creek Book, a novel by Chris S McGee

About the Author

Kyle Andrew McCurry is the author of *The Fleeing Company*, the first book of *The Drifters' Road* fantasy book series. He was born and raised in southeast Michigan. Kyle is one with a hobby for storytelling and reading literature from the past, which led to him becoming an author. Among his favorite writers are J.R.R. Tolkien, Snorri Sturluson, Hans Christian Andersen, and George MacDonald, and among his books are European myths, fairytales, and sagas from long ago. When not reading or writing, Kyle spends his time watching movies, making homemade fudge that was passed down from his grandfather, and following the Detroit Red Wings, his favorite sports team.